The Seeds of Dissolution

Also in the Dissolutionverse by William C. Tracy

Tuning the Symphony

Merchants and Maji

to
drost and Sund

85

- Explore the
Imperium!

The Seeds of Dissolution

A NOVEL OF THE DISSOLUTIONVERSE

William C. Tracy

William C3

Space Wizard Science Fantasy
Raleigh, NC
www.spacewizardsciencefantasy.com

Publisher's Note: This is a work of fiction. Names, characters, places, and inci-
dents are a product of the author's imagination. Locales and public names are
sometimes used for atmospheric purposes. Any resemblance to actual people,
living or dead, or to businesses, companies, events, institutions, or locales is
completely coincidental.

Cover art and Interior illustrations by Micah Epstein
Map by Damijan
Editing by Eschler Editing
Book Layout © 2015 BookDesignTemplates.com

The Seeds of Dissolution/William C. Tracy.-- 1st ed.
Library of Congress Control Number: 2017913728
ISBN 978-0-9972994-4-1

Author's website: www.williamctracy.com

For Dad:
Who read to me about Shelob and the Balrog

CONTENTS

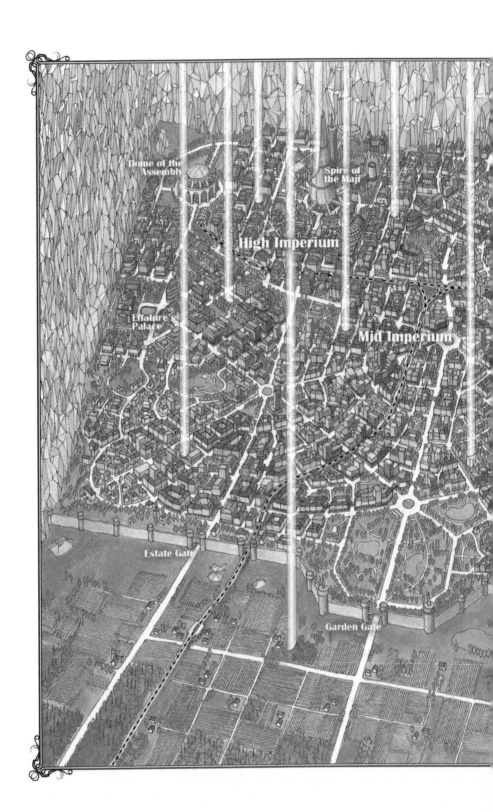

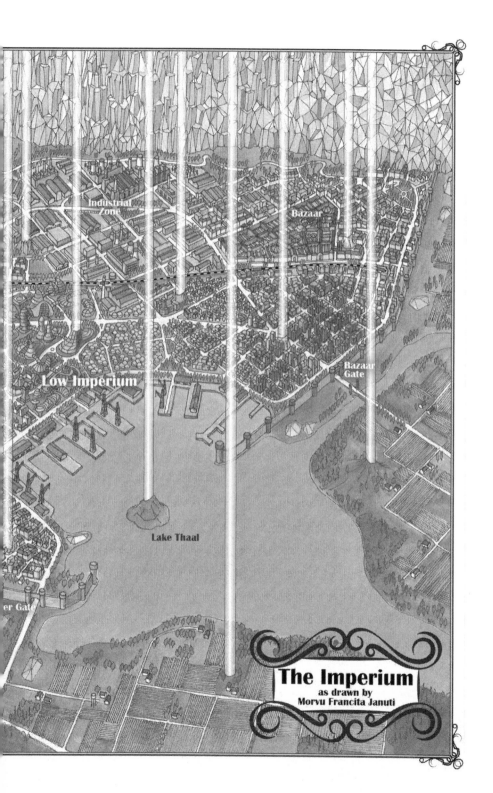

Industrial Zone

Bazaar

Low Imperium

Bazaar Gate

er Gate

Lake Thaal

The Imperium
as drawn by
Morvu Francita Januti

CHAPTER ONE

Shadow over the Sun

-From the start, I was calling the voids "Drains," because of their function. It frustrates me others insist on ignoring or even suppressing my terminology for the phenomenon. It is to be much more descriptive than "void."

Journal of Origon Cyrysi, Kirian majus of the Houses of Communication and Power

Sam was reading when the sun dimmed.

As he looked up from his book, he caught the sky outside his window shading into twilight. Overhead, the light blinked off, then on and the music playing on his laptop—Beethoven's 7th—croaked a discordant jumble of notes before the screen went black. A breath of cold air left goosebumps on his arms.

"What the—" Sam pushed up from the chair as the overhead light faded again. His breath caught in his throat, like he had swallowed a lump of ice. His room was not large, made smaller by the piles of boxes making up his collection, and now shadows rose between stacks of waist-high containers. He wormed through them in the dim light, heart racing. Was this really happening, or was he having an attack? Why now? It took two tries to pick up his grandfather's pocket watch from where it rested on an end table beside his bed. His hands shook, and the thump of his heartbeat nearly overpowered the rhythmic ticking transmitted through his palm. He focused on the mechanical beat—let it inform his body with the regular beat of time.

Calm down. Stillness evaded him, left him unsteady. *Everything is going dark in the middle of the day.* At least the watch was working. He made sure to keep it wound, and kept it safe in his room.

While watching the darkened sky, his other hand fingered the lid of a small shoebox. His collection of boxes contained grass clippings, shells, sand, and other things, bought by friends and customers of his aunt. They reminded him of favorite sights and smells. However, the shoebox contained things more precious than the rest: half a belt, stiff from water damage, and the heel of a woman's left shoe, sheared off cleanly.

No. Can't think of them now. They're gone, and I can't change it. He shivered at another gust of cold air. His room felt like late January instead of August. He eyed the window, but the thought of opening it—letting in the places he didn't know—made his hands sweat. His hand left the box, moving to the windowpane. He hissed and shook his fingers. The window was colder than the house, which meant outside must be too. He breathed out and raised his watch to his ear, listening to the steady beat.

Is this all in my head? He hadn't heard a transformer blow, and there was no storm. It was so quiet his rough breathing was like a train. He rubbed his arms, and a quick touch on his laptop's case nearly numbed his finger. His cellphone was powered down and wouldn't restart.

Aunt Martha will know what to do. Get to safety. Sam weaved through the precise stacks of boxes, trembling. She would be in her sewing shop. Sam wiped sweaty hands on his shorts before pulling a coat from the closet and socks from a drawer. He dropped his watch in a pocket of the coat, but kept one hand on it. If the power outage kept up, he couldn't log in for his shift in technical support. *What will they think? Will they fire me?* He couldn't get his ethics essay done either, and he had to email it in by tomorrow night for the ethical theories class at his online community college.

The chill air in the hall made him regret the shorts, but he shrugged his coat on, then leaned against the wall, pulling his socks on carefully. If the seams were going the wrong way, they'd just distract him, and there was too much going on already. He closed his eyes. *Don't shut down. Keep moving.*

The dark wood-paneled hallway was cold even through his socks, and Sam made a detour to the front door to get his sneakers, adjusting his feet in them, making sure the laces were the same length. It took two tries with his shaking hands. The dark was deepening outside, and by the time he got to the other end of the house, he was using his sense of touch more than sight to navigate.

He met Aunt Martha coming from the small one-room addition that served as her workshop. She held a flickering beeswax candle in her hand. *It's not just in my head.*

"What happened?" he asked. His aunt only shook her head at him. Her posture was precise as always, like the romantic ideal of a noble-woman. He didn't know exactly how old she was, except that her once graying hair was now almost totally white.

She moved slower than when he first came to live with her, but the clothes she made for shops on Market Street in Charleston, plus his job, would let him afford college. His aunt wanted him to go to a real college instead of online, but it was so much easier to learn at home. Since he had started taking classes online, he didn't have to deal with the crowds at high school, or worry if he forgot his homework.

"Do you think the power plant has a problem?" Sam tried again. If his aunt had something to say, she would, but nothing could get her to talk when she didn't want to.

"If it were, all the lights in the house would go out at once," she re-plied. The rounded syllables of "house" and "out" betrayed her Charlestonian heritage. "Haven't you looked outside?"

"Yes, Ma'am." He swallowed. Something was trying to catch in his throat, and Sam put out a hand to steady himself on a wall. His other hand snaked into his pocket to stroke the comforting curve of his watch. He couldn't feel the ticking over the pulse of his heartbeat and his panting breaths.

They watched the candle flame dwindle to a speck, and Aunt Martha cupped her hand around the flame—so close Sam worried she might burn herself. She only nodded impatiently at him to move.

"To the living room, boy." She still called him 'boy,' even after ten years. He moved, but she was at his heels the whole time, urging him on. If she hadn't been using both hands for the candle, she would be poking him in the back. Her closeness was a comfort, in the dark and cold.

The formal living room was a contrast with the rest of the house, filled with overstuffed furniture, throw pillows and doilies—all the accouterments one would expect from a little old lady. Sam shivered violently, and knocked against the curio cabinet with the creaky leg, making the little porcelain figurines inside shiver with him. His aunt was staring at the ancient fireplace, unused since the last big snow, eight years ago.

No dressing down about being clumsy? She is worried. "Wh-what do we do here, Aunt Martha?" Sam's body tried to shiver him to warmth, but even his coat wasn't holding in the heat. *Are the chills from the cold, or the panic?*

"Hush," she said. Then, still shielding the candle, barely alight, she cocked her head toward the hearth. "Lay us a fire."

Sam knelt obediently. Aunt Martha kept a well-stocked hearth. There was a pile of old newspapers, some kindling, and even a small cord of wood, just in case. He placed the fire as quick as he could, hands numb with the cold, stopping every few seconds to rub them together. He snuck a glance up at his aunt, but she watched the tiny candle flame, eyes narrowed. She was shivering, but only what her proud bearing would allow. He laid the fire quickly. *Like Dad taught me.* It took his mind off what was happening, and he felt his shoulders unknot a little, until he thought about what had happened to his parents—the similar temperature, the speed of it. *No. Keep it together.*

"Good," commended Aunt Martha, and creakily, she knelt beside him, both hands still around the candle. He couldn't smell it any longer, in the cold. He steadied her as he could, surprised she didn't wave him away like normal.

Aunt Martha bent forward, hands creeping carefully to keep the flame from guttering, until the little light was just below a corner of newspaper. They both watched the fire—so slowly—blacken the newspaper. It should have caught in an instant and devoured the kindling, but the flame moved unnaturally slow, like the fire was a slowed down recording.

Sam's aunt sat back with a grunt as the newspaper lit, and the fire gradually grew. Her hands trembled as she took them away, and Sam saw the candle was completely extinguished. He reached out to the flame, feeling his hands tingle. His aunt did the same.

"Can we make it bigger?" Sam asked. It was an effort to speak in the freezing air.

Her voice was soft. "There is cooking sherry in the kitchen, but I believe we must leave, instead. We shall warm ourselves, then I shall drive us into town and see if this condition is prevalent over the entire region."

Sam's mouth went dry. "I can't," he whispered. *Crowds. People. I haven't been in the middle of the city in years. It's probably changed. I won't know where to go.*

His aunt only rubbed her palms together. "You shall." She wobbled as if she might fall, and Sam supported her. She put one hand to her chest and swallowed. Sam could see the discomfort she tried to hide. "If you wish to teach one day, you must learn to be around crowds of students."

I can't let her down. His breathing was fast. His application to the College of Charleston was unfinished, in his room. People he knew were one thing, but so many, all together... More warmth was what they needed. "Let me put more wood on." Sam's joints were tight from the cold as he moved.

"No," Aunt Martha said, putting her shaking hand on his. "Let it die, and then we shall leave." The fire was already losing against the cold.

"Let's stay here," Sam suggested. "We can get more fuel, make a bigger fire."

His aunt attempted to rise but fell against him, and Sam caught her awkwardly. "You must go," she said. He was suddenly aware of how much willpower she must be using to stay conscious, to fight the cold that sapped their strength. *She's been strong for me, all these years.* Now she was tiny, leaning against him. Her bright green eyes fixed him in place. "You save yourself. The keys are by the door. Get to the car."

"I don't know how to drive," he said.

"N-no excuses." His aunt shook, and one hand tried to reach for him, failed. She made a small sound he had never heard from her.

"Aunt Martha?" It was like a rock had lodged in his chest. She never submitted to anything. She couldn't now.

"Go." Sam scarcely heard the whisper. Aunt Martha's eyes flickered and her head fell against him, unconscious.

With his remaining strength, he pushed her closer to the failing fire and wiggled onto the hearth. *Something is deeply wrong with the world.* His heart beat too fast, and his stomach clenched. *The air's too thin.* It was as if the very energy around them was leaving, electrical and natural. He struggled to grasp his watch, raise it to his ear. Even the watch was ticking slowly, winding down. He put it back in his pocket. Their only hope was to get warm enough. Then he could wake his aunt up. *She will wake up.*

He prodded the weak flame with the thinnest piece of kindling, hoping to spark the fire back to life, but it wouldn't catch. His hand shook, and he dropped the sliver of wood. He fumbled below the stacked kindling, fingers trembling as he tried to close his hand around the tiny sliver, but they wouldn't respond. *Can I get to the kitchen, to the cooking sherry?* His legs didn't want to unbend. Sam's head nodded forward. *Just a moment to rest...*

Wake up.

Sam's eyes snapped open, as if a voice called him. He jerked his neck up, wondering how much time he had lost. Ice crystals cracked around his mouth, nose, and eyelids. He tried to move, and fell to one side. He was slumped half in the fireplace, his aunt's head on his leg. His fingers and toes ached as if tiny needles bored into them.

He reached down, but when his fingers brushed his aunt's white hair, the strands broke with a tiny *crack* and fell, like little ringlets of glass. He jerked back, then touched her wrinkled forehead. It was colder than his hands, and he winced at the pain in his fingertips. The skin there was dark. He brushed ice from Aunt Martha's skin. Sightless eyes stared back. *No.*

He should feel something, but his hands and his mind were numb. His aunt had put up with him and his fears for ten years. *Should have obeyed instead of questioning.* Sam's eyelids dragged him down to sleep. It was pitch dark, save for a hint of light hidden in the pile of charred wood in the fireplace, like a little campfire in a cave. He was drawn to it.

Take the heat. He reached out to the little light, hoping to delay the inevitable. His aunt's body was a cold weight against him. He wouldn't waste the extra time, however small, she had given him. He wanted to be far away from here, somewhere safe.

The tiny light winked out, and he heard a *plunk* of a bass string snapping in his head, shattering into a thousand harmonious notes. Warmth flowed into him, then away, leaving him colder than before. He gasped as a thick ring of light erupted on the hearth, barely as high as his kneeling form. Two colors intermixed and rotated around the edge of the ring, one color bright, the other shiny, like circlets of gold and silver. In the ring's center was a pool of blackness.

Sam reached out to the glowing circle. His mind was sluggish, but he craved the glow. Instead of intersecting anything physical, his hand passed *through* the darkness, to someplace warm. *That* was where he needed to be. It was not cold there. The world was not dying there.

Another hand, warm and alive, caught his arm in a vice-like grip. Sam's eyes widened, and he pulled back instinctively, but whoever was on the other side of the circle was stronger. He grabbed for his aunt's body, trying to bring her along. His numbed fingers slid across her frozen shawl, down one arm, clutching. His hand closed on nothing as he was dragged head-first through the hole in the air.

CHAPTER TWO

A Portal to the Nether

-Many new maji first use their abilities in a blaze of power, then are unable to use them again for several days. Scholars believe there is an overload of music from one's first contact with the Grand Symphony and the aspiring majus is rendered 'deaf' for a time.
Yaten E'Mez, Highest of the House of Communication, 356 A.A.W.

Sam's head burst into a splash of light and warmth. He closed his eyes tight against the brightness, hands clenching in hard dirt. The air here was a contrast to the still strangulation of his house, but a breeze carried the scent of ammonia and rotting wood. His fingers tingled at the sudden change in temperature, sending up spikes of pain.

Pressure on his arm made him open his eyes. The man who had pulled him through let go, cleared his throat, and stood up to his full height. Sam scrambled to his feet, backing into rough wood siding. There was maybe one body length between him and the next building, behind the man. He had to look up to face him—not something he did often. Nearby, the hole in the air imploded silently, and Sam inhaled, his mind clearing. Aunt Martha was still back home. Had he dreamed her glazed eyes? He grabbed for his watch, in his coat pocket. Stopped. He was hyperventilating.

He lunged for where the ring of light had disappeared, trying to get back, clawing the air as he stumbled, braking before he hit the other wall. He was in a dead-end alley somehow, between buildings with wood slatted siding, far away from home.

He had to get back to his aunt and find out what happened to the house. The warm breeze ruffled his hair, too long since his last haircut. It carried angry trills between two birds overhead, and snatches of conversation. This was not a place he knew.

Lost.

The thought flitted through his mind as his heart raced. Sam's joints locked and he flattened to the dirt like a squashed toad, trying to hold on, to keep the alley from falling in on him. *Too much—too new. I'm not safe.*

"What are you doing, opening a portal outside designated grounds? You are lucky I was the one catching sight of it, in this alley." The voice pulled his gaze up and Sam tried to focus. The clash of color on the long robe the man wore was jarring, half bright yellow, half burnt orange, with a silver belt and stripes of blue and green. He had wrinkled, liver-spotted skin, and hair with small feathery tufts of gray, hints of blue and pink peeking through. The top—crest was the only word—bristled as the man did, a comb rising in the middle of his head. A moustache made of what could only be feathers ran down either side of his chin, hanging almost to the large collar on his robe.

"What are you?" Sam breathed. He had to be imagining things again—so cold he was hallucinating, while his aunt lay helpless beside him. He took his watch out, wound it, his tightness bleeding into the motion, then held it up to one ear, listening for the calming *tick*. It still worked. It had to be real. *Not imagining this. Is that better or worse?*

The man's large purple eyes narrowed at the movement and he cocked his head as he watched. "I am of the Kirian," he said. "You come from Methiem, yes? Your town must not be getting much interspecies traffic."

"I...I'm from America." *What's a Kirian? What's Methiem?* Those words didn't make sense. His heart was trying to strangle him, climbing up into his mouth. One sweaty palm gripped his watch while the other dug fingernails into the dirt. Sam scrambled away, but hit the wall, his right leg spasming. The wood siding rose overhead, blocking his view of whatever was above them. Blocking escape. He looked past the man to the entrance of the alley. Unintelligible sounds wafted in, and a splash of some jaunty music. There were more people out there. Crowds. *No escape that way.*

He was hyperventilating. Breathe deep. Aunt Martha's sightless eyes filled his memory. *No. Not her.* She was his only family.

The man, the...Kirian?...studied Sam. "A fledgling majus? Your first change to the Symphony?" A pause. "I did not make the portal. You were doing that."

He's real. Oh God, he's real. *Where am I?* "I have to get back!" Sam pointed to where the hole in the air had been. He was ready to accept anything at this point. "Can you make another one? I have to get home.

I have to get back to her." He was talking too fast, and tried to stop. "How do I get back?" Sam sniffed hard, then swallowed. His eyes burned, and hot trails ran down his face. Cold flesh at his fingertips, sightless eyes staring up. He would have to...clean up the body. She would accept no less.

"You must be opening another portal yourself." The Kirian was annoyingly calm. Why wasn't he doing something? "Or communicate to me the location. Difficult, if you have not changed the Grand Symphony before."

"How do I do that?" How could music help his aunt? Why wasn't the man helping? Maybe he was hearing things. He held his watch close again, but the ticking didn't calm him. *I already checked that, didn't I? This is actually happening.* He held his breath, then let it out. He was panicking, and he couldn't stop. He had to stop.

The Kirian made an irritated noise, a clicking in his teeth. "Are you able to hear the Symphony?"

"I don't know what that means," Sam said. He heard the words, but they weren't going anywhere in his head. They didn't mean anything. "Just *help* me." He sniffed again, and his nose cleared suddenly. There was an acidic tang in the air, like this place had been used for a toilet. It made him have to pee.

The ridge of feathers on the man's head ruffled, rising like hackles. *Annoyance*, Sam somehow knew. *How can I know that?*

"I have not time to teach a majus, with his song scarcely written, how to access the Symphony. If you are wanting to get back to your home, you will need to learn for yourself or pay for a portal. I am very busy." The man turned, and Sam gasped at an icy spike of fear.

No! I can't be in a strange place all alone. "Wait." He stretched out a hand, and the stranger paused. "Don't leave me. I don't know how I got here. I think she's gone. She was cold, and the fire burned out. Nothing worked anymore." He swallowed past a lump, gulped for more air. "I *have* to get back—" He was babbling, but the man turned back sharply. He wasn't going to leave. Sam ran a hand down the wood behind him, splinters poking his skin. The rough surface had to be real.

"What—exactly—did you run from?"

Sam had to keep him talking. Something his therapist told him bubbled up in his mind: notice what was happening to him, review it, then respond to it. He had to sound reasonable to keep this man here. If he really wanted to teach, then someday, he would have to stand in front of a class of students. If he couldn't talk to one strange man, what did that say about him?

Sam closed his eyes and brought his watch close, letting the ticking set a beat for his thoughts. He was taking quick, short breaths, and made himself hold them. One, two, three ticks.

What had happened? Sam recited, his eyes closed. "I was reading, then it got cold, and all the lights went out, and the sun was dark." His voice got stronger as he spoke. "Aunt Martha and I—" His voice wavered upward, breaking. *She's gone.* "We started a fire, but it burned out. We were freezing, and then the hole appeared." He opened his eyes. "I couldn't take her with me. I didn't have time—"

The Kirian held up a hand, palm out. He had long and thin fingers, each with a nail ending in a wicked-looking curved point. "I believe you are needing to come with me."

Wasn't he listening? "No. I have to go *back*. Didn't you hear me?" Sam straightened, just a little. He could do this. "Who are you, anyway?"

"Ah. I have not introduced myself. I am Origon Cyrysi, majus of the Houses of Communication and Power. You may call me Majus Cyrysi." The first syllable of the last name was hard, almost a click of the Kirian's mouth.

"I'm Sam," he said in a small voice. The man was going to stay. He wouldn't be alone. His breathing slowed to match the watch. He was safe, but he needed to get home. Something the man—Kirian—said nagged at him. He slid up the wall, shaking. His legs fought to stand. "You said I could tell you where my home is and you can open a...a portal?" *Then I can forget all this ever happened.*

The majus' already thin lips compressed to non-existence. After a moment, he stepped closer. Sam swallowed as Majus Cyrysi touched cool fingers to his forehead. *He's going to help, right?* Suddenly, yellow light dripped like syrup along the man's arm, arching toward him. Sam jerked away. "What's that?"

The Kirian twitched, and the color spiraled back up his arm, like mist retreating from the sun. "Do *not* move." The majus looked pale. "I was almost losing part of my song and I do not have extra to lose." His crest ruffled, flattened. "So you are able to see the colors. You can be trained as a majus then, can hear the Grand Symphony." He reached out again. "*Do not* move. Think of your home. Pretend you can be showing the picture in your mind to me."

The long nails pricked his forehead as the swirls of color crept closer. *Anything to get back.* Home was familiar, easy to imagine. This was probably all a hallucination. Sam thought of his room, the boxes in his collection. The cozy kitchen, filled with his aunt's southern cooking. His heart raced at the remembered smell of hominy grits with cheddar and butter. *She's gone.* He grabbed the memory, visualizing Aunt Martha's workshop, filled with scraps of cloth, half-finished shirts and pants, and the sound of a sewing machine. His aunt teaching him to sew on a button. The living room, frozen and quiet, spread out in his mind's eye while silent tears streamed down his face.

Majus Cyrysi's brow eased, and finally, the hand receded. "Reverse communication leaves many questions, but you are acceptable at transferring location pointers."

"Then you can open a hole back to my home?" Things didn't have to make sense in a hallucination.

"Portal. Yes, I believe I am having enough information." The man turned to one wooden wall of the alley. "This is to be highly illegal outside a portal ground, but to catch a Drain like you were experiencing in action is more important. If I were not friends with those on the Council, I would not even be trying this." Sam nodded along, no idea what the Kirian was saying. The majus watched the wall for a moment, then raised a hand, frowning. Then he raised both hands.

As his fear receded, Sam's curiosity grew. *That's not how it happened before.* "Are the colors going to appear again?" he asked. Majus Cyrysi gave him a sharp look and Sam hunched down.

The majus watched the wall, both hands outstretched, then dropped them. "The location is changed too far from your mental picture." He sounded out of breath. "As happened when I was experiencing my own Drain."

"What does that mean?" Something wasn't right, but his heartbeat was slowing. Keep breathing. Three ticks in, three ticks out.

The man ignored him. "This is the second Drain I have encountered. Both times, the phenomenon was powerful enough to warp the environment it was in, breaking down the very fabric of reality. What is happening to the energy—the notes? They cannot simply be destroyed!" He looked back at Sam. "You must be accompanying me back to the Council. Maybe this time they will listen."

Destroying energy? That makes no sense. Was what happened to me one of these Drains? "That's it?" Sam's voice rose, his hands clenching. "Just look at the wall, then tell me I can't get home?" *This hallucination sucks.*

"You are welcome to try yourself." The majus gestured curtly at the wall.

"Maybe I will," Sam said. Anger made his panic lessen. He stood, chest out, staring at the wall, willing the hole in the air to open. It was his hallucination and he needed to see Aunt Martha. He needed the safety of his room.

The faint noise of the crowd grew in his perception, as did the wail of whatever street music was being played. He was fairly sure that wasn't the same thing as the Symphony the majus referred to. The Symphony seemed an internal concept. He closed his eyes and, just briefly, might have heard the same bass *plunk* as when the portal opened from his fireplace.

But nothing happened. He couldn't make a hole through space because that was impossible.

Sam slumped and turned back to the majus, who was watching him like a chicken eyeing a worm.

"Are you finished?" He looked disappointed. Sam nodded wearily. "Then come with me. The Council needs to be seeing this evidence." Majus Cyrysi's robe swished around heavy boots as he strode to the mouth of the alley.

The icy chill seized Sam's chest again. His feet rooted to the ground. *Maybe. Maybe this isn't a hallucination after all.* "No."

The majus looked back. "Why not?"

If this wasn't a hallucination, then the sounds that drifted from the mouth of the alley came from a crowd of people, possibly as strange as the majus. He blinked rapidly, willing the scene to fall away, to see the frozen living room. It didn't work.

This is real. He swallowed. Aunt Martha always wanted him to meet more people. He owed it to her memory to try. What else would he do—live in this piss-stained alley? He took one step forward.

"We will use the maps at the Spire of the Maji to determine where on Methiem you are from," Majus Cyrysi called back from the end of the alley.

Sam's step faltered. "Methiem?" He put one hand to his chest, willed the thumping there to quiet.

The majus frowned. "You are from Methiem, are you not? You are unfamiliar with other species, so I am assuming you know little of the Great Assembly, or the ten species. You cannot be from one of the other homeworlds."

"I'm from America," Sam said again. "On Earth." Questions were piling up, but he had to focus on one thing at a time.

Majus Cyrysi's thick eyebrows drew down. "I have not heard of this place."

"You've never even heard of Earth? Then where are you from?" *I preferred the hallucination.*

"From Kiria, naturally. My birthplace was in a small mountain town called Asbheriton."

"A different *planet?*" *Freezing darkness. Aunt Martha. Holes in the air and aliens. If this was real—*

Sam found one wall with a hand, leaned against it. His breathing was speeding again. Suddenly, fresh tears carved hot lines down his cheeks.

"It is the planet on which most of my species are born," the majus returned, his words sarcastic. "Though some are born in the Nether, or on other homeworlds."

"The Nether?" *No. Too much information. Get home first.*

Majus Cyrysi spun around, robe swishing around his feet, gesturing with a long skinny arm to the mouth of the alley. "This, boy!" he cried. "We are *in* the Nether."

Sam peered out of the alley, keeping his hand on the rough wood of the structure—a point of stability. Before him buildings loomed from all sides. The light outside the alley was wrong, as if from giant fluorescent lights instead of a sun. He shrank back. Strange people thronged a small square across from the alley. They gestured and talked to each other. *Too many, too close.* He would have to go out there. *So many chances to mess things up.* He couldn't just reset, like in a computer game. This was why he hadn't finished his college application.

A red squid-like creature with tentacles sprouting from its head was selling something to another of Majus Cyrysi's species, who was wearing a crazy quilt of a robe. Two eight-foot tall beings strode across the square like faintly blue, two-legged giraffes. They both wore long flowing pants with split skirts, swishing loudly as they moved. They passed a seated figure like them, who blew into a long tube. That was where the music was coming from. Sam's fingers tightened on the rough edge of a plank. He wanted to pull back in the alley, but he also wanted to see more.

There were humans too. A woman wearing a loose wrap of fabric spoke to a being covered in green-brown hair, with sharp blue eyes and a snout. The woman's scarf looked like something Aunt Martha might have knitted, and Sam choked down a sob. How were there humans here when Majus Cyrysi hadn't heard of Earth?

Buildings of wood and stone, reaching far overhead, hemmed in the square. A bridge crossed between the tops of the buildings on either side, greenery trailing from it. Vertigo caught at Sam, and he took comfort in the packed dirt of the alley and cobblestone of the street, pressing back against the wall.

"I can't go out there," he mumbled to his shoes. "It's too much."

"What is this?" Majus Cyrysi said, bending down beside him. "More excuses about your Earth?"

"It's not that," Sam said, looking up into the other's strange face. "I...I don't like new places." His eyes darted to the alley entrance, back down to the ground. "Or crowds."

The Kirian frowned. "I see." He tapped a long finger against his cheek, looking Sam up and down. Did he ever poke himself with those hooked fingernails? "Do you think you are able to be walking through the city just a bit? The Spire of the Maji is much quieter, enclosed."

Sam shook his head. *Not after what happened. How much did the cold touch? Did it affect my house? All of South Carolina? The whole world?* "Maybe later. I need to sit down for a while." With time, he could calm his breathing. He peered out of the alley again and his heart raced.

What if I don't have to go through the crowds? "Could you make a hole in the air to where we need to go?" Sam waved a hand at the alley entrance.

Majus Cyrysi shook his head. "Portals are not working in that manner. There is a limit to how close the endpoints can exist to each other, on the scale of continents. Certainly not within a city. The songs of the two endpoints so close together would cause harmonics overpowering the majus changing the Symphony."

Sam slumped. *So much for having a good idea.*

The majus stroked fingers down his moustache. "Will you stay here for a short while? The information you hold is very important."

Sam looked up. "You're leaving me?" *Alone? Or the crowd? Alone was better.*

"Not long," the majus said. "A friend of mine has experience with fears such as yours. She has techniques to help you cope, if I am bringing her here."

Sam gulped, wiped at his eyes. "Yes. I'll be better soon," he snuck another peek outside the alley, shivered. *Or the hallucination will end.*

"Then I will be back soon." Majus Cyrysi strode to the end of the alley, turned back. "Do not leave, even if you feel you can. It is easy to get lost here."

Sam nodded, and slid down in a corner, pulling his knees in. Alone, he wept for Aunt Martha.

CHAPTER THREE

Moons and Wars

- People commonly wonder how the floor of the Nether is made of dirt, instead of the substance of the columns. By the influx of inhabitants, flora, and fauna through portals, and over thousands of cycles, soil accumulated. I have visited deep windswept gullies, far away from any habitation, where the true Nether floor gleams like crystal in the light from the walls.
   Morvu Francita Januti, Etanela explorer and big game hunter

Origon frowned at the boy still curled in the corner of the dead-end alley, tear-stains on his face, shivering though the air was warm. The fledgling majus hadn't moved since he left, nearly a lightening ago. The light of the walls were shading into afternoon. Was this new majus so scared of existence? If he had been in the boy's place, he would have been halfway through the Imperium by now, warning or not. He hoped the fledgling was capable enough to help his research on the Drains. He had to get the information locked away in that head.

Rilan pushed past him and he stepped aside, anticipating how she would move even so long past the end of their travels together. The bell at the end of her braid jingled as she walked and she tugged at the waistline of her white dress looking, as always, as if she would rather tear it off. That she wore it meant she had been on her way to a Council meeting when he caught her—fortunate timing. Though they had spoken little in the last few cycles, Rilan was his one instance of leverage with the Council, when the other councilmembers thought his research was so much eggshell leavings. What he would give to have the Council of his youth back.

In any case, this boy could influence his next meeting—turn the Council from their obsession with the Aridori to actual threats, like the Drains.

"This is the new majus, Ori?" Rilan asked, breaking into his reverie. "You left him like this?" The boy looked up at the sound, sniffing. His eyes widened a little and Origon let the Nether interpret for him. Surprise, and maybe fear. It was hard to guess at Methiemum expressions without the aid of the Nether, as their topfeathers could not signal any subtle emotion.

"He said he would be fine on his own for a little time. I believed him." Really, there were more pressing matters, like his investigation into the Drains.

"I'm Councilor Ayama," Rilan said, ignoring Origon and squatting down in the stinking alley. She pulled her dress away from a suspiciously dark puddle. "What's your name? Where are you from?"

The boy wiped at his eyes, and took in a deep breath. He still had a death-grip on that pocketwatch.

"I already told him," he pointed up to Origon. "I'm from Earth. My name's Sam. Sam van Oen." Ah yes. That was his name.

"I'm not familiar with that place," Rilan said. "I can get a globe of Methiem—" Origon sighed. The boy was waving his hands again. He was going to get riled up, as before.

"I'm not *from* Meth...Methiem," Sam said, and Origon saw his nostrils flare, sucking in air too fast. "I'm from Earth. My aunt was just—" He swallowed. "There was this cold that took all the power and energy away." Rilan peered closer.

"This is what he told you?" she asked Origon, but the boy nodded.

"He has seen a Drain," Origon answered, "much as I did. You know what happened with the first." Every moment they debated meant it would be harder to study the phenomenon.

Origon's nails dig into his palms, and he carefully kept his crest neutral. The abomination he'd encountered after the crash on Methiem's moon loomed in his mind. So much for the Methiemum's first spaceflight. Not only had piloting the craft deprived him of much of his song, but the off-white, fleshy egg that almost killed him had absorbed the material of the space capsule, changing the crash site so fundamentally that making a new portal to the moon was all but impossible. He still dreamed about it, and now his song wavered like a simple tune, stripped of many of its notes and much of its complexity.

"You claimed the Symphony cannot touch the voids," Rilan said, twisting back to him. "The Symphony's music winds through everything."

"As you say." Now Origon let his crest flatten in disbelief. "Yet both I and the space capsule's crew barely escaped through my portal."

"Space ships?" This at least seemed to catch the boy's attention. "Is that where all the aliens come from?"

"Of course not," Origon started, but Rilan hushed him.

"We travel between our homeworlds via portals the maji control. The capsule Ori piloted was an experiment." She waved a hand vaguely. "One that did not go as planned, because of Ori's void. Did you see the launch of the shuttle? Were you in the crowd on Methiem?"

The boy—young man, really—only shook his head. Origon frowned. They had to get him out of this dirty back alley, somewhere Origon could learn more about the Drains, and where Sam was from.

"Are you well enough to come with us?" he asked.

Sam looked past them, to the open end of the alley, and shivered. His eyes went back to Origon's face. "The same thing happened to you? You know what I went through. Why didn't you tell me?"

Origon stared back. He had said as much, had he not? Or at least mentioned something of it. Why else would he be so interested in the Drains? Was the young man's brain addled? If so, Origon might need a softer approach to get the information from him.

"Up now." Rilan helped pull Sam to his feet, then stepped back so the three of them were in a triangle, looking up slightly to meet his gaze. "You still haven't told me where exactly you're from."

Sam took in a deep, shuddering breath. "Where I come from, there are no aliens, and we call ourselves humans, not Meth—Methiemum." He paused. "And there are no maji. The only symphonies we have are the ones that orchestras play. How does a symphony make colors?"

Origon exchanged a look with Rilan. Many non maji didn't understand what the maji did, and if Sam was new to the Great Assembly of Species, then perhaps more explanation *was* needed, despite the extra time it would take. He seemed calmer now he was conversing.

"The Grand Symphony underlies everything," Rilan said. "It is the music that writes the universe's existence, ever flowing and changing. Maji are those who can hear some aspect of the Grand Symphony."

"Then, a majus can use the notes defining their own experiences to change the music they hear," Origon continued. "As a lit candle produces not just light, but heat, so the changes produce colors, along with the physical or mental effect, based on the aspect of the Grand Symphony that was being adjusted." Origon tapped his robe. "I am of the Houses of Communication and Power, and my strength lies in using air and heat in combination."

He let the Symphony of Communication fill him. Subtle cadenzas representing the buzz of the crowds outside the alley warred against the smooth chords of the wind and pressure differentials. He grasped a few of the notes that made up his song—the reflection of his collected experiences—and used them to alter a chord progression, bringing the notes to a lower register, and speeding the tempo. Yellow spiraled out from his hand as a sharp breeze blew away the smell of the alley. Sam blinked in surprise, but again, his eyes followed the color. He was definitely majus potential.

Origon took his notes back and the breeze died. He spread fingers toward his friend. "Councilor Ayama is of the House of Healing, though her specialty is mental rather than biological."

"I'm a psychologist," Rilan said. Origon grunted. He had just said that.

"I'm studying ethics, and I'm going to go into law," Sam said. "Does your job use magic?" Origon winced at the word. He fluffed his crest and started to answer, but Rilan got there first.

"In...a sense," she said. "Though it isn't *magic*. We can change the tempo and notes of the Grand Symphony underlying the universe, but only of that aspect we can hear. I hear the Symphony of Healing, and so belong to the House of Healing, but any member of any house may pursue a livelihood in whatever they wish."

Sam raised his head a little, holding his watch tight. "Sounds like magic to me." Rilan rolled her eyes. At least Origon wasn't the only impatient one.

"Do you have a way to be helping him?" Origon glanced around the wooden alley. His feathers would mold if he stayed here any longer. "At least to get us somewhere with more resources?" Origon stroked his moustache. An idea was forming.

Rilan held out a hand to Sam again. "Ori is correct. We must get you out of here. I can use my song to listen to yours, if that's acceptable. The House of Healing will enable me to hear what part of your mental makeup does, well, *this* to you." She gestured at Sam, backed into a dark corner.

Origon let his crest ruffle as the young man retreated even further.

This would take all day. He had to be stable, or at least calm, if Origon were to get information about his homeworld, assuming it was not Methiem.

Then Sam came forward, breathing fast, knuckles white around his watch. "You can see why I have problems with new places? With crowds? Can you make it go away?"

Rilan shook her head. "Only you can do that, and likely it will never go away completely. You can learn to cope with it, however. I may be able to help you." Her hand was still extended.

Sam looked to the alley mouth again, bit his lip, then took another small step away from the wood planks. "It's not that I don't like people. I do." Origon let the Nether translate Sam's wide eyes and mouth screwed to one side. Like a crest flattened and swept in a curve. "I'd like to meet more people without being afraid." He swallowed, took yet another step. "Okay, let's try."

Rilan nodded. "Hold still a moment." She shifted forward to touch fingers to the young man's forehead. White and olive blossomed around her hand, shifting into a net that buzzed around Sam's dark hair. Origon could see his eyes tracking the colors, hands shaking slightly by his sides.

"Yes, I can hear the notes describing an overload on neural pathways dealing with the fight and flight response." Rilan's foot tapped in time with something Origon couldn't hear. "Crowds, new places, large areas are the worst?" Sam gulped a breath and nodded, but he must have remembered what happened before. He didn't jerk away.

"You can see—hear all that?" Sam asked Rilan.

"As I said, I'm a psychologist." The fingers of Rilan's other hand were weaving in a complicated rhythm, as though she directed a choir. "I use my song to help me in my job. My house lets me hear the aspect of the Grand Symphony that defines your brain, among other things."

"Oh," Sam said. Origon smiled as he watched his friend work, his crest relaxing. Once, many cycles ago, she had to talk a Lobath child down from where he had gotten stuck on the top of a giant rotting conk fungus—one the Lobath used for housing materials. Origon considered the similarities.

Rilan twisted to him. "He is Methiemum," she confirmed, but her brows drew down. She ran a hand down her long braid, pulling it over her shoulder.

"But?" Origon prompted. He didn't need another impediment. They had been in this alley long enough.

"There are differences in his mental makeup. He's certainly not one of the other species—his psychology is like a Methiemum raised on a different homeworld." She paused.

"I *was* raised on a different homeworld—um—on Earth," Sam insisted, behind her.

Rilan shifted her stance, as if she realized the baby bird she found was in actuality a young nesting raptor. "Or hiding what you are." She passed two fingers in front of her eyes once, twice, in quick succession, in the old gesture to reveal a hidden Aridori.

Origon stared at her, his crest slowly tightening, drawing his skin up. "Do not tell me *you* are now believing the rotten eggs the Council is pushing? Next you will be telling me the Aridori will climb through my window at night and replace me. You have more sense than that."

She dropped her hand, looking only a little guilty. "That's all the Council is discussing today, Ori. It's all they can think about. There are eyewitness accounts coming in from all over the Nether." She looked up, judging the quality of the light, then quickly back, as if Sam would have run off in that time. "In fact, I need to get back very soon." She fixed Origon with a glare. "In the Imperium, in Gloomlight, even in the farming communities and Poler, people are scared the Aridori are coming back. There have been two reported murders this month— someone claiming their spouse had been replaced by an impostor."

Origon watched his old student, his old companion. Her face showed more confusion than conviction. He looked to the young man, who was obviously no threat. "Was there any proof these murderers were not simply capitalizing on panic? They are seeing what? Monsters change shape before their eyes, or shadows in the grain fields? What solid evidence is included? Has anyone brought in an Aridori?"

"Well, no," Rilan admitted. She straightened, chin up. "Though I wouldn't be surprised if someone did. We've had innocent citizens in the Imperium hassled by over-zealous do-gooders, thinking they've single-handedly stopped the downfall of the Great Assembly."

"Excuse me." They both looked to Sam, and he swallowed. However, his eyes were alight, as if he saw where they were for the first time. "What's an Aridori, and what does it have to do with me?"

Maybe there was fire in this new majus after all. "They are but a child's scare-tale," Origon said.

Rilan waved a hand at him. "You must admit there is truth to the tales. The Aridori war *did* happen." She shifted just out of the young man's reach.

"They fought a war with you?" Sam asked.

"It was to be long enough ago no one remembers anything about it," Origon told him. He could at least explain the tales rather than accusing Sam of acting in one. The sooner they got past this distraction, the sooner they could study something real, like the Drains. "The Aridori disappeared after the war was over, so all the stories say, with the last stragglers hunted down by groups of soldiers. The horror tales say they could look like anything, be anyone. For all we know the species fought each other over phantoms."

"'Never trust what an Aridori says or does,'" Rilan said in a sing-song voice, and Origon let his crest flatten again, cocking an eyebrow. Sam was scared enough as it was. "'Slip through a crack like an Aridori.' 'If you lie to the maji, an Aridori will take your place in the night.'"

Sam was looking between them. "So. Do these Aridori exist, or not?"

"No," Origon said. There were serious problems without imagining a monster behind every door.

"Yes," Rilan said. Then she bobbed her head sideways, lips pursed. "And no. I do believe they exist." She flicked a glance up at Origon. "Or did. But, they are no longer considered one of the ten species of the Great Assembly."

"You think I might be one of them?" Sam asked, his voice small.

Origon barked a laugh. "If you are, boy, then you are an actor worthy of the ancestor's praise."

"'Never trust what an Aridori says or does,'" Rilan muttered, but Origon stared her down. She wiped a hand down her face. "No. I don't think you are an Aridori. The Council's fears are getting to me." Tension bled from her.

"Then if we are convinced he has not come to kill us all, can we be leaving this alley?" Origon asked

"We need to get him to the Council," Rilan said.

"I am having a better idea." Origon told her. He tapped the shoulder of her white dress with one finger. "*You* are needing to get to the Council. I will take Sam to the House of Communication and see if we can locate his homeworld. Then we will be coming to the Council." The Drain on the Methiemum moon Ksupara was inaccessible until they sent another capsule, and he was not losing another chance.

"Do you think you can walk with us now?" Rilan asked Sam. "Ori is correct. I need to get back to the Council."

The young man eyed the entrance to the alley again, and Origon saw his breathing speed up. That ancestors-cursed watch came back out. Origon moved to block the view. They didn't have time for this, and he glared at Rilan. "If you are to be convinced he is not some ancient evil, can you please do something for him?"

Rilan took in a breath, but she also glanced up again, judging the time. "There is one thing I can do, but it is only temporary, and will leave you feeling," she waggled a hand, "off."

Sam looked to her, and away from the alley entrance. "Like anxiety medication? I've taken that before, when I had to. I didn't like it."

Origon's friend frowned. "The medical ward attached to the House of Healing has been experimenting with such things. They are common, where you come from?"

Sam nodded.

"Hm. I mean to do this with my song, though it will be a permanent use of my notes." Rilan rubbed her chin. "A physical form of this medication would save much effort from maji of the House of Healing."

"Permanent?" Sam asked.

"Not to you," Rilan answered. "A permanent change to the Symphony means I do not get that portion of my song, my being, back. The change is non-reversible."

"If I were to add heat somewhere with the House of Power," Origon explained, "I could later reverse the change to be recouping my song, as I was doing with the breeze you felt."

Except, in the space capsule, he had spent hours spending his song like spare Nether glass to keep them from crashing.

"This change—to the Symphony—would act like anxiety meds?" Sam dry washed his hands.

"I think so," Rilan said. "I can block that phrase of music for a short time, lessening your fear of crowds and spaces, but it is artificial, and never as good as working through the issue—" she broke off to Sam's furious nodding.

"Do it," he said, then pointed to Origon. "Like he says, I have to get out of here. When I'm somewhere safe I can work through it on my own."

Rilan nodded. "Hold still." She cocked her head, listening for several seconds, then placed both hands on Sam's head. They blazed white and olive, and the color made an organic-looking map once again, pulsing in time to something Origon couldn't hear. This time the net slid into the young man's flesh and disappeared. Rilan removed her hands and took a deep breath in, tilting her head side to side as if a headache was imminent. Sam relaxed, and sighed. He lowered his watch. His eyes were slightly unfocused.

"I've silenced the music of several of your mental connections," Rilan told Sam. "It is not the best method, but it should work for the moment." Origon pushed down his crest. Rilan giving up her notes sent his memory spinning back to piloting the capsule. She looked up to him, as if she knew what he was thinking. "The cost is small enough. I've done it before."

Origon nodded back, making his crest loosen. He turned to Sam. "Are you ready to be finding your homeworld?"

CHAPTER FOUR

Through the Imperium

- The Spire's structure was one of the first built after the Imperium was founded. All species in the Great Assembly accepted the idea, as the Spire was destined to be the center of education and governance for the maji. The maji's portals brought the species together, and it was deemed necessary for maji of different species to continue their association.

From "The History of the Spire," a work by the Festuour philosopher Hegramtifar Yhon, Thinker

Sam blinked at the majus. Majuses. Maji. Everything was muddy, like strong anxiety meds. He peered around the councilor and Majus Cyrysi to the end of the alley. *Is my heart beating faster?* He couldn't summon the will to care about it. He edged closer. There were layers of cotton wrapped between what he saw and the fear that usually rose up.

"Is it working?" The councilor sounded tired.

He took a few more steps forward, and when he looked down, his shoes were outside the wooden walls of the alley. There had been a question. "I think so."

Before him, swirls of people passed by, all shapes and sizes. He took another step, pulled despite himself to the chaos. It was like a big party he'd been invited to, or so he imagined. He was never invited to anything. He hoped that would change when and if he got to college.

He stepped out, between a family of humans, or whatever they were called here, and two women of Majus Cyrysi's species, one with skin the color of mahogany, the other's like desert sand. Both sets of bare legs ate up the ground in long strides, their crests waving and stretching as they gestured to each other. He was already past the first vendor stalls, stepping around a sputtering motorized cart holding a glass tank of fish, when the other two caught up. The majus' clawed hand came down on his shoulder, holding him back.

"It's so colorful," Sam told him. He pointed to a squid-like bipedal creature, with rubbery skin and three head-tentacles in place of hair.

"What is that?" There were lots of the creatures here, now he looked more carefully. His finger wavered, pointing out more of them.

"*She* is one of the Lobath," Councilor Ayama said, pushing his arm down. She peered up at the Kirian, around Sam's shoulders. "I may have blocked a few too many connections."

The buildings around the plaza grew on each other, sprouting up like mushrooms after a heavy rain. *So many buildings.* They stretched on, built up and around. A glint of light caught his eye above the line of structures, reflecting from a giant curved surface. It pushed through the fluff in his mind, and Sam staggered at a moment of vertigo. He swallowed and grasped for his watch, feeling a little more himself.

"What is that glass thing?" *Did I just point at a whole bunch of aliens?* He glanced around, but no one besides the two maji were paying attention.

"You are meaning the column?" Majus Cyrysi followed the surface with one hook-nailed finger. Sam's gaze went higher and higher, and he could feel unease scratching at his mind behind the cotton. "The columns are spaced more or less regularly, through the Nether. They connect the floor—" Majus Cyrysi pointed *down*, as if through the dirt beneath their feet, "—to the ceiling, far above." His finger speared upward. The immense cylindrical surface protruded from the buildings lining the square, reaching upward until it was lost to sight. Reflections shimmered across it, and buildings crowded around like small animals bundled near a larger one for warmth.

"There's a ceiling?" Sam asked. The column disappeared from view as they passed under an archway, moist, earthy scents pungent in the enclosed tunnel. Small ferns and moss dotted the sides of the streets, and Sam pulled his arm close before he brushed a wide, furry alien. His stomach turned over, and he swallowed bile, though he didn't *feel* afraid.

"The Nether is enclosed," Councilor Ayama said, from just behind. Sam blinked back at her, trying to understand. The fog in his mind was slowing everything. "The first maji found their way to this place long ago. The ten species came from different stars and galaxies, like you did. Normally, one must have detailed information of the endpoint of a portal, except for the Nether. This is the one place maji can reach without knowing where they are going beforehand."

They exited the tunnel, hurrying across a wide tree-lined street where carriages and vehicles puffing smoke passed each other at a walking pace. Sam tried to pay attention both to the councilor's words and to his surroundings. One of the nearby trees had fluffy blue fronds instead of leaves.

Majus Cyrysi's robe was bright as they walked through pools of light and shadow. "The first maji to come here remembered the way back home, and were starting trade between their species. It was what grew to be the Great Assembly."

They passed through a square where the walls were a wet-looking brown resin. Long bushy ferns hung from windows, and the flat fluorescent lighting cast shadows from strange directions. A fishy smell permeated the air, mixed with something like mushrooms in take-out Chinese. Sam slid through people, trying not to let them touch him. A jangle of music made him turn to another street musician, one of the giant blue-ish aliens like he had seen outside the alley. This one had a thin stringed instrument taller than him, and was singing in a high reedy voice along with his plucking. They seemed a common sight here. Haggling, speeches, and casual conversation washed by, and hands of anxiety clawed at the cotton in his mind, reducing its thickness. *Why are they blurry? Can't quite focus on faces.*

"Through this market, then up above street level," Majus Cyrysi called back, his voice almost lost in the voices around them. "Once we exit the Lobath district we will be in High Imperium."

I can feel my heart beating. Should I be able to? Maybe it's because we're walking fast. Sam realized his watch was in one hand. The constant influx of new places was overcoming the councilor's magic. *If I break down in the middle of the street, will they leave me here?*

"I have not been visiting E'Fon's curio shop in many a cycle." Majus Cyrysi pointed at a recessed section of wall with a bright blue door. Did the Kirian not see Sam's distress? Did the councilor? The majus gestured at a display of writhing insects behind a red-tinted piece of plate glass. "Murienta's shop has the freshest maggots. Much tastier than those half-dead things they serve at the Spire."

They turned into another open square, all the buildings made of green, glowing stone. There was a crowd of people surrounding a platform made of old crates, shaded by two tall, leafy plants, like banana trees. On top of the platform, a human and one of the very tall aliens were shouting out into the crowd. Some people were holding signs. The fuzziness was evaporating, and Sam knew this was wrong, especially when both maji stopped dead.

Sam peered at a sign, willing his eyes to focus. A sequence of circles and dots wavered, and suddenly he was reading English: 'The Assembly is lying to us,' and 'The Aridori are hiding in plain sight,' and 'Don't let the maji dictate your life.'

"Not this way," Councilor Ayama muttered, and grabbed for him. She held her other arm in front of her dress, as if she could keep others from seeing it. Majus Cyrysi was frowning, his crest spiking in all directions.

Sam stared between the signs, resisting the councilor's pull. There was someone else on the platform, a gangly, hairy person on their knees between the two others. "What are they doing?" he asked.

Majus Cyrysi came up next to him. "Rilan, they are holding a Sureri prisoner." The councilor's grip lessened on Sam's shoulder.

"So much for avoiding this," she said, no longer obscuring her dress. She strode toward the crowd, her shoulders back, and white and olive green bloomed around her throat as she called out.

"What's going on here?" Her voice was thunderous, rolling over the shouting figures on the stage.

Majus Cyrysi, seemingly at random, grabbed one of two humans in leather leggings and lace shirts, talking about a restaurant's high prices and ignoring the scene. "Find the civic guard, now. Bring them here."

The person hesitated, as if she would refuse, but the majus' face must have changed her mind. She took off at a fast trot, and Majus Cyrysi turned back to the crowd, pulling Sam along. He trembled. This was no longer an exciting walk.

"Stay close," the majus said. Yellow and orange were curling around his fingers and something tickled the back of Sam's mind, like a band playing several blocks away, but the blood pumping in his ears nearly drowned it out. He held on to the majus' robe, dizzy.

They came up behind the councilor, who was already in heated debate with those on the stage.

"—is an Aridori!" The man on the stage pointed down at the person on his knees. Several members of the crowd passed fingers in front of their eyes as the councilor had done to him. This close, Sam could see the prisoner trembling. *I'd be doing the same, in his situation, or just faint.* The councilor's magic was the only thing keeping him from a complete breakdown. He could feel the anxiety battering at his mind, but it slid away, as if against a steel door. *Can't pass out. Stay up.*

"What proof of this are you having?" Majus Cyrysi called out. "The Aridori are long dead." They shuffled farther into the crowd, keeping pace with the sidling walk Councilor Ayama had adopted. Getting closer, but not threatening.

"They've been hiding. Pretending they were gargoyles like him, all this time," the man shouted back. The kneeling figure's face was distorted and hairy, almost bat-like, and Sam realized he wasn't human, but one of the alien species. "We don't need the maji to tell us what to do! You've been helping them hide!"

"Shield, Ori," Councilor Ayama hissed, and the air shimmered in a sphere around them, glowing yellow and orange like a soap bubble in the sun. Something struck and bounced, above Sam's head, and he cringed down. His heart hammered in his chest. *Need to get out of here. Can't go alone.*

"Take us in," the councilor said, and shuffled forward. Ori crept along behind her, hands waving as if tying knots in the air.

Sam stumbled forward with them, his eyes trying to take in everything at once. There was a faint music in the air—or in his head—though he couldn't make out the notes. *Is that the Symphony they keep talking about? How did I get in this situation?* His hands shook so badly he couldn't keep hold of the majus' robe.

They reached the stage, the man hurling insults at them, and climbed up a set of crates serving as stairs. People around the edge of the crowd were leaving.

The councilor's throat still glowed with white and olive, and she leaned closer to the raging man.

"Hush!" she bellowed at him, and shocked, he fell silent. She knelt to the trembling prisoner, the bubble following them as Majus Cyrysi closed in, enveloping the prisoner. She laid hands on his head as she had done to Sam, her colors flowing between hands and the alien. Then she stood.

"This is no Aridori!" she shouted, and her voice filled the small plaza. She pointed to the man on the stage—the tall alien that had stood beside him had since climbed down and was hunkered down in the crowd. "He told you correctly that I am a majus, and I have used the Grand Symphony to determine that this person is Sureriaj, through and through."

"And do you take the word of a lying majus, or of someone who's telling you what's really happening?" the man shouted, but more people were leaving. Sam hugged himself, sick to his stomach. The cotton in his head was unraveling, and he drew a thumb over the comforting texture of his watch. He looked away from the staring eyes.

Then a troop of guards entered the plaza, in uniforms with polished metal armor, holding long, fluted rifles. The councilor crossed the distance to the shouting man on stage in an instant and touched him, her colors flashing once around his body before he slumped down to the ground.

The next few minutes passed in a blur to Sam, as if time sped up, then stood still. *It must be the medication.*

The guards were dispersing the crowd. The councilor and Majus Cyrysi were talking to the guard, handing over the distressed alien and the unconscious man. Majus Cyrysi's bubble disappeared with a pop, and the faint music that had been running through Sam's head vanished as if someone turned off a radio.

Soon, he found himself on a side ramp curving up and around buildings, leaning against a railing. *Did I black out?* The other two were walking, no colors visible around either, and he pitched forward to catch up.

"—Aridori are becoming a big problem, Ori, real or not," the councilor was saying. She wasn't even out of breath, though Sam was panting. "No one has seen your voids but you and him, while crowds like that are convinced the Aridori are real, and the Council and Assembly are covering it up. Some have even spoken against the Effature himself."

"This was an isolated incident, easily handled," Majus Cyrysi protested, his boots *thock*ing against the stone.

That was easy? Sam was calm enough to realize the cotton in his head was still holding.

"The crew of the shuttle saw the Drain as I did. Are they to be ignored as well?"

Councilor Ayama shook her head. "Several have admitted they may have been confused from the stress of the flight or the crash. Two of the eight members flatly refuse they saw anything, now." They turned a corner, Sam struggling to keep up. "The Aridori problem is bigger. I have to report to the Council while you take him to the House of Communication."

They passed three Kirian children, their faces as wrinkled and liver-spotted as Majus Cyrysi's, arguing over who would win in a race. The majus' crest was spiky with suppressed anger, Sam somehow knew, but the Kirian held his tongue, fuming.

They pushed through a revolving turnstile, past which was a tiled floor, wrought iron lanterns giving off an orange light. Sam tried to keep his gaze up, but the cotton in his mind was too thin. The ground was safer. There was a deep groove in the floor, then more tile on the other side, littered with discarded papers and trash. Bannisters sectioned off people standing in rows, or at least their feet. Suddenly, he realized they were at a tram station.

"This will take us to the houses of the maji, and the Spire," Majus Cyrysi told him. As Sam's head cleared, he was putting pieces together, trying to figure out this place before he had another panic attack. He tried to forget the crowd and the kneeling alien.

"How can I read the signs?" It was the first thing that popped into his head. He looked up the majus' colorful robe to his face. *Just focus on him.*

"The Nether," Majus Origon answered, his lips opened in a pointy smile, like a shark's. He seemed unconcerned about their encounter with the protest.

"Oh, give him a straight answer, Ori," the councilor said. She tapped a toe, looking down the track for the shuttle. "The Nether is alive, in a sense. It translates for us."

"The Nether bridges differences between its inhabitants," Majus Cyrysi said, still unconcerned. "If you were on one of the homeworlds, you would not be seeing this mix of beings." He waved an arm at the people waiting with them. "Sometimes there are conflicts, yes. Not all learn the Trader's Tongue, though here it is not mattering."

"So you're not speaking English." The longer they stood there, the more Sam got used to his new surroundings. The haze in his mind was still there. He looked around, carefully.

"Certainly not." Majus Cyrysi looked offended. "Whatever that is. The Nether deciphers not only words, but intent." The Kirian's crest ruffled, and *something* pushed a meaning toward Sam. Majus Cyrysi was pleased to pass on knowledge.

"Then the Nether is in our minds?" Sam asked. "You didn't say it was telepathic." Was that allowed? Did he have to sign something to give his consent? He reached for his watch. The ticking made the clock jump a little in his hand. *Regular, like your breathing.*

Councilor Ayama put one hand on his shoulder, squeezing gently. "The Nether helps us out. You don't need to be afraid of it." She sighed as a silver coach arrived with a smoky blast, auras of brown or red around the moving parts.

"Systems," Majus Cyrysi told him when Sam peered closer at a cam shaft that fed into the brake mechanism.

"System of what?" Sam asked. Wood doors with filigree inlay swung open, and a tentacled alien in a jumpsuit bowed them in. Sam forced his feet forward.

"Systems are collections of changes to the Symphony, held together through the workings of a maji of the House of Potential," Majus Cyrysi said. One hand described the aura around the cam shaft. "It will last for some time, at the cost of notes from the maji who created the change. Normal changes to the Grand Symphony fade quickly if the majus involved does not keep adjusting it with their song."

They chose seats facing forward, with glass windows to the side and above. The interior of the tram was dark polished wood with metal accents, decorative as often as not. Sam breathed a sigh of relief. Motion, at least, didn't bother him much, and he could let the thin barrier in his mind hold the anxiety back. He would have to do this sort of traveling if he went to the College of Charleston when he got back—riding on busses between classes.

The kneeling alien tugged at his thoughts, though he tried to let the memory of the crowd go. *Majus Cyrysi and Councilor Ayama handled it. Stop thinking about it. Ask something else.*

They shot forward, and a flock of large insects followed, the size of birds but with clear wings. Sam could hear them trilling to each other.

"How many houses of the maji are there?" Majus Cyrysi talked about them like they were fraternities.

"Six," the councilor told him. She folded her dress so it didn't take up as much space, shifting next to him. "Strength, communication, power, grace, healing, and potential."

"You can make people fall unconscious?" he asked.

"The Symphony of Healing contains the music that relates to biology, and living things, so yes," she said. "But those in the House of Healing can do many different things."

"I am better at manipulating the physical sides of the Houses of Communication and Power," Majus Cyrysi volunteered. "The House of Communication holds the Symphony of air, but also those of words and intents. The music that is forming heat transfer is contained in the House of Power, but so are those related to political and societal connections between objects and people."

The councilor leaned forward. Her smile was taut, but he could tell she was trying to soothe him. "You'll learn all this soon. Look up. You don't want to miss this."

The tram jerked around a turn. Sam's hands were sweaty, but he made himself watch. *I want to see it all.* He wanted to push through the fear that kept him back, though it would return when the councilor's work dissipated.

Massive columns rose through the city, spaced almost at random. The giant cylinders were translucent in the odd light, reflecting, or maybe even producing it. They were lost to sight above, not in fog, or darkness, but simply because he couldn't see that far. They were *miles* tall.

"You are seeing much of the Imperium," Majus Cyrysi said. He carefully arranged his robe, covering a flash of ankle, pulling his sleeves down so his wrists didn't show.

"The Imperium?" Sam tried to keep the tension out of his voice.

"This city. The oldest in the Nether, and the capital."

"There's more than one city in the Nether?"

Majus Cyrysi snorted. "Many, boy. Are you thinking columns that big are supporting the area of only one city? Look now, High Imperium is coming up."

Sam gaped as the tram rounded another bend. A gigantic dome rose above the rooftops, which were tiled in ornate blue and green and orange slate. These buildings were in straighter lines, the streets wider and cleaner. Motorized vehicles passed under them, along with fancy carriages drawn by two, four, and six-legged animals. Not far away from the dome, a spear-like building rested against a column.

Sam shifted in his seat, trying to peer around the buildings. Something made a backdrop to the city, but he couldn't tell what, until the difference in scale clicked in his head.

Towering above everything were two massive walls. They formed not quite a right angle corner directly behind the dome, shining with the steady permeating light. The columns might reflect the light, but this was where it originated.

Sam put his hand on the seat in front of him, trying to keep his balance against the vertigo that battered at him.

"What are those," he paused, mouth dry, "those walls?" He would have called them cliffs, but they were too smooth, too shiny. The nearest vanished in the distance above, like the columns, and stretched to his left as far as he could see. The intersecting wall did the same in the other direction.

"They are the edges of the Nether," the councilor said, her voice soft. "The Imperium was built close to this corner so it would be one of the best-lit cities."

Majus Cyrysi pointed to the dome. "That is the Great Assembly, where representatives from all ten species meet, built directly beneath the light of the walls." The majus shifted his outstretched finger to the spear-like building shooting up higher than anything around it. "That is to be our destination—the Spire of the Maji, where the Council sits. The houses of the maji surround it."

The Spire was at least forty stories tall, hugging close to one of the giant columns. Bridges stretched from it to six smaller buildings. Around the column, a wide area was filled with bushes and trees.

As the tram sped on, open spaces popped through breaks in the buildings, and trees passed beneath, some blue, some red, some with large flowers at their crown. Rooftop gardens boasted flowers, shrubs, and crops. Another group of flying creatures kept pace with the tram for a moment, shrieking as they chased a gliding predator, which tucked long leathery wings and dove into the mass of buildings below.

It's beautiful, he thought.

"Get ready," the councilor told him. "The Spire is the next stop."

CHAPTER FIVE

Patterns of Stars

- The question of the uniformity of the species in the Great Assembly has come up many times among groups of thinkers. There are differences between us, but none so great that the Nether cannot allow communication. Is all life so uniform? Or does the Nether somehow select those who find it?

From "Ruminations of the Nether," collected by the Kirian philosopher Yufariti Helbramitus

The tram opened its doors on a platform directly across from the Spire, several stories in the air. Sam and the maji got off behind two of the fuzzy aliens. Sam swallowed at the wooden threshold. The councilor's presence pushed him forward, but the layers of cotton had reduced to shreds of silk from the protest, and from travel through the new city. He shook, clutching his watch close to his ear. *I can do this. Just have to keep walking.*

"Not much farther," the councilor whispered. The tram whipped away, trailing a group of the large winged insects. The enormity of the open area weighed on his mind, and he grabbed a banister for support.

"I'll be with the Council," Councilor Ayama told them, fixing first Majus Cyrysi and then Sam with her eyes. "The inside of the House of Communication should feel safer for you." She strode off to a connecting bridge that arced far above the ground, ending at the Spire.

"This way," Majus Cyrysi said, pointing to a ramp that thankfully led down to ground level.

Keep it together. Almost away from the crowds, the stares of judgment. They had to see him trembling. He wanted to experience everything, but he was barely keeping his hands from shaking. The councilor's fix was all but gone. *Just have to get to the majus' house.* There was safety. He followed the majus into a looping stairway that deposited them between two rows of a sweet-smelling hedge with silky-haired leaves.

Sam could hear each of his breaths, like a bellows inside his head. *Have to do something to keep the panic away.* There were too many people here, too many unknowns. They turned a corner, weaving through a maze of bushes and trees. The Spire and its column rose above, and the tops of the six buildings—the houses of the maji—that surrounded it, peeked over the foliage.

"How do you not get lost in here?" he finally asked, his knuckles white on his watch.

The Kirian gave him a disturbingly pointy grin. "As always, the answer is: the Nether." Sam tried to smile back, but the expression slid off his face. The majus must have realized something, and his face became serious, crest neutral. "It is to be an instinct," he said. "A feeling or guiding sense. With a destination in mind, I am walking in the best direction. It may calm you?" The last question was unsure. Sam thought the majus had no idea how to help his anxiety, but at least he was trying.

"I see," Sam muttered. *More of this telepathic place invading my mind.* He wiped his hands, as if he could wash away the Nether's influence. Someday, he'd have a story to tell when teaching. If anyone believed him. If he got back.

"The House of Communication is there." Majus Cyrysi pointed at a tall rounded building, like a watchtower backlit by the immense wall, sparkling iridescent, that rose above everything. It was not as tall as the Spire, but it was the tallest of the six houses. Sam kept his eyes on the building, trying not to think about the columns, the wall, or the dizzying expanse of the Nether.

The towering House loomed closer as the majus threaded through hedges, the park-like grounds interspersed with areas for seating. An occasional sculpture would rise up from behind a tree or bush. Some were representations of the alien species Sam had seen on the way, others were abstract. Several generated tinkling music, twisting in a breath of cool wind. Sam's skin broke out in goosebumps at the chill. *How is there weather when the Nether is enclosed?* He clutched his watch closer. *Enclosed, but still huge, and unknown. Just need to make it inside.*

At last, the tower loomed overhead, carved wooden doors before them. The doorframe, easily twice his height, was painted a bright and sunny yellow. Majus Cyrysi pulled on a door handle, and the door swung open silently, soft music rolling out from inside. Each door was as thick as Sam's forearm was long.

As his foot crossed the threshold, he let out a long breath. *No people to tell me I'm not right. A roof above my head.* It was another strange place, but he could see the extents of it, accept it. A staircase wide enough for ten abreast twisted up into the height of the tower, and Sam glanced up before bringing his eyes back to thick rugs that decorated the marble floor. They showed scenes, he assumed, from the homeworlds, each one inhabited by a different species—Methiemum, Kirian, Lobath with their head-tentacles, and so on. Music played from an unknown source, some theme composed around a low reed instrument.

"The map is downstairs," Majus Cyrysi said. He threw out a claw-tipped hand to the staircase, which Sam now saw went down and up.

At least it's not a long climb.

"Afterwards, I will take you to my apartment on the top floor to clean up, and we will take one of the bridges to the Spire." Sam stared back, then pursed his lips and traced the ridges on his watch, secure in his coat pocket. He was getting hot in the temperate atmosphere of the Nether. It was even warmer in the House of Communication. Maybe he could leave the coat in Majus Cyrysi's apartment. On the top floor.

Of course that's where he would choose to live. I haven't had this much exercise in years.

Sam followed the Kirian down the staircase, and away from the music playing in the lobby. Thoughts of his house and Aunt Martha rose up from where they had been pushed aside first by the cotton in his head, then by crossing the Imperium, and the crowd of people. He hoped the map showed how Earth was connected to this strange place. The longer it took to get back, the more food would go bad at the house. And other things. Sam stared at the polished wooden railing, sliding under his hand as he went down the steps, trying to keep his breathing even. Between the telepathic semi-sentient Nether, the aliens, his aunt's death, and his distance from home, he was probably in shock. His stomach gurgled and he suddenly didn't feel well. *Keep it together.* He swallowed bile.

Sam huffed down several more flights, dreading the journey up. The building looked as tall as a small skyscraper. Below, the stairs ended in a gently glowing doorway.

"Through here," the majus called as he turned out of sight.

Sam followed. Glare from the light of the floor partially obscured the room after the darkness of the stairwell. Then his eyes cleared, and his breathing sped up. The room was a cavern, lit by a glow from the uneven floor. It highlighted walls of carved stone, and a vaulted ceiling of marble. *Buildings shouldn't be this large.* Sam took a hesitant step in, shading his eyes. *It's just a room.* It was big, but this was nothing compared to the Nether. He took another step. This was a part of the house where Origon lived. *Part of a home. Safe.*

"Coming?" The majus was halfway across the shining floor, heading to a pedestal in the middle of the room.

"Just...getting my bearings." Sam felt the comfortable weight of his pocketwatch. Majus Cyrysi glanced back and his eyes flicked to Sam's pocket. *Calm the breathing. There's nothing to be scared of here.* Sam stomped a foot on the floor. His feet had purchase, as if on dirt or rock, but the surface was like glass shifted into gentle waves and valleys. It glittered with an interior light. "Is this like the columns and walls?" he asked.

Majus Cyrysi looked down. "This is to be the true floor of the Nether, beneath centuries of buildup." He gestured up to ground level. "Underneath the layers of dirt, this floor is connecting to the bases of the columns and joins with the walls at the Nether's extremes."

"Why didn't they smooth it out?" Sam scuffed a small crystal hill.

The Kirian laughed his breathy laugh. "That is impossible, boy. The substance of the Nether is impervious to any material but itself."

"What about your magic?" Sam saw the Kirian wince, the feathers on the top of his head flattening.

"A majus may hear the Symphony of the Nether, but as physical implements are unable to cut or break it, the melody is so resilient no majus has ever changed it."

Sam peered at the floor. It gave him a moment of vertigo, and he braced his footing. The crystal was translucent. Like the distance to the roof outside, there seemed to be no end. He could see facets and reflections, like ice cubes stacked together without end. He pulled his gaze up, blinking. "What's on the other side?"

Another laugh. He didn't think the Kirian was being mean, but the laugh sounded condescending. "That may be a more metaphysical question."

"How's that?"

"The Nether is not, precisely, existing *within* the universe," Majus Cyrysi answered. "It is separate. Many are thinking this is why maji are able to open portals to it before seeing it the first time, when that is impossible with any other location."

Sam lifted one foot. He suddenly wanted to be back on the stairs, and took one step back, but didn't let himself take another. "Not *in* the universe? Then where are we?"

"That is why it is metaphysical, is it not?" the majus waved a hand, dismissing the question. "Though we are here for a purpose. I wish to find this world of yours, and the Drain. If you are truly not from Methiem, the starmap may be helping us."

"Starmap?" Sam looked around, keeping his eyes off the floor as much as possible. *I suppose it has to be a map of stars, doesn't it?* His eyes widened as the thought sunk in. *I've traveled away from Earth.* The last of the film in his mind was shredding away, leaving him vulnerable. His stomach tightened convulsively, and he wiped his hands on his pants, trying not to vomit.

I'm in space. No. Don't think about falling. No. Going to die. No. He staggered, looking for something to support him, but the room was empty except for the pedestal in the center, waist high.

"Come." Majus Cyrysi went to it, poking at the surface. Sam shuffled his way across the translucent floor, watching the majus' motions, every muscle tight. As he came nearer, he saw the whole pedestal was wood, carved and ornamented. The majus pressed small inset buttons, each labeled with a number. They looked like ivory, polished to a warm glow. Carefully, Sam placed one hand on a space with no buttons. He didn't want to push anything that might mess up what the majus was doing. He was nervous enough already.

The Kirian spared him a glance. Was he disappointed? *Maybe I'm supposed to be asking questions.*

"What are you telling it to do?" His voice only shook a little.

"I am inputting the calculations for the section of space I am wishing to view." The majus turned a crank and Sam heard a crunch of gears from inside the pedestal. Colors exploded out from the pedestal and he hastily stepped away, eyes wide. The swath of color expanded, passing through him, filling the entire room.

"What is it?" he asked, looking up and around.

"It is to be another System, maintained by the House of Potential when more notes are needed." Majus Cyrysi pushed more buttons and flipped a switch. The colors spun. "Now, can you tell me where you are from?"

The dizzying cloud coalesced from distinct hues—yellow, orange, blue, green, brown, white—into blobs and swirls. Sam's balance was thrown off, between the uneven floor and the colors in the air. He staggered, then righted. *It's some sort of information, but what? What does the majus want from me?*

"Where I'm from—?" He turned in a small circle, watching the play of colors against each other. It was like a three-dimensional painting, or a visual interpretation of music.

"Where you are from. Planet, solar system, anything useful?" Majus Cyrysi jerked his head toward the cloud. His crest was spiky—frustration.

Sam turned again, watching the colored blobs sink toward each other, moving lazily in an orbit around them. Understanding snapped like a rubber band against his skin. *Galaxies of stars, planets around stars, moons around planets. I'm in space, I'm in space.* The scale made him rock back. It was too big. His muscles clenched and he looked away and down, needing to get away from the yawning expanse of open space in which he floated.

Looking down was a mistake. *That's why the starmap is on the floor of the Nether.* The stars reflected—or perhaps extended—through the floor, turning him into a giant, drifting through space. Sam was unmoored, his stomach clamped, and he vomited onto the crystal floor. His breath came in short rasps as his vision narrowed. He curled in a ball and shut his eyes, holding the pocketwatch close to one ear. *One breath, one tick.* He panted. He couldn't slow it down. He was falling.

"—to be the problem? Are you hurt?" The voice came from solar systems away, terrifying in power to reach so far. Sam shivered.

He felt a claw-like hand grasp his shoulder and try to heave him to his feet. He resisted, pulling in tighter.

"It's...too big," Sam got out through clamped teeth. He was thousands of light years from anything. *It's a model. It can't hurt me.* Focus on what he felt. Three breaths to a tick. Two breaths. One breath.

"What can I be doing?" The majus sounded apologetic, for once.

He had to respond. *Turn it off.* No, then they couldn't find Earth. His mind whizzed. *Think logically.* It was a projection. The majus had control of it.

"Can you make it smaller?" Sam asked, his eyes still closed. There was a rustle of Origon's robe. He was still in the House of Communication. It was safe for him to be here. He heard the thunk of ivory buttons releasing and gears rotating against each other.

"It is done." Sam peeked one eye open, swallowed vomit, and wiped his mouth. The vast field of stars and galaxies had receded to an arc overhead, well above the floor.

It's contained, like a big TV screen. Sam pushed against the crystal floor, not looking down. Carefully, he stood up. *Breathe deep. Have to find Earth.* The pocketwatch was slick in his sweaty hand. He took two steps closer, suppressed a hiccup of anxiety. He pressed his hands together to keep them from shaking, took another long gulp of air.

"Sorry about the—" Sam gestured at the floor. Majus Cyrysi eyed him, nervously picking at his moustache with one hand. His crest was spiky with agitation, though Sam could tell he was trying not to show it. "I'm alright now, I think," he said. Hesitantly, he reached out a hand, passing it through a spiral galaxy. His hand left a wake of stars behind which then reformed, undisturbed. "It's beautiful." His physics teacher would have loved to see this.

"Can you—" The majus looked him up and down. "Can you be finding something familiar?" He went to the mess on the floor, one hand glowing orange. The patch smoked, then glowed, the liquid evaporating, and the majus slumped. Then the smoke disappeared and what was left solidified into a cold lump. Majus Cyrysi drew in a deep breath. At Sam's questioning look, he said, "I was changing the notes of the Symphony of the temperature with the House of Power, first to warm the spot, then cool it as I was reversing the reaction and reclaiming my notes. I will get someone to clean the rest."

Sam nodded, embarrassed, then studied the galaxies hanging in front of him. *It's like an astronomy app, except using a hologram. Or the Symphony, I guess.* He hadn't made a habit of stargazing, back on Earth. He could find the moon and maybe the Big Dipper on the rare occasion he looked outside at night.

"I don't see anything I know," he said. His breathing was almost back to normal. *Just don't look down.*

"Over here." Majus Cyrysi poked a finger at a set of stars. When Sam stood beside him, the cluster compressed to something like the letter 'J.' "This is the Scimitar; a common constellation the children of Methiem learn."

Sam shot him a look. "I'm not from Methiem." *How can we find Earth if he doesn't even think it's real?*

"Of course." The Kirian's crest spiked. Annoyance. "Maybe we should try another view. This would be much easier if we were to use the whole room."

"No," Sam said quickly. "No bigger than it is now."

"Very well." Majus Cyrysi zoomed the view out and back in. Sam closed his eyes against the motion. When he opened them again, the stars were stable.

"This is the Festuour homeworld, on the other side of the galaxy they share with the Methiemum." The majus said. The view centered on the fourth planet orbiting a large red sun.

"What about the other eight species?" Sam asked. *I've only seen humanoids,* he realized. *They could just as easily be intelligent bananas.* He'd need to find books, read up on the different species, what sort of laws and government they had. It was a lot easier than asking people questions.

"Our objective is to be finding your home, where I will be able to study the Drain you escaped."

"Humor me," Sam said, smirking as the majus' crest fluffed. The last vestiges of his brief panic were fading. Maybe he could get used to this place. Turn the unfamiliar into the familiar, his therapist told him once.

Majus Cyrysi slid the view back as he pushed buttons. Sam kept his eyes open for this change, though it almost made him lose his balance. Large swaths of space were unfilled with data. Nine points of light emerged, artificially highlighted.

"This galaxy is the one we were observing," Majus Cyrysi pointed at a collection of stars, "containing the homeworlds of the Methiemum and the Festuour." The other eight lit galaxies were in no order, six in a loose group. "Aside from them, only one planet in each galaxy is to be inhabited, as far as we know," said the majus quietly.

"It's so big," Sam said, He swallowed and fought down the sensation of falling.

"Yes, and empty." Majus Cyrysi's voice was low. "We are knowing little of the shape of the universe."

"It'd take years to find my home in this," Sam said, waving a hand through the starmap. Displaced galaxies snapped back into place afterward. *I'm alone, very far from home. I still don't know what the Drain did to the house.* A memory of Aunt Martha sewing tugged at him. He wondered if the Nether had sewing machines. He had sewn a few things, and the back and forth motion always calmed him.

"We can try," said his new mentor, but his voice was less confident. "What differentiates your homeworld, your sun?"

Sam thought. "There are nine planets in my solar system. Eight if you want to be technical." *My Very Earnest Mother—*

The majus cocked his head, feathers ruffling in thought. "I am believing the Pixie system has eight planets. All the others have either too many or too few."

"There are big planets farther from the sun, small planets closer," Sam said. "Earth is the third planet out."

Majus Cyrysi made a sound of annoyance, his crest separating, resettling. "This is not telling me anything useful. Do you think we are able to see planets in another solar system? Our best telescopes can barely tell us about other stars." He poked at the starmap, his other hand pressing buttons. The view slid into one of the home galaxies, and Sam realized the representation was crude. The view centered on one system.

"This is my home," the majus said. "Kiria is here." He poked at the fourth planet out of twelve, white with clouds and blue with ocean. "But farther," the view slid back to incorporate several star systems, the rest merely blurs of color, "we are not knowing. If you could give me a constellation of stars, finding the system would be much simpler."

"Oh," Sam mumbled. His shoulders hunched in, muscles tightening. Thinking on this scale made his heart race. He listened to the rhythmic ticking of his watch. *What else can I tell him?*

"The Big Dipper is a constellation I know."

"Good, good. What stars make it up?" The majus' crest spiked forward.

"Um." He had no idea, and even if he knew, would it look the same from here? "It looks like this." He drew the shape in the air, but Majus Cyrysi only frowned at him. *Well that won't work.*

"How about this: Earth is in a spiral galaxy." *What is the Andromeda galaxy? That's the next nearest, right?* Sam had known, once. "Um, the sun is a yellow star?" He couldn't think of anything else.

"That is to be some help," the Kirian allowed. He selected several buttons on the pedestal, turned a crank. Gears clanked and the view slid out again.

Sam swayed and looked for something to steady himself in the empty room. He caught a glance at the bottomless floor and pulled his eyes back up. *Not helping.*

More than half the shapes in the starmap lit up. "These are spiral galaxies the ten species have recorded," Majus Cyrysi said. "All have yellow stars, though the fact is lowering the possibilities significantly. Can you tell me more about where yours is to be located?"

Sam slumped. *Hopeless, without knowing how to stargaze, or at least an internet connection.* He turned to the majus.

"I had no idea there were so many." His eyes burned, but he would not cry again. "I want to get home."

Majus Cyrysi grunted assent, stroking his feathery moustache, but Sam could tell he was about out of suggestions. "Maybe if I am showing you views from the other homeworlds, you could be recognizing familiar views."

Sam shrugged. He watched Majus Cyrysi fiddle with the pedestal's controls, certainty settling over him like a stifling blanket. *The only thing I truly remember about Earth is the inside of my house, but the Drain might have affected the whole East Coast. Aunt Martha always wanted me to go out more, meet more people. Now it's too late.*

"I'm not going to get home, am I? I had a plan, or part of one. I was planning to go to college, train to teach students about laws and ethics." The unfinished application was still lying on his desk. But with Aunt Martha gone, what did he have tying him to Earth any longer?

At the question, the majus straightened and looked directly at him, large eyes earnest. "I will not lie, chances are seeming small. I would help you back if I could. Your home is holding the key to researching the Drains, important to me as well. However, until we gather more information, you are," Majus Cyrysi's crest twisted, "welcome here." Embarrassment was a strange look on the Kirian.

"Here—in the House of Communication?" Sam looked around the vaulted basement. He was getting used to the space, though he hadn't seen the aboveground portion.

A strange expression flickered across the majus' face. He stared past Sam, his crest relaxing completely, then puffing up. His eyes focused again. "Well, what is stopping me?"

"Stopping—what?" Sam felt the conversation leaving him.

"You were creating the portal here from Earth. There is some part of you which must remember another location. We only need to draw it out. To train and apprentice you, as a new majus. I am not having an apprentice. You want to learn to teach? I was a professor of philosophy, in my younger days. It could be beneficial, for both of us."

"You want to—to teach me?" *Teach me philosophy? Magic? To change the Symphony?* Sam stared at the stars and planets, made by other maji.

"Yes, yes." Majus Cyrysi paced back and forth across the floor, his strides taking his head through the lower half of a galaxy. Sam didn't think he noticed the bits of the map trailing his crest. "The portal—it was surrounded with yellow, yes? Maybe with another color, rare for a novice, but not unheard of—"

"What...what are you talking about?" Sam tried to remember the hole in the air, connecting his home and the Nether.

The Kirian stopped abruptly, staring at him. "A majus may only teach another of the same aspect, or house. This is to be obvious, as each house can only hear the Symphony they were born to, that portion of the overall Grand Symphony that leads the universe in its dance. You were having yellow around your portal, which means you must be of the House of Communication. If this is the case, then I *can* teach you of that Symphony. When you know more, perhaps you may be finding your way back to your home."

"That seems like it will take a while." Months, even years before he could send that application in, if he even wanted to go back to an empty house and no family. His heart was speeding. He should have finished the thing when Aunt Martha first told him. Then at least he'd have some deadline for when he had to get home.

"It is a lifetime of study, to change the notes that create our universe," Majus Cyrysi said. "To be granted the ability by the ancestors is a great honor, but you may also be finding peace doing so. Of course, if you are wanting to discuss philosophy, or law, I can be doing that, too." The Kirian smiled, showing a mass of pointy teeth.

Sam looked back at the starmap—Earth was in there somewhere like a single bead lost in a pile of sand. Back to Majus Cyrysi, whose eyes were wide, crest erect in anticipation. *Which I can tell because the Nether is invading my mind.* Honestly, it was more surprising he hadn't broken down completely, lying comatose on the floor. *It's the only way, isn't it?*

Slowly, he nodded. He was going to be a majus. Could he still teach if he was a majus?

"Excellent!" Majus Cyrysi rubbed his long hands together. "Then we have even more to tell the Council. Come, we must be on our way." He punched a button and the starmap sucked back into the pedestal, leaving Sam blinking in the absence of the display. "New evidence of Drains, a lost homeworld, and now a new apprentice. We will drag the Council's nose out of those inane Aridori rumors after all."

The majus made for the door, leaving Sam to scuttle along behind him. He cast one last look back at the now dark pedestal. *Can I lead a full life here, if I never get back to Earth?*

The Council of the Maji

-The Aridori war was more than a thousand common cycles ago, waged across every homeworld. We know the species' attack was unexpected, and pitted all the species in a joined effort against them. At the end of the war the insane beings were completely extinct, hunted by Sathssn-led extermination squads. What was the reason for the attack? The war destroyed many records from that time, and we are still finding "new" history buried in forgotten ruins across the assembly of homeworlds. One such piece has speculated a societal shift centuries before, given little heed until too late. But can we believe any hypothesis which takes the Dissolution as an accepted fact?

From "The Great Assembly through the Ages"

The trip up to Origon's apartment was tedious, with the young man complaining about the stairs on every flight. What was the Methiemum's problem with a little exercise? Losing one's home must have put him out of sorts, though Rilan complained almost as much, on her increasingly rare visits. That was more a ritual, though. She had earned the chance to grumble from so many repetitions of this climb. Origon let his crest wriggle in amused remembrance. A strange species. The view from the top of the House of Communication was worth the climb.

He looked out one of his windows toward the Spire as he listened to his new apprentice—apprentice!—shuck out of his heavy coat. When he turned back, the young man was carefully hanging it in a closet. Origon would rather have thrown the thing somewhere and been on their way, but Sam was deliberate, if nothing else. He washed his face and used the facilities while Origon tapped a foot. The Council would be in session most of the day, but that did not excuse such slowness. By all the ancestors, it was like being mentor to a turtle, though any wait would be worth getting to research the Drains.

"So what does being your apprentice mean?" Sam asked.

Origon drew away from the window. It was worth a brief

explanation before they went before the Council. "I will be showing you how to listen to and change the Symphony of Communication." He held up a hand and let the music defining the air currents in the apartment fill him. "Do you hear the Symphony?"

Sam squinted, then shook his head. "Maybe a little. Like someone playing music a long way off."

"It will be coming to you in time," Origon told him. It wasn't unusual for new maji to have difficulty. There was time to teach him later. For now, he grasped for the notes that made up his being, and a portion of his self separated, like a bandage ripped away. He placed those notes in the soft sonata that was the air. They doubled the tempo, making the music allegro, and a breeze blew through Sam's hair, which was slightly longer than Origon's topfeathers. The young man's eyes tracked the streams of yellow, visible only to another majus, and his body seemed to relax for the first time since he had arrived.

"I can see the colors," Sam said, and a shaky smile appeared on his face. "Beautiful."

Origon drew his song back, trying to ignore how much it took out of him. The breeze reversed for a moment, then faded away, as did the color. "Any majus will see any other majus' colors, though we can only hear that portion of the Grand Symphony that is defining our house. It is what naturally divides the maji's abilities. As I have said, mine are better suited to the physical side of the spectrum, though I can introduce you to other sides of the House of Communication. For now, though, we should be going."

The young man agreed, and they were off, Sam trailing him down the spiral stairway as he had going up. The bridge to the Spire was only halfway back to the ground. Origon kept a careful eye on him while they crossed high above the Spire's garden. This bridge was enclosed. Others were not.

"Are you to be experiencing problems with this height?" he called back. Sam was several paces behind, shaking and face pale, one hand to the plaster wall of the bridge. The other hand was in a pocket, no doubt clutching that pocketwatch of his.

"I'm okay," he said, though he didn't sound convincing. No crest to show his emotions, but the Nether told him Sam was not happy. "It's not the height so much as the view. I have to find Earth, and that means I have to learn about your world. I have to make the effort." He took another small step forward and Origon frowned. Maybe getting food in him was in order, after meeting with councilmembers. He certainly felt better when he ate. Too late to get any now—he would just have to hope Sam didn't collapse.

"Not *my* world—that would be Kiria," he answered, "Though I am seeing your point. Keep up then. We will soon be free to explore the Drains together, and in the process, find your homeworld again."

Sam mumbled something in agreement.

The bridge deposited them into the main atrium of the Spire, and Origon did another dance, coaxing Sam out from the bridge, getting him used to the vaulted ceilings, the sight of the sheer walls on this floor of the Spire, the orange auras of Systems glowing around the lamps, providing light as long as the majus' song that fueled them still played.

A few minutes later, Origon burst past the door guards into the Council chambers, Sam trailing behind him. Rilan should have prepared the rest of the members for his entry. A shame he hadn't thought of taking Sam as his apprentice in time to tell her that.

The six heads of the houses of the maji—who made up the Council—were spaced around the semicircular wooden table they used to variously debate policy and interview maji who came to them with problems or suggestions. Origon's eyes were drawn to a spot on the table's impressive center carving of the ten species, working in harmony. His eyes went straight to the chip in the Sureri figure's ear, a reminder of a meeting many cycles ago where he had...disagreed with the then head of the House of Communication. Her replacement, if possible, was even more contrary.

Light spilled in from windows set high in the rear wall of the room, illuminating the pile of paperwork in the middle of the table, sheets pulled toward one councilor or another. Rilan sat with arms crossed and mouth open, as if she had just finished making a point. Several of the others scowled up at him as he and Sam entered.

Rilan gestured as if to introduce them, but Bofan A'Tof got there first. "You were supposed to enter when called. Rilan has already informed us you are here about your *voids* again." The Lobath head of the House of Power looked like a stuffed sausage: his reddish skin bright on his cheeks, his old maroon jumpsuit about to shed its buttons. Even his three head-tentacles looked about to burst. He was nominally in charge of Origon, since with being able to hear two of the six aspects of the Grand Symphony, Origon's second allegiance was to the House of Power. That didn't keep Origon from disagreeing with almost everything the Lobath did.

"Drains," Origon corrected. "Yes, I am here with even more evidence. Not only that, but I have an important announ—"

Jhina Moerna Oscana cut him off, large watery eyes glaring. "Tell us about the boy with you. Rilan mentioned him briefly." Jhina was the head of the House of Grace and also the Speaker for the Council, in the Great Assembly. Like most Etanela, her words flowed together, and she topped the other councilors by at least an arm span. She bobbed her head at Sam, mane of dark hair waving with the movement.

Origon glanced back at Sam, whose mouth was open, eyes wide and darting. "He is newly touching his song, and has created his first portal to escape a Drain," he told them. "You are having another witness now to these abominations. In addition, I have decided to—"

"More of your conspiracy theories," hissed Freshta. Origon let his crest flare this time at the interruption. He drew a long breath in through his teeth. The Pixie was a weak choice for the head of the House of Communication, and he had protested her elevation, three cycles ago. Freshta's wings beat furiously, lifting her small body off her chair. Her compound eyes glittered black, reflecting the lamps spaced around the walls. "First assassins, then impossible voids. Now you conjure allies when even the space capsule crew retracts their absurd claims." Jhina laid a calming hand on the Pixie's shoulder and Freshta settled back with a frown.

"I am not making up claims—"

"Councilor Freshta is correct, *Majus* Cyrysi." Jhina stressed his title. Her words rolled over each other like a tide coming in. Origon forced his crest back to neutral. "We are occupied with escalating indications of the Aridori, who may have replaced or killed several families in the grainlands of the Nether, according to the newest reports. You yourself were present today when Councilor Ayama kept a mob from turning violent on a lone Sureri. As such, we have no time for unfounded crises."

So Rilan was the one who stopped that rabble single-handedly? No matter—he didn't need credit. Origon threw one hand out to his old friend, whose lips were compressed to a thin line. "Yet you do not listen to your own councilors? I have given you proof, Speaker Oscana. The entire crew of the Methiemum capsule gave reports on the Drain they saw, even if you were pressuring them to recant."

"Does anyone want to ask me?"

Origon almost jumped at the voice. He hadn't expected Sam to speak. When he looked back, the pocketwatch was out, in one trembling hand, but the young man, surprisingly, stood tall. The councilors looked interested, so Origon stayed silent.

"What is your name?" Jhina asked.

"Um. Samuel van Oen," he replied nervously.

"Tell them what you told us," Rilan said. She sounded calm, but there were honey colored spots showing through the normally dark copper of her cheeks. He was not the only one annoyed with the other councilors.

Sam recounted the same panicked explanation of his escape. Rilan's mental bandage must be all but gone, shaky as the young man was. He ended in a whisper, but got across the same details he had told Origon and Rilan about the Drain affecting his home. That would have to get the Council interested, especially when Origon told them he was taking Sam as an apprentice to help study the—

"This happened where?" Bofan asked. "On Methiem, I presume?"

Sam only shook his head, eyes down. He was breathing fast and Origon let the Nether translate his emotion state—near panic. He likely couldn't do anything to help, but he at least abandoned announcing that he was taking on an apprentice for the moment. This was the most interested the Council had been in the Drains. "He says he was raised on a separate homeworld, not one of the ten," Origon told them. "This tells us the Drain's area of effect is larger than I originally thought."

Freshta's wings buzzed in agitation and she cut one small hand through the air. Sam did a double take at the sound and stepped back. The Pixie's eyes had that effect on some people. She addressed Origon. "First conspiracy theories, now you bring a Methiemum with outlandish stories to help you. Go back to your wandering and let us work on real problems, like Aridori."

"Real problems?" Origon asked her. He let his crest rise in anger. Freshta barely had a handle on the politics of the House of Communication, much less the Great Assembly. He could have done a better job as head of house, if he desired that job. "How is panicking over phantoms a thousand cycles dead a larger problem than that which destroyed the Methiemum's space capsule a few ten-days ago?"

"Have you seen reports?" The Pixie waved a paper at him. "No. Because you are not on Council of Maji. You have been traveling outside Nether; have not seen protests here over Aridori threat. Have not seen unrest in Low and Mid Imperium. You do not get to decide what maji do."

Origon's thoughts went to the crowd and the frothing Methiemum who led them, and he glanced to Rilan. She locked eyes with him, then looked away, obviously thinking of the same thing. Was it really that big of a problem? "I know enough about the Aridori—a scare-story being brought up every few cycles to satisfy ignorant people's fears. I know—"

This time Rilan cut him off. "The Aridori problem is not going away, Majus Cyrysi." Her use of his title, and her clenched teeth, convinced him to quiet. She jerked on one arm of her dress. "Whether it is real or not, perhaps we should return to the reason you are here."

"Indeed. What do we do with this newcomer?" a deep voice cut in. Mandamon Feldo, head of the House of Potential, stared at Sam through dark glasses. Sam shrank down beneath the focus. Pouches and strange instruments hung from the councilor's deep brown formal suit. Feldo turned heavy eyes on Origon, who just stopped from stepping back himself. The house head was a dusky-skinned, stern Methiemum, with a thick bushy beard and mane of hair, once black, but now more white than not. He had kept the Council on course for many cycles, since before Rilan had been raised to majus.

"That, at least, will be settled easily," Origon told them. Finally. He straightened, settling his crest. "The portal he came through was ringed in the yellow of the House of Communication." As well as another color, but no matter. Training would bring the young man's secondary color out for sure. "I am taking Sam as my apprentice, both to help my study of the Drains and to help him find his homeworld."

There was a collective shuffling as the councilmembers sat

forward—even Rilan. Origon let the corners of his mouth pull up. *That* had made them pause. "Then it is no problem if you would rather take on the *threat* of the Aridori. I will be collecting maji on my own to study the Drains." He looked over the six councilmembers. "And report my findings, of course."

Freshta buzzed up off the chair, her wings twitching in agitation. "No. We need apprentices to track Aridori. If he is Communication, then I can take him." Origon stared daggers at her. Sam made a small noise and Origon glared at him, letting his crest rise slowly. Sam closed his mouth. Now was not the time.

"*My* apprentice and I have already come to that decision between us, as maji and apprentices have always chosen."

"Maji usually are choosing who they shall train while enmeshed in the culture of the Nether," said the last member of the Council. Scintien Nectiset, head of the House of Strength, absently tugged her pink and green shawl tighter around her fleshy bare arms. Now she joined in the Council's debate? She was as useless as Freshta, though Scintien largely kept silent, knowing her weakness. The Kirian's topfeathers ruffled in anticipation of stymieing him. "These times call for stricter measures in making sure our apprentices are adequately prepared."

"Yet the final decision still belongs to the majus," Origon stated.

"Does it? Then maybe time to look at apprentice processes again," Freshta said. She darted a look at Rilan. "With so much crisis over Aridori, what does Council say of revoking maji rights to choosing apprentices, for a limited time?"

Scintien actually looked thoughtful at the ridiculous request. That egg-sucking daughter of a grub-digger. Origon thumped one fist into his thigh. First disbelief of the Drains, now interfering with a majus prerogative? "It should not be questioned whether I may take Sam as my apprentice." He risked a look back. The young man's head was up, scanning across the faces of the councilors. "Am I needing to make this an issue for all maji? Perhaps during an Assembly meeting? I am certain others will have objections as well." The whole Council could not be so wrapped up in this drivel about the long-lost Aridori species.

"A vote, then," Jhina said. "If the Council agrees to Councilor Freshta's suggestion, you may make an appeal formally, if you wish, though the boy will be hers for the time being." As Speaker, she had authority to call consensus votes, and Origon felt his crest go rigid with anxiety, but he had no response. Surely a majority would back him up? They could not take this away. He was so close to discovering more about the Drains.

"All for the new proposal?" Freshta raised her hand for Communication, as did Bofan for Power and Scintien for Strength. His own houses, *and* his own species voted against him. He kept his crest down, grinding his teeth together.

"Against?" Jhina asked, and Rilan raised her hand. After a moment, Councilor Feldo raised his as well, watching Sam. Jhina looked over the other councilors, one long finger tapping against her chin. Was the Etanela actually *considering* voting against him? She was the voice of the Council to the Assembly. She was supposed to be impartial, enacting the rules and traditions of the maji. As Speaker, she had the final vote, and counted for two in a tie. Origon realized he was holding his breath. With his song so disturbingly reduced after piloting the Methiemum's capsule, he needed all the support he could find to raise word of the Drains.

"Even apprentices can be of use in our situation," Jhina drawled, musing. "They can open portals, helping traffic between the homeworlds and the Nether. Even if they do not have the control of a full majus, they would be icons of authority, helping to quell fears of the Aridori. They could be sent to the different cities of the Nether and homeworlds, where allowed, improving our reach. There is something to be said for the Council directing apprentices where they will be of most help to the Great Assembly of the Species."

Now Origon let his crest flare in utter incredulity. Was she really suggesting they abandon the approach the maji had taken for hundreds of cycles, letting apprentices learn the topics they were most interested in, bettering themselves, and rising to the top of their professions? There was a reason maji were regarded as near celebrities, besides their small number—several thousand, compared to the billions on the homeworlds. Squashing new maji into whatever space was left over in their house would lead to dull minds and incompetence.

"Do I get a say, since I'm the one being sold off like a slab of meat?" Once again, Sam surprised Origon. He turned to the young man—no, his apprentice, whatever the Council would say.

"Let the boy speak," rumbled Feldo. Rilan nodded, and Jhina waved a hand in acceptance.

"I don't...don't think I'll be much help to you," Sam told the Council. He was stiff, breathing fast. Origon saw a bead of sweat roll down his face, but Sam swallowed and carried on.

"I don't know how things work here, so I won't be much help as an icon of anything. I'd never heard of the Aridori until this morning. Before that I was trapped in a freezing house—" Sam cut off, staring forward, bottom lip pulled in. The Nether translated it to Origon as possibly fear? Maybe grief.

Sam drew in a breath. "I'm not good with new people and places, so I won't be going through portals until I get my bearings, if then." He blinked rapidly, hands in pockets, then smoothing out his shirt, then back to his pockets.

"Even if you forbid me, I'll still help Majus Cyrysi find out about the Drains. I...have to. One killed my aunt." He looked down, then back up, eyes red. "I have to find out what happened." He looked across the Council again. "That's—that's all."

Origon heard one of the windows creak in the silence.

"Hm. You have an interesting apprentice, Origon," Jhina said, steepling her fingers. "Frankly, I would rather him be a burden to you than to a majus working toward the Council's goals." She looked across her fellow councilmembers. "I vote against."

Origon slumped, hearing Sam give a quiet cry of triumph. "Will the others concede?" Jhina asked. The Council always showed a united front outside of chambers.

"Bah." Freshta waved a hand in the air. "I don't have time for apprentice anyway. Especially not this one." Bofan and Scintien watched her, then nodded their assent. The Pixie glanced to where Rilan sat on the end. "I think we will revisit this concept, though."

Origon watched Rilan, his one-time student, his old confidant, whose brows were creased in a frown. She would have to keep fighting the Council on this half-hatched idea by herself for now.

He bowed to the councilors. "I am thanking you for your consideration." Like pulling feathers from a live raptor. "I believe my new apprentice and I will be having much to do."

"Time to go," he murmured to Sam, and the young man nodded vigorously. They left the Council chambers, Sam right beside him.

CHAPTER SEVEN

A Crisis of Apprentices

-The Sathssn are unusual among the ten species, in that nearly eighty percent of the population follow the same religion—the Cult of Form. Only around the hottest tropical regions of Sath Home do inhabitants fully spurn the concealing black robes, gloves, boots, and religion, which typify this founding species.
    Excerpt from "A Dissertation on the Ten Species, Book V"

Rilan started awake at an insistent knocking.

"Uh. What? I'm coming," she called blearily. She pushed out of the warm covers, grumbling around the room until she found enough clothes to be decent. The council meeting had lasted until late last afternoon, debating new policies to enact in the face of the rising panic over the Aridori. Terrifying as the reports were, Rilan didn't want to change long-accepted traditions in the maji. But Freshta had been adamant about revising the apprenticing process, so they had ended with no resolution.

She had met up with Ori and Sam for a quick dinner before they left to requisition a bed and some basic supplies for the young man. Apprentices lived with their mentors and Ori had never had one. The past few ten-days had been the longest she had spent with him in the last several cycles, though thankfully his attention was on Sam. That kept her from foolish actions like inviting Ori over for late night drinks. They had been too long apart. Her place was on the Council, not gallivanting across the ten homeworlds.

More banging on the door. Rilan pulled on her shirt and glared out a window—a perk of the apartment for the head of the House of Healing. It was around fifth lightening, the light from the walls barely strong enough to make out details, and far too early for anyone to be hanging on the knocker.

"Hold on!" She bumbled to the door and jerked it open. "Who are you and what do you—oh." Rilan's eyes were drawn down to the Pixie buzzing happily, then back up to the short girl beside her. Just because the gods-cursed bugs didn't sleep didn't mean they had to inflict it on everyone else. "What do you want, Freshta? Who is this?"

"This is new apprentice, for you," the councilor said. Her face was serious, compound eyes wide and innocent, but the Nether didn't let Freshta disguise her body language. If her wings were any indication, vibrating every few seconds, she was viciously happy about foisting this girl off on Rilan.

"*My* apprentice? I didn't agree to this. Wasn't the debate in the council chambers yesterday enough to remind you maji choose their own apprentices?" The girl held her head high, though her dark eyes flicked between the Pixie and Rilan. Her hands were folded in front of her red silk shirt, tucked into sturdy canvas pants, but her fingers tapped as she listened to the exchange.

"We talked a bit, after you left," Freshta admitted. "Rest of Council was unanimous. More apprentices need quality training to get ready for Aridori threat." The girl twitched at that, her head turning to the blueish Pixie half-floating beside her. Anyone would get nervous at the mention of those monsters, especially treated as reality.

"Why me? Why now?" Rilan pressed. Training, hogwash. The Council was tying her down with work so she couldn't make waves around Ori's voids. "We've only had three new apprentices able to hear the Symphony this cycle. They don't just appear out of portals."

"This one did." Freshta's smile stretched across her face. "Very strong. House of Healing." She urged the girl forward with one small hand.

"My brother and I were recently orphaned." The girl finally spoke, her voice on the knife edge between control and grief, and Rilan reassessed her age a few cycles higher—a woman, not a girl. Might be around Sam's age, or a little older. She was compact, for a Methiemum, one of the Northern continent ancestries, maybe from the Ofir archipelago.

"What's your name?"

"Enos, Councilor."

"Anything else?" Maybe names were different up there.

"Just Enos."

"So. You get along," Freshta broke in. "Must get back to important work. Your friend has good ideas, taking on apprentice now."

Shiv take that Kirian, Rilan thought, as Freshta buzzed off. She wondered how many other councilors would get new apprentices to "prepare" for the Aridori. If any did, they were likely able to choose their own. She drew in a long breath, let it out.

"You might as well come in," she told the young woman, backing into her apartment's entrance hall. Enos followed, as stiff as if she'd been stuffed.

Rilan led the way into the receiving room, one of several rooms in the larger than average suite given to the head of a house. She yawned, and took her usual chair. Enos—her new apprentice, unless Rilan could convince the rest of the Council to reverse their stance—stood, until Rilan waved a hand and the compact woman sat in the chair across from her. *Formal, that one.* Enos' eyes quickly took in her decorations, originating from all over the ten homeworlds. Rilan nodded slightly. Observant.

"You want breakfast? I have some flatbread and yogurt left over."

"That would be...nice." Enos was sitting on the edge of a stuffed chair like it was going to bite her. Rilan shook her head and got breakfast, setting it on a low table between the chairs. She had chosen the artistically styled piece as a centerpiece for the room after buying it in Karduniash on Methiem on a trip two cycles ago. The wood of the base was polished to a dull shine, carved like twisting tree trunks. Flat slabs of heartwood, in imitation of a canopy, created the surface of the table, at staggered heights.

As she chewed, she watched Enos, who watched her back. Enos was nervous—who wouldn't be—but Rilan thought there was more hidden in her straight-backed formality.

Rilan cleared her throat, searching for what to say. She was more comfortable addressing the Assembly as a group than she was one young woman. "I haven't had an apprentice before, though I have talents in several parts of the House of Healing. I have also developed new techniques in the psychological community." Enos stiffened, but nodded, jerkily. Rilan bit back more words. They wouldn't mean anything to someone so new to the maji. She was babbling, and changed tactics. "I will have less time than other maji because of my duties on the Council. You understand that?" *Not as much time as some buffoons who sit on their backsides 'researching' and eating up the Council's funds.*

"Yes, Councilor."

Had Rilan been this prim and irritating as an apprentice? Surely not. "What do you know of the maji?"

Enos fidgeted. "I am afraid I know little. I have seen much of Methiem, and the other homeworlds. I have passed through many portals with my family, before—" She broke off.

Rilan raised an eyebrow. An orphan, she had said. Her thoughts went to her father, her only living relative. It had been too long since she last saw him. "May I ask how long ago?"

"Six ten-days." Finally a little emotion pushed its way onto Enos' face, forcing her mouth down. "I, I wish I had someone—some*thing* to fight back against, but it was a—an accident."

Rilan wanted to comfort her, but Enos' posture still warned of getting too close. Some other type of comfort, then. "Maji may follow any profession they like, you know." Enos' eyes hardened and Rilan continued before she lost the young woman. "My father is a poor craftsman in Dalhni, but he provided me with the education and drive to end up here, after I first heard the Grand Symphony." He still rationed the money she sent home, as if he had to hide it lest it undo his cycles of labor. "If you wish to make sure such an accident doesn't happen again, you can. It's better if your area of study ties in to your house, though one of the best doctors I know is not in the House of Healing, but in the House of Grace. He's saved hundreds of lives." Rilan put her flatbread down and dusted her fingers off.

"It cannot reverse what has happened," Enos said.

"No, but you can help yourself," Rilan told her. "I have studied the mental aspect of the House of Healing for many cycles. There are several ways of installing mental links I have found which—" She broke off at Enos' horrified expression. "What?"

"I wish to have nothing to do with the mental tricks of the House of Healing. Among my family it is considered a great insult to pry into another's mind, in whatever capacity."

Rilan cocked her head, then pinched the bridge of her nose with a forefinger and thumb. *By Devi's holy feet, I get the one apprentice that won't have anything to do with my entire field of expertise.* "Well, I won't be very good at teaching you physical healing, though you're welcome to what I know." She looked over her hand at the young woman. "It's not my," Rilan hesitated, searching for the right words, "strongest field." That was an understatement. If Enos was interested in healing, Freshta couldn't have made a worse choice. The Pixie knew Rilan's skill set.

"Let's move on. How progressed are you in using the notes of your song?"

Enos twiddled her thumbs for a moment. "I am able to hear the Symphony, but I have not yet been able to manipulate the notes. My brother is much better than I."

"Your brother?" Freshta had not mentioned the sibling was a majus. The ability to use the song rarely ran in families, and if it did, it was by generation. It was rare to have a sibling with the ability. Rilan sat forward, flatbread forgotten.

"Yes, my twin. Did you not know? Majus Caroom of the House of Strength apprenticed him a ten-day ago."

More news the Council declined to tell her. Twin maji would be a powerful force, and very rare. The talk of siblings reminded her of a crazy theory from the first time she traveled the worlds of the Assembly with Ori. She would have to dig into this later.

In any case, she approved of the choice of mentor. Caroom was a solid person, a member of the Benish. "Interesting. I'll have to talk with Majus Caroom soon. I'm sure they can show your brother much about the Symphony of Strength."

Rilan rose to her feet. "Well, if you're going to be my apprentice, we need to get you a room. Good thing Ori just went through this with Sam. That will make it easier for us." Rilan mentally rearranged her schedule for the next several days.

"Who is that?" Enos looked curious, and an idea began to form in Rilan's mind. Maybe the Council hadn't tied her up completely.

"Ori—Majus Cyrysi—is a good friend of mine, and he accepted an apprentice yesterday. Let's settle you in, and maybe I can introduce you. Apprentices are encouraged to work together, after all."

* * *

Sam bulled through the rest of his first day in the Nether. He managed to avoid another anxiety attack, mainly because he spent most of the day on the highest floor of the House of Communication. Majus

Cyrysi's apartment was a dusty, uncared for penthouse.

This morning, movers had delivered the low bed, a few tables, and the dresser with mirror they ordered, and shoved them into the corners of Majus Cyrysi's spare bedroom. For breakfast, the majus had ordered him something like porridge. Sam had been too hungry to question it, though at least it was dead. The Kirian's meal was still twitching when he started to eat it, and Sam stopped watching.

He was supposed to learn about the maji today, and Sam was feeling surprisingly composed so far. *Is the Nether getting into my head, keeping me from panicking?* Possible, but he chose to believe it had rebooted his brain, in a way. Every time he felt overwhelmed, he remembered advice from his therapist. Stop, acknowledge what he was feeling, then figure out what to do. It didn't make the anxiety go away, but it helped. There was a plan: learn how to be a majus, learn about the Drains, get back home—however long that took. *Have to be friendly. Can't afford to offend my new mentor, or any of the other aliens here. Aliens. Wow.*

Sam sat on a mint green couch across from Majus Cyrysi, in a chair, in the majus' living room. Light came in through a side window, giving a close view of one of the cliff-like walls. The majus was wearing a different robe today, half dark blue, half electric green, with orange and yellow spirals. Sam still wore his T-shirt and shorts from the day before.

He had learned to tell time here, after a day. The wall's light was strongest at noon, during what people called 'tenth lightening.' It was just past that, and the walls were dimming. After the ten lightenings, there were ten darkenings, which took the walls down to the barest glow, the equivalent of midnight. Sam had no idea how long the cycle was, but a lightening seemed slightly longer than an hour, compared to his watch. It wasn't very useful to keep time any longer, but the shape and sound still comforted him.

He closed his eyes again, fingers in his ears, trying to focus as the majus told him. *Calm the mind, block out the senses, listen to the part of the Grand Symphony you can hear.* He had practiced mediation on a few occasions, on advice from his therapist, but never with a clear objective—only in an attempt to calm himself.

After a few moments, he flopped his hands into his lap and opened his eyes. "I still can't hear anything."

Majus Cyrysi gave a heartfelt sigh and opened his own dark eyes.

"You never will, if you are continuing to cease your meditation. You have interrupted yourself twelve times, now."

"Why don't you have to do all this when you use magic—" he saw the look in the majus' eyes "—use your song?"

"Practice." Majus Cyrysi sat back with certainty and closed his eyes again. Sam took a long breath in and followed suit. At least they weren't running around the Imperium again. *I think I'm getting used to it a little, though if I don't die from falling off a balcony, the exercise will kill me.*

Sam's eyes popped open of their own accord a few minutes later.

"What if I can't do this magic, since I'm from Earth? Maybe there's something wrong with me."

"By the ancestor's egg teeth, boy, you already have." The majus' crest looked like it had been caught in a whirlwind. He frowned at Sam, his thick eyebrows nearly merging. "It is not magic. I have been telling you this. It is a science. I am a scientist, as is Rilan—Councilor Ayama. The best in her house."

Sam spread his arms, thankful for the interruption. "How can this be a science? I'm listening to music I can't hear with my ears, to change notes that only exist in my *mind*."

"This is repeatable. It is consistent." The Kirian tapped his fingers, curved fingernails clicking. His crest ruffled continuously as he spoke. "You will learn to hear your house's melody as a part of the Grand Symphony. When you do, you can be imposing notes of your song into the universe's music. This will only happen when you are attuned to the Symphony. It is made of the subtle vibrations from every existing thing in the universe, so you must *listen* to it." Sam sat back and glowered, and Majus Cyrysi waited a beat. "If you are to be through with questions, let us *practice*." He growled the last through clenched teeth, and firmly shut his eyes, just as a knock echoed through the apartment.

"Ancestor's beards and bile, *what now?*"

Sam got up as the majus opened his door, ready for something new.

"If you are not having the best of reasons to interrupt me—" Majus Cyrysi broke off as Councilor Ayama, in her brilliant white dress, pushed past, ignoring him. As she came closer, Sam noticed the dress had olive-colored filigree at the shoulders and waist, just like the councilor's colors. Aunt Martha would have liked the design.

A short girl, about his age, with shoulder-length black hair, trailed behind her, and Sam craned his head to get a better look.

"Ori, five members of the Sathssn delegation are *seceding* from the Great Assembly." Councilor Ayama stalked into the room, her long braid swishing as she moved. "An emergency session is called at second darkening. All speakers and the full Council are required. All other maji and representatives able to come are requested."

"Why would the Sathssn be seceding?" Majus Cyrysi asked. "They depend on aid from the Assembly more than the other species, for disease testing on their livestock and crops."

"It's the Most Traditional Servants." The majus grunted in recognition, though it meant nothing to Sam. He eyed the new girl again. She was stocky, skin coppery, lighter than the walnut hue of Councilor Ayama. She was following the conversation with interest, looking between the two. As if she felt him looking, she spared Sam a single glance, taking him all in at once. Sam's mind froze and his stomach tightened. *Someone new. How's my hair? Don't throw up. What am I wearing? Oh no.* Belatedly, Sam looked down at his T-shirt and shorts. Aunt Martha would have had fits about what she called "entertaining" dressed as he was. He pushed away a stab of guilt for not thinking of her more, as if he needed more anxiety right now. His heart was already pounding. He really needed to find some new clothes, and he tried to part his messy hair with one hand, but it flopped back as it always did. *I probably look terrible.*

"Rilan and I are needed in the Great Assembly," Majus Cyrysi told him. "This will likely be taking most of the day, so you will be on your own."

"Not completely," the councilor added. "My new apprentice won't be accompanying me either." She threw an arm out to the girl behind her. "I assume you two can keep each other out of trouble while we're in the Assembly."

"Yes, Councilor," the newcomer said. She was watching him—no, his clothes—and Sam brushed hands down his shorts nervously. *Going to be alone with someone new.* He had to stay calm. She was just one person, not a crowd. It wasn't like at school. *She is pretty, though.* That didn't help his anxiety at all.

"Apprentice?" Majus Cyrysi asked. The councilor rolled her eyes.

"Secession first. Then I'll tell you about it." She looked over her shoulder. "I'll be back later, Enos. Get to know Ori's apprentice. He's new here too." Councilor Ayama took a firm grasp on a sleeve of Majus Cyrysi's bright robe and marched him out of his apartment.

Sam's stomach gurgled, and he hoped the councilor's apprentice hadn't heard. It had been several 'lightenings' since breakfast. *What about lunch? How do I order something? What if she doesn't like what I do?*

A leather pouch plunked against the rug covering the apartment main room. Sam was relatively sure the majus couldn't read minds. "Lessons are to be done for the day," Majus Cyrysi's voice floated from down the hall. "Try to get out and see the Imperium."

Sam picked up the bag and opened it to see clear chips, trying to ignore how the air felt too thick to breathe. Money? He showed the pouch to the councilor's apprentice—Enos, whose eyes widened.

"Enough for lunch?" he asked. *Should I have showed it to her? Maybe she's not hungry. What if—*

"How much do you plan to eat?" Enos said. One side of her mouth quirked up in a smile.

* * *

Rilan kept a grip on Ori's robe as they moved down the corridor of the House of Communication. The faint music that permeated all the houses hung in the air, played through hidden Systems. Some maji liked it. Others, like her, thought it only interfered with hearing the real Grand Symphony.

"I am able to be walking unaided," Ori finally said, and Rilan released the sleeve of his obnoxiously bright robe. He patted the offending section, as if it would make the thing any more palatable. She could see his dressing habits had drifted back toward the vomit-inducing while he had been playing around the homeworlds.

"What is the Most Traditional Servants' reason for causing trouble this time?" Ori asked.

"The Aridori. They say the recent increase in accounts has them worried. Yesterday there was another sighting in the grainlands. An Etanela farmer claims a hybrid between a Benish and a Pixie killed her cow and nearly strangled her husband before she drove it off."

Ori made a rude noise. "Such a hybrid is impossible. There is still no proof of these ghost stories."

"Supposedly there will be today. The entire Sathssn Cult of Form, not just the Servants, is terrified of an outsider masquerading as one of their own, perverting their ideal Form. They keep bringing up the Sathssn leading the extermination teams after the Aridori war, as if the Aridori are holding grudges against them especially, even after a thousand cycles. The Most Traditional Servants are planning to cut off all relations, retreat to their diocese on Sath Home, and close their borders." Rilan glared at him. Just like when they used to travel together; she was practically running and he was keeping up with little effort. Shiv take those long legs of his!

"I am assuming these are the fundamentalists who still practice ritual euthanasia?" Ori's lip curled and his crest laid back. The ritual had largely been abandoned by the rest of the Cult of Form, with advances in medicine by the House of Healing. Only this small group and a few others still used their ancient culling method.

"Yes, this is them." Rilan had spearheaded several measures to propose alternate techniques, but the Cult always resisted. If the Council had backed her proposals rather than letting the Assembly shoot them down—

"Why not let them secede? It will only ease relations."

"I agree, but that's not the point." Ori was almost purposefully dense sometimes. "If they secede over the Aridori threat—" she ignored Ori's snort, "—others might do the same. You've seen how weak and ineffectual the current Council is. My people are already edgy over the loss of their investment funds for the spaceflight you piloted. The reprimand the Council gave Mayor Nandara has several other governments primed for any chance to call foul against the Assembly, and the Effature hasn't spoken for or against." She had been working overtime with the speakers for Methiem, but they were nearly as stubborn as the Council.

They walked for a few moments in silence, navigating the top of the spiral stair, before she continued. "The last thing we need is infighting between the homeworlds and the Nether. With pressure from enough species, the Great Assembly could grow shaky. If the Assembly fails, what happens to the Nether? Without it, we are little more than ten planets, floating alone." It wasn't her responsibility to keep them together, but someone had to do it.

"Doubtful," Ori countered. "We have yet to be seeing any true evidence of the Aridori." He was taking the stairs down two at a time. Rilan huffed along behind him. "Yet I know of two Drains, unexplained phenomena which seem to bend or break natural laws. This is a physical danger which cannot be ignored."

"According to only your testimony and that of a boy prone to panic attacks." He half turned to her and she held up her hands, stopping a few steps above him. "I believe you, Ori. I do. I just don't see the same urgency. Please, don't bring it up. We have enough problems without your voids." It was the request of a councilmember to a majus. She felt the distance between them, grown larger over the cycles. She wouldn't have commanded him like that when they were traveling together. Before that, he had been *her* professor at the university.

Ori watched her a moment, his crest writhing. Then it settled. She knew he recognized the same space she did. "Drains," he insisted.

Rilan rolled her eyes as he turned back. He would not give over on that stupid name. Nearly as stubborn as her father. It was a factor that drew her to him, so long ago. "Call them what you like. Let's get one crisis dealt with before we introduce another to the Assembly, unless you really do want panic."

They continued downward. "So this is why the Council was not letting me address the Assembly on the problem when it first happened?"

"You know it is, Ori. There was too much uproar over the failure of the space capsule without also worrying about an isolated occurrence on a moon." The people who made decisions didn't see it, and that meant it wasn't an issue.

"Which has now happened on the surface of a planet. No longer isolated. If I am able to produce hard evidence of the Drains, while this Aridori rice paper flaps in the wind, what then?"

"Then we'll see," Rilan amended. "Let's get through this session first and see if we *have* an Assembly afterward."

Ori grunted again, and his crest flared with annoyance, but he shifted topics. "What is this about you also having an apprentice? Jealous?" He smirked at her, but his crest rose, taking the sting from his words.

"Like you wanted one to begin with," Rilan shot back. "You only took him on because of your voids. Does he know you've never trained anyone?"

Ori opened and closed his mouth a few times. "I will be using my experience teaching at university. It cannot be so different." Rilan pitied Sam if he was in store for anything like Ori's philosophy classes. As smart as he was, Ori could befuddle an entire class of students in record time. They clomped down the next set of stairs. "You have still not explained."

Of course her deflection wouldn't last. "You were in the meeting yesterday. Freshta got an idea in her head and then, the Council decided I needed one," she sighed. "Enos just came through a portal made by her brother. Some family tragedy. I haven't gotten the details yet."

"Then it is a way to keep you out of Council matters. Again." Rilan bit her lip at Ori's words. He was right, even if she didn't like it. "The last time you were having to develop an algorithm for determining where more new maji appeared before they paid attention to your insights."

"Cost me half a cycle," Rilan said, letting the argument take her in despite herself. She stopped at the bottom of a landing, making Ori stop as well. "I've been on the Council for eleven cycles now." Just because she had been the youngest majus raised to the Council, her ideas were 'fresh' and 'experimental.' Yet she still carried that stigma, to the older members of the Council. "Freshta only has a few cycles but they agree to her wild ideas. When are they going to start listening?" *I'm not stupid, or weak, like others I could name.*

Rilan thought she kept her face neutral, but something must have given her away. Even after all these cycles, he knew her too well, could see the uncertainty she kept tucked away. Ori came close, raising a hand to her face, then dropping it as she pulled back. His crest showed embarrassment, maybe even resentment. They had been apart too long.

"May I?" He raised his hand again.

Rilan felt her resolve waver for an instant. "I suppose."

He brushed the back of one hand down her cheek, but then she stepped back, shaking her head. It was a bad idea. They hadn't been together since shortly after she'd been elevated to the Council. She could not make policy in the Nether and traipse around the homeworlds at the same time.

"The Council is too set it in its ways," he said. "Its members too old. You are too good for it. If you had stayed, traveled with me—"

Rilan moved up another stair. "I didn't, and I wouldn't alter that. I've changed the Assembly for the better, with my position on the Council. Have you done the same, wandering the homeworlds?" She shook her head as his mouth opened. "Come on. We'll be late to the Assembly at this rate, and we need a few people with sense to be present."

* * *

"Um, I think we can get into the cafeteria downstairs with Majus Cyrysi's membership." Sam ran his fingers through the clear chips in the bag—triangles, squares, and circles. *I probably look like an ignorant bumpkin.* Enos wrinkled her nose and Sam swallowed a spike of panic. *What did I do wrong?*

"I am not going to eat there," she said. "The chef boils everything until it tastes like mud. At least the House of Strength has better produce." She smoothed back short black hair, tucking it behind her ears. "The House of Healing is decent, but no culinary wonder. There is no reason to stay inside the houses, with the whole Imperium around us and that bag of Nether glass." She jerked her head toward the pouch Sam still held. "There's a Lobath spice and mushroom buffet close by. A lot of apprentices eat there as it has the cheapest food, but with that amount of money you could take *all* of them out to eat."

Sam looked at her. *I've been to the Spire already. How much worse can it be?* He checked his pulse furtively. Too fast. *When was the last time someone asked me out to eat?* He felt the tears rise at the thought of home, burning the back of his nose and throat. *Stop it.* His hand strayed to the pocket with his watch, but he pulled it away. He wanted to make a good impression, and he was sure he wasn't.

He swallowed. Enos was looking as if she might run after the councilor after all, so he took one of the glass or crystal pieces out of the bag, knocked it carefully against an end table. It certainly wasn't glass. *Look casual.* "I...I could manage a few blocks," he said. *I won't panic.*

"My brother would love to join us, I am certain," Enos added. Sam looked up in time to catch her eyeing his clothes again. "Afterward, maybe we can find something a little more *dignified* for your station as a new apprentice."

That's more than a few blocks. "Brother?" *Is he as handsome as his sister?* Aunt Martha would have approved of her clothing choices. Her silky red shirt had small silver flowers stitched into it. Sam wanted to meet more friends, but he was breathing too fast, just thinking about going out. *What if she doesn't like me? What if he doesn't? Maybe I should stay here.*

"We are both new apprentices, like you," Enos said. "I am apprenticed to Councilor Ayama, and my brother has been working with Majus Caroom for almost a ten-day already. We can pick him up from the House of Strength on the way out."

The House of Strength isn't far. I can manage that. He had thought he was calm from the morning's meditation, but that tranquility was melting away like dew in the sun. *If I'm going to be here for a while, I'll have to go out in the Imperium. I need something else to wear.* He felt Enos' eyes on him and realized he was picking bits of lint off his shirt. His clothes weren't going to get any better if he pulled on them.

"Well?" she said. "Would you like to meet him? Get some lunch?"

Sam was staring, breathing too fast, and sweating. He realized he hadn't answered, so he tied the pouch to a loop in his shorts, swallowed, and fingered his watch in his pocket. "After you." *I better not faint.*

Enos swept through like she expected no less. He sighed, and followed her out into the hall and down the stairs. The climb down was long, but gave him time to get his mind around the concept of going *out*, with *people.* He focused inward, listening for the Symphony, letting the action calm him. Was that a few notes he heard, or the music that constantly played in the house? It was hard to tell them apart.

For now, he was within the boundaries of the houses of the maji. Majus Cyrysi and he had walked across the grounds yesterday, to put in an order for his furniture. He would figure out how to go farther when he got there. *The panting is just from all the steps.*

When they got to the bottom, Enos pushed open the heavy wood doors, letting in the flat light of the Nether. Sam took a deep breath, feeling slightly more composed, and followed. He clenched one hand around his watch tight enough that he could feel the ticking through his palm, like a metronome for life.

The houses of the maji were arranged in a circle around the focal point of the Spire and the column, stretching up and out of sight. The column itself was the size of a stadium, the Spire leaning against it like a listing skyscraper, each house an edifice. Sam didn't look up, though he had crossed one of the bridges above his head the day before. *I can do it again.* The space between the buildings was open, like pictures Sam had seen of universities. Other people—maji, he assumed—wandered the paths, most heading away, into the Imperium. It was much less crowded here than in the warren of buildings. *Good.* The second time somewhere was always easier for him, and the lack of crowds helped. *Watch the grass. It's different here, redder, like leaves, more than blades.*

He followed behind Enos, who wandered through an archway in a row of hedges, each clipped into renditions of fanciful animals—probably real animals, on one of the homeworlds. What looked like scale armored squirrels with fan tails scurried between bushes. Enos seemed to know where she was going, and Sam followed silently, trying not to think about the Nether's eerie telepathy getting into his head. *Watch the ground. It's not far.* They aimed for the next building over from the House of Communication. Rather than a tower, this one was low and squat, with a fenced off area connected to each side of the building.

"Maji may ask us where we're going, but apprentices are free to enter the other houses. We're not wearing any house colors, in any case." Sam looked up just enough to meet her eyes. Thankfully she was shorter even than Councilor Ayama. *She's looking at my clothes again. I really need to get new ones. Out in the Imperium.*

Sam grabbed at the conversation. Something to take his mind away from the immense column looming to his right. "What does that mean?" He slowed as they approached the squat building's doors—twice his height, these of heavy-looking purple wood.

"Surely you have noticed the maji wear a token of their house color and their personal color? The councilor's dress is white and olive. Your mentor must have his colors somewhere in those robes he wears."

"Oh." Sam carefully looked to the emerald green banner hanging above the doors. "The House of Strength, I assume?" he asked.

"Right," Enos said. "Come on." If she recognized signs of his anxiety, she didn't show it. She pushed past one of the towering bluish aliens, an Etanela, who was exiting the House. This one was nearly eight feet tall, wore flowing pants, and a light vest that left her slender arms bare. She didn't even look at the two of them. Sam stared after her, and saw the sequence of green and rose ribbons tying her mane of hair into a bun on top of her head. Green for the House of Strength. The other color would be the majus' personal color, something Majus Cyrysi said came after cycles of training.

Once inside, Sam's tension lessened. He listened for the Symphony again, not that he thought he would hear much, as there was also music in this house, but like a cello sonata played on a bass, lower than in the House of Communication. This was a new place, but enclosed and finite. Since Enos was in front, he raised his watch to his ear, letting the ticking time his breathing, his heart. She didn't look back, and he nervously checked the doors and hallways for maji who might accost him. Was there someone in charge of people entering and leaving?

Enos knocked on a wide, arched doorway, and the sound of shrill laughter cut off abruptly. *Her brother? Laughing at what? Who?* Enos sighed, her back to him. He straightened and put the watch away. Sam swallowed. He was as calm as he would get.

A young man, within a couple years of Sam's age, opened the door. The similarity to his sister was immediately obvious. The same stocky frame, same coloring, the same straight black hair—his tied back—and the same intense eyes, though not as serious as his sister's. He wore a dark green shirt, a similar sleek material to Enos'. Sam couldn't imagine that high laugh coming from his throat. Especially since this man's mouth was pursed.

"Sister." His eyes flicked to Sam, who tried out a tentative smile. The eyes glanced down his clothes. *Not again.* "Who's this?"

"Another apprentice." Enos pushed through the doorway. "He belongs to a friend of my mentor. Sam, Inas. Did I hear Rey's braying?"

"That yer did," came a higher voice, and Sam peered around the doorframe. The brother—Inas—made a gesture with his free hand and Sam stepped the rest of the way in, clenching his hands together so they wouldn't shake. Inas closed the door behind him. Seated in a wooden chair wide enough for three was the ugliest human Sam had ever seen, almost comically so, with a turned up nose, large pointed ears, and fine hair covering his entire face. There was something funny about his torso, too, like it was too short for the rest of his body.

Sam narrowed his eyes. No—this wasn't a human, or Methiemum, he should say. It was one of the other species. In fact, the last one Sam had seen had been on his knees between two agitators yelling about the Aridori.

Don't think about that. There are three people here to deal with. Enos. Inas. Rey. He wouldn't embarrass himself by forgetting their names. So much else could go wrong. The very thought made his skin heat.

"He started a few ten-days before we did," Enos said in explanation, gesturing to the alien. "Inas has become good friends with him."

"Nara Reyhorer I am, yet yer can call me 'Rey'," the alien said. The heavy brogue washed over Sam and he wondered about the Nether's choice of translation.

"Good to meet you, and Inas." Sam included Enos' brother in his glance, hoping he was doing this right. The siblings next to each other made a handsome pair. Inas gave him a hint of a nod, and one side of his mouth rose in a smile, just like his sister.

Sam addressed Rey again. "I'm new here. I don't mean to offend, but which homeworld are you from?" Maybe he could learn more about what he had seen.

"Ah, it's no skin off me," Rey said, lounging back, one boot up on the chair support. "I'm a Sureri, me. Yer don't see many of us toddlin' about here on account o' the family back home."

"The Sureriaj are very family oriented," Enos said. "Many elect not to visit the Nether, or even other homeworlds. Rey must stay here while he goes through his apprenticeship."

"Eyah, and not even a visit to me mother and fathers until I learn how to fling open one o' them portals." Rey turned his gargoyle face into such a rubbery expression of despair that Sam had to laugh. He quickly covered his mouth, afraid at the noise, but Rey was chuckling too and Inas had that half smile. "So, wha's the occasion?"

"Lunch," Enos said. "Then new clothes."

"Mushroom and Spice?" Inas asked.

"Of course." Enos opened a hand toward Sam. "He's paying." Sam caught that cue at least, and jangled the pouch attached to his belt loop. He tried on a shaky smile. *So far, so good.*

"How much are yer plannin' to eat up?" Rey asked.

Sam lost his smile, and shook his head. "Majus Cyrysi must have a lot of money." Enos tipped her head in agreement.

"I know a good tailor," Inas said, walking to Rey and offering him a hand up. Standing, the Sureri was of a height with Sam, but would have been dangerously thin for a Methiemum. Sam started as Inas clapped a warm hand on his shoulder, and squeezed. "We'll teach you all you need to know about being an apprentice while we eat."

CHAPTER EIGHT

The Great Assembly

-There are six founding species of the Nether. The Methiemum were one of the first, closely followed by the Kirians and Lobath. Then came the Etanela, Sathssn, and Festuour. One theory claims the Aridori were as much a founding race as the others, but any truth was lost during the destruction of the Aridori war. Today, the theory is largely considered apocryphal, though the same theory assumes the Aridori destroyed any records of their involvement.

Excerpt from "A Dissertation on the Ten Species, Book I"

Rilan settled into her chair on the crystal floor of the Great Assembly, built on the uneven bedrock of the Nether. She tried not to look down. Even after many cycles of sitting in this seat, staring into the never-ending expanse of faceted crystal made her slightly nauseous.

There were sixty-six other chairs like hers: six speakers from each species, six members of the Council of the Maji, and the Effature, who handled administration of the Nether. The giant stadium was structured like an inverted cone, with a stone wall making the floor of the Assembly into an arena viewed by the seats above. In the first several rows sat the maji, in six sections around the circumference. Ori, never one to assume a modest view of himself, took a seat on the row closest to the floor. At least he stayed in the section reserved for the House of Communication this time.

Above the maji, the lesser representatives, delegates, and senators from the ten homeworlds watched. They would pass questions down to the speaker who represented them. Similarly, the maji passed down information to the head of their house, who would then feed their information to Jhina.

Rilan fiddled with her dress while the rest of the Assembly filed in. The shoulders restricted her range of motion, but formal attire was expected of councilmembers, and she didn't like wraps. If she had her way, she'd dress in something that let her fall into the moves of *Fading*

Hands at a moment's notice. Not that martial arts were particularly needed in the political forum.

The white bell hanging from the tip of her long braid chimed as she turned her head to a patch of dark-robed Sathssn delegates milling about higher up. The familiar sound gave her some comfort before what was sure to be a difficult session.

"Please be seated." Jhina Moerna Oscana's amplified voice boomed through the System the maji laid over the Assembly, and representatives drifted toward their seats, breaking up little groups discussing the day's schedule. Jhina bent her long neck close to the Effature. *Probably urging him to get this meeting started.* The little man nodded sagely, light catching the diadem on his bald head while his eyes roamed the rest of the arena. His long polished fingernails tapped the arm of his chair. Anyone who didn't know him would not see the tension in him.

The Effature had been caretaker of the Nether for as long as anyone could remember, and his iron will held the Great Assembly together as firmly as the peace accord the species had signed after the end of the Aridori war.

The Effature put a hand on Jhina's, then rose from his chair. Quiet fell in waves through the Assembly, as the last delegates scurried to sit. The afternoon light from the Nether walls shone through the sheet of crystal covering the top of the Assembly—the same construction as the walls and the columns, though no one alive remembered how it was created. The Effature tilted his head back to address the Assembly.

"Friends, today there is a topic of importance to us all." His voice was like melted chocolate, rich and warm and much deeper than anyone of his size had a right to. "I call for level heads, and a willingness to hear all sides. This meeting of the Great Assembly is begun."

The Effature sat down, green and purple scaled robes of office spreading out beneath him, long sleeves draped over his armrests. He nodded once to Jhina, as even though the councilmembers were given seats on the floor, only Jhina, the Speaker for the Council, would address the Assembly directly.

"Thank you, Effature." The Speaker for the Council, head of the House of Grace, was tall even for an Etanela. The speakers for her species were on the other side of the rotunda, and she commanded an instantaneous presence, sitting between shorter beings. Runners began carrying messages down from the seats to the floor.

"For months, talk of the threat of the Aridori has been higher than in living memory, with multiple reports coming in of sightings. Yet to this date there has been no true confirmation of the rumors." Jhina's words rolled over each other in the fluid way of the Etanela, and she looked around the circle of speakers. "Today a faction of the Sathssn, who favor increased isolation, will speak to this point. Speaker Veerga, you have information to bring forward?" She addressed one of the six Sathssn speakers, who rose and came to the middle of the floor.

Rilan squinted at him. It was often hard to tell Sathssn apart. They were a short species, comparatively, and nearly all of them, even the maji, held that the body was sacred, not something to show about. She had no problem with that, but she had never got an answer to why they only wore black. It was like watching a parade of phantoms. *If only they wore some color, I might be able to tell them apart.* At least the Sathssn maji showed their colors in an insignia on their chest. She didn't know what orator, long ago, had convinced them of that—probably a Kirian—but she commended their memory to the gods.

"Yes, Speaker Oscana," the Sathssn said. Like many of his species, his words lingered on the sibilant syllables. "The Most Traditional Servants of the Holy Form, they are concerned for their welfare. They believe this Assembly is no longer capable of protecting their group from outside threats, and wish their political faction to be allowed to withdraw from the Sathssn delegation. The Servants, they also wish to close their borders to any blasphemers—" Speaker Veerga broke off at a rising murmur among the delegates, the dark cowl covering his head whipping back and forth. "I apologize. I merely mean those who do not follow the Cult of Form. No offense is meant to the other species."

Rilan flipped through a pile of dossiers next to her chair as ripples of comments ran across those assembled. *Veerga is a new speaker, raised this cycle.* Hence his mistake. She flipped back a few pages, then raised her eyebrows. *Three of the six Sathssn speakers are newly raised, as their predecessors died of...natural causes. Right.* That could mean a multitude of reasons among the Sathssn, including their body failing to meet the strict limitations of the Cult of Form.

"I assume proof is here?" One of the Pixie speakers cut in to the Sathssn's request for the Servant's secession. She should have waited for the floor, but the Pixies weren't big on procedure.

Veerga turned to the Pixie. "We, that is the Most Traditional Servants, have proof in a direct eyewitness of the Aridori—" The roar from those above drowned out the rest of his words. Diplomats, maji, and even a few speakers swiped their fingers across their eyes.

Rilan peered at the speaker, trying to see under his cowl. The Council had been briefed beforehand, but she would bet her belt knife this Veerga was one of the Most Traditional Servants. That meant he would exit the Assembly with them, should the Assembly approve their request. A hole in the ranks of speakers was not that uncommon, but what if he took the two other new ones with him? Or all of the Sathssn speakers? How many other non-Servant Sathssn would follow this group in their exit from the Assembly?

"How is this proof better than any of the rest we have heard?" asked one of the Lobath speakers. Zie had hir head-tentacles wrapped close around hir head, a popular style among the wari Lobath—those of the third gender.

"This witness, he had direct contact with multiple Aridori," Veerga said over rising murmurs. "This, I will let him tell you."

Another figure was descending the long set of stairs from an entrance in the middle tier of the Great Assembly. The witness. As he drew closer, Rilan was surprised to see a Sureri. Where the Sathssn were generally specist, the Sureriaj were just plain xenophobic. The two usually had little to do with each other.

The Sureri was typical of his kind—tall and painfully thin. This one was paler than most, and the fine silky hair covering his face was nearly invisible. He wore thick leather leggings, a white ruffled shirt, and a bulging tan jacket over top.

The Sureri walked to the center of the rotunda, and put one hand on a hip, glaring around defiantly. Veerga nodded to him and went back to his seat. The Sureri sneered after him.

The silence stretched, until Jhina cleared her throat. "You have something to report, sir?"

The Sureri cast her a suspicious glance before speaking, as if he wasn't sure whether she was who she appeared to be. "Naiyul Tadisoful I am, but until recently Baldek Tadisoful I was. Yer can call me 'Tad'."

"You have been disgraced?" Jhina prodded Tad.

"Eyah. Me whole cousin-group were killed off by Aridori—" the rest of his words were drowned out by a rising drone of conversation. The Sureri quieted, glaring around.

Jhina caught his attention when the noise died down. "You were saying, of the Aridori?"

"They killed everyone, excepting me, and me bein' left, the matriarchs weren't too happy." His gargoyle face crumpled in sadness. "They've turned me out, they have. I'm one of the Naiyul family now."

"You have corroborated this?" an elderly Etanela speaker asked Veerga.

"That is correct, Speaker Humbano," Veerga answered. "The Sureriaj Baldek family reports that all sixty-two of Tad's Baldek sub-family is deceased, from the Grand Matriarch and her two mates all the way down to the youngest child—" Veerga consulted a sheet of paper, quietly hissing as he searched it. "One Baldek Tyrgithan, aged eight Sureriaj cycles."

"Aye, it were horrible," Tad put in. "Them Aridori burst in the family home. Yer'd think they'd have knives and guns, but no." He shivered elaborately, and held up one hand, tightening his long fingers into a blade. "Their very flesh changed to sharp bone, and claws. I defended me kin as best I could, but they were too powerful." Tad wiped at one eye, his voice cracking. "They killed us all, even me old grandmothers. They were monsters, like in them stories. Took nuthin. Only wanted to kill us fer their own entertainment." He fiddled with something in his coat. "Bess and Widdershins were shootin' like angry hornets, but it still weren't enough."

Tad suddenly pulled two short guns from inside his leather coat. In a moment, guards appeared from the corners of the rotunda, as a hundred panicked conversations started up. The Effature held up one hand and they quieted.

"Those were taken before you entered the Great Assembly," he said quietly. Tad's eyes were wide, as if he realized what he had done. He pointed the guns down to the floor, keeping his fingers away from the triggers.

"No offense meant, yer Honor," Tad said. "Haven't been off me homeworld before, yer see." He made some sort of cowing gesture, probably a sign of surrender among the Sureriaj. "They go everywhere with me, and seein' as the Aridori are back, I don't feel much comfortable without their protection. They're nae loaded up now, yer honor. Them Snakeys tried to take 'em away, but I snuck 'em back in." Rilan saw the entire Sathssn delegation stiffen at the slang.

Jhina spoke. "You thought bringing them here was a good idea?"

"I would nae come without. Not with Aridori traipsin' around. Can't trust no one. Lucky them guards didn't search me again."

"You will have to give them up to continue to speak before the Assembly," Jhina said.

Tad nodded, a jerky gesture, and laid the weapons to one side, stealing glances at them.

The Effature spoke a word to a runner next to his chair, who sped forward and gathered up the guns. He opened one hand to Jhina, who sighed. "What did the Aridori look like?" she asked.

"Ah well, yer know, like Sureriaj." Tad cocked his head. "They were hiding their true shapes, like in the stories, lookin' like me family. But once they started changin', we could all tell what they were. Slimy beasts they were, all teeth and claws. It were too late, then."

Conversations whispered through the Assembly. Murder inside a sub-family, and even inside a great Family-nation, were rare, though there were wars between Family-nations. It was a strong piece of evidence for Tad's story. Still, something didn't sit right with Rilan. There was another piece else here—something familiar. She pulled a hand down the pleats of her braid, thinking.

"As you can see, Speaker Oscana," Veerga said from his seat, "the Aridori, they are coming back from where they have hidden the last thousand cycles." He raised a gloved finger. "The Sathssn, may I also remind you, they historically headed the extermination squads that hunted down the last remnants of the Aridori after the war, and as such, our species no longer feels safe. Even now, these beasts may be in the Nether."

There was more muttering and warding signs against Aridori at the implication, and Rilan watched the thousands of members of the Great Assembly. Any one of them might already be replaced. *No. That's stupid. Get a grip on yourself. Ori's most likely right that these tales are being blown all out of proportion.* She hoped she wasn't just rationalizing.

"We must protect and insulate ourselves," Veerga said. "Therefore the Most Traditional Servants maintain their petition to withdraw."

* * *

Sam followed the gangly Sureri, Enos and Inas. This was his third time across the spreading grounds of the Spire, but he kept his head down. *I've been here before. I'll be here a lot.* He noted a tree with a curving branch that bent to the ground. A little further was a rotating sculpture with panes of some material that sang in the slight breeze. Landmarks, for future walks.

They passed around the curvature of the column, like a wall of solidified light. The three others were joking and talking in front, and every so often Inas or his sister would look back, but they seemed content to let him bring up the rear. Sam trailed a hand across the crystal surface of the column and the six colors of the maji cascaded behind him, following his touch. Faint music spun through his head, too far away to make out the notes, though he mentally grabbed at them. He could see inside the column, where the base met the floor of the Nether several stories below. The House of Grace, on the other side of the grounds, was refracted and distorted when viewed through the column. The vision made his head swim and he looked away.

He paused at the delineation from the purple and blue leaves of grass to cobblestone, taking in a deep breath. *Past this is the Imperium.* He held his watch up to his ear for a few moments, timing his inhalation. The others didn't notice him lagging. *I've been across the Imperium before.* He practiced one of his breathing exercises. *The buildings are closer together, like it's inside. Think of them as rooms of a house.*

He pressed after them before he could think too hard, passing down several wide streets and around a few citizens of the Nether. Rey chattered excitedly to Inas in the front, throwing out a long-fingered hand to some of the obviously expensive shops selling jewelry and fine furniture. Music filtered from one—a hired street performer singing a folk song. Inas had a hand on his friend's shoulder as they walked. Enos dropped back next to Sam and he turned to her eagerly. *Anything to help me stop thinking.* He focused on Enos' round face. Human contact helped.

"The restaurant is not far," she told him. "We are near the divide between High and Mid Imperium. Any farther and apprentices would take too long at lunch." Her brow furrowed. "Are you well? You seem upset."

Sam waved a hand, realized his watch was in it, and stuffed it back into his pocket. "I'll be fine. I just...It's all so new, here. A lot to take in." *She's going to ask something else and I'll have to explain, and that will make me nervous, and—* He grasped for another topic, nodded forward. "They're good friends. They can't have known each other that long."

"About twelve days," Enos said. She still eyed him, but was evidently willing to let his tension slide. "Rey is friendly, for a Sureri, and you know them. He's taken a liking to Inas."

Sam cocked his head at her. "I don't, actually." *Maybe I can learn about these species.* He tensed as something lizardlike ran from a hole in one wall, in front of them, and up the farther wall.

Enos ignored the scuttling creature, and raised her chin after a moment. "Ah. Well, the Sureriaj have two fathers and one mother. Their species is about two thirds men, so Sureriaj men on their own often gravitate to males from another species."

"What about you?" Sam asked. The more they talked, the more he could ignore the unfamiliar buildings crowding up and around, and the occasional view of a silvery column. They passed a Lobath and an Etanela, one shorter than him and rubbery, the other half again as tall. "Have you found any friends here?" He tried to hold her gaze, but nervousness made him look away.

I could be one. I could have a friend again.

He needed all the friends he could get, and Majus Cyrysi and Councilor Ayama didn't really fall in that category.

Enos paused a moment before answering. The city was changing from straight streets to the warrens of Mid Imperium, and Sam forced his breathing down to a regular cadence as the walls started to close in overhead, trailing purple vines with white trumpet flowers.

"My brother finds friends easier than I," she said.

Sam could see how. Inas was smiling with Rey, joking back and forth. He also had the kind of wide face, high cheekbones, and expressive eyes that made Sam like him on instinct. Enos shared his features, but she held herself tightly, closed off.

"Where are you from?" he asked. Enos skipped a step. "I mean, I can see you're human, that is, Methiemum, like me."

"We spent several cycles in the northern mountains near TaiRapa."

At Sam's blank stare, she added, "On Methiem."

"Is that a big city?"

"We did not stay in the city. My family moved around often, in our caravan. We were merchants, you know, so we had to go where we could sell." Enos watched her feet.

"All over Methiem?" That sounded scary, but also exciting. *Living in a moving home, always under the open sky.* He suppressed a shiver.

"All over the ten homeworlds," she corrected, looking up. Then she looked thoughtful. "Though most of the time was on Methiem." They skirted around a trio of Methiemum talking and laughing. Sam ran his fingers along the stone blocks of the nearest building, letting the cold material ground him.

Another topic. Anything to keep his mind from settling on one thing. He clasped his hands, using the motion to check his pulse, thumb on wrist. Too fast. The buildings swirled around them. *Ask something else.* "I haven't seen any of the homeworlds yet," he said. "Are they pretty?"

Confusion drew Enos' thin eyebrows down. "You were born in the Nether, and you still don't know about the species and the maji?"

"Oh no," Sam laughed, a shaky thing, then sobered at her frown. "I really just got here. I come from Earth. I think I'm the first." That sent his mind spiraling back. *Freezing air, crumbling white hair, sightless eyes. I'll get back again. I promise.* The strain was building, threatening to take him down, but Enos' steps slowed. Sam took smaller steps to accommodate. If he stopped moving, he wouldn't start again. He tried to focus on her instead of himself. His reaction was normal, to what happened back home. He was normal. He couldn't let it paralyze him.

"You are Methiemum, surely?" Her round face showed confusion.

"That's what they tell me. Councilor Ayama said we share the same biology. But where I come from, we call ourselves 'humans'."

Now Enos looked faintly sick. "She can tell all that by talking to you?"

Sam shook his head. "She looked in my head, with her song."

"We're here, so cease yer jabber," Rey called back. Enos turned away, pulling her arms in, hands clasped together in front of her chest. *Did I say something wrong? She probably thinks I'm an ignorant bumpkin.* He checked his pulse again. *Will she want to talk to me anymore?* He couldn't tell if it was the walk or his nervousness making his heart race.

They turned into what at first appeared to be an alley between two buildings, both of cut marble, reflecting the walls' light from an obscure angle and turning it into a cozy glow. Then Sam saw the fungal growth stretching from wall to wall overhead. Fleshy gills gaped underneath, sheltering him from the ceiling of the Nether. He relaxed, a little, then saw the rows of dishes set out. Bowls of brown, gray, and red pastes were displayed below a rainbow of powdery spices. Whole mushrooms, some with stalks and caps, others flat and wide, sat on trays between the two. Inas gently pushed Sam toward a podium with one of the squat rubbery creatures behind it, three head-tentacles braided together and pulled across shoulders like a fleshy scarf. Sam squinted as the Nether clued him into subtle features, letting him know this person was not what he would consider male or female, but a third gender. His mind spun at what to call the person and the Nether nudged his memory toward specific words. Sam squirmed at the mental intrusion, though he was thankful for the reference.

"Welcome to the Mushroom and Spice," the attendant said. Hir voice was thick, as if zie spoke through a bowl of water. Zie had a look of perpetual surprise, as hir large silvery eyes did not blink. "Buffet is on special today."

"Um." Sam froze, feeling the alley start to spin around him. He couldn't remember the last time he ordered something in person. He always ordered delivery online. *What if I do it wrong? The others will laugh at me.* He suddenly felt the absence of his cell phone. He sniffed his fear back and dug a hand through Majus Cyrysi's bag of crystal coins hanging from his belt. The attendant's slit pupils followed the motion, flicking down his shorts. Zie wore what looked like a brown jumpsuit, the many pockets buttoned shut. Zie pointed a long orange finger to the sign above hir head, which contained a confusion of descriptions and numbers. *At least I can read it, even if I don't understand it.* Sam stared helplessly until Inas coughed next to him. He jumped.

"Here," he said, and dumped a pile of coins into Inas' hands. Sam's hands were cold from nervousness, and he felt the heat from Inas' open palms before he drew back. He had a sudden urge to cover the other man's hands with his own, to share in that warmth. Sam put his hands at his sides, biting his lip.

Inas' eyes widened slightly at the mass of reflective money, then he picked several small triangles and squares out and handed them to the attendant, who separated them into clay jugs by hir podium and waved a hand at the collection of tables and chairs in the alley, deeper in the shade of the gilled fungus that spanned overhead. Inas gave the rest back to Sam, who dumped them in his pouch with a sigh of relief. *Well, they haven't left me yet. Now to get through a meal.*

Enos showed him how to sample a pinch of the different spices, then mix the flavors into the base paste of his choice, made from ground mushrooms in some manner. The whole mushrooms between the offerings doubled as utensils, the flat ones as mini-shovels, the others, with thick, woody stems, as a way to scoop up paste. No one mentioned his gaffe at the podium.

Once safely at their table, conversation started again, though Sam stayed quiet, watching the three. He grasped for the calm the others exuded. *I won't have a panic attack here, at least.* He held on to his watch when he wasn't eating, surprised at the range of flavors available from the pastes. Rey told several jokes he didn't get at all, and a few more which were surprisingly funny, given he recognized none of the people or places.

Inas laughed at all of them, and eventually turned to Sam, sucking the last bit of paste off a mushroom with a lengthy stem. He had been using it to clean out the corners of his bowl. "Enos says you are new to the Nether and the homeworlds?"

"That's right." Sam scanned the three faces as he spooned in a mouthful of his red paste with a flat mushroom. *Don't think about Aunt Martha.* Eating gave him time to push away the sadness threatening to burst back out his throat. "It looks like I'm staying for now. Can you help me learn how to be an apprentice?"

Inas waved the hand that still held his mushroom. It wobbled with the movement, and Sam's eyes followed it, then back to Inas' friendly face. "Do not worry too hard. Mostly, it seems the maji leave apprentices to learn theory on their own. Or with friends." His mouth lifted in that crooked smile and Sam followed the smile as it rose through Inas' dark eyes. "Basic theory, at least, is shared between the houses, even if specific rhythms and musical phrases are not. As long as you can hear the Grand Symphony, the maji are content to let us practice by ourselves, and sometimes show off what we've learned." He paused, frowning. He must have seen something on Sam's face. "You can hear the Symphony, can you not?"

"I...Majus Cyrysi and I haven't had much chance to practice the basics yet, but I've heard bits of music a few times. It's like the most complicated song I've ever heard, but everything works together." *Maybe I should have concentrated harder this morning. Can everyone else hear it so easily?*

Inas nodded, his face grave. "Then you have heard it."

"The Majus seems," Enos hesitated, "flighty."

Sam felt his mouth purse. "He probably hasn't settled down completely. I think he's been traveling." *I can hope.*

"Yer mentor will want yer to find out where to focus yer study." Rey's face screwed up as he spoke. "Bein' a bit mechanical-minded, I'm plannin' on focusing on how the House of Potential fuels some of the more recent contraptions maji are devising."

"What about you?" Sam asked the twins. *Maybe they could help me study.* Surely he had something in common with them.

"She has only started today," Inas gestured with his mushroom, "though she has been practicing for the past few ten-days. I have been working with Majus Caroom for only nine days so far. They said it will take a few more ten-days before I'm ready to choose."

A few ten-days. It was their equivalent of a week. Suddenly the time involved hit Sam. He had only been here a little more than a day. To have to study for weeks, months, *years*—

He swallowed a sob, hoping the others wouldn't hear it. He covered his mouth and looked down, but it didn't help.

Sam jumped at a light touch on his shoulder, then hunched inward. Enos had a hand on his shoulder. "You have lost your home." It wasn't a question, but Sam nodded anyway. "I'm sure you will one day find your way back."

He rubbed at his eyes. Too late to hide anything now. He sat back and watched the others, heedless of how he must look. "No, I won't. Majus Cyrysi already tried. My home is gone. The only place I remember well enough is 'changed too far from my mental picture' for a portal." He tried for a rendition of Majus Cyrysi's airy tone, but ruined it by sniffing afterward.

Inas studied his face. "What happened?"

"It's nothing."

"Out wi' it," Rey said. The harsh command shocked him, for just a moment. "We're all homesick and pent up-like. Yer not the only who's missin' his home. It's good to be sharin' yer troubles with friends." The usually jolly Sureri stared at him, thick eyebrows drawn down.

Sam looked at the twins, their faces open, willing to listen. *If I start, I won't be able to stop.* He resisted, but heard the words roll from his mouth. He told of his home, his collection, Aunt Martha, and finally, the Drain. He even told of trying to find shelter with the small village in Alaska—so many suspicious people—after his parents were killed, though he left out the specifics of their deaths. That was still too personal.

"That's tough, mate," Rey said after he finished.

Enos and her brother shared a long look. "You say Majus Cyrysi knows of only one more of these 'Drains'?" she asked.

Sam blinked. *That wasn't the response I expected.* "Um. Yes."

"We have also encountered one of these 'Drains'," Inas told him.

CHAPTER NINE

Clothes Make the Man

-Some delegates in the Great Assembly whisper the Council of the Maji has too much power. They control transportation, imports, and exports between homeworlds, and have the ear of the Effature. I believe the Council must work in the best interest of the Great Assembly, for if not, they could reduce us to ten simple planets, spread wide across the universe.
Rabata Liinero Humbano, Senior Speaker for the Etanela

Rilan watched the speakers question Tad, thankfully now devoid of his guns. What was so familiar? It wasn't him. Rilan had never met Tad before. Was it his family?

Baldek. The Sureriaj family name rumbled around in Rilan's head, and her eyes narrowed at the implication. Around her, the Assembly argued over Speaker Veerga's insistence on the Servants seceding. *Tad is lying.* It took several minutes for the Effature to calm everyone. The Most Traditional Servants had been much more influential a thousand cycles ago, when they led squads to exterminate the last of the Aridori. It was understandable they were scared now, but manufacturing a panic based on Tad's testimony was foolish.

While the others probed the Sureri on the details of the crime, Rilan hastily scribbled a note and sent an attendant over to Jhina, as Speaker for the Council. She caught an interested frown from Feldo over his round glasses, and suspicious glance from Bofan A'Tof, who was re-tying his head-tentacles, but she ignored them, raising her eyebrows at Jhina. She caught the willowy Etanela's subtle moment of shock—a widening of her large eyes. Jhina remembered. Surely, at the peril of losing a section of the Assembly, it was past time to let the secret of the Baldek medicine go?

Then Jhina slowly shook her head, and flicked her eyes toward the Effature. Rilan followed her glance and saw him watching her. Of course he had already figured it out. He closed his eyes and made the tiniest negative gesture.

Aridori had not killed the Baldek clan, because the Aridori were extinct. This was like every other wild rumor popping up over the cycles. They had only the testimony of Tad, a disgraced Sureri. The cloaked Sathssn representatives had listened to him because it furthered the worst-case scenario they feared and reinforced their prejudices.

Rilan wrote another note to Jhina: *Ask him his sub-family's name.* When she looked over, the speaker took in a long breath, but signaled agreement with one hand. Rilan watched the five Sureriaj speakers on the floor of the Assembly, all male, reflecting their unbalanced gender ratio. That, and the women were far too busy running the country-sized families to deal with interspecies politics. One of the Sureriaj speaker seats had been vacant for several months. They watched their fallen son nervously give testimony from the center of the floor.

Rilan tried to pick out the family groups. Each family was as big as a province on Methiem, its members all related, led by the oldest of the family matriarchs—ruthless and effective women. There was at least one speaker from the Nara and Frente families, and maybe one of the Roftun. None from the Baldek, as far as she could tell. She looked up into the seating, trying to catch sight of an unusually pale Sureri—the nominal sign of the Baldek family. None she could see, but that family was isolationist even for the Sureriaj.

Jhina broke into an Etanela speaker's questions. "Naiyul Tadisoful, formerly Baldek Tadisoful, will you give us the name of your Baldek sub-family?"

Rustling conversations in the Assembly went quiet, and Rilan leaned forward. It was considered very impolite to ask for more names than those a Sureri gave. Within their species, additional names pinned down ancestry to at least eight generations. They weren't shared.

Tad drew up to his full height. "What's that got to do wi' anything?"

"Do you have the sub-family title, Speaker Veerga?" Jhina addressed the Sathssn who introduced Tad. The cloaked speaker shook his head. Jhina turned back to Tad. "As I understand, being disgraced to the Naiyul family releases you from all ties to your former family. Is this correct?"

"Eyah, 'tis," Tad said, "but—"

Jhina rode over him. "Then you should have little compunction about telling us, to further a matter which concerns the very integrity of the Great Assembly of Species, an organization that has lasted for thousands of cycles." The Etanela's ever-present movement had stilled, lending her the air of a predator about to strike.

Tad shrank, his hands drifting to where his guns would have been holstered. He swallowed and glanced to his species' speakers. They did not meet his gaze.

"Meneltec." The word was nearly inaudible.

Rilan pushed a fist into her thigh, looking again to Jhina, who closed her eyes. *Got him.*

This was not an Aridori attack. The Meneltec sub-family was one Rilan knew of from four cycles ago. They had likely committed mass suicide after discovering their increasing sterility, which was a punishment enacted by, and known only to, the highest echelons in the Great Assembly, including the Council. Rilan mentally praised the band of merchants who had first brought her information on the plot against the Methiemum. She had personally arranged for the tainted supplies, disguised as relief for an epidemic of the Shudders, to be slipped back into that sub-family's own medical stocks. It had worked better than she expected.

Little conversations were starting up among the higher ranking speakers. Most of the Assembly did not know of the Baldek Meneltec plot, but those who wielded the most power—the Council and the Effature, the senior speakers, even some of the longest-serving diplomats—they knew. They were the ones who, in the end, guided the course of the Great Assembly of Species. Tad watched a senior speaker for the Methiemum lean over and whisper something to a Festuour speaker, who then looked to the disgraced Sureri. Tad slumped. His removal from the Baldek family was probably for not following his sub-family's lead. The questions would continue, but it would be downhill from here. The Most Traditional Servants would have a hard time using this pawn to further their secessionist agendas.

Rilan glanced up to where Ori sat, his crest lifting and flattening as he followed the discussion. Despite herself, she was starting to think his voids might be the more important issue, especially with the continued lack of evidence supporting the Aridori threat. She had trusted him implicitly, at one point. Were they such different people now that he had to struggle to prove everything he told her?

"With this new information, and if there are no more questions—" Jhina began, but a runner appeared at her elbow. "There is a request for comment from—" She speared a glance toward Rilan, who frowned back, feeling a drop in the pit of her stomach. She hadn't been paying attention. "The House of Healing?" The drop in her belly became a chasm. Why had the majus not come through her?

Her eyes moved to a small figure standing above, in the section of maji from her house. She recognized the dark hair, the carefully trimmed goatee, the prideful head tilted upward.

Vethis. She closed her eyes, just for a moment, and inhaled. *Shiv's teeth.* Rilan felt her hand drift to her belt, but of course her knife wasn't there. Jhina was busy approving the request. Little surprise Vethis would ignore her authority as one of the Council. Nothing had changed since they were apprentices.

"This is not the only recent activity of the Aridori," the man said, the System projecting his voice across the Assembly now that Jhina had approved him. He emphasized the lisp his rich friends in High Imperium affected. He thought it made him sound sophisticated, but instead it made him sound like the ass he was. "I have on good authority the Council of the Maji has suppressed another report of an Aridori assassin—one connected with the ill-fated Methiemum expedition to our moon."

Vethis didn't know the Baldek Meneltec had tainted medical supplies. He wasn't high enough in the maji's ranks. He would undermine her plan with his nonsense, whatever his current scheme was. It was known there had been an assassin—just not that he had been a disguised Methiemum guard. She almost gestured for Jhina to cut off his access to the voice projecting System, but stopped. If the Assembly saw her interrupt Vethis' tirade, it would only cement his noise in their minds as reality. She gritted her teeth. Those who looked for conspiracies feared the power of the Council of the Maji.

Vethis poured out all he knew of the Methiemum assassin disguised as a Sureri—something the Council had desired to keep quiet for the moment. It was more than the majus should have known, but not everything. However, in his version, the assassin was not paid by the corrupt mayor of Kashidur City, but a free agent. Not only that, he had been an Aridori, capable of looking like whomever it wished. She saw the other councilmembers shifting uncomfortably in their seats. She would hear the snide comments and bear the disappointed looks for not keeping a tight enough leash on those in her house.

One of the senior Etanela speakers stood up. "If I may break in for a moment, Majus Vethis," the tall woman said, cutting through his tirade. Rabata Liinero Humbano was a very old Etanela, a dominate female. Her ancestors had led the Etanela speakers for the last three hundred cycles, and her descendants would likely lead for that much longer. Speaker Humbano was on no one's side but her own, but she was logical. The head of the House of Strength gave a sigh of relief next to Rilan.

"May I ask where this information has come from, and what proof you have of your claims before you throw the entire Assembly into chaos?" Speaker Humbano rotated to stare up at Vethis, and the whole Assembly grew quiet, waiting to hear the answer. Rilan started to breathe easier.

"I have this on the best authority, Speaker," Vethis countered, puffing his chest out. "I have many sources of information on multiple worlds. All of them can see the benefits of being close to one of the maj—"

"I did not ask for your boasts of how many toady to you, majus," Speaker Humbano interrupted. "I asked for proof."

Through the amplification of Vethis' voice, Rilan clearly heard him swallow. Few crossed the elder speaker. "There is a guard in the mayoral house who owes me a favor, Speaker," Vethis mumbled. "She told me she personally saw the shooter, who was a Methiemum. At the scene of the assassination, the man appeared as a Sureri, with similar build and face. It is obvious he changed his shape, like the stories of the Aridori."

"That's ridiculous!" Rilan stood, but her words were subsumed into the growing conversations coursing through the rotunda. More representatives were making the gesture warding against Aridori. Bofan, down a couple seats, shook his head at her and tapped one ear hole. Rilan clenched her fists. Common sense would say the assassin had merely been disguised, rather than a member of a long-dead species, but common sense seemed to be lacking today.

The System that served the Assembly picked up parts of different arguments, defeated by so many speaking. Rilan heard agreement, disagreement, mutters that the Aridori were attacking, and even a few say the Dissolution was coming again. She rolled her eyes. Shiv's eyes—was the Assembly made of children and gossipmongers these days?

Vethis might as well be working for the Most Traditional Servants. He was an ass, but usually his target was the Council. Speaker Humbano was trying to speak again, but the amplification System was picking up too many different conversations to project the old Etanela's voice. Rilan caught a movement to her left.

The Effature rose to his feet and cleared his throat. The amplification System took it and echoed it around the Assembly, making it into a vast rolling drumbeat, overwhelming the noise. The Effature rarely spoke in sessions, preferring to let others come to their own conclusions.

"Speaker Humbano, you have the floor," he said into the new silence, and sat back in his chair.

The speaker gave him a creaky bow of thanks, and addressed the Assembly. "Majus Vethis, you say this guard's perspective proves the Aridori still exists, but is it not easier to assume this man was wearing a disguise to fool others?" Rilan mentally thanked the woman. One did not get to be senior speaker for a species of several billion without a little rationality.

"That is what some would assume, Speaker," Vethis said, tugging on one lace-trimmed sleeve. "The woman who told me this wasn't lying. I have a skill at knowing when people speak the truth. It's well known. All the time, people compliment me on how I can tell what's truth—"

While Vethis babbled on, Rilan saw Ori shoot to his feet, crest rising, in the section reserved for the House of Communication. At the same time, Councilor Freshta was frowning down at a message a runner had brought her, passing it on to Jhina. He must have been waiting to stand until the message got down here.

Rilan closed her eyes again. *Ori, don't do this,* she thought up at him. He had been warned once already, but even more than Vethis, he had never been one to follow rules. When she was younger, that had been something attractive. Now, she could tell he had waited the whole session for the best moment to push his agenda.

Almost before Jhina gave him permission to speak, Ori was addressing the Assembly.

"Councilors, speakers, representatives; you are seeing that the threat of the Aridori is a rice paper fiction, not worth your time on the matter." Mutters of disagreement. "I bring you a far greater threat, truly worth the fright of the Most Traditional Servants." He nodded toward the Sathssn delegation.

What are you doing Ori, you arrogant cockatoo? Rilan thought at him furiously. *You're going to cause more panic than that ass Vethis!* As with Vethis, any reaction from her would only confirm the suspicions of others. She could shout him down eventually, but it might take longer than keeping quiet.

"I have personally witnessed an aberration of nature, a Drain of energy that is to be untouchable by even the Grand Symphony itself." Further side conversations started, and several maji called out for Ori to sit down. Only they would know what an impossible statement Ori made. When Rilan talked of the Grand Symphony to non-maji, she could tell they thought of it a supernatural thing, as powerful and mighty as a force of nature.

"This was to be the true culprit behind the failure of the Methiemum space capsule. It was nearly killing the entire crew, myself included. These Drains are able to eat away the nature of reality itself—and there is more!" He was shouting now, to make himself heard over the competing conversations and shouts for him to cease. "I have recently saved a fledgling majus from certain death, rescuing him from yet another of these Drains. Forget the Aridori—they are not to be worth your time. Instead we must focus on these aberrations before they destroy the worlds beneath our feet!"

There was no way to bring the Assembly to order. Rilan shook her head. The Effature came to his feet again, with little effect. So much for a resolution on the Servant's secession. They would not see the end of this today.

* * *

Sam sat up straight, rubbing his face. He pushed the bowl of paste away. "You've seen a Drain? How?"

"Our merchant caravan held our parents, all our cousins, aunts, uncles, and other relations," Enos said. She curled her hair over an ear and sat back, then put the hand on the table. Inas covered it with his own. "Our last trading run was from TaiRapa, bringing their glazed pottery to Etan. The Etanela will pay high prices for Methiemum mountain-crafted pottery, and we were one of the only caravans to travel that far into the mountain district of Prishna."

Enos fell silent, and her brother squeezed her hand. Rey watched, his expressive face like a kicked puppy's. *He must have heard this before, and it's not a happy story. I shouldn't have asked.*

"Since TaiRapa is so remote, it does not have ready access to a portal ground," Inas said. "We had five days' travel to the nearest town with the services of a majus." Now he paused, taking in a large breath. "On the third night, my sister and I were tending the System Beasts that pulled our caravan when we heard our family cry out." He stopped again, and pinched the bridge of his nose with his free hand. His eyes were wet.

"I remember little of that night," Enos said, "except the cold, the screams, and the skin of the thing, like a giant boil, sitting half in the ground, half out, consuming everything. We tried to come near enough to help, but the cold was so fierce it kept us away." Her chin was up, but her mouth trembled.

Sam reached over, hesitant, then put his hand on top of theirs. *They're not pulling away.* A thrill ran through him, despite the topic. He had had a few dates, one with Phillip, a quiet transfer into his school from Arizona, and a couple with Molly, though that hadn't gone anywhere. His anxiety always held him back. *This is not the time.*

Rey was looking up at the fungus awning. "It was a Drain?" Sam asked.

"I believe so, after what you told me." Enos sniffed and wiped her nose on fabric napkin. "We did not have a word for it. I would not be here if my brother had not saved me."

Sam looked to Inas, taking in his wet eyes, his hair coming out of the knot on top of his head. "How?"

"We eventually ceased trying to approach the Drain, after it ate most of our caravan. Using some instinct to escape, I created a portal, as you did. It was my first time using my song." Inas shook his head. "I do not know why the portal opened to the Nether. We had only been here once, when we were very young, to visit the Great Bazaar—it is quite expensive to travel here."

Enos added, "Only later did I find out I was also to be a majus."

"We have to tell Majus Cyrysi about this when we get back," Sam told them. Something rose in his chest. *Maybe home is not so far.* "He's trying to find out more about the Drains. He saw one too. You can help us stop them." Now Inas did pull his hand back, and his sister brought hers together, rubbing them nervously. Without their touch, Sam felt a chill on his skin. He pulled his hand into a loose fist, then back to his lap.

"I am not sure I wish to go back there again," Enos said, and Inas frowned. Sam looked between the two. He wanted to go back to his home, if only to see what happened. Why didn't they?

"All the maji're bogged away in that big meetin' today anyway," Rey said. "Mebbe after, yer can talk to him, if nothin' worse has happened."

Sam let Rey's question distract him. "What is it about, anyway? The councilor dragged Majus Cyrysi off in a hurry." None of the others said anything. "Who are these Aridori everyone is frightened of? We almost got trapped in a mob chasing one yesterday, but the councilor proved they—" He stared at Rey for a second. "They caught an innocent person," he finished lamely.

The reactions were instantaneous. *I've said the wrong thing, again.* Rey's face could only be described as a sneer, and the siblings both sat bolt upright, faces taut.

"They are monsters," Enos said.

"Nah, those Aridori aren't but a gaggle o' stories made up to scare kids to sleep," Rey said, his voice harsh. Sam watched the siblings, who were both silent. The Sureri followed his glance. "Some more than others." He waved a thin hand at Inas. "Buck up there. Yer've a full belly and we can get back to Majus Caroom's apartments for a game of Hidden Chaturan."

"Not yet," Inas said. He set his shoulders, his face softening into its usual placidity. "We promised Sam we would get him new clothes, re-member?" He dusted his hands off, pushed his empty bowl to the center of the table, then stood up.

Sam and the others followed. Inas gave him a warm smile. His worry about the Aridori seemed to have dissipated. *He's pretending.*

He's still upset. Though that might be Sam overreacting, as usual. He looked to Enos, who, if not as composed, had at least wiped away the look of shock.

Sam turned at a warm hand on one shoulder, and Inas reached up to grasp his other shoulder, looking him up and down. Sam leaned into the contact. *I need someone to ground me—keep me from freaking out.* Was Inas simply checking his clothes, or did the touch mean something more? He watched Inas' lips as he spoke.

"I would bet you tidy up nicely. Let's see, shall we? I told you I know a good tailor. My family—" Inas paused, took in a breath. This close, his pain was barely hidden. "My family did a little business with him." He turned Sam toward the exit, and Sam let himself be directed.

"Hapt's place?" Enos asked, and her brother nodded. She eyed Sam again, from his bare knees to his gummy T-shirt, but this time Enos was appraising, as if seeing him wearing something to her taste. Sam resisted the urge to cover himself, and forced his eyes to meet hers. *Am I reading them wrong?* He raised his head and followed the others out of the Mushroom and Spice. *Thinking they—and me—there's no way.* Still, he couldn't deny his attraction. They were striking, side by side.

He had opened himself up too much to the others. Thoughts of Aunt Martha dogged him. Memories of the cold numbed his fingers, and he followed the others mechanically, eyes turned inward until a breath of wind tugged at his shirt. Sam froze and realized where he was. *There's no roof overhead. I'm back in the unknown. Lost. Everything's new.*

"What's with yer?" Rey asked, as Sam sagged against a wall of cut stone. He held up a hand as claws of ice reached up his spine. *No. Not now.* He had kept it back all the way here, but now his feet were pinned to the ground, one hand scrambling inside his pocket for his watch. He closed his eyes, trying to catch hold of breathing exercises, to the meditation the majus showed him—anything to make the well of panic go away.

He jumped when a hand fell on his arm, then recognized Inas' warmth. He opened his eyes again, keeping his gaze at Inas' eye level, below his, focusing only on the densely-packed buildings. Enos was close on his other side, and Rey had a confused expression on his hairy face.

"I'm okay," he told them. *They don't know about me yet.* He took in a deep breath. *Better to jump to the explanation.*

"I...I don't like new places, or crowds," he said. There were few passersby on the alleyway, though he could see a busier street, through two buildings. "They make me, well, uneasy." That was a weak word for an anxiety attack.

"Is that all?" Enos said. She had one hand to her chest. "I thought you were having a reaction to the food. Lobath cuisine doesn't always sit well with everyone." Sam frowned at her. Dismissing his anxiety wouldn't make it go away.

"Four's not a big crowd, hey?" Rey asked.

"How can we help?" Inas' dark eyes were on Sam's face. Worry marked his mouth, eyes, and forehead. Sam blinked, swallowed, and almost unconsciously, clasped Inas' hand, squeezed. He didn't pull back. *He's really not pulling back.*

"Um. Just stay close, if you don't mind." He watched Enos, whose strange half-smile was back. "Both of you." He looked to Rey as well, nodding his thanks. "Crowds bother me. Friends don't." He hadn't had many friends, but he would have had more if he could. The Sureri tipped an imaginary hat.

What set me off? Aunt Martha? The city? Both? Whatever it was, he accepted it. *It's alright to be scared.* He had to choose what to do. He chose to keep moving.

"I'm ready." He took comfort in the other apprentices—no, in his friends—around him. He kept Inas' warm touch and Enos' half-smile in his mind. *Think of them. Not where you are.*

They turned into a long stone-roofed arcade filled with shops selling expensive-looking merchandise on either side, the stonework reminding him of pictures of buildings in Italy. Sam caught sight of a store selling ladies' shoes, and his mind went to the shoebox in his room—the sheared off shoe, the half a belt. His parents would have liked it here. He wished he could have shared this with them.

Enos kept close on one side, her brother on the other. Sam kept a firm grip on his watch. It was another connection to Earth, and a metronome. Rey walked a few paces in front, while other people moved around their group. "We're almost tae Mid Imperium proper," he called back.

On the other side of the arcade, the buildings were even closer, looming overhead in a confusion of styles and stories. Sam relaxed a little. Though unfamiliar, this warren would be easier to handle than the open sky—ceiling?—of High Imperium. Lilting music came from a Methiemum woman with a wooden pipe, sitting at an intersection.

The streets were barely wide enough for the three of them to walk side by side. Beings brushed past, Kirians, Lobath, Methiemum, tall Etanela, and others, and Sam recoiled inward, hunching his shoulders. The siblings to each side provided a buffer against the attack. A few creatures with long rat tails, scales, and leathery wings scurried past. Rey suddenly pushed a Kirian in a dirty robe away. Sam jumped.

"Geroff! Filthy beggars." He turned back, pointing to Sam's belt. "Yer should nae be wearing such a tasty treat on yer belt, in this part o' the city. Best to hide it in yer shirt or an inside pocket, or someone may relieve yer of it."

Sam's hand went to the largish pouch, jingling slightly as he moved. He untied the bag and hefted it, trying to figure out where to put it. *My T-shirt and shorts don't have a lot of storage, and it won't fit in my pocket.* He pressed his back to a wall of rough fiber, letting the glint of the clear coins inside distract him from the panic of the crowds. *Just a few seconds to get my bearings.* His pulse was getting too fast, and pins and needles stabbed his fingers and toes.

"These are a lot different than the coins back home," he said. His friends made a wall between him and the rest of the Imperium.

"They are called Nether glass," Inas said, "used in the Nether and as official trade in the ten homeworlds." Sam let Inas' calming voice wash over him and fend off his anxiety. "They are also used by maji, since a full majus gets paid a stipend by the Assembly. Outside of the Nether, many don't deal with them directly. Our caravan—" his voice hitched, "—used them as a standard, since they are impossible to counterfeit."

"Impossible?" Sam looked up. *A distraction.* "To counterfeit glass?"

"They are not actually glass," Enos said. She was looking around, potentially for others who might steal the purse. "They are made of the same material as the Nether."

Sam squinted at the others. Beings passed by them, stuck like barnacles to the alley wall. "Majus Cyrysi told me the material of the Nether was unbreakable."

"It is," Enos said. "That is why the coins cannot be counterfeited."

"But...then how are they made?" Sam picked up a square coin with a hole in the middle, seeing the cobblestones through the translucent surface.

"Ah, yer've got the gist of it now," Rey added. "Most don't pick up on that juicy piece."

"It is something guarded by the Council," Inas said. "They also act as mint for the coins."

"I'm get the feeling the Council holds a lot of power," Sam said. He remembered people watching Majus Cyrysi and Councilor Ayama.

Rey waggled a hand. "Eyah, there's a mite o' anti-majus sentiment at the best of times," he said. "No one is too pleased they—we—" his face showed surprise for a moment, "—hold the only way to throw open portals between homeworlds."

"The maji charge tariffs to travel through a portal," Enos said, and Sam's head swiveled to her. His heartbeat was slowing. "It is expensive to travel from homeworld to homeworld, and even more expensive to travel to the Nether. The Assembly's Guild of Merchant Interests has always been in opposition to the Council of the Maji." Sam could feel her trembling beside him, and remembered that he was not the only one who had lost family.

"Our parents would not have been thrilled we were to become maji," Inas said. His voice stayed steady while he spoke, until the last word, which wavered upward.

"It's been worse of late," Rey said. "Some naughties are getting folks all screwed up about the Council's power again. Yer can bet something will happen before too long, or I'm a Pixie."

"I'm sorry." Sam shook his head. "I didn't mean to bring all this up. I just needed a minute to get out of the crowd." He watched the passing beings as if one would turn and accuse them, then passed the bag of coins to Inas. "Can you carry this somewhere safe for me?"

"Of course." Inas smiled back, though his eyes were red. He tucked the bag inside his vest. "Hapt's shop is not very far."

"How do we get there?" Sam asked as they began walking again. Then as he wondered, intent blazed in his mind. He stumbled with the new knowledge, looking to the end of the street they were on. They should turn left between the next two residences.

"Oh," he said. A shiver ran through him at the invasion.

Rey chuckled. "Yer'll get used to it. The Nether likes to be helpful."

I'm not sure I want this thing in my head. He found his watch again, feeling lightheaded. *One breath per tick. No more.* He watched the Sureri's shaggy head in front of him. He was even less human than Majus Cyrysi. How much did the Nether blunt differences between species? If it could translate words, and not just that, but intent and idiom, it was surely doing other things to help the ten species get along with each other. On the one hand, it was a violation. One the other hand, Sam tried to imagine the different countries on Earth co-habiting peacefully with the Sureriaj, or the Kirians, or the Etanela. He didn't think it would happen.

They walked a few more minutes through close streets made of polished cobblestones, the Nether's direction guiding Sam's feet. He would have to stop again, soon. He felt panic rising. Occasionally, a cart or carriage would go past the other way, pulled by a two or four-legged beast. A few looked as if they were carved of wood or metal and then animated in some way. Even more rarely, a motorized cart rumbled by, steam coming from pipes in the top, the clanking of its passage making him wince.

He stopped halfway down a narrow alley, the others around him, and studied a door with *Morphonyion Hapt, Dresser* etched in the glass. The urging in his head faded away.

Inas opened the door, and they piled in. There was a lively jig piping from a wheezing mechanical contraption in a corner. Sam examined the walls and counter slowly, a smile growing on his face, and calm filling him. This was familiar. Aunt Martha would *definitely* have wanted to come here. It was almost like being in her workshop.

There was every variety of cloth and fabric, some already made into shirts and pants. Leather jackets and hats hung on mannequins of all shapes and sizes, from ones eight feet tall to a few that only came up to Sam's waist. Gears and screwshafts showed how the mannequins were adjusted in height.

A movement behind the counter caught his eye and he froze. *Bear in a top hat.* Then he realized he had seen this species before, often in the little shops that peppered the Imperium.

"Ah, how're my favorite merchant twins?" the Not-A-Bear-In-A-Top-Hat said. "With some new friends? In need of clothes?" His glance passed over Sam. "Morphonyion Hapt, Dresser, at your service. You can call me Mister Hapt. What may I do for you this fine day?"

"Our friend is in need of a new wardrobe," Enos volunteered before Sam could speak. "He is a Festuour," she whispered to Sam. "Many of them are merchants in the Nether. Our family sold him bolts of silk from the Ofir archipelago."

The words meant little to Sam, but it didn't matter. He was the most relaxed he had been since arriving in the Nether. He almost expected his aunt to walk in from the next room, and swallowed past a sudden catch in his throat. Instead, Mister Hapt bustled out from behind the counter, taking a monocle from underneath his top hat and screwing it into one bright blue eye. Sam did his best not to goggle. *Bear in a top hat with a monocle.*

Mister Hapt did not actually look like a bear. His snout was more pronounced, and there were the very intelligent blue eyes looking over Sam. The fur covering his body had a greenish brown hue. He wore nothing but the top hat, monocle, and a belt cinched around his waist, full of pouches with scissors, thread, measuring tape, pins, and other supplies.

The Festuour smelled of cinnamon and sage, with something musty underneath. Large but gentle three-fingered paws touched the fabric of Sam's shirt. The three digits were spread wide to allow for much dexterity.

"Smoother than a sheared woolrat, though dirty," Mister Hapt commented on the fabric. "Fearfully simple, I say. Let me show you some styles."

He led Sam off to a corner of the shop to demonstrate the stretch and feel of a section of blue fabric with a sequence of black stitching running through it. Sam could tell from the care the alien gave the cloth that he would be here a while. *Fine with me.* His aunt had friends like Mister Hapt, and Sam had joined in their conversations every once in a while. While sewing, he could follow a pattern and know it would come out as he expected. He glanced over his shoulder. Enos gave him a raised eyebrow and a shooing motion with one hand. Inas was fingering a leather hat, comparing it with another style. Rey stared hard at nothing in particular, his expression drooping. Sam gave over to Mister Hapt's ministrations.

A bit over one lightening—or maybe darkening, as it was after noon—later, Sam emerged from the shop into the cramped alley, wearing a new set of clothes, with a lighter purse, Mister Hapt's card, and a promise for the rest of his wardrobe to be delivered to Majus Cyrysi's apartment in the House of Communication.

Sam brushed a speck of dust from his new green vest, layered over a cream undershirt. The vest had lines of subtle yellow texturing he had to squint to even see, and a special pocket just for his watch. All were cinched together with a new belt, intricate, yet still easy to put on. His baggy cloth pants had hefty pockets in the hips, and were tucked into brown leather boots. They pinched a little, but he was sure he'd break them in soon. The smells of leather and cloth reminded him of Aunt Martha's shop, but subtly different. Soothing.

"Much better," Enos said as they made their way back to the main street. She stopped him a moment to re-arrange the collar of his shirt, her hand sliding off down his arm. Sam's heart sped, but in a good way this time. He smiled back. *Even the crowds can't break this mood.*

"I told you he would tidy up nicely," Inas told his sister. He took one of Sam's vest sleeves, pulling the shirt underneath out a little farther. "There." Sam grinned, watching the twins fight over him.

He pulled them close on impulse, and they didn't resist. *Is this real?* "Thank you."

"If I blabber on about how nice ye look, will ye nae stop in any more clothes shops?" Rey pleaded. "I've had me fill for a month. Reminds me o' me second father's mam. Couldnae pry her out her wardrobe wi' an iron bar."

Sam joined the twins' laughter, then stretched his shoulders. *I feel lighter.* The anxiety was a permanent presence in the back of his mind, but the Nether felt a little more familiar, a little safer. He settled his new shirt. His clothes were more like the others they passed, with the same sort of fine detailing, and he realized how much he had been *other* before now. Inas and Enos' silky shirts had small trails of blue trim, and even Rey's plain leather jacket and thick denim pants had patterned indentations.

Aunt Martha would have loved to see the clothes these aliens wore, and Sam swiped a hand under his eye. He would find his way back home eventually, but for now, he fit in.

CHAPTER TEN

Lines Drawn in Secret

-A number of animals have migrated to the Nether along with the ten species. They brought domesticated animals, but also scavengers, insects, prey, and predators, gathered from every world in the Great Assembly. Ecologists speculate the Nether was barren when it was first discovered, and new species always look to fill out niches in the ecological web.
From "The Flora and Fauna of the Nether"

Origon winced as Rilan slammed his apartment door shut behind them. He didn't need the Nether to tell she was furious with him. He remembered how she used to ask for his opinion, to depend on his knowledge of the homeworlds back when she was first made a majus. Now she commanded, as often as not. He missed when they used to travel together, to be together.

"A lightening and a half devoted to arguing about your voids, Ori. This session was supposed to be about the Sathssn wishing to secede. The Council gave you direct instructions not to bring the subject up!"

"Would that have made them any less likely to be seceding?" Origon countered. His crest fluttered up in annoyance and hurt, and he didn't bother to flatten it. Just because she was on the Council, she thought she knew everything. He saw the political undercurrents as well as she did. "As it is, they will have to think about their position carefully before they are maintaining their petition."

Rilan snorted. "Don't even try to tell me that was your aim. It was a far second, if that."

"They did not secede," Origon insisted.

"No, the Most Traditional Servants didn't secede, despite every-one's best efforts to the contrary." Rilan sighed. "The Great Assembly is the shakiest I've seen in cycles, probably since they debated entry for the Lobhl, though that was before my time. To hear Bofan tell it, there was nearly a civil war."

Origon waved a hand to shoo away the off-topic comment. "I do not remember it being so dramatic, but it was more than fifty cycles ago—I was only an apprentice at the time."

"Who are the Lobhl?" came a voice. His new apprentice poked his head around the door to the next room. As he entered, Origon saw he had gotten new clothes, thank the ancestors. Rilan's apprentice, a stocky Methiemum, and a Sureri followed him.

"The Lobhl are the latest race to join the Great Assembly," Rilan told the young man. "They required some adjustments to the Assembly chambers."

"I was surprised at how many of the Methiemum were agreeing with my assessment of the Drains," Origon said, trying to steer the conversation back to relevant territory. Sam looked at him, his mouth quirking. The Nether told him it was annoyance. Not his fault if the boy didn't have topfeathers to signal his intentions. At least he was calm, in the apartment. He'd shown a lot of courage, coming even this far from the shivering wreck he'd found in the alley.

"Of course they did," Rilan said. "They've heard gossip of the space flight. It's still not enough to give your voids more attention than the Aridori."

"Drains," Origon corrected. He cocked his head at the apprentices. There was something going on in the group. The three young Methiemum were speaking in low voices, and Sam had his hands on the young woman's shoulder, pushing her to the front with words of encouragement.

"Enos and Inas have information for you," Sam said. "It might help me find Earth again."

Enos looked down, hands clasped. Sam nudged the other Methiemum male, who pursed his lips, then took in a breath and pushed his black hair behind one ear.

"My sister and I have seen what you call a Drain."

Origon felt his crest expand in shock. He was across his living room in a second. "Where? When? Can you be taking me there?" He barely kept from gripping the young man's shirt to get him to talk.

"Why didn't you tell me?" Rilan said from behind him. "That means this is more than just Ori's ravings."

"I could have brought this to the Assembly today." Origon threw a glare backwards. She needn't be so harsh. His thoughts raced. When was the next session?

"We did not know the issue was of such import," the young woman answered. Her voice was tentative, wavering. "It is an emotional matter for my brother and me."

"How is the Drain emotional? Dangerous, yes. Needing to be studied, yes." He looked back and forth between the two. If they had been Kirian children their crests at least would give something away. Maybe if he shook them he would get more out of them. Why didn't anyone react with the proper amount of concern?

"We lost our family—" the young man—the brother evidently—broke off with a choking sound. Origon cocked his head again. Regrettable, yes, but how did this tie into the Drains? He needed more information.

"They lost their whole family to the Drain, Majus Cyrysi," Sam said. He sounded accusing. The Sureri in back patted the brother on the shoulder.

"Oh, I see." That would make it hard for them to express what happened. Origon thought about how to rephrase so it would cause them less grief to answer. Kirians were much more philosophical about death than Methiemum. Rilan brushed past him, almost knocking him aside.

"Just ignore him," she said, catching Enos' shoulders. "I am so sorry. I can help you—both of you. If you want any counseling, or if I can do anything with the Symphony to help you through—" Rilan raised a hand, offering, and white and olive green sparks swirled around it.

"No." Enos backed up quickly, bumping into the doorway with a grunt. "I—we will work through it on our own." Her brother had backed up too, crowding the young Sureri. Sam looked from the two to Rilan, confused. Origon shook his head. Rilan was one of the best at ferreting out what caused mental strife. She'd take his head off if he said it directly, but he thought she might be too reliant on how the House of Healing could change mental activity.

"Then if you are recovered," he said, "could you tell me where the Drain was occurring?" He tried to keep his words calm, his crest down. "The more exact the location the better."

"I—I do not—" Enos looked as if she might burst into tears, and Origon frowned. Time was wasting.

"It happened halfway between the towns of TaiRapa and ChinRan, in the Prishna district," Her brother started, "I was the one who—"

"Good," Origon cut him off, "I could make a portal to ChinRan—tonight, if you are ready." He looked around the room. No one else seemed to realize how important this was. He had fled as the last Drain was forming, with no way to get back to it. This was a chance for him to study the abominations.

"The Drain is no longer there," Enos told him, her face flushing. Anger, the Nether told him.

"How are you knowing this?" Another one lost? He could feel his crest spiking in alarm. Would he never get to research an ongoing Drain?

"My brother's mentor, Caroom, took us there two days after it happened. We wished to find out what happened to our family." She shivered, her shoulders folding in.

"And?" Origon peered down intently at Enos. His nails dug into his palms.

"There was nothing left but pieces of wood and half of a carriage." Inas said. He took in a deep breath. "Our family was gone, destroyed by that thing."

"No residue? Nothing like a yellowing skin?" Origon prodded. Surely the Drain would leave something behind. It could not simply disappear.

"There was a perfectly spherical crater in the ground, wider than one of the columns here. It erased my entire family from existence." Enos wiped at her eyes.

"Now stop goin' on about it," the young Sureri told him. "Can yer nae see they're all bodged up about it?"

Origon ignored the interruption. Methiemum emotions would have to wait. Was there anything else the two could tell him? Probably not. "I must go," he told them, and turned to his bedroom. He had a bag under the bed for just such an emergency.

Rilan caught him by the arm. "Later, Ori," she said. "It will still be gone tomorrow, and the day after." She tilted her head to the sibling Methiemum, who were both teary-eyed. Origon opened his mouth to argue and Rilan raised her eyebrows at him. "Later."

He didn't push. Rilan understood Methiemum better, naturally, and if she thought it was important, then he would wait. Besides, she could have the Council bar him from studying this at all. He didn't think it likely, but with the panic over Aridori sightings so high, anything was possible. "It must be before the next time the full Assembly is meeting," he insisted. Waiting galled him. "A few days before. I will be needing time to analyze any deposits I find." He had work to do, had to get ready.

"The next session is a ten-day away." Rilan answered. "You can let them rest a couple before dragging them off to where their parents died."

"Then so it must be." Origon pointed a finger at her. He felt his crest rise, though he tried to keep it flat. "Only a couple of days."

* * *

The next few days passed quickly for Sam. He clung to his new friends, though his mind screamed they would get tired of him. However he agonized, they seemed to enjoy having him around. It made the Nether into something welcome, a place he belonged. The open grounds of the Spire, and the massive column in the middle still set his heart racing, but as he tentatively made more trips into the Imperium, he found the close walls, of so many types and materials, almost exciting. Every trip presented new sights to see, and if it was too much, then Enos would rub his shoulder, or Inas would put an arm around him, and the resounding panic inside would fade. Even his new clothes, though they would have stood out back on Earth, were plain compared to some outfits he saw. They were normal.

They tried out an Etanela seafood place the second day. Sam had tried to give the pouch of money back to Majus Cyrysi, but the majus waved him off, telling him it to keep it if it would help him get used to the Nether quicker, so Sam treated his friends. The restaurant was near a festival hall and closer to High Imperium, so Sam only had to bring out his watch a few times. He explained to Rey how it came from his grandfather, showing off the engraving around the face. He knew the wavy crisscrossing lines by heart, tracing them so many times with his fingers. Enos, with a practiced merchant's eye, approved of the manufacture, the timing mechanism, and even the silver of the casing.

The day after that, they went back to Mushroom and Spice. Sam was eager to try the combinations he hadn't gotten to the first time, as well as some of the spicier mushroom stems Inas liked. By unspoken agreement, he didn't mention Earth, or Aunt Martha, and the twins didn't bring up their family. Rey talked about whatever came into his head, but most of the time he was complaining about the crowds, the heat, or one of the letters his first father had sent him, asking when he would be getting back to "civilization."

"Eyah, he's a specist, but most o' the old-timers are. First Father's getting on a bit compared to Mother and Second Father." Rey stood and stretched as they finished their meal. Inas shook his head, helping Sam pile the bowls in the middle of the table. Sam's hand brushed Inas' ever-warm skin, and his dark-haired friend gave Sam a one-sided smile. *He didn't pull back.* Sam gently brushed fingers down Inas' knuckles. He imagined his hand on Inas' cheek, pulling his head in closer—

"All Sureriaj are specist," Enos interrupted Sam's thoughts. "If they did not have other species to complain about, they would likely complain about the other families."

"Oh, they do, mate," Rey said. "They do." He wiped mushroom paste from the fine hair covering his cheek.

"What about Methiem?" Sam ventured. He moved from watching Inas' face to his sister's, to her neck, as she raised her chin. She'd opened up, in the last few days. "What is it like?" They had compared plant and animal species, and Methiem had a similar selection to Earth.

"We have mostly traveled in the northern continent," Enos told him. "Many of the richer cities are there, save Kashidur City, of course." They made their way to the entrance of the fungus-shrouded alley, and Sam waved at the Lobath attendant, who waggled long fingers back.

"It is colder there," Enos continued, moving close to Sam's side as they walked down the street. "Very mountainous." Inas took his regular position on his other side, and Sam placed a hand on each sibling's shoulder, ready to pull back. *One of these times, they're going to tell me to stop, to go away.* They didn't this time, and he relaxed a little, taking comfort in the closeness of his friends against the unknown of the Imperium. Rey walked a few steps in front.

"Is that what they wear up there?" Sam asked, nodding at Inas' silky shirt. Today he also wore steel bracers detailed with bronze inlay, and a heavy vest covering most of his shirt.

"Many do," Inas said, looking down at one arm. "Though it is too warm in the Nether to wear an overcoat. You would like them. Very stylish."

Sam took a moment to imagine Inas in heavy coat, maybe with a fur collar setting off his hair. *Could I wear something like that one day, lecturing to a class in the Nether?* He nodded in appreciation and Inas gave his half-smile.

"Yer not goin' to start on about clothes again, are yer?" Rey called back. *Think of a joke—something to deflect him.* Before he could, they almost collided with a stream of people hurrying their way. They were in the same stone arcade they had passed through the first day. Sam felt his shoulders tighten at the crowd, seeking comfort in the barrier the twins made.

They stumbled the other way down the street, trying to keep ahead of the crowd, which was comprised of several species. A few like Rey, gangly limbs and faces all covered in fine hair, pushed past them. Sureriaj, drawing quickly ahead and around a corner.

"In here," Sam heard Enos say, and he felt a strong hand on his shirt. He followed, in turn catching Inas by a hand.

As the rest of the crowd passed, Sam looked around to see where they were. It was a sort of left-over vestibule, nestled between the arcade and another building that didn't quite line up. The entrance was only wide enough for one person to enter at a time, sideways. It was dark and musty, but in a comfy way, and Sam relaxed a little, until Rey spoke in a hiss.

"They're chasin' me people," he said, and Sam could just make out his face, crumpled in anger.

"Who is?" Sam asked.

Inas poked his head out of the pocket. "I do not see anyone following," he said. "Let's get away from this smelly corner."

Rey grabbed his friend's arm. "Wait a tic," he said, voice serious. "No telling if there're more clumpin' along after. Best to stay planted where we are."

"Why?" Sam asked. "Who's following?" *Are they looking for Aridori?* His thoughts went back to the crowd that Councilor Ayama and Majus Cyrysi had stopped from doing—something—to that Sureri. His heart sped, and one hand reached for the pocket with his watch.

"Concerned citizens," Rey said. "Getting uneasy-like about the Aridori rumors, and some o' them think they should take it into their own hands rather than letting the Council and the Assembly handle it, like rational people. I nearly got me own backside handed to me the day I got here. Had to run and hide for a whole lightening to escape that mob."

"Why you?" Enos asked.

At least I'm not the only one confused.

"It's like they're targetin' the Sureriaj," Rey said. "I cannae say why, but they think Aridori are hiding among us—it's ridiculous! Sommat to do wi' what's happenin' in the Assembly, I gather."

Sam felt the tension running through Enos at the mention, from where her shoulder touched his arm. "We can't stay here forever," he said. Something with lots of legs climbed up his pant leg and he shook it off with a shiver. *Maybe this corner isn't so cozy.* "It is safe yet?"

"I'll check," Rey offered. He peeked an eye around the corner, first the way the group went, then the other. "Looks clear."

They emerged, blinking, into the light of the walls again. The street was strangely silent after the crowd passed. No birds flew overhead, none of the lazy lizards climbed the trailing vines on the walls.

"Are they gone?" Inas' breathing was heavy. *Anxiety? In Inas? He's always so strong.* He put an arm around his friend's shoulders, holding him close.

"Long breaths, it'll help," he whispered.

"I think—back in the dark!" Rey hissed, but it was too late. Sam heard footsteps getting louder. *I knew it was too quiet.* The Imperium usually sounded like a kicked wasp's nest.

Sam pushed Inas back into the alcove as a second crowd of aliens turned the corner—Methiemum, the flash of fur from a Festuour, several Pixies furiously beating their wings to keep up, and even a tall Kirian woman, wearing a garish patchwork dress and waving a bare arm in the air.

"There they are! I saw a gargoyle," one shouted. Sam heard Rey make a sound of disgust. "Down there." The footsteps came closer as all four crammed themselves into the tightest corner of the vestibule. Sam felt frigid water trickle down his neck, but didn't dare move. Next to him, Inas was panting. Sam, oddly calm, pulled his watch out, holding the timepiece between his ear and Inas'.

"Listen," he said. The ticking was loud in the tiny dark cave. After a few moments, Inas' breathing slowed a little.

Then the entrance to the alcove darkened and a Methiemum peered in, his eyes dark. "They're in there," he said. "There's a gargoyle. Probably one of the shapechangers in disguise."

Sam almost spoke, when a stone the size of his fist whizzed by, clattering above his head.

Enos struggled to the entrance to the vestibule. "There are no Aridori in here," she said, the heat in her voice surprising Sam. "It would be best if you left."

He felt Inas duck, and a stone hit Sam on the shoulder. He inhaled in pain.

When his friend came up again, an aura of green—the House of Strength—glowed about him, settling into his skin. It cast no light into the dark alcove. He shuffled in front of his sister, and the next stone hit him square in the jaw. Inas didn't flinch, but turned sideways and exited. "Your stones will not hurt me," he said. "Please leave."

Sam heard whispering in the crowd. *Can't see past him. Don't they know he's a majus?* No. They couldn't see the aura blazing around him.

Rey, evidently emboldened by Inas' protection, stepped outside next. "Aye, there's a Sureri in here. I'd like to see ye try to take me on." Rich brown swirled around his hands, the color of old earth. Two Pixies had a bulky cobblestone between them. They hefted it forward, and Rey held up his hands to meet the incoming missile. As the cobblestone reached him, it slowed, then reversed direction, shooting back into the crowd. Someone grunted in pain, and Rey's footing shifted backward a notch, as if he had been pushed. The brown aura faded as Rey slumped. Now whispers of 'maji' floated from the crowd.

Another stone flew through the air, and Rey grunted and staggered back into the wall. Sam was half out of the alcove before he knew it, Enos beside him.

"Are you okay?" he asked. Rey was holding his ribs. *I should be panicking. I should be huddled in the back of that corner.* He found only anger burning. He looked up to the crowd, and something wavered on the edge of his hearing, like a single note that split into dozens before fading away.

"We are not Aridori!" Inas roared, and took a step forward. Wisps of green spiraled down his legs and into the ground. His boots popped the cobblestones beneath them with sharp *cracks*. Several of the crowd drew back, the fearful whispers getting louder.

The Methiemum in charge raised his voice. "They're barely more than children—not worth the effort. Let's find the *real* Aridori." Mutters answered him, and the crowd of angry aliens began to move again, first in confusion, then with purpose, farther down the street.

"That's right!" Rey called after them, one hand to his side. "Best not be pickin' on the maji—ow." He curled over his ribs.

"Thank you," Sam told them. Inas waved his thanks away, the green aura around him fading. He staggered to one side, and Sam caught him.

"Enos, can you?" he pointed to Rey.

"Councilor Ayama has not taught me to heal wounds with my song," Enos said. "I am not certain how capable she is in healing." She bit her lip, then carefully pressed Rey's side, a shaky white aura like mist around her hands. He grunted in pain. "Bruised at least, maybe broken. Can you get back?"

"I'll be dandy fine," Rey said, but he was pale, one thin hand creeping to his side.

They moved the other direction from the crowd, but Sam saw the Kirian woman and a couple Methiemum stop to pry loose stones out of a nearby wall. *We have to tell the councilor and Majus Cyrysi about this.*

A few more corners, away from the mob, and Sam slowed. The rush of adrenaline was leaving, and his hands were shaking. The others slowed with him as he dug out his watch, holding it to his ear, timing his breathing.

"Another attack?" Inas asked, eyebrows drawn low. Sam saw understanding in his eyes and nodded, trying to keep the feelings back. *It's not going away. I can't keep it back this time.* He couldn't breathe. He crouched, counting cobblestones. He got up to thirty before Inas spoke again. "We are willing to help if you tell us how."

"Distract me," Sam said. *The Nether is supposed to be safe. If it's not safe, I'll be stuck in Majus Cyrysi's apartment and never find a way home.* "Why are they chasing the Aridori?"

Rey stared at him, incredulous. "Ye really dinnea ken?"

"No one will talk about them," Sam said through chattering teeth. *They think I'm stupid, I'm useless.* He shook his head. He was stupid for thinking that. "They say the Aridori have been gone for a thousand cycles, or they were horrible monsters, or are coming back somehow. But *who* were they?" He looked up at Enos, who frowned at him, and Inas, who wouldn't meet his eyes. *What is so bad the twins can't even talk about them?* Sam shifted back toward the stone wall of a shop. The street was still clear of anyone else.

"I cannae say I believe all the old stories," Rey said, scrunching up his bat-like face, "though there's too many to all ring false. The greatest story, no doubt, is their ability to appear as some aught body."

"Shapeshifting. I've heard that." Sam almost had his breathing under control. "Why is that so bad?"

Rey raised a hairy finger. "It's *what* they did, not how they were goin' about the task. Not a one knows much from the Aridori war. Many things from before then are lost. The stories are all that's left." He turned a little, wincing, and put a hand to his ribs again.

"What did they *do*?" Sam took his pulse. Too fast. The twins were looking away. *Will they leave me here with Rey? Did I ask too much?*

"The Aridori made war on the other species, but sneaky-like, so the story goes." Rey watched the siblings too, then shrugged. "The war started everywhere on the same day. That much all the stories cry the same. Families and friends across the universe were torn up. The critters planned it for many a cycle, slowly replacing bodies, one by one. From childhood even, yer best friend might be an Aridori in disguise, playin' the role, passing information about yer family to his people."

"No one is just *evil*," Sam argued. He pushed up the wall, feeling the chill of the shadowed stone through his vest. They were hidden from the great walls of light here. "They'd come to like the people they grew up with, right? They wouldn't turn on their families." *Adopted or otherwise.* Sam glanced between his friends. He didn't want this discord.

"They were terrible. Why not leave it at that?" Inas interjected.

"Who's tellin' the story?" Rey asked, and Inas looked away, arms crossed. After a moment, Rey continued.

"The Aridori did nae target just officials, or politicians, or maji. They slid themselves in with farmers, and clerks, and workers. They were predators, lookin' fer weakness to exploit. Mebbe it was they joined the Great Assembly fer this one reason—to cause chaos." He spread his hands. "What if, one day, the buddy you've known fer ten or more cycles changes, and yer faced with a total stranger. Except this stranger knows were yer mam lives, and what yer sister likes and hates, and he can look like anything. Even like yer self, as a dutiful son goin' home to visit his mam and fathers. With intent to do her harm."

"That's—awful," Sam said.

"You have given this some thought," Inas said. "Why waste time on it? They are gone. No one wants to think about this."

Sam stared at Inas. *We should at least know the history, if they're really coming back.* He put his watch away. The stabs of panic were getting smaller, held back by curiosity. "How were they stopped? How were all the Aridori killed off—if they were?"

Rey shook his shaggy head. "The Sathssn led trained teams to hunt down the last of them. Got real fine at figurin' out who was who. Gave rise to this," he passed two fingers in front of his eyes, as the councilor had. "Supposed to show if there's an Aridori hiding in the body yer seein'." He shrugged. "Dunno if it works, but no one's seen hint of a real Aridori fer a thousand cycles. They must've all been wiped out."

"Except now people think they're coming back," Sam said.

Rey shrugged. "From where, I cannae say. Many times there've been rumors of the Aridori, so me mam and fathers say. This time is different. Yer saw the mob—people are scared. Maybe some Aridori are still alive."

"Can we stop talking about this now?" Enos asked. Her fists were white, by her sides. "I have had enough already today with that mob, without bringing up the...the Aridori." She looked like she had bitten into something rotten.

"If we do not wish to be caught in a second mob, we should head back to the Spire," Inas said. "We need to tell the councilor. Are you two able to walk back?"

Rey gripped his side, but nodded.

Sam took a deep breath in. "I'm better now." He pushed up the wall, hoping for a hand from Enos, or Inas. They didn't offer. "I'm sorry to bring this up. I want to understand."

"Understanding is good, but obsessing over stories a thousand cycles dead is unhealthy," Inas said.

As they walked, the alley walls pressed against Sam. The twins were not at his sides as usual, and he struggled to keep the panic at bay as the Spire came closer.

CHAPTER ELEVEN

A Time to Learn

-The other species often mistakenly consider Lobath dull or lazy. This is as much a stereotype as saying Pixies are always aggressive. Many Lobath live a hard-working agricultural life on their homeworld, farming crops of flavorful moss or fungus in their forests. However, their larger cities are works of art, with massive engineered structures, efficient streets, and the cleanest sewer systems among the species.
Excerpt from "A Dissertation on the Ten Species, Book II"

Rilan was just about to leave to meet a few friends for dinner when someone began beating at her door.

"Hold on!" She hurried to the door, and pulled it open to find Enos and three other apprentices. Sam stepped back, his eyebrows going up, and Rilan adjusted her expression from "going to eat you" to "annoyed." The group looked shaken enough as it was, and the Sureri apprentice was holding his side.

"Well? Why are you trying to cave in my door?"

The four piled in, Enos dragging her brother around the table to the couch. Sam helped Rey limp to a chair across from them. Something bad had obviously happened. Another protest? She had told the Effature of the one she had disrupted, and he had promised to increase the patrols the Imperium guards made.

"We were attacked," Sam said over his shoulder. His eyes were dilated, and Rilan saw his hands shaking as he eased Rey down, who winced, cradling his left side.

"Attacked?" Panen and Gompt would have to wait on her for dinner. "By who?"

"A mob, looking for Sureriaj," Enos' brother said.

"For Aridori," Rey wheezed. Sam hovered over him, wringing his hands, until Rey shooed him away. "It's not so bad, mate. Go sit, eyah?"

"Aridori—" Rilan rolled her eyes. "Of all the stupid things." Lately, stupid was becoming commonplace. It was worrying. She closed her apartment door and went to Rey. "Let me look at that."

She slipped into the Symphony, separating out the staggering melody of the Sureri from the frenetic rush of Sam and the oddly syncopated rhythms of the twins. If Enos would only let her listen to her mind—there was something slightly off about the two, especially when they were together.

She ran one hand down Rey's tunic, the motion bringing his music into focus. White and olive trails followed her fingers. There. She moved up his chest a bit, reaching inside his shirt to make skin contact, finding the place where one refrain broke from the harmony, its notes jangling and off-key.

"This is second report I've heard this ten-day of a group of low-lives with nothing better to do accosting residents of the Imperium. The Civil Committee is going mad over the disruption to their watch roster. Double overtime." She watched Sam nestle next to the twins, giving them a shaky smile. Enos patted his hand.

"I'm afraid healing is not my forte," she told Rey, "though I can block the pain receptors for a time. The change to the Symphony will eventually reverse, of course."

He nodded quickly, eyes squinting up at the movement. The tips of his ears were curled in pain. Rilan dove back into his melody, taking a few notes of her own song to bridge from one cadenza of his brain to another, bypassing the pain. She would take her notes back in a few lightenings so the change would not be permanent. Rilan next turned her attention to the off-key phrase of his ribs, attempted to grasp the chords, but as usual, they slipped away from her grip. *Brahm-cursed physical injuries. Like I'm an apprentice with Vethis showing me up again.* She wouldn't be healing that.

Rey relaxed back, his face slack, and Rilan pushed to her feet, straightening her vest with a tug. She turned to the other three.

"Now. Tell me details."

The three stumbled over each other, laying out how they hid and the stone throwing. Sam excitedly praised Inas and Rey for using their song to fend off the attackers. Rilan frowned at Enos' brother.

"We don't need to give them another reason to hate the maji," she said. "Vish knows there's enough anti-maji sentiment as it is." She peered closer at Inas. He looked tired. "Cracking the stones like that, it was a permanent use of your song, wasn't it?"

The young man blanched a little, and Sam stared at him. "It was unintentional, Councilor," he said. "I was upset by the mob, and the melody of the stones was so close, so easy to put a few of my notes into them to disperse the themes—"

"Talk to your mentor about it," Rilan told him. "Caroom would teach you better than that, I know." She swung to her apprentice. "And you." Enos shrunk down, and Rilan realized she was channeling her inner councilmember at them. They were hurt, and confused, and she didn't need to compound that. She took in a breath, held it for a moment.

"It's on me for not teaching you about healing. It's not easy for me. However, there are other ways to work around pain." Her father taught her that, with long hours helping him tool leather and stitch thick cloth. "Don't just think of the physical part of healing. The nervous system and mental states can also be adjusted." *Gods know I've had to work around it.*

"Yes, Councilor." Enos still looked cowed. Next time, Rilan would handle things better. Having an apprentice was not like bringing errant maji before the Council. There would be chances later to train the young woman properly. For now, she put it out of her mind.

"The Sureriaj," she mused. "They have made some interesting speeches in the Assembly. They seem to be targets as much as the Sathssn are afraid of *becoming* targets." With the question of the Sathssn secession question ongoing, she didn't want to add another species' voices to those calling for separation. "I'll bring this up to the Council. If four apprentices getting attacked doesn't make them come to a decision, I don't know what will." She looked to the door. "Anything else before I go? I'm already late meeting with some maji." She gave it a moment, and was almost ready to leave when Sam spoke.

"Councilor, I...do you think...would you be able to, to see if I'm alright?" He had that watch back in his hands, playing with it. She looked him up and down. His anxiety had seemed more controlled since he'd found friends and gotten new clothes to wear, found a schedule. Now he was sweating and shaking again. He was close to a full attack, just barely holding it together over something. She had been so focused on Rey's physical injury, she hadn't paid attention.

"Certainly." She scooted Inas aside, and the boy took the hint and stood. Enos tried to stand as well, but Rilan glared at her until she sat back down. There were some parts of teaching an apprentice that *were* like sitting on the Council. "Do you mind if Enos assists me?" she asked Sam. He looked to the other apprentice, and a look passed between them. He shook his head.

"Councilor, I do not need—" Enos began, but Rilan overrode her.

"You must be able to use all parts of the melody to which you are attuned. I am passable at anatomy, though that is not my specialty. You must learn of the mental aspect of the House of Healing, if you are to be my apprentice." Enos swallowed, but stayed sitting. "Observe the Symphony with me, and try to follow the phrases as I do."

Sam sat, hands clasped with his watch between them, breathing heavily. Rilan put a hand on his shoulder, listening to the frenetic timing of his melody. White and olive dripped from her hand. Enos screwed her eyes shut, laying one hand on Sam's other shoulder. There was a faint sheen of white around her. Good.

She touched Sam's forehead with her other hand, feeling him shiver under her fingers. The phrases defining fear, worry, embarrassment, and loss were much faster and louder than they should be, as expected with Sam's type of anxiety. She could artificially tamp them down as she had before, but the effect was temporary, and draining. Better to come to an understanding and cope with the anxiety.

"How many attacks have you had since you got here?" she asked. "Any I haven't seen?" She watched Enos, who looked as if she wanted to run away. Her eyes were wide, shoulders tense. Maybe Rilan could forge just a little into her apprentice's mind, through the connection with Sam. It might tell her why she was so afraid of the mental aspects of the House of Healing.

"I've been out with them most of every day," Sam told her, and Rilan's attention was drawn back. "I wanted to see more, to be with them, but there's so much here." She could feel his muscles cramp up.

"You can't keep pushing yourself. Save time for training and relax- ation." Rilan traced a thread of his melody. Too much pent up, over too short a time. "Where has Ori been? He's supposed to have been teaching you. Is that man stupid or just self-involved?" Not that she needed an answer, with Ori so focused on his voids. She sighed, and Sam flinched. "Shiv's toenails, I'm not going to eat you."

She reset her fingertips on his forehead, nodding for Enos to do the same. Hesitantly, her apprentice copied her. "Listen to how his melody changes compared to your own song." Sam was trying to eye both of them at once, and she heard a snort of laughter from Rey. Sam's shoulders vibrated under them as he tried not to join in. Even though she had done nothing, Rilan heard the phrases defining his panic unraveling. Laughter was as good as many other medicines.

"Feeling better?"

Sam nodded slightly, skin wrinkling under fingertips.

"You do seem like you're getting used to this place a little at a time. You're doing a good job, but you have to take it slowly, and tell your mentor to do his job." She narrowed her eyes. "Or he'll answer to me."

Sam smiled back, and his shoulders relaxed. The frantic rhythms in his mind were slowing. She drew her hand back, letting the side of her finger brush Enos' for just a moment.

Another melody erupted through her mind, and then was gone as Enos jerked back. Rilan kept her face neutral. There *was* something different about her, like how Sam seemed a Methiemum raised on a different homeworld. It could be her merchant background, traveling with no fixed home, but Rilan needed more time with her to make sure. Enos was eyeing her, jaw tense. She had likely felt some of the invasion. What was she hiding? Rilan looked away casually, her gaze passing over Inas. There was another chance to find out more, but tampering with another majus' apprentice was even more frowned upon than the brief glimpse she had stolen inside Enos' mind.

Rilan stood up. "Well, if that's all, I need to be going." She stabbed a finger at Rey, who was sitting up straighter. "Be careful. Even though you can't feel the pain now, you still must be careful not to injure yourself further. The sensation will return soon." She looked back to the others. "At least no one was hurt more. I'll bring this attack to the Council's notice. I have a feeling we haven't heard the last of this. You apprentices must be more careful when you go out."

She left to a chorus of agreement.

* * *

Origon knocked on the door of a lab tucked into the back of the university. In the background, a machine chuffed to an unknown beat. He hadn't visited the University of High Imperium for several cycles, and had taken the chance to swing by his old offices to see what they had done with the place. That had been a mistake, as usual. Some Pixie had taken over, repainting his office walls to a dull shade of nothing and removing all the furniture. Thankfully, he had taken everything he needed when he left the post.

He burped. Another reason, besides the endless bureaucracy, he didn't stay for long periods in the Nether. Those bog grubs at lunch had been virtually dead—probably sitting in the back of the kitchens for a ten-day. He preferred wandering the homeworlds, seeing what was really going on between the ten species, and enjoying fresher food.

There was no answer, and Origon knocked again, then peered through a tiny window in the door. The sign outside had the correct name, though he hadn't been this way in maybe fifteen cycles. He hoped the ancestors would smile on him today, because if not, he was out of options.

Another knock, and still nothing. Origon sighed and turned the handle. Fortunately the door was unlocked.

The clanking, grinding sound that had been muted in the hall was louder here. A boxy construct puffed steam into the air, chewing on a ream of paper. Farther into the laboratory, half-empty flasks sat beside racks of chemicals on wooden blocks discolored by cycles of use. He tapped one as he passed, listening to it chime.

Mhalaro Ipente Riteno was hunched over one of the metal tables, fiddling with a sample of rust-colored material. He did not look up as Origon approached.

"I can be finding you much dirt to look at outside, Mhalaro," Origon said.

Mhalaro started and spun on his stool, eyes widening behind his tiny round glasses. Even sitting, the Etanela's head was even with Origon's. A smile split his thin bluish face, and he rose to his feet. Origon craned his neck and clasped forearms with the scientist.

"What a surprise to see you after so many cycles, Origon!" Mhalaro said, his words flowing together, like all of his species. "Have you been back in the Nether long?"

"Nearly half a cycle, old friend," Origon let his crest fluff in pleasure to see his former associate. "Are you still to be teaching recalcitrant youngsters?"

Mhalaro tipped his head forward on his long neck. "Still teaching, yes. You should have stayed. The philosophy department has been pitiful without you. Pluatri is too aggressive in her teaching. I think the old Pixie has scared off more students than you graduated, before you started your—travels."

Origon waved a hand, his crest flattening. His university time felt like another life, before he met Rilan, and discovered her fiery spark. "I would not have done it differently, given the choice. Though I have not simply stopped by to speak of old times. I have a proposition for you."

"Oh? What is this? The famous adventurer has finally found dirt interesting?" Mhalaro's face turned serious, and he brushed stray bits of his auburn mane of hair back into shape, tied down his long neck.

Origon took a proffered wooden stool, perching on it across from the scientist. He had yet to meet as sharp and analytical a mind as Mhalaro Ipente Riteno. "It was beginning with the Methiemum's space capsule," he began. Even Mhalaro had heard of that disaster. Shortly, he outlined the danger posed by the Drains, and the inability of the Grand Symphony to touch one. Why had he not thought of his old colleague before? No one else had taken him seriously. "I am wondering, if maji and the Grand Symphony cannot touch the Drains, perhaps manufactured scientific equipment can determine their makeup."

Mhalaro was silent for several moments, staring over Origon's head. Then he abruptly went to the far side of the laboratory, coming back with an object as long as his arm, made of bent, burnished metal and a blown sphere of glass, with protrusions on each side.

"What is it?" Origon asked.

"A device for measuring the spectrum of material of a sample. A fairly new invention, created since you left." Mhalaro cradled the device as if it were an infant, eyes glinting behind his little glasses. "It can break down a specimen—it runs using a System crafted by the maji I have been working with—and let me see what else has come in contact with the sample."

Origon sat forward. "This could show what objects touched a Drain?"

"Indeed," the Etanela answered. "The masseous spectrum-analyzer can even show if there have been changes to the material itself."

Origon made a note to light a candle for the ancestor who sent him to visit his old friend. "What do you think about making a camping trip to the Prishna Mountains on Methiemum?"

* * *

Sam sat in meditation in the room Majus Cyrysi had given him. His legs were crossed on his bed, a throw pillow propped against his back. Based on the councilor's advice, he had decided to stay in today. After the mob of people the day before—he shivered. He needed some time to himself. *I'm still not sure if Enos and Inas have forgiven me. I'll ask them tomorrow. A day will let them cool down.*

Meditation sometimes helped him over a particularly rough day, and in any case, Majus Cyrysi had told him in no uncertain terms to practice when he related what the councilor said. Silence permeated the apartment, except for the far-off ticking of a clock the Kirian kept in his room, and the answering pulse from his watch, laying on an end table close by the bed. The majus was off on an errand and Sam was alone. *I've been around too many people, too many new places over the last few days. Am I flailing with the twins? I feel like they like me.* His eyes popped open. *Will they make me choose between them?* Enos was stern, but kind. Inas was warm, gentle. Did he have to decide one over the other? He felt a bond with both of them, and he thought they felt the same. Aunt Martha had encouraged him to get out more, find friends and have relationships. This was about as far as he could be from his house.

The memories of the frozen room still stabbed at him—icicles of grief—but every day they melted a little. He hadn't even seen the Drain that affected him. *Now I know more about them, how big was mine? Did it affect my house, or all of Earth?* Learning was the only way to get back.

Sam pushed the thoughts away. *Don't let your mind run wild. Concentrate.* Meditation didn't help if his brain spun like a gerbil in a wheel. No sadness. No anxiety. No fear or even happiness or affection. He shut his eyes and leaned back, forcing his body to relax.

The tick of both clocks made a syncopated music in the silence, and denying it anything else, his mind fixated on it, hearing the two beats combine, separate, and combine. There was a pattern there, if he could only figure it out. Was his watch slower, or the majus' clock? Did they even define a second the same way here?

A steady chord joined the two timepieces, weaving between the two. Sam almost opened his eyes to see if someone else was in the apartment, though he knew the majus was out. *Breathing steady. Mind calm.* He tried not to be aware of his body, even while bringing his focus to himself. The chord was still there, like the thrum of several deep reed instruments, just on the edge of hearing.

Then the reeds multiplied, chords overlapping each other. Sam inhaled at the complexity, the beauty. *Don't lose it.*

The chords split again, competing harmonious Symphonies, all in the same low register. The clocks were lost in the background. Like a fractal spiral, the melodies split off until Sam thought the sounds would fill his entire head. His breathing came in short gasps, though he could somehow keep track of each thread of music. Slow, fast, loud and quiet, he could hear each Symphony, each one more complicated than the last. The pure sound was beautiful—it was primal and *right*.

Shoulders down. Hands unclenched. He opened his eyes, slowly. The sound was still there, in his mind, and now he could match the Symphony of Communication to what it meant. The Symphony contained a multitude of information, not only dealing with communication, but with air and pressure difference, with the way signals interacted, with speech patterns.

The quick, quiet trill was air leaking in through cracks around the window frame. He could tell it would be windy in the Imperium the next day by a far-off rumble of bass—a horse at full gallop. A fluttering tremolo gave him the path of a group of birds passing by the window. The brightly colored creatures shared with each other the locations of fruits growing in the gardens of the Spire. The almost martial beat of another Symphony outlined the path insects made on his floor, communicating locations of crumbs. Even far away, he felt the paths of speech in a chaotic, discordant chorus as aliens spoke far below on the ground of the Nether.

He blinked away wetness, and reached out with his mind, trying to change one of the melodies he heard. *I'm made of notes too.* There was a flowing and ever-changing melody that defined him as a body, as a personality. He tried to catch an individual note, but it slipped away like an oiled pebble between his fingers. *If I can catch them, I can change the beat, the volume, the order of the music.* He could insert his notes into the songs around him, adjusting them to meet his will, changing the makeup of the world.

His body was outlined in a faint yellow glow—the visual representation of the House of Communication. He tried once more, straining to catch his body's notes and the music in the air currents circulating through the room, but as he did the fractal Symphonies collapsed into themselves like a whip, and the resulting thrum slid across his soul. The glow around him faded.

Sam slumped, empty, then drew in a ragged breath. He was calm. *I'll be scared and anxious again in the future, but right now—it's peaceful.* This was what Majus Origon spoke of. Whether magic or science, Sam could touch his song, and songs around him. The House of Communication. He wiped the tears from his face and settled back to try again.

* * *

Rilan sat in a hastily called session, consisting only of the sixty-six speakers and the Effature, three days after the apprentices reported the anti-Sureriaj mob. The Most Traditional Servants had urged all six of the Sathssn speakers to call the Small Assembly to formalize their faction's secession. The full Assembly was divided on the issue, but speakers were the ones whose votes counted, and they reached the two-thirds majority. Rilan clenched her fists as the Effature counted red and black pebbles from an urn in front of him. She was fairly sure even two of the Council had voted for the Servants to leave the Assembly. They would take their section of delegates with them, and at least two of the six speakers. *So who was bribed and blackmailed, and who's tired of listening to the Sathssn fanatics whine?* She was, but she also understood the risk the Assembly opened itself to by allowing factions of species to leave their protection. *Others will try, after this.* It reduced the Assembly's effectiveness and reputation. If part of a species was not represented, yet still wished to use the resources of the Nether and the maji, such as portals, would they be regarded as smugglers? Did they pay taxes? It threw unnecessary complications into the works.

At least Ori was absent, not being a speaker. He had been on her for the last half a ten-day to leave for Methiem, and she had to block three more of his attempts to proposition the Council with his talk of voids destroying them all. Once he got his evidence, there was nothing to stop him from bringing it before the full Assembly, and that would only panic them more. The xenophobic Sureriaj might vote to leave the Assembly, citing the attacks on their citizens, and that would be a whole homeworld gone, not just a faction, like the Sathssn.

Back in her apartment in the House of Healing, Rilan was stripping off the hated formal white dress when the communication System in her bedroom pinged for attention. She left the thing on the floor and shrugged her jerkin over a shirt, cinching it closed. She would be decent enough for a communication, even if she wore no pants.

She sighed and pressed a button.

"Yes?"

Feldo's face swam out of the mist of colors that made up the System. "You are to attend an emergency session of the Council at the Dome of the Assembly," the councilor for the House of Potential said. He sounded shaken. Rilan felt a shiver run down her back. Nothing fazed the elderly councilor.

"We've been at the Dome all day, Feldo," Rilan said, careful keeping her voice neutral, despite the claws of dread pulling at her spine. None of the maji on the Council were spontaneous. It came with the job. "Why not at the Spire?" She waved a hand behind her, the direction where the building rested against a column. "Why an emergency session now?"

"The Dome. *Now*, Councilor," Feldo growled, and cut the connection before she could reply.

"Then you're getting me looking like this," she told the empty communication platform, and looked down. "Fine. Once I put on pants. Shiv's nosehairs. Can't I get a moment's peace?"

At least Enos was out—probably with Ori's boy again. The four apprentices were bonding nicely, though she wondered at the dynamic between the twins and Sam. She wasn't sure what was going on there, but he was practically Sureriaj in nature. Still, she saw him accepting the Nether more every day. She thought his anxiety issues might be more controllable now he had emotional support.

Jhina, as Speaker for the Council, had likely stayed behind to talk with the Effature. Maybe he was the reason for the emergency meeting. Rilan walked quickly, letting the Nether guide her footsteps in the dimming glow from the walls. It gave her time to think. She edged around a male and a wari Lobath cuddling and strolling, their long fingers intertwined. The roads were still crowded at this hour, but nowhere near as bad as at tenth lightening.

They had to be ready for others to secede now the Most Traditional Servants had shown it was possible. Possibly the Effature was trying to create a stopgap through the maji. The Council could withhold portals to and from a homeworld, in an emergency. It had not been done since before she was born, but the Aridori scare could not be allowed to gain any more momentum.

Someone bumped her shoulder and she whipped around fast enough to see a dark cloak in the twilight. This was High Imperium, but as she checked her surroundings, she saw she was traveling through a warren of alleys, which the Nether prompted her was a little shorter today. The light from the wall barely reached here, and few shops were still open, turning the path she followed into a series of lit oases between dark seas. Only the most desperate or stealthy cutpurses operated in High Imperium, and they usually gave maji a wide berth.

She spared a glance down as she walked. "Vish's ever-beating heart," she cursed. She was out of uniform. The old hunting leathers her father had made her were comfortable, but did not show her status as a majus. She checked her possessions. All there.

She picked up her pace, only to swerve out of the way of another figure, this one's face hidden by a low, broad hat. Even the Nether had limits to guiding one's path. Maybe everyone was in a hurry today.

Someone else bumped her, and she tensed as a rough hand gripped her jerkin, pulling her roughly to one side. The fractal orchestra of the melody flowed through her quick as thought and emotion fell away. Trills of pheromones played against sloppy beats of sweat. Arpeggios rose from eagerness to violence. She hadn't been attacked in *cycles*.

She twisted, crossing her right hand to grip and lock out the arm holding her. She blocked the measures connecting muscle to ligaments and ligaments to bone with notes from her song. White only a majus could see flowed down her arm.

Her other hand came up underneath the man's elbow, little spikes of her olive green stabbing into the tough's arm. There was a slight resistance, and she felt the elbow dislocate. Then bone broke with a wet snap. She took her notes back as the man screamed and dropped, letting the connections between sinew and bone strengthen again.

Two other Methiemum, a Lobath, and a Kirian were surrounding her. The one whose arm she had broken—a tall blob with a nose like a potato—looked like he had been in charge. The other two Methiemum, one short, one tall, both thin, were on guard. One took a step back.

Rilan disregarded them for the moment and focused on the Lobath. She didn't feel like diving into the Kirian's mind—Ori's mind was bad enough, and she knew him. A strange Kirian would make her feel disoriented afterward.

She waited for the others to approach, still holding their fallen leader's limp arm loosely, turning to keep the others in view. The man dangled in her grasp, his eyes wide, and short wordless gasps came from him. He turned gingerly with her, attempting to keep his broken arm from more injury. He was out of the fight for the moment.

It was easier to do this by touch. While she waited, she created a counterpoint duet to the Lobath's mind with her notes. Lobath as a species were logical and hardworking. Though stereotypical, the underlying formula was sound. She would have an instant to make changes, and this was her strength.

Once the Lobath was close, Rilan let go of the leader and sprang forward, tapping her between the roots of all three head-tentacles. A net of color burst into being, sinking beneath the orange skin. As it did, Rilan heard the makeup of the Lobath's mind and made instantaneous adjustments in her artificial melody.

"Defend me!" she commanded, and saw the shock come over the Lobath—the compulsion to do what Rilan told her. Fortunately no other maji were watching. *Old Farha Meyta would turn in his grave if he saw me using mental compulsion like this, but it's my skin on the line.*

The Lobath faced her companion, arms rising, and the Kirian backed away, pursued by his former ally. She watched until they disappeared around a corner, then glared at the two other Methiemum. They turned and ran.

Rilan gasped and staggered at the loss of notes. The compulsion would wear off quickly, the parts of her song reverting to her. Meanwhile she had to get what information she could.

A kick to her back sent Rilan stumbling forward, and she converted the movement into a spin, facing the leader again. He was holding his arm, upright, but with his face white. Rilan grinned at him. He frowned, but held his ground.

"You don't push around Oswald's gang!" he shouted, and ran forward. That was a mistake. Rilan sidestepped him, and put a boot into his knee. It buckled, and the man went down. Rilan knelt over him. He was trembling, cradling his ruined arm. Both the fore and upper arm bent at odd angles.

Might have weakened his bones a little too much. At least she was used to combat. Another majus might have killed their attacker by accident.

"Who sent you?" she asked quietly. He didn't respond. She touched his arm, using a few more notes to dull the forte of pain down to piano.

"Did you know I was a majus?" she asked. If this was only a gang targeting single pedestrians, she'd let the city guard know. However, if they were stalking maji—

He blinked bleary eyes at her, finally acknowledging her presence. "You maji are hidin' the Aridori, lettin' them replace us while we sleep. Liam Oswald ain't dumb!"

They *had* known she was a majus. "Who sent you?" she repeated.

"Not tellin' you nothing!" he gasped.

"Then I'll bring you into the Council and you can tell them."

She reached for him and the man growled, swinging his good hand at her head. She deflected it easily. "Fine. I can do this the hard way, if you want." Rilan sighed, and touched his arm again, removing her notes blocking his pain. She added a trill to the phrase and the man's back arched, feet kicking. She gritted her teeth against his expression, looked around to make sure they were still alone. *Don't have time to wait for the others to return.*

She reversed her change to his melody, blocking the pain again, and raised her eyebrows at him.

He panted, fingernails scraping across the cobblestones, then swallowed and spoke. "My gang is—" he glanced around, realizing his friends were nowhere to be seen, "Word's got around we need to take things into our own hands. We know the Assembly is hiding them Aridori—and the maji are controlling them. They want to replace us regular folk. Corrupt politicians stealing our hard-earned coin."

It was stupid, but people had believed worse. "*How* did you know I was a majus?"

"We seen you leave your fortress."

"The Spire and houses?" They were hardly fortresses. Parts were even open to the public.

He glanced down at the ruin of his arm, then rolled his eyes away. "Don't matter what kind you was—you're all out to get us normal folk. I got proof now." He tried to spit at her, but Rilan scooted out of the way, a flash of heat rising.

"What would you have done if you caught me? Kill me? Hold me for ransom? Try out a little fun with a majus?"

He was silent.

"Are there more like you thugs?"

The man regarded her sullenly, until she started to reach for his arm. The others might attempt to return soon, and she didn't relish fighting all five of them at once.

The man was breathing fast. Going into shock. "There're more of us than you know. We won't be pushed out of our homes by you maji. We'll be on top again, before you know it."

Rilan stood up. "I don't have time to deal with this. I'll alert the first city guard I see. Have your friends get you to a doctor as soon as you can. What I did will not last forever—you'll begin hurting soon, and you're in shock." She stopped before offering to set his arm. What would he have done to her?

Rilan backed away, keeping her eyes open for sign of the man's friends. Whoever was running this hoax about the Aridori was planting rumors about the maji, too. People were always eager to believe ill of the maji. They controlled transportation between worlds and aided in natural disasters, but they were also an unknown and powerful force in the universe. At least she could tell the guard his name.

The Great Assembly was already shaky, and the Council of the Maji all but inept. Was there an intelligence behind all this, or was she jumping at shadows? The Aridori scare stories had her paranoid, even if they were nowhere to be seen.

Fortunately she was familiar with fighting, and knew how to control this situation. Maji weren't trained to fight. A surprised and threatened majus might have made wild changes in the Grand Symphony and killed themselves, or the attackers, or both.

She watched faces as she walked—nearly running. A few blocks away she found a guard and gave her directions to the injured man, then promised to give a full report through the Council and the Effature.

The Dome drew close, and once inside, Rilan hurried to the side chamber where the Council met when not in the Spire. She was late, but whatever news they had, hers was more important.

She burst into the room, taking in the two empty chairs of six around the semi-circular table. Then she wasn't the last to arrive.

"What happened to you?" Jhina asked her, and Rilan looked down at the tall Etanela's words. Her leather jerkin was unbelted, her shirt underneath untucked. It must have happened in the attack.

"That's why I'm late, Speaker," Rilan said, tugging her clothes back into place. "Before we start this emergency session, I have news. Where is Bofan? I don't want to repeat what I have to say." She crossed to her chair.

"Councilor Bofan is the reason we are meeting," Feldo said quietly. She glanced toward him, thrown off by the old man's shaken tone. "Bofan A'Tof was killed this afternoon by Aridori."

Rising Fears and Discoveries

-Many large cities on the ten homeworlds will have an area prepared as a portal ground. The maji run these areas, and connect, for a price, that city with the greater civilization of the ten species. While the funds from the portals go largely to the maji, to help pay for their services and research, a good portion is also set aside for upkeep in the Dome of the Assembly. In addition, a percentage goes to relief funds for those impacted by natural disasters where the maji have assisted in recovery efforts.

Methiemum grade school textbook on economy

"The Aridori attacks are a hoax." Rilan collapsed into her chair, behind the Council's semi-circular table.

"I am not thinking Bofan agrees," Scintien Nectiset said. The Kirian swept a clawed hand at the empty chair for the House of Power.

"What happened?" Rilan asked.

"He was set on by eight attackers," Feldo said. "At least one was Aridori. Possibly all of them."

"Eight Aridori? No one has seen one for almost a thousand cycles and now there are eight? How can you know?" Rilan stared at the older man. He was the last one to jump at wild stories. She looked over the other councilors. She respected Jhina and Feldo, but Scintien was weak-willed at best, and Rilan still hadn't forgiven Freshta for apprenticing Enos behind her back.

"Councilor Feldo was able to determine what happened at the scene," Jhina said.

"There was skin and blood under Councilor A'Tof's nails," Feldo rumbled, smoothing out his wild silver beard. "The body also had several bruises and cuts, one containing a sliver of metal. With the House of Potential, I traced the energy of the materials, which gave me eight different paths of probability. Nine, with Bofan."

"Attackers, yes. How did you know they were Aridori?" That was a question better suited to the House of Healing. Rilan crossed her arms, aware the other councilors were staring at her, as if she had been called to the schoolmaster's quarters. She fought the emotion away, careful to let none of it show on her face. Bofan had once been a good councilor. Now he was—had been—on the margins of maji policy, trying not to make waves. He had been too old, hanging on to his position for far too long. Something else, however unlikely, could have happened.

"That...was more difficult." The old councilor was normally certain in everything he did. Councilor Feldo had probably forgotten more techniques with the Grand Symphony than Rilan had learned. "Truthfully, you might have been better to diagnose the scene, Councilor Ayama, but for the speed at which this was resolved, I could not contact you. Unfortunately, the traces I read have already been disturbed, and will not be of much use to you." His eyes flicked to Jhina.

Rilan nodded. She could have read biology and history in the attack better than one of the House of Potential, but the Grand Symphony resisted multiple changes. Still, she might find something if she were to examine the body herself.

"Several of the cuts were from an attacker's hands," Feldo continued, "but the shapes match none of the known species, and there were no energy signatures of animals at the location of the murder. More than that, the injuries changed depth and form mid strike. A weapon could not have done that. So from the shape of the body and the force of the blows upon our late councilor," before she could interrupt, Feldo raised a hand, creased from cycles of working with reagents, "I determined that the assailant was in the act of changing its shape."

Rilan frowned back at him. "That's sloppy," she said, daring him to disagree. It was also evasive. Feldo always delivered certainties, not conjecture as fact. Was he hiding something? "You should have waited for me to investigate, or called another from the House of Healing to corroborate." Feldo rewarded her with a slight tip of his head—as much as a vigorous nod from someone else.

"This was deemed to be a matter only for the Council," Jhina said, her words streaming together. Typical of the Speaker to force a decision so quickly.

"Again, you should have waited for me." *We're right back where we were before—circumstantial evidence of the Aridori, at best.* Though now even Feldo seemed to believe, and logic drove the old man even more than it did Rilan.

"Time was of the essence to give us a chance to catch the attackers," Jhina countered.

"But you didn't catch them," Rilan said. "I'm still not convinced the attackers were Aridori. Why target a member of the Council? That's the quickest way to bring a hidden species out in the open."

"Yet we will not spread either version of the story," Jhina said, her large eyes unusually sharp. "The Council intends to declare that Bofan A'Tof died of natural causes. We do not dare risk panic in light of this discovery."

Something clicked in Rilan's mind. "You've already disposed of his body. That's why there's nothing left for me to examine. You had to get rid of the evidence before anything got out and caused more panic in the Assembly." She shook her head, gritting her teeth. Deciding without her, again. It was left over from when she joined the Council, surrounded by members much older and more experienced than her. That was no longer the case. "If you had left some evidence for me, I could tell you if the group that attacked Bofan was similar to the one that attacked me."

"Attacked you?" Freshta buzzed a handbreadth above her chair.

"When?" The sharpness was back in Feldo's voice.

"On the way here," Rilan said. "The reason for my disarray and tardiness." She briefly explained what happened, leaving out certain pieces the Council would not approve of. "The man who led them knows others who feel the same. *That's* who you should be concerned about—the citizens of the Imperium attacking maji, not ghost stories *still* without solid evidence." By Brahm, Ori was getting to her. Though he had reason, and was more logical than these blowhards, save Feldo perhaps. *Back when we traveled the homeworlds, sleeping together under the stars—* No. No time for that now.

Rilan looked to Feldo, his eyes hidden behind a reflection in his glasses. His mouth was pulled tight. "I'll wager you the same people encouraging these groups are planting the seed of secession with the Most Traditional Servants." Rilan glanced over the others. No one responded. "The man that attacked me certainly wasn't Aridori, or he would have fixed his broken arm. We don't even know what the Aridori can do, if they *are* still around."

"Organization of citizens against the maji, influencing Assembly decisions, is preposterous," Freshta said. "Now is time to elect new councilor, not chase rumors."

Now who was diverting the Council from its investigations? Rilan ignored her, and watched Jhina and Feldo. Jhina shook her head, but Feldo only watched Rilan.

"It is as Councilor Freshta says," Feldo agreed. "Whether your claims are true or not, we have no way to discover proof in Councilor A'Tof's murder, now the immediate evidence is gone. The most pressing matter is to elect a new councilor for the House of Power. Only with a full council can we investigate your claims."

"How long will that take?" Rilan asked. "When Karendi died it took nearly a cycle to elect Freshta. Can we ignore assaults on maji for that long? Feldo, they *knew* I was a majus. No one in their right mind attacks maji, and I was set upon by five." *Yet Bofan required eight.*

"Then with these attacks at hand, we must decide quickly," Jhina said. "We must hope no other maji are assaulted in the meantime. We should release a statement warning the houses immediately, though perhaps not in the same statement with Bofan's death."

"So no one gets suspicious," Rilan said. The others glared at her. She glared back. This was ridiculous. If Karendi had still been alive, Speaker for the Council instead of Jhina, the old Kirian would have tolerated none of this hesitancy. Feldo was naturally cautious, but Karendi had known how to draw out his genius at deductive analysis.

Suddenly, Rilan wished she hadn't stopped Ori when he tried to leave for Methiem, most of a ten-day back. At least he was trying to do something, even if it was about his voids. With the lack of evidence of the Aridori, they were at least as important as these attacks.

"We must be fully represented, and put this matter behind us as quickly as possible, for when the Assembly resumes over the matter of the secession of the Most Traditional Servants," Jhina said. She leaned forward. "We intend to have them rejoin the Assembly."

Rilan rolled her eyes. "They're all the way home with the doors locked!" she exploded. "The Servants are gone. Shiv's teeth, people— you're far too late, and you're not looking at the most pressing matter at hand. I'm not convinced the Aridori exist, but someone is trying like blazes to make us think they do. They're *attacking* the maji and you're trying to win back the favor of a group no one even wants around? We need to make sure no one *else* leaves, first and foremost. The ten homeworlds depend on each other. Perhaps one of the newer species will decide we don't really know what we're doing? The Lobhl are already ostracized, and we've put significant expense into making sure they are represented as well as the other nine species in the Nether. Do you want to explain to the Effature why we've wasted that investment, in time, money, and majus notes?"

She heaved in silence for a few moments, watching the other four. Freshta and Scintien looked away, and Jhina wouldn't meet her eyes, staring fixedly straight ahead, head raised on her long neck. Only Feldo still watched Rilan, though she couldn't have said whether he agreed or disagreed. *Shouldn't have shown anger. I have better control than that.*

Rilan took in a long breath. "Surely the Effature agrees we need to regroup?" she tried. "Have you even brought this to his attention, or were you too busy hiding it?" She grasped at her thigh with one hand, under the table, squeezing to keep from thumping the wood to make a point.

"We have not. Without a new councilor—" Jhina began icily.

Rilan threw up her hands. "Fine," she interrupted. "You want to know who I think should be the next councilor for the House of Power?" She had their attention now at least. "Hand Dancer."

There was a gasp from Scintien. "The Lobhl?"

"Who better to show we intend to honor our commitment to them? We pick councilors from the best and brightest of that house, right? Do we still do it that way?" Rilan speared a glance toward Freshta and Scintien. "Hand Dancer has some of the best control of power and connections of anyone I've seen. Have you seen the majus play?" Among other things, the Lobhl was an accomplished musician, handling the complexities of their unique instruments. "Imagine how much we could learn with Hand Dancer on the council—about the Lobhl people, and the way they think."

"We will take your nomination under advisement," Jhina said, her voice several degrees cooler than the room. Rilan knew what that meant. Like every other time, they would come to their own decision and she would be forced into agreement with whatever they decided.

"Do with it what you will," Rilan spat. She pushed up from the table. "If no one else wants to cultivate good councilmembers any longer, then assume I will abide with your 'unanimous' decision, but I certainly won't hold back from letting the Lobhl know what the Council thinks of them. Now if you'll excuse me, I have more important things to do." She gave a mocking bow, turned, and stormed out of the chamber.

* * *

Origon strode toward the furious pounding on his apartment door. "I am coming," he called. "Try not to be breaking the door." Sam had a key to the place, but was probably still out with the other apprentices. It was dinner time, and the last few days, the young man had been inseparable from Rilan's apprentice and her brother. He hoped it helped the young man accommodate.

The banging stopped only when he jerked the door open, which protested loudly on its hinges. It revealed Rilan in her traveling clothes, or maybe after a fight in them. Her hair was wild, coming out of her severe braid. It reminded him of when they escaped the squalpoid pack on Loba. Origon realized he was staring. He blinked and hastily showed her in, or rather got out of the way as she stomped inside.

"Tell me what you have been doing," he said. *And who you have killed*, he bit back at the last moment.

Rilan's story flowed out in a rush. Telling him how both she and Bofan had been attacked on the streets of the Imperium, her frustration with the Council. Her usual rational speech was buried in a torrent of anger and frustration. Origon watched her worriedly as he listened, catching sight of a bruise on her arm, a small cut on the side of her face. He would have insisted she let him bandage her up, save in her state, she was as liable to start shouting at him. Two members of the Council being attacked was nearly as bad as the news of his Drains.

Finally her speech ran down and she sat—fell, almost—into a chair.

"So I came back to the one person who has as much sense as I do," she said. "Ori, I want to go to Methiem. Now. Or tomorrow. Soon. There is something else behind all this. I can feel it. Even your voids—"

"Drains." She still wouldn't accept his name.

"—Whatever. All this can't be happening at the same time. At least we can research the twins' void without being under the thumb of the Council."

Origon pursed his lips at her refusal to call the Drains what they were, but wisely held his tongue. He kept his crest neutral—no need to show too much excitement, though this was like the young woman he used to bring on adventures across the ten homeworlds. A thrill ran through him at the prospect of another adventure, or even another night, close to her.

When she had been elected to the Council—the youngest member in many cycles—he knew he had lost her for a time; almost eleven cycles, as it turned out. Maybe a change was coming. He forced his crest down. No need to look like an overeager schoolboy—she could read him well enough as it was.

"I have been speaking with Mhalaro Ipente Riteno these last several days," Origon told her, keeping his voice level. "He believes he has a new device that may let him investigate the Drains where the song cannot."

"The professor?" Rilan asked. "Have you even spoken to him since we...since I joined the Council?" Since they had gone their separate ways, she meant.

"We were catching up on old times, and I was persuasive," Origon said. If he was convincing enough, then maybe there was another chance for the two of them.

Rilan grunted. Origon kept silent, watching her, his crest rising despite his control. She would have to be the one to initiate their plans. She had nearly used her position on the Council to forbid him, before. If all went well, he might be able to research the Drains with Rilan accompanying him.

"We'll have to bring the apprentices," she said. Origon let out a breath.

"If you talk to yours, I will be addressing mine," he said. "Tomorrow, you said?" He almost said more, but stopped. He didn't want to risk her changing her mind.

After a moment, Rilan gave one sharp nod. "Tomorrow morning, we travel to ChinRan."

Now Origon let his pointed teeth show in a smile. His crest was expanding in anticipation. "I am already packed. Would you like to be getting some dinner downstairs?"

"I thought you'd never ask," Rilan said, pushing up from her chair.

* * *

Sam rubbed grit out of his eyes, squinting against the brightening light from the walls of the Nether. It glistened off the Spire's column, perfectly curved to focus the flat light on his face. He looked around the little open space, lost among the flora and sculptures that dotted the open areas between the houses of the maji. An orange thing like a rabbit crossed with an armadillo hopped into the bushes across a bricked path, which ended in a wrought iron gate. He hadn't been here before, but something from the previous night was still dulling his anxiety. *That, or I'm too tired to care.* Sam pinched the bridge of his nose.

He had come home late last night to find Majus Cyrysi sitting in a chair, staring at the door, his crest like he had been electrocuted. *Didn't even let me get washed up before he started talking.*

It had been his first tentative foray into a Festuour tavern. The others had booked a private room with the majus' money, to keep most of the noise and music at bay. It was in High Imperium, but the twins kept close on the way there. They had forgiven his questioning about the Aridori, and after a couple days of rest, Sam was ready to go back out, noting new landmarks to guide his way in the strange environs.

The Festuour food had been rich, filled with the furry alien's equivalent of butter and cheese. The bubbly drinks had been powerful—not exactly alcoholic, but including some ingredient that made Methiemum hazy.

He had a vague recollection of Rey, standing on the table, telling an outlandish story about a creature that lived in the basement of the House of Potential. The aliens' drinks had pushed Sam's anxiety far down, where it didn't affect him. *One hand cupping Inas' cheek, the other holding Enos' hand. Did I kiss him? Kiss her? What will they say? Whatever happened, I think I enjoyed it.* He'd made out with both Molly and Phillip, back home, but no further. He had always been too nervous. This was different, like a puzzle piece falling in the right place. His home was very far away, but right now, he could accept it.

Rey, at least, was sleeping it off back at the House of Potential while Sam was out here, in the far too bright light from the walls, and underneath the hulk of the Spire. Sam glanced up at Majus Cyrysi. The Kirian was pacing as if they had a timetable, his aqua robe—with bright green and yellow slashes—swishing as he passed. They had been out here for more than half a lightening.

"Where are we going again?" Sam finally asked. The majus' excited speech last night had been almost too fast to follow, and Sam hadn't been thrilled about talking this morning. The majus' pacing, and his large yellow leather duffel bag beside the iron gate, was raising Sam's heartrate, despite his fatigue. He gathered it was something about the Drains, but they couldn't be traveling yet, could they? He hadn't had enough time here.

Majus Cyrysi stopped his pacing to watch Sam for a moment. His feathery hair was all over the place. "You are seeming to be fitting in to life in the Nether well," he said, incongruous.

"Ye-es." Sam drew the word out. He swallowed, now uncomfortably awake, taking in more of his surroundings. Behind the gate was an open space, fenced on all sides. One lone being stood in the middle of it—a Methiemum, from the height and build. Sam patted at his pockets. *Still have my watch.*

"Your practicing is going well, yes?"

Sam nodded. *Not that you helped.* He had been able to hear the Symphony six more times since his first success, but the notes still slipped through his grasp when he tried to change the music. "What are you getting at?"

The majus opened his mouth, and then closed it again as a look of relief came over his face, looking over Sam's shoulder. His crest laid flat.

"Rilan—finally," he said. "You are bringing your apprentice. Good."

"Are we ready?" the councilor asked. She also had a large duffel bag, hers of a dark cloth. Gone was her usual white and green dress, replaced by sturdy, clothes. A jerkin, dark and tanned, fit snugly against her chest, over a loose shirt. She had a pair of soft leather olive green gloves and boots, which Sam thought might even stop—or at least slow down—the long sheathed knife hanging at the hip of her heavy cloth pants. If she had ever looked uncomfortable in her formal attire, she looked like she had been born in these clothes.

Sam made eye contact with Enos, behind the councilor, trying to get an idea if she knew what was going on. *Or what she remembers about last night.* Oh lord. There went his heart again. He palmed the watch, raised to one ear. Enos gave him her half-smile, but was obviously distracted, eyes flitting in all directions like she expected one of the trees to pounce on her.

"We are, as soon as Mhalaro gets here," Majus Cyrysi said, hefting his bag. It looked heavy.

"Where are we *going?*" Sam said, louder.

The councilor looked to Majus Cyrysi. "You haven't told him? Come on, Ori. He needs time to accept changes."

"We *are* leaving the Nether, aren't we?" Sam said, one hand creeping to his stomach, the other still clutching his watch. Now he wished he wasn't so awake. He glared at his mentor, who looked away, crest drooping, and scuffed one boot against the ground. "New places, remember?" Sam bent his knees, blowing out.

"Rilan came to me last night, while you were out. She insisted we leave this morning." Even to Sam, the majus sounded like he was making excuses.

"I did *not* insist you breeze the idea past your apprentice, who has a known aversion to traveling. Really, Ori."

When Sam looked up, the councilor was in front of him. She pressed a cool finger to his head. There was a flash of olive and white, and his nausea dissipated, though he was still agitated. "We are traveling," she continued, speaking low for Sam's benefit, "but it is necessary. Apprentices must travel with their mentors. Knowing Ori, he probably didn't tell you I was attacked yesterday."

Sam looked up sharply. "Attacked? How? Why?" The focus pushed his anxiety back a little.

"A long story," the councilor said, shaking her head. The little white bell at the end of her braid chimed. "I believe it has something to do with the fears about the Aridori. The Council is," she hesitated, "undecided at the moment, but I feel it is best if I put distance between myself and the Imperium for the time being. We're going to Methiem, to investigate the void Enos and Inas told you about. The nearest portal ground is in ChinRan."

Sam heard his mentor mutter something about Drains under his breath. "Why can't we go straight there?" he asked. If he had to travel, they could at least cut down the time he was away from Majus Cyrysi's apartment.

"There are to be specific places where portals are allowed, by order of the Assembly. Another control of the maji," the majus answered. His crest signaled irritation with the limitation, though his attention was obviously not on the conversation. He was watching the space between two of the houses. "We could not be making a portal from ChinRan straight to the site of the Drain either, as they are being too close together. Portals must connect distant points. Any closer than a quarter of the way around a homeworld puts undue strain on the majus involved due to the songs of the two endpoints overlapping."

"But you can make a portal across the universe with no problem?" Sam asked. His mentor nodded agreement.

"Ah, here is our other member," Councilor Ayama said, gesturing. Sam looked to see one of the hugely tall Etanela lugging a hard leather case half as tall as he was in one hand and a small bag in the other. He set the bag down on the ground, as he neared them.

"Councilor, majus," he said, nodding to the maji. "I assume these are your apprentices?" He peered down through little glasses. Even with the Nether translating, his speech slurred together. "I am Professor Riteno."

Sam swallowed again. He hadn't talked to one of the Etanela yet. *What if I say something stupid?* He tried to think of a greeting, but the bluish alien was already engaged in strapping the hard case over his shoulder. Sam looked to Enos, but she was staring the other direction. He needed to talk to her about the night before, at some point.

Majus Cyrysi was already at the wrought iron fence. The Methiemum inside came toward them.

"Good morning, ah," Majus Cyrysi paused for a moment.

"Alphonse, sir," the man said. "You were at my raising to full majus, three cycles ago."

"Of course," the Kirian said. "I was thinking you looked familiar." Alphonse was a large man with a sad, drooping face, and a scraggly moustache. "We will be needing a portal to Methiem. If you are not minding, I will handle it myself."

Alphonse frowned, but opened the iron gate. It was wide enough for three to pass through. *Is this where they make portals to other worlds?* Sam's hands were sweating. *Where is my bag? Did Majus Cyrysi pack something for me?* Light struck his face and he glanced up the length of the column, blinking it away. It was a clear morning, but as usual, he couldn't see the top of the Nether. For once, that was a lesser concern.

"Come on, Enos," Rilan said. The maji and the professor were inside the fence, and Sam forced one foot in front of the other, looking down at where the iron fenceposts pierced the ground. The blades of purple grass curled around the black metal. Enos was fiddling with her own, smaller bag.

I really hope he has a least a change of my clothes packed.

Sam's mentor paused near the center of the clearing, one hand to his head, crest fluffing as if in a breeze. "Have you got it?" Councilor Ayama asked him.

"Yes. It has been several cycles since I was in this part of Methiem. I am simply remembering details."

"Don't put us in a tree or anything," the councilor shot back. Majus Cyrysi took the time to glare at her before returning to his concentration.

"Will the transition be safe?" the Etanela said, nervously rubbing a hand over the case he held. Their voices were tinny, like they were talking at a great distance.

We're leaving. We're leaving the Nether.

"It'll be fine," the councilor assured him. "Ori does some of the best portal work I've seen." She turned around. "Come *on*, Enos. Stop dawdling. It isn't like you."

"Yes, Councilor," Enos said from outside the gate, only just loud enough to be heard. "I am checking my bag. I may have forgotten something."

"Aha." Sam swiveled back to his mentor, heart racing. Majus Cyrysi's feathery hair was slicked back now. He opened his hands wide and rings of color surrounded them, orange and yellow.

We're going. We can't go. But we have to find the Drains. I knew this would happen. I should be ready. He closed his eyes, trying to hear what the majus was doing. *Anything to keep from thinking about traveling to a different planet.* Something low buzzed at the back of his mind, a harmony, and then a fractal of harmonies. A new theme entered, as if from a separate piece of music, and Sam's eyes flew open. In front of his mentor, a hole formed, pitch black, ringed in shifting orange and yellow. It grew to Majus Cyrysi's height, and then taller, until even Mhalaro could fit through without ducking. Sam took a step back, hand grasping for the solid iron of the gate. *I have to do this. This is the only way back to Earth and Aunt Martha.*

"I will be needing to go through last to close the portal," Majus Cyrysi said.

The councilor was still watching Enos. *Why is she out there? Why isn't she here, helping me?* Sam reached a hand for her, but Enos had her bag closed, looking back toward the other side of the circle of houses.

"I am ready," she announced, and walked through the gate into the portal ground. She moved close to Sam, rubbing his shoulder. "You can do it," she whispered. Behind her, he saw two other people, one running, and one moving slowly and methodically, legs pumping like pistons. The first figure resolved into Inas.

"I was able to convince Majus Caroom only at the last moment," Inas said, puffing slightly.

Sam felt Enos' hand loosen on his shoulder. *Both of them, and they're not pulling away. They can both keep me steady, keep me sane, on this field trip.* Sam's knuckles were white on the gate post.

"You told your brother where we were going?" Councilor Ayama was not smiling. "Shiv's bloody eyes, girl, this is supposed to be a secret. How many others know?"

"None," Enos said, no trace of apology in her voice. "I told you before, I must keep close to my brother."

The councilor looked a question to Majus Cyrysi, who shrugged, his crest rising in anticipation. "I am only happy to be going," he said.

"Fine." The councilor crossed her arms, then one hand strayed to her belt knife. "I should send you all back home, but it's too late. I hope you like sleeping under the stars." Her face was pinched like she'd bitten something sour.

"I am sorry to be late," Inas said. "I slept in after last night." He reached out, and Sam grabbed his arm as the other man came closer, the prospect of camping raising his anxiety level even more. Bolstered by both twins, he made his way toward the portal. "I was unable to convince Majus Caroom to run."

His heart rate slowed a little, surrounded by his friends. *Shame Rey is missing this.* Sam looked back as the final person stumped up to the group. They—the Nether pushed the non-specific gender into his head—were the first of this species he had seen up close. Majus Caroom was large, and wide—almost three times as wide as Sam, but no taller. The skin on their arms was craggy and dark, like driftwood polished to a shine. Gnarled toes, pointing several directions, gripped the ground. Sam wasn't sure whether they were wearing pants, but a faded, no-color shirt covered their torso.

"Rilan, Origon," Majus Caroom rumbled, nodding with a creak. "This one was, hmm, persuaded to come here for the sake of my apprentice." They made an odd breathy sigh when they spoke, like wind gusting through a tight spot.

Sam let go of Enos long enough to hold his watch to his ear, and Majus Caroom's bare head, like burnished mahogany, twisted to him. There was a sound like straining wood, and their tiny eyes bored into Sam. They were solid green, without pupils, and glowed with some inner florescence.

"You have, hmm, not met one of the Benish before, have you?" they rumbled. "We are an old species, but not often, hmm, seen around the Nether. We prefer our own homes."

"Pleased to meet you," Sam breathed. He shivered in suddenly chill air. *I will not have an attack here.* Caroom's eyes dimmed for a moment in acknowledgement.

"Caroom is something of an adventurer among their people," Majus Cyrysi said.

"Are we going to chat here all day, or get on with it?" Councilor Ayama said. She moved to the portal hanging in the air, and disappeared through it. Mhalaro went next, hugging his case to one side with one elbow, his bag dangling carelessly from a loose finger. His mane of hair just cleared the top of the portal.

Enos pulled at Sam's hand. "We are both here for you," she told him. "I'll go through first. It's easy."

Don't leave me. Enos gently disengaged his hand, went to the portal, and through.

"It will be good to see Methiem again," Inas told Sam, squeezing his hand. "Our positions may be reversed when we get to our destination. I may need your assistance." Sam let him go, his hand trailing Inas' motion as he went through, Caroom stumping after him without a word.

It was just Sam and Majus Cyrysi. "Well, on with you, boy," the Kirian said. "I cannot be holding this portal open all day." He looked pale, nearly as short of breath as Sam.

Sam stepped forward, hesitated. *I can't see where it goes. It could end up in the air, or in space. How does anyone use these things?* The air felt thick.

He turned back to the majus. "I can't," he said. His knees were jelly, and he stretched a hand to catch himself against the grass if he fell.

Majus Cyrysi looked him over, crest spiking, then lying flat. His clawed hands shook, yellow and orange still flowing across them. "I am realizing this is soon for you." He breathed in, then out. "You have lost much recently, but if you wish to find your home again, you will be needing to step outside of what is comfortable."

He can't hold it open much longer, Sam realized. If the majus lost control of the portal, Sam would be stuck here, without Enos or Inas, without a way to learn about the Drains. *I have to do it, no matter the cost.* Sam met Origon Cyrysi's eyes, nodded his head. He straightened his knees with an effort, and shuffled toward the dark hole, ringed with yellow and orange. *Don't look at it.* He made himself inhale deeply and closed his eyes.

I can't. I can't take that step. Sam cursed his brain for failing him. *If I can't take a step, then—* He leaned forward, purposefully off balance. *A little farther. A little more.*

Sam fell forward into the portal.

CHAPTER THIRTEEN

Of Caravans and Drains

-The economy of the ten species balances on the backs of the merchants and traders. In their domed caravans, these travelers are responsible for bringing rare and hidden goods through portals to worlds which have never seen such things before.
From the notes of the Effature, approx. 763 A.A.W.

Sunlight hit Sam's face for the first time in weeks. He began to shake.

Not here. Not now. He crouched down, looking across grass—green grass—which edged up to another fence. He had his watch at his ear, but his heartbeat was too fast.

Too new. A new world.

He saw Enos' shoes next to him. Inas' hand gripped tense muscles in his shoulders, squeezed. "We are here for you," his friend said. *Then he's still willing to be near me.*

"I've got to go back. I'm not ready." Sam spun in a tight circle, still crouching. The blackness of the portal behind him disgorged Majus Cyrysi, then shrank to a pinpoint, collapsing in a ripple of orange and yellow. "No! Keep it open!" he called.

The majus shook his head, crest limp. There were no clues here to say what that meant. *Not in the Nether anymore.*

"One cannot be going the other way through a portal," Majus Cyrysi told him. "It will be a time before one can again be opened to the same place."

"But I have to get back. I have to—" Sam clung to Enos' arm, knowing he was putting all his weight on the smaller woman. *She'll hate me for it, leave me here. Why can't I do anything right?*

To one side, there was a flash of white and olive, then the cool touch of Councilor Ayama on his forehead. She must have pushed Inas aside. Sam could still hear him, breathing, not far away, barely audible over the beat of his heart, pounding through his head.

"I can apply the same patch to your thinking again." the councilor said. She smoothed his hair, an oddly maternal gesture. "It's your choice. Your thinking will be fuzzy."

Sam pushed her hand away. "No," he panted. He knelt down on the grass—*getting my new pants dirty already*—and put one hand down, flat, feeling cool, damp blades bend beneath his fingers. The other hand held time, chopping seconds off near his ear. *One breath, one beat. One breath, one beat.*

He couldn't tell how long he knelt there. At some point, his breathing equalized, his heart slowed. Sam raised his head, swallowed, gasped for air. There was still a hand on his arm, and he looked up at Enos. "Thank you."

She stared back, eyes wide and worried. Slowly, Sam stood back up. *It's like Earth.* There were trees, just outside the portal ground fence. He let his eyes rest on an oak. *Like in the yard back home.* Except that triggered thoughts of frost, and Aunt Martha, lying cold—

He shook his head, trying to get rid of the vision. There were buildings nearby, a rural city, well-kept but obviously not wealthy. The structures were predominately wood and stone, only two or three stories.

"Are you able to come with us?" Inas asked. "They need to open another portal and cannot with us still here." he pointed to a man standing near the fence gate. There was something about him that told Sam he was the majus working this ground. Maybe it was his blue vest and matching pants, like a uniform. Behind him stood three men and two women, looking impatient. Behind them was a woman with a little boy hanging on one hand and a traveling pack in her other.

The rest of their party was gone. *How long did I take? I'm holding everything up.*

"I think I'm ready," Sam told the twins. "Thank you for staying with me."

"We are not eager to be here either," Enos said, and Sam realized her eyes were not just wide with worry for him.

It's not all about me.

They exited the portal ground, and behind them another dark hole appeared at the majus' gesture, this one ringed in blue and magenta. The first group of Methiemum gave a pouch to the majus, and stepped through, either to some other homeworld, or according to Majus Cyrysi, to the other side of Methiem. Sam wondered where the woman and child were possibly traveling to. Off to see someone she knew in the Nether? Visiting a friend or family member on one of the other homeworlds? The scope of the ten homeworlds drove Sam close to Enos and Inas, marking trees as they followed a stone path to a collection of one-story buildings. *It's like Earth. It's not so new. Keep it together.*

There were differences. His steps felt heavier than in the Nether. The ambient light was like Earth, though the sky was bluer. Soon they got to ChinRan proper, and Enos and Inas kept his attention by pointing out odd buildings, or adding little bits of history. A few times someone passing them exchanged greetings as if they knew the twins.

Sam only saw Methiemum here, jarring after the riot of species in the Nether. Though it had been morning when they left, here it was closer to noon, from the length of the shadows. The air was crisper too, and Sam burrowed within his vest. *Did Majus Cyrysi pack me any clothes, or am I stuck in these for however long we're here?*

Soon they caught up with the others, standing outside a low building with parked carriages and a large fenced area to one side. Professor Riteno seemed almost as confused as Sam, nervously curled around his case, and both he and Caroom drew stares from the inhabitants. Majus Cyrysi and Councilor Ayama were bargaining with a teller in a little office.

Sam's breathing was getting faster again, and he stared at the maji in the office, his watch clutched in one hand. Where were they going?

"Can we talk about something?" he asked Inas. His friend's head snapped around from where he had been contemplating the town.

"Are you going to—"

Sam shook his head, cutting Inas off. "Just...I'd like to talk. It helps to distract me."

Inas pointed to the fence, where several sturdy horses had their heads down in a trough. Four others had the shape of oxen, but were hairless and made of wood. Polished dark wood gleamed in the sun. A handler walked to them, lifting a smooth board from one side and flipping a sequence of toggles. The ox tossed its head, then followed him, and the three others followed the first. The handler led them in front of the building.

"See those System Beasts?"

Sam nodded. He had seen some of them in the Nether, made of metal, wood, or even stone, in all sorts of shapes. "What are they?"

"Majus Cyrysi has bought us an expensive ride," Enos said.

"I don't think he cares much about money," Sam said, and she turned her hands palm up in a shrug.

"System Beasts are constructions of the House of Potential," Inas said, "and expensive to maintain. Maji from the other houses must permanently contribute notes from their songs to propel and fuel the creatures, and to allow them to take instruction."

"Why would they be so wasteful?" Sam asked. He put his watch back in a pocket.

"They are a sign of prestige, though the maji use them more often than others," Inas said. "Our parents—" he paused, "they used living creatures to pull our caravan, but wealthy merchants use them to pull loads far heavier than a normal beast of burden might. In richer cities and in the High Imperium, there are other, smaller forms of System Beasts, used to guard dwellings and shops, or even just to look pretty, though it is hard to imagine being wealthy enough for that."

"Are they worth it?" Sam asked.

"Are you ready? We cannot be waiting around all day." Majus Cyrysi strode by, heading for the largest carriage parked in front of the store. The wooden oxen were being hitched to the front. The professor was already loading his case, tying it carefully to the top of the carriage.

"You will see." Inas gave his half smile.

"Still alright, Sam?" Councilor Ayama asked as she passed. Sam nodded. *I am, for the moment. Strange.*

Mhalaro folded his tall frame to fit through the door, Caroom pulling up jerkily afterward.

"The owner was telling us where the site is," Majus Cyrysi called back, as he threw his bright yellow bag on top of the carriage. "It has attracted attention from both ChinRan and TaiRapa. I am hoping no one has disturbed the site too much." He waved an arm forward. "We are wasting daylight, as it seems a long way off."

Soon they were bumping along the city streets in the carriage, the seven of them squashed together. Sam was between the twins, trying to bleed away his tension. Mhalaro's knees were in Sam's legs, and Caroom took up two seats.

As they left the town, Sam was pushed back by a sudden rush of speed. They tilted into a curve and Sam clutched at Inas' knee, his other hand digging for his watch.

Inas laughed, the movement pulling his lips wide. "Look outside."

Sam risked a glance across Majus Cyrysi's chest. They were flying across the landscape, at least thirty or forty miles an hour, but the carriage's suspension had smoothed to a gentle roll. Sam stared back to Inas, then to Enos, on the other side.

"There were too expensive for our—our family to use." Enos barely paused on the word. "System Beasts are useful for quick transportation, and I do not think Majus Cyrysi wants to wait any longer."

Their conversation fell off, and Sam listened to the snatches back and forth between the Etanela professor and Majus Cyrysi about what they would do when they got to the site of the Drain. It was over his head, both magically and technologically.

The whole time, the System Beasts' pace never faltered, and the carriage swayed gently side to side, though the road was simple packed dirt. One of the maji—probably Councilor Ayama—had thought to buy flatbread, a cheese spread, and dried fruit for the road, and they ate on the way, Majus Cyrysi grumbling about how none of the food moved. Sam judged the journey was a couple hours long, but it gave him time to cool off. *I have to be strong for Inas and Enos when we get there. It's like if they went back with me to the house.* Thoughts of Aunt Martha traded off against spikes of adrenaline when he looked out the window. He let his mind work through things, safe against the warmth of Inas and Enos.

They were hot from the stifling carriage when it finally stopped near a giant depression not far from the road, the sun sinking. Everyone piled out, and Sam looked around for something else to mark this place. He expected panic to tug at his throat. *Am I getting used to new places? I should be frozen, with so many new people and places in one day.* He would need a day to himself when they got back, but for now, his breathing was under control, his heartbeat only a little fast.

Caroom creaked like a tree in a storm, stretching their arms out wide. Inas brushed dust off his yellow silk shirt. Majus Cyrysi and the professor stomped off, talking back and forth at high speed. Councilor Ayama had her hands out toward the oxen-like System Beasts, white and olive ringing her hands. Steam was rising from the creature's backs, and Sam was surprised to see they bent their necks, tearing chunks of grass and leaves away from the ground and nearby bushes.

"I didn't know they ate—" He turned to the twins to find them pale, watching the depression where Majus Cyrysi gestured next to the professor. The Etanela was unpacking things from the case that caught the sun's light.

"We don't have to go over there," he said quickly. *Is this what it would be like if—when—I go back to Earth? What if I went back where my parents—* "Come on." He grabbed for Inas' hand. "We can sit in the carriage for a little—"

"Sam, you should be practicing the application of song with me," Majus Cyrysi called from a distance. Sam winced.

"Go, if you are able," Inas told him. "We will be fine here." His voice was steady, but Sam saw how his friend clasped his hands together. Enos had her chin high, looking across the treetops further down the road.

"Sorry," Sam told them. The words were not enough. *They've helped me so much, and I'm walking away from them.* He looked away, guilty, and walked toward the majus and the scientist. His steps were shaky. *It's not like something's going to swallow me up. This is my chance to find out more about the Drains. Keep going.*

Majus Cyrysi was standing at the edge of a vast, raw chasm of dirt, the towering Etanela next to him looking like an oversized cotton swab with his mane of brown hair waving in a slight wind. Sam carefully stopped a body length away from the edge and peered down. It was large enough to make his heart race, and his throat tighten.

"We need to be getting a sample of dirt from the center of the depression—as close to the Drain's epicenter as possible," Majus Cyrysi said.

"Can we—can we climb down?" Sam asked. The sides were strangely smooth, like the dirt had been compressed and polished. He could see rocks, and further down, boulders, cut in half and polished to a reflective shine.

His mentor shook his head, crest rippling. Frustrated? Dismissive? It was harder to read the Kirian now they were out of the Nether. Nothing gave Sam any hints. He found he missed the mental cues.

"Much easier to be using the Symphony, and it will give us a chance to practice. Be following my lead." Majus Cyrysi raised a hand, swaths of yellow sweeping from him down over the side of the pit. Sam closed his eyes. Each time it was easier to find the music of the Symphony. *Stay calm. It's there. Prove you're useful for once.*

There was buzzing, as if a huge bee flew nearby, then the melody of this area erupted in his mind, and Sam gasped. The amount of interconnected melodies threatened to overwhelm him. Small animals nearby twittered in cadenzas of desires and threats. The air was a turbulent fugue of shifting patterns. Even the trees and earth passed metronomic messages of time and shifts in the ground. Sam stepped further from the ledge, panting. *Too much.* He looked away. Professor Riteno was connecting pieces to a large contraption of metal pipes with a glass bulb at the end. It looked scientific.

"Focus, boy," his mentor said. "I am certain you can do this too. Simply listen for what I do."

Sam forced his way into the melody swirling though his mind—the Symphony of Communication. He ignored most of the music, listening to a forming counterpoint in the fugue of the air, new notes playing over and over, countering those that defined the wind. At points around the bottom of the chasm, little dust storms gathered samples of dirt. Beside him, Majus Cyrysi was pale, but kept his hands moving, long fingers splayed as if he was conducting. Sam heard more music appear, coming, he knew, from the majus' own song.

I can do it this time. Always before, he had failed. Sam breathed in crisp mountain air. *Maybe this will help Enos and Inas, too, make up for me leaving them.* He grasped at the little rondos of air currents, notes slipping away from him.

Like this. Form these notes. Keep them in your head. Put them here. Change the Symphony to your purpose.

Like someone was showing him the way, he found the notes of his own melody, coursing through his being, like musical DNA. He struck each note, heard how it behaved. They could be placed to affect the physical world. He gripped one and tore it away from his being, kept it from slipping back. He took more, feeling as if he were running up a steeper and steeper slope. Each note he placed into the melody of the air, copying the rondos Majus Cyrysi made.

Another patch of dirt stirred at the bottom of the chasm—a feeble wind compared to his mentor's. Sam looked down, realizing he was reaching out, yellow droplets forming like beads of water at his fingertips. They dripped, fading to nothingness.

"That is the way," Majus Cyrysi said, and the approval in his words jostled Sam back to reality. He only kept hold of the music with an effort. "Keep at it. Your wind should be following mine."

There is no anxiety in the Grand Symphony, Sam realized. There couldn't be. The effort took all of his concentration. He added more of his notes to the little melody, bringing the whirlwind toward them. He held his breath as it moved, skimming bits of dirt closer.

The professor had laid a plate beside his device of metal and glass, like something seen in a mad scientist's lab. Majus Cyrysi's winds obediently placed their samples of dirt in little piles, then dissipated. Sam's followed slower, erratically, as he bit his lip, adjusting measures in the strains of music. Where Majus Cyrysi's composition was a classical masterpiece played on a Stradivarius, Sam's creation was a squeaky recital. His hand, still outstretched, shook with the effort to bring the whirlwind to the plate.

"Reclaim your notes," the majus explained, "and the wind will die."

Sam blinked, then grabbed at the little rondo he had made, the notes slipping back into him. The wind died, depositing dirt in a swath, half on, half off Professor Riteno's plate. Sam breathed in deeply, as some part of him he hadn't realized was missing returned. *I changed the melody.* Then he saw the mess of samples on the scientist's metal plate.

"Oh, I'm sorry!" he told the Etanela, who gave him a confused look from several feet above Sam's head.

"A good first attempt," his mentor congratulated him. The Kirian was breathing heavily, his crest in disarray. "Maybe I will be bringing you outside more often when I want you to understand what I teach."

Professor Riteno was looking back and forth between then with a blank look.

Sam realized his hands were shaking. "I did it. I didn't have an attack. I did it." He looked up to the Etanela with a smile. "I can help organize the samples."

Professor Riteno stared back through his little glasses, head moving left to right, his body never quite still, as with the other Etanela Sam had observed.

Majus Cyrysi glanced between them quickly. "Ah. I am forgetting. It is to be your first time outside the Nether. You will be able to understand others here, as you are a majus and have been in the Nether, but they will not know what you say unless you speak in their language."

Sam's mentor turned to the professor and repeated a similar explanation, though it seemed to be in the same language. Had the two been speaking in professor Riteno's language the whole time?

He wanted to ask more, but his mentor held up a hand. "You will be tired, and Mhalaro and I have much work to do, determining what and who has left impressions on this material. Maybe later, you will be helping to gather more samples." His crest was waving, and Majus Cyrysi kept glancing to the plate while he spoke.

Sam let them get to their experiment. His thoughts went back to the twins. *Are they alright without me?* He left the two talking animatedly.

The councilor and Majus Caroom were setting up tents, and Sam eyed the hastening twilight. His hands clenched at the thought of sleeping under the sky. *Maybe the twins—*

"Where are they?" he asked the councilor. He didn't see them.

Councilor Ayama brushed a stray hair back that had escaped her braid. "They went off that way." She pointed, then made the hand into a warning. "They need to do this, Sam. I'm sure you understand getting used to changes in your life."

Cold, seeping into my hands. Aunt Martha's eyes, staring at nothing.

"I'm going to be with them," Sam told her.

"This one is certain Inas would appreciate your, hmm, company, Sam," Majus Caroom said. They were methodically connecting braces, to a chorus of pops and creaks. Sam wasn't sure how many came from the supports and how many from the Benish. "That one has told much of you, and in this one's experience, a friend may be able to, hmm, dull many troubles."

The councilor pondered Majus Caroom for a moment. "You know, I think you're right." She turned back to Sam. "Enos obviously enjoys your time with her, though she doesn't share quite as much as Inas seems to. Go help them out."

The affirmations blazing in his chest, Sam backed away from the maji. He found Enos and Inas on the far edge of the crater, next to what used to be a vehicle of some kind. Small metal and wood wheels held it just off the ground. It was in the process of collapsing into rusting metal and gray wood, deteriorated far past where it should be in a few weeks' time. Half of it was sheared away. As he came abreast of the ruin, the profile lined up with the edge of the crater, on a smooth curve. The cut through the metal was clean as a razor's, the material shiny. The twins were standing close together, silent. They shifted apart to let Sam slide between them, in his usual place with Inas on his right, Enos on his left. He grasped for their hands, for once not even feeling his own anxiety.

"I'm sorry," he told them.

"You apologize a lot for things that are not your fault." Enos turned her half-smile on him. Even for a smile, it looked sad.

"Can I do...anything?" Sam asked.

Inas shook his head, then rested it on Sam's shoulder. "Just stay with us. We must grieve, and then we will be in harmony again."

Aunt Martha's head, heavy on my leg. Cold.

"My aunt raised me since I was eight," Sam said. He swallowed. He hadn't meant to say the words. "After my parents died, when we were on a vacation, she took me in. She was a strong woman. If the Drain hadn't—" Sam broke off, trying to breathe around the hard spot in his throat. He forced the words out. "If the Drain hadn't killed her, I think she would have lived a lot longer." His voice wavered higher.

There was silence for several minutes. *Did I say too much? Did I not say enough? Did I talk about myself too much?* He had almost decided to step away, to leave the two in peace.

"Our parents were the heads of our caravan," Enos said. "There were not—are not—many people like us left—" She stopped suddenly, taking in a deep breath. Inas, on Sam's other side, lifted his head away and Sam instantly missed the warmth.

"Your family—you mean merchants?" He didn't even know what to ask about them. This was a completely different world.

"We traded with all the species of the Great Assembly," Inas said. "Father would show us how that species lived, what their customs were. We learned so much, but never really belonged anywhere."

Sam hugged both of them closer. "Even if none of us have families, we still have our friends."

Calamity

-Dalhni is one of the largest cities on Methiem, rivaling Kashidur City. But where Kashidur City is tall, polished, and gleaming, Dalhni is sprawling, foggy, and murderous.
From "A Travel Atlas of Methiem"

"Tell me you have something, Ori."

Origon shook his head at Rilan. The sun was just climbing over the horizon. Mhalaro, Caroom, and he had worked all night, and he was exhausted.

"We are finding nothing about the Drain," he told her, feeling his crest spike in frustration. "If I had been able to study the occurrence on Methiem's moon with the song—but that is the whole issue, yes? The underlying vibration of the universe cannot touch it, and we are having similar problems with scientific equipment."

"Every test is the same," Mhalaro muttered, approaching with Caroom. "I've stripped out all of the variables, but there is nothing left." The Etanela took off his little glasses and rubbed at his eyes, red from staring at numbers all night. His words strung together in his emotion, almost no space between. Rilan squinted her eyes at him; even Origon struggled to understand when the professor was tired.

"Tell me I haven't risked the wrath of the Council for *nothing*," Rilan asked, stumbling over words. She was less fluent than he in Etan's dialects, and Mhalaro was woefully ignorant in the trader's tongue. "Ori? Mhalaro? Caroom?"

"There is, hmm, no burning, no melting, no atomic deconstruction," Caroom answered. They scratched one arm with a sound like a rasp on bark. "It is as if this ground has always been thus."

"It was no mistake Origon's skills as a majus could not touch it," Mhalaro said. He looked like he was only half-following the conversation. "There is no trace of what caused this. It can't be natural."

Rilan leaned in. She spoke slowly, probably in the main dialect of Etan, though Origon couldn't hear the difference. There were downsides to being able to understand all languages. "You say it isn't natural. As in, someone made it, or not of this universe?"

Mhalaro thought for a moment, frowning. "Either, or both. There should be residue. With as many tests as I have run, I should find a change at the boundary layer."

"Then if there's nothing, we have to go back," Rilan said to Origon. "I know Mhalaro's reputation as well as you do." The Etanela straightened a little at the compliment, even under the extra weight the Methiemum homeworld put on his shoulders.

Origon let his crest flare in disbelief. For the effort to come out here, they could at least run a few more tests. It was not like her to give up so easily. Her mouth was pinched, and a suspicion crept over Origon. "You are in a hurry. What is it you are not telling us?"

Rilan drew in a long breath, wearing an expression he had only seen a few times, in the over twenty cycles he had known her. "I may not have told you everything two nights ago."

Origon screwed his eyes closed, dreading her next words. He treasured Rilan's tenacity, while foraging through the swamps of Lobath, or the deserts of Sath Home. That tenacity had gotten her elected as the youngest councilor in recent history, and she was good at it, too, even if it had taken her from him. However, Rilan could get so focused it clouded her better judgment. The results were always spectacular. What had she done this time?

"I told you both I and Bofan were attacked, and the Council wanted to pin both on Aridori, though they clearly were not responsible."

Origon nodded, hesitant. "I am remembering that."

Rilan bit her lip. "I escaped relatively unscathed—" She paused, looking to Caroom and Mhalaro. The Etanela looked confused. So she wasn't speaking for his ears. Caroom's green eyes were dim with concern. "Bofan did not. He's dead, and the Council will vote on a new head of the House of Power, while keeping the whole thing quiet. I gave my recommendation, though the Council won't listen." She looked at Origon, her skin blotchy with anger and embarrassment. Origon drew in a slow, long breath, his hands clutching the sides of his robe. This was bad. No, this was unheard of.

"Councilor Bofan A'Tof is, hmm, dead?" Caroom said, their voice carefully level.

"You left the Nether in the middle of that sort of crisis?" Origon asked. "I could have come with Mhalaro. You did not need to pacify me. Your work is as important as learning more about the Drains." Or nearly.

"The Council is keeping it quiet," Rilan said again. She squeezed her mouth together until it was a brown line. Now the truth was out, Origon knew she would move fast, all business. "Now we have found nothing, we must go back." She looked toward the tent the three apprentices had shared, talking late into the night. "Wake them up."

* * *

"What is going on?" Rilan craned her neck out the carriage window as they drew close to ChinRan. The traffic jam was bigger than this little town should ever see. There were merchant caravans, personal transports, horses, cows, even people with belongings loaded on their backs.

"It looks, hmm, like an exodus," Caroom said. Rilan marked the dirty clothes and crying children. These weren't travelers, they were *refugees*. What happened, and where?

She slid out of the carriage as soon as it stopped near the trade store. They could only be coming from the portal ground. The others bundled out after her.

"What is this?" Ori sidestepped a running group of children, his crest spiking in alarm.

"I thought this was a small town." Sam was near the twins, breathing heavily as he watched the crowds flood ChinRan, his watch clutched to his chest as if someone might take it from him. Enos and Inas supported him, one on each side, though both were still reserved and long-faced after seeing the place their parents had died.

Rilan looked a question to Caroom, who was helping Mhalaro pull his case from the top of the carriage. "This one will take care of the return," they assured her. She plopped a handful of Nether glass into their rough hand, not even bothering to look at the denominations. She had plenty of Council traveling funds to go around. She grabbed Ori's arm and made for the portal ground, wading through streams of people. Halfway through Ori took the lead, opening a path with his height and his wildly colored robe waving around him. Rilan smiled. Just like they used to do, cycles ago.

Outside the town, people were streaming out of a portal a majus held open. The woman's back was rounded with fatigue. It was an effort to make the Symphony of two places converge for even a short time, and for this many people to arrive, she must have been here a while.

"They are almost all Methiemum," Ori observed. "Wherever they are coming from is on this planet." The Great Assembly could not exist without portals, but they had limits. The closer the endpoints, the more strain the majus would feel.

They pushed through the refugees to the side of fenced area. "What happened?" Rilan called. The majus was dressed in a simple blue wrap. Rings shone on all her fingers. From the colors around the portal—sapphire blue and creamy beige—she was from the House of Grace. The rings finally jogged Rilan's memory. Bosyln Vadeert—that was the woman's name.

"Something in Dalhni," Bosyln said. "Every portal ground on Methiem far enough from the city has been accepting refugees for hours."

"Dalhni? Your father." Ori looked to her, his eyebrows drawn down, his crest askew.

"Do you have any details?" Rilan asked, a shock of ice running through her core. Dalhni was halfway around Methiem. She should know—she had grown up there. Rilan barely kept from reaching for the woman. She looked as if she might fall over.

Bosyln shook her head. "Nothing confirmed yet, and I'm running out of notes to keep the portal open. Majus Szaler opened the first portal, early this morning, but he's recuperating in the inn." She pointed, one hand ringed in blue and beige drifting up. "I've held this one open nearly two hours."

"Was Szaler saying anything?" Ori asked. Rilan flicked a glance toward him. His crest was up—she couldn't be sure without the Nether, but she caught a note of excitement. She shivered, anticipating what the woman would say.

"He only said the city was losing power," Bosyln said. "Refugees tell me of fires and candles going out, or Systems running down—"

A man stopped, new from the portal, hearing the majus speak. "There's something growing in the sky, like a giant ball," he said, hefting the bag over his shoulder. It looked like a bedsheet, square corners distending the shape. Fear pulled the man's face into a grimace. Others pushed past him, but even as Rilan watched, the flow was decreasing. "It's so cold there." He hurried on.

Bosyln stared at them, leaning on the gate. "I can't take much more. Do you know what this is?"

"Vish preserve us," Rilan whispered, her hand to her mouth.

"A Drain," Ori breathed beside her.

One of the others would have to warn the Council, because Rilan had no intention of staying away, not when her father, one of the most stubborn men she had ever known, was certainly still in the city. *Gods let him have left.* She raced, Ori a step behind her, back to the rental shop where Caroom was finishing up with the merchant. Rilan gathered the group around her, making sure she spoke in the Etan main dialect so Mhalaro could understand her.

"There's an emergency, and we must go to Dalhni, another city on Methiem," she told them.

"Another city?" Sam asked. His eyes were widening, face flushing. Now was not the time for a panic attack. The twins pressed close to him on either side.

"You won't have to worry, Sam," she said. "You aren't going, but there's a void, happening right now." She ignored Ori's mumbled correction beside her. She wasn't going to call them that. "Caroom, can you take the apprentices back to the Nether, and tell the Council? Mhalaro, I would ask you come with us. This will be dangerous, but I think you may be essential as the only non-majus, if Ori is correct that the Grand Symphony cannot touch it." She looked around the small group. "Agreed?"

She started to turn away, but was stopped by a rumble from the Benish.

"Hmmmm." The sound was a low vibration, like a bass holding a chord. Rilan sighed.

"Yes, Caroom?"

"It occurs to this one," Caroom drawled, a thick fibrous finger to their chin, "that Origon's arguments in the Assembly have, hmm, not been taken fully on faith." They stopped, and Rilan waggled a hand at them to get to the point. She was having trouble not opening a portal to the Nether here and now and pushing the Benish through. Caroom had a good head on their shoulders, and it paid to listen to them.

"Well, hmm, this one must admit to interest in seeing Origon's voids. In addition, if we were to observe one and deem it as important as Origon seems to, hmm, think," they opened a wide hand toward Ori, "this one would then lend weight to your arguments in the Assembly. This fact let Inas convince this one to come along to see yesterday's site."

Rilan paused. Only a few days ago, she had thought Ori's complaints a stumbling block before the issue with the Aridori fears and the Servant's agenda. His crest was standing nearly straight, and he was vibrating, as ready to go as she was.

"You make a good point, Caroom," she said. "I'd welcome help in putting this to the Assembly, when we return, but what about the apprentices?" She'd be willing to trust Caroom with them, but not to send them back to the Nether on their own, with the threat of anti-majus groups. Both places were dangerous, but in Dalhni, they'd be with three full maji.

She bit her lip, but the decision was easy. Her father was in Dalhni, and so was one of Ori's voids. She wasn't the youngest elected to the Council for no reason. If nothing else, the post taught her how to make decisions. They had to go, whether it was the right decision or not. She glared at the three apprentices, and Sam hunched in protectively.

"You are coming," she said shortly. "You will stay out of the way, behind us at all times. If something happens to one of us, you are *not* to try any Shiv-cursed heroics." She had all their attentions now, even though Enos and her brother still looked wan.

"I can apply the same patch in your mind, Sam, but I would prefer not to."

Ori's apprentice stared at her, then shook his head. "It will slow me down."

She held all their gazes for a moment longer. "Let's go save my city."

* * *

Rilan stepped out of her portal and narrowly missed being run over by a family of five, towing a cart behind them. She jumped back, then shivered in the chill. It should be warmer here than ChinRan, in the northern hemisphere. It felt more like winter in Ibra.

She turned back and grabbed for the notes linking this place to ChinRan. It was harder than it should have been, even considering the two cities were just above minimum portal distance. Slowly, the white and olive swirled and condensed around the dark hole in the air, compressing it to nothing. Rilan took in breath, her song full again. It didn't help with the chill in the air, and she pulled her vest tighter.

The others were standing to one side, the apprentices behind the maji, all staring as one above the city. Mhalaro had even loosened his death grip on his precious case of instruments, his pointy chin hanging slack.

Rilan spun. The void hung, like a malevolent toad, above the sprawling, low buildings of Dalhni, giving off an air of *wrong*. It was as wide as the center of the city, pulsing with some sort of sick heartbeat. The skin of the thing was as Ori had described, off-white, like a wound full of pus.

"We must be getting closer to study the Drain," Ori said quietly. "If possible we should be getting underneath to see how it started."

Rilan nodded, scanned the town, and drew in a sharp breath. Her father's house was at the lowest curve of the void. She sent a prayer to Vish that he had enough sense to leave. She knew he hadn't.

"Follow me," she told the others. Her chattering teeth made her words choppy. "I know the city."

The others followed, Inas and Enos supporting Sam. He was gasping, clutching at them, but still putting foot in front of foot. Every time she looked back, his eyes were locked on the thing above the city, face gone gray with barely restrained panic. She didn't know if she would have the strength to make the adjustments he had, over the last ten-day. There was no time to reassure him now. When they got back, she would work with him one on one.

There was no chance of securing transportation. Vehicles of all kinds were abandoned by the sides of the roads, powerless. Their Systems were gone or mechanisms stuck fast. Inas at one point tried to pick up a cycling frame, but the pedals would not even turn, no matter how he pushed. It was if the mechanism was completely frozen. They ran, or jogged, Mhalaro easily keeping up with his loping steps, and Caroom stumping along at a respectable pace for their thick figure. Moving kept them warmer in the biting cold. Their breaths made clouds of steam.

They were not dressed for this temperature, and Rilan felt her ears and nose going numb. They had to move fast. Bright red spots were on the cheeks of the other Methiemum, and Mhalaro began to move jerkily. Caroom seemed less impacted than the others.

No lights burned in the houses they passed. It was past the middle of the day, but the void cast a heavy shadow over the city, sucking light from all around. Farther into the city, they saw the first animals, dead of exposure. Horses and oxen were still hooked to carts, stray dogs and even animals that had obviously been family pets lay in the street. Past the first wave of animals, there were Methiemum bodies.

He had to get out. Even he is not that stubborn.

Their pace slowed, the cold eating their strength. Soon she had only Ori to one side and Mhalaro to the other. Behind her, Sam sagged between Enos and Inas, the three clutched together to keep warm. All of them were panting. Caroom brought up the rear, and waved a hand at her. They were nearing the center. *Father's house.* The void sat overhead, a moon tethered to Dalhni.

"I have to check on him, make sure he got out," she told Ori. He nodded, crest flattened.

Rilan almost missed the side street. At this time of Methiem's cycle, early spring flowers covered the arch above it, but these were dead, flattened against the walls they grew on. The cold—the void—had sucked the life from them.

"I must check my father's home," she called back to the apprentices and Caroom. *Just to make sure he got out.* There were more bodies here—people who didn't leave early enough before the void sapped their strength.

"This one will make sure they are not, hmm, lost," Caroom boomed. Even their voice was muffled, quieter than it should have been. Rilan paused only for a second, then nodded. She would only be gone for a few moments. *I have to do this.*

"Come on," she told Ori, and Mhalaro followed them. Her breath was a thick mist as she spoke, and breathing in numbed her nose and lungs. She was dressed warmly for ChinRan, but the cold near the center was oppressive. Her hands were numb inside their gloves, feet numb in their boots. She rubbed her hands together as they moved along the side street, pinched at her nose to warm it. She looked to Ori. "Can you do anything?"

Ori caught her meaning and narrowed his eyes, presumably listening to the Symphony of Power while they walked. Rilan couldn't hear it, but Ori could control the music of heat with it.

"There is not to be much to be working with," Ori said in spurts as he pumped his long legs. "I am only able to move the power inherent from one place to another. There is so little left, and I am still weak—" he cut off, lifting his head. "I will do what I can."

An orange aura grew around him, leaking to objects they passed like an octopus, moving energy from them to him. Ori was one of the best she had seen with the naturalistic function of his houses, moving heat or changing the medium of air as if conducting vast orchestras. Eventually, his aura encompassed both her and Mhalaro. The air stopped getting colder, even gained a few degrees as they squeezed together. Rilan knew he would have to take back his notes at some point, or risk losing even more of his song. After the disaster with the space shuttle, he could little afford it. He was moving slower, puffing through pointed teeth. She realized this was the closest they had been to each other, physically, in a long time.

She turned onto a last narrow street, and heard Ori grunt behind her. He was tired, though she could tell he was trying not to show it. *Only a little farther, just to check. Just to make sure. Then back to the void.* They were almost directly under it now.

It had only been a few months since she last saw the little shack, but it looked as if twenty cycles had passed. The chickens were silent lumps of feathers in their cage, cold and dead. The grass was wilted, and the new flowers that had bloomed around the porch listed like drunkards, blackened and shrunken.

There was a pile of rags and sheets on the lawn. Her father had probably been trying to save as much as he could before he left. Stubborn man. She wondered which city he went to.

She nearly passed the pile on her way to the shack, before she realized its shape. Her knees buckled, hitting the hard ground.

Brahm, no. Her hands shook, and she grasped them together, on her legs, on her face.

"Rilan," Ori started, but she shook her head. She couldn't speak. The freezing air seemed only an inconvenience now.

It might not be him. She bent to move an arm, covered in multiple layers. He must have worn as many layers as he could stand in, trying to outlast the void. The arm was solid and cold, unmovable.

"I will check for you," Ori volunteered.

Rilan forced her tongue to move, forcing air out of frozen lungs, whispering. "No. I have to see for myself." It could be someone else on the ground, collapsed while running away.

She reached, ignoring the protests of her joints in the below-freezing air, and pushed the top layer back over the head. It was stiff, and resisted. Without her asking, a tendril of orange detached from their combined aura and warmed the wrapping enough to give it flexibility. She pulled it back.

Her father's lifeless eyes stared directly into hers.

Rilan fell forward on him, ignoring the freezing ground burning her skin. *Stubborn man. Why would you never do what was easy?* If she had only gotten here sooner. He could have been here for hours, or minutes. It was impossible to say, with the void above. She put fingers to his cold, frozen eyelids, but they wouldn't move. Icy tears halted, halfway down her face.

"Ori?" she breathed. It would cost him, but her friend detached another strand of power and heat, touching her father's face. There was a moment of warmth, and the eyelids closed under her fingertips. She withdrew her hand, as Ori withdrew the heat. Ice spread over her father's face. She strained to look away, didn't, held herself rigid until it was done. Only after the layer of frost had coated what used to be her father's face, did she turn to the others.

Maybe we can reverse the void somehow, give back heat. Have to fix it.

"We've spent too much time here, and we need to get to the center." Talking was a chore, and her voice cracked. There was no sense wiping away the frozen tears. Rilan didn't look up at the abomination sitting above them.

Ori raised a hand as she passed, sending a patch of warmth into her shoulder. "Rilan, what can I do for you?"

"No." She stepped forward, away from his hand, catching Mhalaro's sympathetic look out of the corner of her eye. "The void first. We must find out how to stop it." She couldn't break, not here.

Rilan led the others back out of the alley to a blaze of green. Caroom and the apprentices were surrounded in a glow of emerald and tan, centered on the Benish. They must have been fortifying melodies with the House of Strength. The aura was lopsided, another spike centered on Inas, his face twisted in concentration. Good. That would help them stay alive longer. *Have to stay alive. Have to stop this void.*

She put everything but that goal out of her mind, and led her group to Caroom's.

* * *

While walking beneath the oppressive presence above, Majus Caroom did something with the House of Strength, and Sam felt the cold recede. A green glow surrounded them, and Inas whispered about a 'constitution chorus.' Soon, Inas had his own shine of green. Sam couldn't hear what his friend did, but he burrowed closer between Inas and Enos, letting the shield buffer him from the cold, trying not to look up. He could feel the Drain getting closer as it grew. *Like the house and Aunt Martha, but I have friends now. I could have saved her if I knew what I do now.*

A fiery orange wall emerged from the side alley, as Councilor Ayama, Majus Cyrysi, and Professor Riteno rejoined them. The extra heat was like sunlight on a chilly day, and the two auras merged, swirling in a wobbling mix of green and orange until Majus Cyrysi and Majus Caroom adjusted their notes to coincide with each other's music. Though he could hear neither song, Sam felt the impact of the music in the back of his mind, just out of reach. He was stronger and warmer, and Enos raised her chin, breathing in. The air was still freezing, but no longer burning their lungs.

They continued beneath the dark shadow of the Drain, and Sam gripped his friends, feeling tremors run through their muscles. *We are all equally terrified here.* It was almost refreshing to know they had the same shortness of breath, the same tightness in their chests.

It was nearly pitch black this close to the center, underneath the bulbous skin of the thing, and Majus Cyrysi concentrated part of his orange aura into a pinprick in his hand. The pinprick began to glow, not with the non-illuminating light of the song, but with real flame. The Kirian faltered. *Is he okay? Was that change permanent?* Caroom put a wide hand on Majus Cyrysi's shoulder and the green aura intensified around him. Majus Cyrysi straightened. His tiny flame pushed the shadows back, though not far. It cast harsh shadows into the councilor's face, giving her a stern, fixed expression.

There are even more dead this close to the Drain. Sam and the twins stepped around two bodies, arms entangled. There was no smell to the city, as cold as it was.

It was hard not to see the off-white skin pulsing above him, very faintly luminescent in the blackness, growing as they trudged toward it. *If only I was House of Power, I could help Majus Cyrysi.* The Kirian's crest drooped and his steps were much slower than normal.

Even with both auras around them, strengthening and warming, they faltered in the last few sprawling blocks near the city center. Councilor Ayama stopped, and let the others go by her, touching each as they passed. Enos shied away.

"I will do the same for Inas and myself," she whispered to the councilor. "I can hear the changes you are making." She shifted to the other side of her brother, and Sam instantly missed her heat. A white glow surrounded Enos, buffeting Inas' green.

Councilor Ayama reached for him. "This is a physical change. It'll make it easier to move," she told him. Her face was closed, tired.

"Do you have enough notes?" he asked.

The councilor nodded. "It's not permanent. I'm changing the way your joints and skin work, just a little. They will move easier, and resist the cold. I'll reverse the change when we get out. You wouldn't like how this feels in normal weather."

"Like changing the oil in a car in winter," Sam said. Councilor Ayama shrugged, a gesture of exhaustion, and touched a gloved hand to his arm.

White and olive dug into him, and Sam nearly stumbled. His joints were loose, almost floppy, but in air this cold, they moved easier. He felt slightly warmer.

"Thanks," he said. Speaking made his throat hurt.

Two blocks later, Majus Cyrysi called a halt. It was pitch dark, but for the majus' little flame illuminating their circle. Sam watched the multi-hued glow around them, which gave no light. He wondered how the professor saw things, without the colors around every majus.

They're all doing something useful but me. Even if I'm not panicking, I'm still useless. His skin felt stretched, like his muscles were pulling away from his bones. Even with four different songs grounding him, the largest pull was from the Drain above. He felt it sucking at his essence.

"We cannot be moving closer. I must be saving energy to work against the Drain." Majus Cyrysi was dragging his feet.

The councilor looked up, and Sam felt his head lift with hers. The Drain was above them, ripples moving through the mass of the thing as it slowly increased in size. It gave just enough light to see. *This was above my house. This killed Aunt Martha.* His knees wobbled, and he sank, pulling at Inas' arm.

"Are you well?" Inas asked, but Sam nodded his head, not trusting himself to speak.

Can't take more from him. Have to do my part. Sam forced himself up, watched the thing above. The bottom almost touched the tallest buildings, and a layer drifted between them and the skin of the Drain, like it was stripping dust away. *It's grown since we arrived. We'll have to leave soon, unless we can stop it.*

Professor Riteno knelt, setting up his equipment as fast as he could with shaking, jerking movements. *I can help there at least.* The panic that gripped him when they entered Dalhni was a low buzz, but there were no crowds, the scenery was unchanged. *Just a physical threat to my existence.* Sam pulled Enos forward. They were the only ones free. The other maji and Inas were maintaining their respective auras. Councilor Ayama was on the other side of Majus Cyrysi, hand spread out in front of her, white and olive glittering between fingertips.

"The very life is leaving this place," she said after a moment. Her voice was scratchy and flat in the still air. "The air and ground are dying. Animals too small for you to see are falling from the sky." She turned to Majus Cyrysi. "Your song can't touch it?"

Sam's mentor nodded. "That is correct, but I will bring a sample from its edge for Mhalaro." Majus Cyrysi reached a hand up, and the yellow glow of the House of Communication mixed with the orange surrounding him. The flame in his other hand dimmed, the yellow glow flickered, and the majus stumbled.

"Sam, help him," called Councilor Ayama. Majus Cyrysi protested weakly as the councilor and Majus Caroom supported him from either side. Sam stepped from the equipment to his mentor. They were grouped as tightly as they could and still move.

"What can I do?" *Anything. Let me help.*

"Listen for the—" Majus Cyrysi paused for a breath. "For the Symphony. I am needing a sample of particles near the Drain."

Sam concentrated, and the low ringing in his head expanded into a fractal Symphony. *Every time is easier.*

"I've got it." The others were around him, comforting presences, damping fear before it could overtake him. He frowned and his lips, chapped with cold, tugged painfully. The Symphony was sluggish, missing beats and notes. He winced at the discord in the music. "What's wrong with it?"

"It is the Drain," Majus Cyrysi said.

"It appears to be deconstructing the, hmm, energy that makes up the Grand Symphony," Majus Caroom observed from where the bubble of green and tan was concentrated. Their eyes glowed more fiercely than usual. "This one would not believe it if not present. Where is the, hmm, energy going?"

"It is being destroyed," Majus Cyrysi said. He reached stubbornly, the yellow glow struggling to leave his fingers.

You're going to hurt yourself. Sam felt a strange flash of affection for his mentor. He closed his eyes and reached for the notes making the Symphony, but they shifted out of his grasp. *No. I'm stronger than the last time.* He grabbed again for the notes. Learning about the Drain was the only way to find Earth again.

Here is the song. Find where the Grand Symphony falters. This is how you change the music. The thoughts sounded alien in his head, but his eyes shot open as he found the notes and chords. Understanding flooded him.

"To destroy energy is impossible," Majus Caroom said, and it was the most surprise Sam had heard from the Benish.

Sam intercepted the decaying rhythms of the air between the tops of the buildings and the skin of the Drain. He took notes from his song to create a cadenza, wafting the faraway dust to him. Yellow swirled around his fingers, reaching out to the faltering notes from his mentor.

"Equally impossible is a place where there is no Grand Symphony," Councilor Ayama answered Majus Caroom. She raised a hand, palm up. "Listen." The Drain was affecting all of the Grand Symphony, not just that of Communication.

Sam and his mentor brought swirls of dust back to Professor Riteno on breaths of air, taking precious minutes. The Etanela captured the dust—combined from earth, plants, and disintegrated objects the Drain had swallowed—in a container and fed it to his equipment. Sam grasped his notes, rejoining them with his song.

Several ages passed, as the professor studied the sample through a small viewport. Sam eyed the Drain as the lumpy surface grew, ripples passing along its surface.

Finally, the answer came. "Nothing," the Etanela said. "These particles have everything I would expect to find in a city of Methiem." His words rolled together. "Nothing to indicate they were affected by *that*." He gestured upward.

"We must be trying again, closer," Majus Cyrysi said.

"We must consider there isn't anything to see, Origon," Professor Riteno said. "If your song cannot touch it, there may be no physical residue either."

"I will not accept that." Majus Cyrysi swiped a hand through the air. "We have no time to debate. Once again, Sam. Remember, the Symphony cannot be changed the same way twice."

Sam nodded. *It's getting more fractured.* The swirling melody of the air was missing parts. He could hear the changes the majus made, one note here, another there. Rather than a whirlwind he was guiding the dust to them on a corridor in the air currents.

Sam added his notes to the song, this time finishing the majus' creation when Majus Cyrysi faltered and bent forward. His crest rippled and he shot a glance toward Sam. *Was that thanks, or annoyance?*

"Collect a sample from as near the skin as possible," the majus said, but it was Sam who was pushing out, creating bridges and phrases in the halting melody to reflect what he wanted it to do. *I am conducting a composition out of air.* He had always liked music, but never thought he would be making it. It was natural to him. Despite the cold, the fear, he felt elation as he tweaked a measure, bringing the corridor of air closer.

Majus Cyrysi was providing support at best, and he was pale and drawn, his crest limp. The music spoke to Sam, guiding him as much as he guided it. *A little closer to the skin of the Drain, to get the particles nearest to destruction.* The glow of yellow was mere feet from the surface, and Sam urged it closer, feeding more notes to the composition.

The pulsating sphere touched the tops of the buildings and *surged.*

Sam gasped at the same time as Majus Cyrysi, notes ripping from him. The ones he had committed to the song of the air corridor melted away. He hadn't lost his grip on them—it was like they never existed. Sam swayed toward his mentor, Majus Cyrysi's thick cloth robe rubbing against his sleeve. Part of Sam's self was...missing.

"Too close," Majus Cyrysi said, panting. Their heads were close together, and Sam's vision tunneled. "The Drain obliterates what we create in the Symphony." Sam clutched his stomach, sick and even colder than before.

"Again," Majus Cyrysi said, though the word was pulled from him. "We must—get a sample for Mhalaro—"

"Move!" Councilor Ayama cried suddenly, and Sam looked up, his eyes clearing with the shock of noise. The Drain had grown into the tops of the buildings, and was eating them, growing much faster than before. A spike of cold stabbed into Sam's skin and the other maji slumped as their auras shrank.

Professor Riteno stuffed the long metal and glass object back in his case, and left the rest of his equipment where it lay. The councilor had Majus Cyrysi's arm, pulling him behind her. He was still staring at the Drain.

"Can we make it?" Sam called. His heart was in his throat, his hand in his watch pocket. The satisfying ridges of the watch case fell through his fingers. He moved to Enos and Inas as they staggered away from the epicenter of the calamity.

"We must," Inas said.

Like a race in slow motion, they trudged toward the edge of the city. Maji Cyrysi and Caroom's aura covered them, but barely. Inas clenched his hands as Sam pushed him forward, Enos on his other side. "Can't lose the chorus," he muttered.

Sam looked up every few seconds, gauging the Drain's distance. Even his panic couldn't force him to stop. It was growing faster, buildings flaking away like crackers crumbling at the touch of a giant finger. Something crashed into the street next to them, and Sam jumped, yelping at a piece of masonry fallen from at least four stories up. *Keep moving. Keep moving.* His breathing was too fast, choking him. He stumbled, caught himself on the pavement. Inas reached down for him, but he waved the other man away, groaning to his feet. *He has more important things to concentrate on.* The sustaining orange and green auras were shrinking back to those who made them and Sam shook violently, almost biting his tongue.

He glanced back to see Enos trailing. No auras surrounded her, and Inas was consumed in keeping his meager one going.

"Stop!" he called, or tried to. His voice was a ghost of frozen air. The Drain loomed over Enos' shoulders, halfway down the buildings, off-white haloing her dark hair. He pushed toward her, the warmth and strength of the auras decreasing at each step. Only Councilor Ayama's change sustained him.

"Go," Enos said when he was close enough to hear her. Her feet were scarcely moving. "I will catch up to you."

"No, you won't," Sam whispered back. "I don't know if any of us will get out of this." *Please let us get out.* The others were getting farther away. He pulled on her, trying to move her faster.

Enos hissed in pain at his touch. "You are hurting my arm."

Sam didn't let go. "I'm not letting you fall behind."

"The change I made was not as successful as Councilor Ayama's."

"You can make it," he urged. "Just a little faster." He let go of her arm, wincing at the dark spot where he touched her, and fell in beside her to help. *We have to go faster. Have to catch up. Can't be caught here, in the cold, the death.* His heart raced, arrhythmic.

Enos shook her head, frost glittering in her hair. "You must go on. Comfort Inas, if I do not get out in time."

"No! I'm not leaving you," Sam said. *Don't look back. Looking won't speed us up.* His body wanted to find a hole and crawl in it, but he overrode it with everything he had gained in the last ten-day. The others were out of sight. *Did they turn down a side street?* In the gloom, the road under his feet was almost invisible.

Sam recognized the arch of dead flowers above the street to his right. It was the one the councilor had come from. *Of course.*

"In here," he told Enos. "I think it's a shortcut."

"How...know?" He could hear Enos' teeth chattering. Her hands were icy.

"Why else go in?" The air made speaking difficult. "Shorter way back."

They walked slowly, Sam's arms around Enos, half-carrying her. Everything was numb. The alley turned sharply, back the way they came.

"Wrong...way," Enos shivered.

"I know." *Damnit. Damnit.* The shame and embarrassment of a wrong decision coated him, tightening the skin of his face even more. *No time to get out. Going to die.*

Overhead, the skin of the Drain blotted out the last bit of sunlight and the street around them fell into complete blackness. Sam hugged Enos close, but even that warmth dissolved away.

They sank to the ground, leaning against a brick wall, his vest riding up.

"We shall die here." Enos' voice was a shiver in the air.

"I know," Sam shuddered. He let the panic boiling in him come out and clutched at Enos. *It doesn't matter anymore.* He burrowed into her side and her fingers slid down his arm, too frozen to grip.

It was too dark to see, but Sam could feel the Drain coming closer. Even in his terror, the Symphony was still there. *It's been in the back of my mind since the city center.* There were only fits and starts left, a measure missing half its notes, a disharmonious chord. It was dissolving into the Drain. Impossible.

They clung together in the darkness, shaking. Sam could hear Enos' breathing slow, become shallower. His chest was a vice.

"Enos?" he ground out, but there was no response. What the councilor had done to his joints and skin stripped away, and he cried out as the cold speared deep to his core. Then even that sound was absorbed.

All feeling disappeared, and Sam was left with nothing, not even the feeling of Enos' body. He was panic. He was fear. He was reduced to shivering statements of fact, and then to darkness.

CHAPTER FIFTEEN

Moral High Ground

-The method by which the Council of the Maji chooses new members is a secret. Often it appears to be by merit or strength, but occasionally, a junior majus is chosen. This can cause chaos with the Council's consistency until the new member is fully settled. Several times, the Assembly has proposed rules to control the Council's makeup, but the proposals have always been vetoed at the extreme urging (and sometimes threats) of the Council.

Economic and Judicial assessment of the Ruling Parties of the Great Assembly

Origon stumbled as he burst through Rilan's portal back to the Nether. Despite the danger, the thought repeating in his mind was how Sam had taken the composition from him. His apprentice had completed the music, and the fact made twin spikes of annoyance and pride flow through him. He was far too weak. How could he teach the boy when he could barely make basic changes to the Symphony?

He faltered the few steps to the fence for something to lean against. Even away from the Drain, the portal had resisted Rilan's attempts to open it. This end opened in the Spire's portal ground, and the lighter pull of the Nether was a relief to his aching muscles.

Ancestors curse the Drain for taking more of his notes! At this rate his song would be reduced to nothing, and him to a mere husk. His song had only begun to grow from his losses piloting the Methiemum shuttle. He needed rest, to recuperate and experience more life to fill his song again, though full healing would take many cycles.

Mhalaro emerged from the portal next with his case, followed by Caroom and Inas. The others had fallen a few steps behind.

The open portal rippled as moments dragged on. The majus who opened it had to be the last one through, but it would tax Rilan's strength to hold it open so near the Drain. He watched the hole in the air. How far away were Sam and Enos? He hadn't looked back in—how long? He had been keeping the measures describing the temperature from collapsing into low notes and silence, but he still should have been looking after the two. His apprentice was fragile, but had the potential to be a great majus someday, if his current control of the Grand Symphony was any indication.

Mhalaro tapped a foot, and Inas wrung his hands, staring at the portal. Origon ran his nails down the front of his robe, trying to keep his crest flat, maintain the calm that Caroom exuded. Was the portal entrance shrinking? Was it being deconstructed by a Drain? No use worrying the others. He swallowed.

"Where are they?" Inas finally asked. "Where are Enos and Sam?"

Origon pushed away from the fence. "They will be appearing momentarily." That didn't sound reassuring even to him. "The portal is still open, so we can be sure Councilor Ayama is alive and well. She will bring them through." The portal would not be open much longer if it continued to shrink at this rate. Origon clenched one hand.

"I saved the sample you took," Mhalaro said unexpectedly. "I left expensive material there, but I saved the last sample, and my masseous spectrum-analyzer." He hefted his case. "I may have missed a variable—I processed the sample in a rush." The scientist was babbling, his words running together. "Maybe I will be able to tell you something else once I get back to my lab. I can run more tests there, find out if I missed anything else." He cut off suddenly, shifting from foot to foot, looming over them.

Origon nodded absently and watched the shrinking portal, praying to any of the ancestors that Rilan's white and olive did not wink out. It was wavering, like a puddle of water someone stepped in.

"This one believes it may be time for these here to begin, hmm, worrying about the councilor," Caroom rumbled. Even they were tapping one set of beefy fingers against their leg.

"You may be right," Origon answered. He forced his hands open. "Can we make a portal back to her location? I was unable after the Drain on Methiem's moon changed the area."

"Shall these ones try?" Caroom asked.

Origon nodded at the Benish. He let the Symphony flow through his mind, trying to tie the music of this place to that of Dalhni. His very song ached at the repeated abuse.

Before he could mesh the two melodies, Rilan stepped through the portal and it closed behind her with a *pop*. Little creases around her mouth smoothed away when her notes returned. Origon stared at her, and she stared back, white faced. If he reached to help, would she pull away?

"What about my sister?" Inas asked. "What about Sam?" He was halfway to the councilor when she held up a hand, let it drop back to her side.

"I couldn't find them," she said. "Came through just before the void would have collapsed my portal." She shivered. "It was close. Very close." She pitched forward into Origon's arms, unconscious.

* * *

Rilan awoke at Ori's apartment, lying on his horrible off-green couch. When she grimaced at it and tried to sit up, a long-nailed hand gently pushed her back. She was surprised at how little effort it took. Ori was beside her, Caroom leaning against the far wall.

"Our apprentices," she said. It was immediately followed by a vision of cloth and flesh, a body face down on the cold ground. She gulped back a scream that rose from the bottom of her diaphragm. No time now. The apprentices had to be alive.

Ori shook his head. "Still gone." His eyes were hollow. "Neither I nor Caroom were able to be going back to Dalhni. The surrounding area had been changed too much for the portal songs to merge, just as with the others. We will have to be waiting until another of the House of Communication travels from there and communicates the new geography. We should not have left them." Ori opened his mouth again, then closed it.

"What is it?" Rilan's vision blurred with tears, but she stared defiantly back at him. Ori was hiding something. He was a terrible liar.

"You are needing more rest. I cannot be troubling you now." His crest was drooping, his face as concerned as it ever got.

She struggled against his hand until she got to a sitting position. "Spit it out."

Ori sighed, and glanced at Caroom, who did a fair approximation of a shrug for a being with a neck as thick as their head. "You have received a summons to appear in front of the Council this afternoon."

Was that all? She thrust down the tightness clenching her chest and throat. She had expected something else to add to the mountain of guilt pressing her down. "Yes. I'll have to give details of the void. The Council must vote on the new member, as well. There are probably some other minor issues—"

Ori was shaking his head, his crest flattened out in agitation. "Not a summons to appear *with* the Council, but *before* it." He looked to her, looked away. "They were very specific."

Rilan sat straight up, wincing at the hammer pounding in her head. *Don't think about him. Can't change it. Have to keep going. Too many problems.* She would not collapse like a weakling. "Can you get me a glass of water? I think something died in my mouth."

While Ori was in his small kitchen, she got up and dabbed at her eyes, re-braided her hair. Her formal Council clothes were back at her apartment. If they were calling her before them like a common majus, then she would appear like one. Her clothes looked like she had spent a few nights in them, with good reason. Tough.

Caroom's flickering eyes watched her. They hadn't lost their apprentice. Or their father—progenitor—whatever the Benish called their parents. Rilan punched one hand into the back of the couch, but it was too soft, and the sound was unsatisfying. She ground her teeth instead.

"What is your stance on this?" she asked Caroom. "You've never been much involved in the politics of the maji, have you?" They preferred to tend exotic animals in their veterinary clinic in High Imperium.

Caroom didn't answer, while Rilan tried to straighten some of the wrinkles from her clothes. *Don't think about father. Don't think about the lost apprentices.* She had asked them a purposefully vague question. Caroom was a keen observer of the animal-based organisms with which their species shared the Nether.

"This one believes the Council lately has had too much power while the maji have veered away from public service and into, hmm, self-service, as it were." They waved a thick finger in her direction. "This one is one of two I trust out of our councilors, but this one, hmm, may well be outvoted on important matters. It depends on for what purpose the Council has called this one to them."

Rilan sighed. She hadn't been expecting anything quite so on-the-nose. She straightened her shoulders as Ori came back with her water. *Time to work.* It would take her mind away from things she couldn't change. "I think you're right." He put the glass down on a nearby table. She glanced at it, then back up at him.

"You are going?" He was unsurprised.

"I am," she answered. "I'll let you know the latest news when I get back." She'd get a bite to eat on the way.

The rest of the Council was in their chambers in the Spire. The way seemed longer than usual, Rilan's feet covering less distance than they should. Pain and sorrow dogged her thoughts, but she refused them entry. She was a psychologist. She knew how the mind worked. She could work around her feelings and come back when she had time.

Rilan held her chin high as she studied the guards on either side of the door—the Effature's guards. Usually she would walk right in, summons or no, but with the guards, she raised her hand to knock.

"Come." Rilan heard Jhina's voice through the door. She pushed it open.

Six pairs of eyes stared back at her. She had been expecting the Effature, once she saw the guards at the door, but not *him*. Rage bubbled up from the pit of her stomach.

"What's *he* doing here?" she said, pointing toward Vethis, who managed to lounge even while standing. He flipped a lacy cuff at her.

"Scared your indiscretions have finally come to light?" Vethis sneered back. He was dressed in a blindingly white suit today, the lace at his cuffs and neck in his secondary color, a deep—almost black—blue. He sniffed and ran a finger along his carefully trimmed moustache.

"What indiscretions?" Rilan said, off balance. Her eyes were burning already, and she blinked. *I will not show weakness to this toad.*

"Your misuse of mental practices in the House of Healing, of course," Vethis answered, careful to emphasis his lisp. He knew it annoyed her.

Rilan was about to reply when the Effature's slight cough brought her up short. "Perhaps we should begin these proceedings officially," he said from his seat at one end of the semi-circular table, in his capacity as an honorary member of the Council. Rilan had never seen him use that privilege before.

The Nether's caretaker was in his customary green and purple scaled suit, the sleeves draped expansively over the sides of his chair. The diadem gleamed on his head even in the room's soft light. His glance landed on her, like the touch of a butterfly, then transferred to Vethis, who hunched his shoulders.

"Yes, let us begin this inquiry," Jhina said.

"Inquiry?" Something dropped in her belly and Rilan very much regretted not using the restroom before she entered. "For what?" *They know about Enos and Sam. I don't know how, but they know.*

"For your indiscr—" Vethis broke off and took a step back at Jhina's swift glare.

"A matter has come to light requiring the rest of the Council to inquire into the nature of your work, Councilor Ayama," Jhina said formally, her words slurring together. Her face betrayed nothing, but her ever-moving fingers were tying themselves in knots. "This will decide what course we take."

Feldo, sitting beside her empty chair, on the opposite end from the Effature, looked grim, but that wasn't out of the ordinary. His brown collared uniform was strung with arcane equipment as always. His only sign of tension was one gnarled hand, stroking his flowing white beard. Scintien and Freshta looked almost pleased. Rilan's eyes paused on Bofan's empty chair, then hers, one on either side of Jhina.

The Effature's presence was the more concerning, because of his hands-off approach to letting the Council conduct their business. Vethis' appearance meant he was the one that had brought up the case against her. Rilan clenched her hands to keep them from wiping at her eyes. *Brahm help me, no weakness.* She could feel Freshta and Scintien scenting for blood.

"Have a seat," Feldo told her, his voice gruff.

She eyed the single chair on this side—the wrong side—of the table, but couldn't keep her glance from going to her chair, on the other side of the table. Why of all days was this coming up now?

Rilan sat down, her mind racing. Just this morning she had been outside of ChinRan. Her hands plucked at her pants, straightening wrinkles. Her father had made them for her. She swallowed, sniffed, caught a brief whiff of her own body odor. *Two days without a shower. If I had known, I would have changed.* She had to focus.

"Majus Vethis," Jhina said, voice too loud for the room. "What is your complaint?"

"I accuse this councilor," Vethis extended a finger toward Rilan, his moustache bristling, "of misusing the House of Healing to unduly influence the behavior of members of the Assembly and of her own apprentice. I saw her specifically with Majus Cyrysi's apprentice."

Feldo coughed something into his hand. Rilan thought it was, "dramatic fool."

"Councilor Ayama, what is your reply?" Jhina said.

What is this farce? What are they talking about? Rilan stared back. *I could be traveling to Dalhni, taking care of—* She squashed the thought. "It's completely false," she said—the only thing she could think of. The bile in her stomach was turning to pure anger. "This accusation is obviously made up. I have important news for the Council."

"Don't try to sidestep the issue," Vethis warned her. He was silenced by another scowl, from Jhina and Feldo, this time.

"Majus Vethis, now you have made your accusation, you are not *required* in this inquiry," Feldo said. "I suggest you reflect on that before your next comment." Rilan's old schoolmate had enough sense to keep his mouth shut, for the moment, at least.

"As Councilor Feldo says, this is an inquiry, not a trial," Jhina said to Rilan. "Still, we would like evidence to refute Majus Vethis' claim."

Rilan crossed her arms, fingernails digging into her palms. Her stomach was threatening to bring up the curry she had slurped down on the way. "What proof does *he* have for my supposed 'behavior influencing'? Show me that first."

"Vethis says he saw you affecting Majus Cyrysi's apprentice," Freshta said. Her wings crinkled the folds of her yellow tunic as they vibrated. "Tells us he saw a mental net created. Is only used for affecting someone's personality."

Rilan's thoughts flashed back to the few days after she had been raised to majus, her first journey to another homeworld with Ori, and Vethis' part in that disaster. *He doesn't remember it. I was thorough. No one knows but me and Ori. Is a repressed memory emerging?* Her heart beat faster and she was sure the guilt showed on her face, but she spoke in a loud voice, clearly.

"The boy has anxiety issues," she said. "I gave him a mental repression patch to help him overcome his fear of moving through the

Nether. I've worked with him several times over the past ten-day. He could have seen one of several times. Yes, it's not the ideal way, but it isn't criminal." *When did Vethis get that information? How closely is he watching me?* She almost added that they could ask Sam, but caught herself. It wasn't time for that explosion. Vethis still looked smug, picking his nails, in his rich clothes. "Got anything else?" *This is ridiculous.* Was this something from cycles past, or just petty spite? He had been jealous of her rising to majus before him, twenty cycles ago. He had protested when she gained a place on the Council, eleven cycles ago. Just because he thought he could buy his way into anything he wanted—

Scintien waved a batch of papers. "Letters sent to Origon Cyrysi, expressly telling him *not* to bring up the topic of the supposed voids in the Assembly. He was bringing it up anyway, and Vethis stated you were seen with him before the Assembly meeting in question. You were affecting his mind to disrupt the meeting."

Rilan didn't even try to keep her eyebrows from raising. Were they really this gullible? "Where is your proof? Have you *met* Ori?" she asked. Heads jerked at her volume, and she clutched her pants. *I don't have time for this.* "How often has he barged in here with no warning? Do you think it's more likely I used illegal practices on one of my closest friends, or that he went off all half-cocked like he does *all the time*? Give me something better or I'm leaving, and coming back when you're less dense. I have important matters to discuss."

Vethis puffed his chest, sucking in a breath. Feldo stared him down and Vethis deflated.

"He also reports you attacked him last night," Feldo told her, peering under his thick black eyebrows.

"I—what? That's impossible. I wasn't even here." The words came out before Rilan could stop them. She clenched her jaw until her teeth hurt. *Stupid.* She blinked back hazy vision. She couldn't be mourning *and* angry at these fools at the same time.

"Then who was it, an Aridori?" Freshta asked. The Pixie bubbled out a laugh, then glanced at her fellow councilors, who were staring back, eyes wide. "Heh. Maybe another discussion. What do you mean, not here?"

"I was—" Rilan paused. This was not the way she wanted to break her news. She gritted her teeth. "I was not in the Nether at the time."

Feldo cocked his head. "Then where were you?"

Rilan pursed her lips. This was in all the wrong order. She should be telling them about the voids. Her hand drifted down to her belt, but of course she had left her belt knife back at Ori's apartment.

"Councilor?" Feldo prodded.

"I was in ChinRan, on Methiem." Rilan forced out the words.

"On family matters?" Freshta asked, her wings vibrating. "You do not live in this place."

Rilan almost broke. *Vish's knees.* She wiped at her eyes, a slashing, angry gesture. *No weakness.* "It was not family matters."

"Business of the maji?" Jhina asked.

"Of a sort."

"Can others support this claim?" Feldo asked.

"Yes." There was a question she could answer. "There are six others who can—" She swallowed, regathered her wits. Two of those were missing—probably dead. "Excuse me. There are four others who will report my presence near ChinRan for all of last night."

Feldo narrowed his eyes, peering over the tops of his glasses. Rilan's gaze flicked to the Effature, silent. He leaned slightly forward in his seat, his scaled suit catching light from the overhead candelabra.

"Shall we bring in your apprentice to corroborate your story?" Jhina said. "She must have accompanied you."

Rilan clenched her hands until her nails hurt her palms. *Shiv take you, Vethis.* "She cannot do that."

"Apprentice was not with you, when out of Nether?" Freshta rose a little from her seat, wings buzzing furiously.

"She was with me," Rilan said. *Just drop it.* That was hoping for miracles.

"Yet she cannot back up your claim." Feldo's head was cocked, disbelief sketched on his face.

Rilan closed her mouth tightly, and looked between the councilors. *Have to take control.* She swallowed back spicy curry.

"Councilor Ayama," Jhina said.

She jerked her head to Vethis, lounging against a wall. "I want him out of here before I give any more information. This is a Council matter."

Vethis' head came up at that, and he popped away from the wall, mouth pulled down like a pouting toddler. "I demand satisfaction for my claim!" he said, before anyone else could answer. His voice was high, shrill, and Rilan would have laughed if she didn't feel so sick. "There is no evidence this matter is anything but what I have said."

Rilan caught Feldo's sigh, though he tried to hide it. "I...must agree with Majus Vethis," he said. *'Unfortunately'* hung unsaid. "You have not yet said anything to show this is a matter only for the Council."

Rilan watched the others, weighing her options. Her chance to control the flow of her story was gone. Vethis would not stop until she removed his made-up accusation. Vague evasions would never work with Feldo. *The truth, then.*

"My apprentice cannot add her voice to mine because I do not know where she is. She was separated from me early this morning when we encountered one of the voids Majus Cyrysi warned you of. You should be receiving reports, if you haven't already, of a city on Methiem destroyed by a void."

There was silence, then everyone began talking at once. Rilan didn't even try to parse five different conversations. She watched the Effature, the only other silent one. He watched her back, but his bland, kindly face was sad.

Finally, Jhina thumped the table with a fist, and the room quieted.

"We have had preliminary reports of some disturbance in Dalhni. It is time for you to tell us your important news, Councilor," she said. "You have our attention. All of it."

"First, he leaves," Rilan said, swinging a thumb at Vethis.

Jhina nodded, her mane of hair waving back and forth with the motion. "I believe we all regard the matter raised by Majus Vethis to be satisfactorily answered."

There was a squawk of protest from the majus, but Rilan had said enough to ensure this was treated as a Council matter. *A small victory.* She wished the she could feel any satisfaction, instead of nausea. Jhina looked quickly to the other councilors to receive their nods of acceptance.

"You will repeat none of what you heard here, majus," Feldo cautioned. He leaned forward, staring into Vethis' pale face.

"But—" began Vethis.

"Not a word," Feldo growled. "We will check."

Vethis opened his mouth again. Rilan was surprised he had the compunction.

Feldo raised his eyebrows. "You wish to debate the Council?"

Vethis closed his mouth and glowered, fingering his moustache. After a few moments he gave a half-hearted bow. "By your leave, Councilors," he said stiffly.

"Go," Jhina said.

Tension left with Rilan's odious rival. *Now I just have to deal with the worst news I can think of, and— Father.* She kept her face neutral with an effort, but there were tears in her eyes again. *No weakness.*

"He won't keep silent," she said. "You should have let me raise this as a Council issue."

"We have ways to deal with him," Freshta countered. "Am still waiting for explanation of why apprentice is missing." Rilan tightened her lips. The other councilors were more tactful than the Pixie, but their expressions said the same.

Rilan took in a deep breath, let it out. *Just make it through without breaking down.* She began her story.

* * *

"She has been gone for quite a long time," Origon said, pacing the length of his carpet. He had checked the dimming walls every few minutes, it seemed. It was getting close to night. Rilan had been gone for over three darkenings.

"This one has made such observations several times," Caroom said placidly. They had elected to stay until Rilan returned, and both they and Inas now occupied Origon's living room. The young man was pale, and had his knees up under his arms on the couch, staring at nothing.

"I worry for her conduct with the Council. Not only are our apprentices lost, but with her father—" Origon turned to the Benish. He ached to focus on Sam, and Enos, to contact Mhalaro and what the scientist had found out about the Drains. But Rilan's *father.* He had met the man several times—admired him, in a sort of morbid, terrified way, though the man was only a couple cycles older than him.

Rilan's father had been the kind of man who could survive anything, pushing until the forces of nature gave way in front of him. It was easy to see where Rilan got her determination. The Drains were not a force of nature. They were abominations. He had to stop them, for his lost song, for Rilan's father, for Sam and Enos.

"I greatly respect the councilor, and by extension, that one's progenitor." Caroom was leaning against a wall, as the Benish were not well equipped to sit. Their torchlight eyes twinkled as they regarded Origon. The Nether translated the expression as a sign of true grief. "However hard the last few days have been for, hmm, all," they waved a hand at their apprentice, watching them blankly from Origon's couch, "these here must now concern ourselves with the voids—the 'Drains'. This one believes that term may be more accurate, now one has been seen. In any case, they are, hmm, more important than they appear." Caroom's gnarled toes gripped the carpet as they pulled upright.

Origon forced himself to stop pacing. Finally, another majus accepted his term for the anomalies, and thought the Drains had to be stopped at any cost. His eyes fell on Inas, white-faced, and trembling. Origon hoped he wouldn't be sick on his carpet. Still, the young man reminded him of Sam, when he first arrived in the Nether. If not for the next generation, why were they stopping the Drains?

"How are you faring, Inas?" he asked.

"I must get my sister back," Inas whispered. His voice was raw, eyes unfocused. Origon frowned. This was not Sam's panic, but something quick-growing and wild. The boy was devoted to his sister, surely, but the physical signs were concerning, and Origon wished Rilan were here to tend to Inas. Comforting people was not his strongest attribute.

"We must be waiting for news from Methiem," Origon said. On a whim, he went to the communication System buried in the knick-knacks on a display table. He barely ever used the thing, preferring face to face communication, but tonight it was broadcasting official news from Methiem. The news of Dalhni had flown across all ten homeworlds in the last several darkenings.

The System arose in a swirl of colors. A non-majus wouldn't be able to see that part, of course. They would only see the image it projected. The Systems were fairly expensive, both in cost and in song, contributed by maji. Every full majus was required to have one, paid for jointly by the offices of the Effature and the Council. Non-maji could buy them, at great expense.

An emergency report about the situation on Methiem scrolled in letters the Nether translated to Origon's brain. It was the same message as it had been. Origon was about to switch it off when another line of text appeared. "There is news."

Caroom stumped over to the terminal. Inas stayed on the couch, rocking slightly. Origon watched him for a moment to make sure he didn't do anything stupid.

"Dalhni is mostly destroyed by the effects of the void—the Drain," Caroom read. "The city's Symphony is too changed for maji who have been there to, hmm, return, but a majus has traveled there from a nearby town, and made a portal to the Nether to re-establish communications. Survivors say the, hmm, disturbance in the sky is no longer in evidence, ceasing to grow this afternoon, then suddenly drifting away into the, hmm, atmosphere."

Origon beat a fist into his other palm. "They will have to spread the new melody of Dalhni through the maji before we can be making a portal there. Once again, we lose the chance to study it."

"Would this one have preferred the Drain stayed?" Caroom asked.

Origon shot a look at them. Of course he didn't want more damage and death. "I am not in favor of more chaos, especially not with my apprentice missing, but the aberrations must be studied. It is the only way to stop them from causing more damage."

"This self agrees," Caroom said. "Though if these here are to, hmm, apply logic instead, there may be more answers than thought."

Origon eyed the other majus. What had the Benish neglected to tell him? "Meaning?"

"This one knows of three Drains, yes?" They gestured to Origon.

"Four," he said. "The first on Methiem's moon, the one at ChinRan, the one that was driving Sam here, and the one in Dalhni."

"Hmmmm," Caroom rumbled for a moment. "That is unfortunate."

Origon raised his thick eyebrows. He wanted to shake the information out of the Benish.

"Otherwise," Caroom explained, their voice agonizingly slow, "all Drains have occurred on or near Methiem. It is enough to draw conclusions. The, hmm, outlier is Sam's."

Origon hadn't thought of that pattern. "You are right," he mused. "Maybe there is to be something special about the Methiemum. Sam is one of them, even if he comes from another homeworld. Rilan has confirmed this."

Caroom nodded their head with a creak. "Then there is a possibility the Methiemum have been, hmm, targeted."

Targeted. A thrill of excitement lifted Origon's crest. A small difference in wording generated so many more questions.

"You are saying the Drains are not natural occurrences." Origon stared at the wall, letting the Symphony run through his head, tagging the trilling phrases defining the airflow and speech in the room. It helped him think. He had been so busy trying to find out how to stop them, he hadn't considered where they came from. The Drains were the opposite of natural. They defied all laws of the universe.

"It is a possibility," Caroom repeated.

"Someone is trying to hurt me and my sister?" Inas said from the couch. His voice was still weak.

Origon frowned at him. "I am doubting that," he said. Both he and Sam were overly dramatic at times. Origon shook his head at the over-simplification of youth.

"The question stands," Caroom said. "What one would, hmm, do this thing?"

Origon was about to reply when the door banged open. Rilan stood in its frame, pale, with bruises around her eyes. He wondered if she had been sick. She did not take care of herself when she was stressed. Origon went to her quickly, pulling her inside.

"Are you well, hmm, Councilor?" Caroom said. Their eyes flickered in concern.

Rilan's face went even whiter, somehow, and she clutched at Origon's arms, putting a significant portion of her weight on him. She was lighter than he remembered.

"I'm afraid not, Caroom," she said weakly. "You will be the first to know. It's no longer 'Councilor.' It's just 'Majus'."

Origon blinked at her, not comprehending. "You no longer wish to be addressed as 'Councilor'?" He felt stupid, even as the words left him.

"They removed me. Unanimously." Rilan took a few aimless steps away from him, then turned back. "All of them. Even the Effature voted." She stopped, hands grasping at nothing. "He was only there to stop Vethis, he said, but after what I told them—" She stopped again. "I *lost* two apprentices, Ori," she said, then collapsed into a chair. "And my father." Her gaze was far away.

Origon stared back, his mind blank. His crest was rippling with anxiety, and he couldn't control it. He didn't know what to say.

Rilan pushed back out of the chair. "I'm going to bed. I'm done for today. I pray to all the gods that tomorrow is better." She walked toward the door, then stopped, as if she didn't know where to go.

"Stay here," Origon told her.

"Thank you." Rilan's voice was soft, her back to him. "I will."

"Should I come with you?" he asked.

Rilan turned, watched him for a long time. Caroom and Inas faded from Origon's notice. They had not shared a bed for many cycles, and he had never offered directly, after they parted ways. He had no idea what made him say that, now of all times. He waited, like a small animal trying to avoid a predator's notice.

"No," Rilan answered eventually. "I want to be alone tonight. I'll use the spare bed, since Sam isn't—" She broke off and swallowed, then closed her eyes for a moment. "Isn't here." She turned to go, turned back. "Thank you."

Origon watched her retreat, braid swinging side to side. He also hoped tomorrow would bring a better day.

CHAPTER SIXTEEN

Lost

-*"The Dissolution is coming, and to counter the death that will ensue, we must create a coalition of those standing for life."*
Slithen the Dreamer, Sath Home, 902 A.A.W.

Sam lifted his head. *Not dead.* He blinked bleary eyes and shivered. It was cold, but not the numbing, deathly cold of before. It was a brisk winter day, though sunlight touched the ground instead of the pitch blackness of before.

Before.

The claws of panic rose up, and he huddled into the brick wall. Enos stirred, buried in his side. She raised her head, eyes hollow and pained.

The Drain. It was gone, and the sky was visible through a small gap in the buildings above them. Frost dusted the ground. *Where did it go? Something that big can't just disappear.*

"We are alive." Enos pushed away, and Sam instantly missed her warmth, missed her resting against him.

We are alone. Lost, in an unfamiliar, dead, city. He felt sick, and tried to grip the ground with one hand. The other dug into his vest pocket, and found his watch still there. He hadn't lost that, too.

"I can't—can't move," he breathed. Panic thrilled through him. The brief moment of alertness was fading into the morass that accompanied a full attack. His vision dimmed to Enos' round face. His hands dug at his shirt, his pants, scraped the watch down his side. *Can't get back.*

"...having one of your..." Enos' voice faded in and out. He was barely conscious of her getting to her feet. He clutched at her boots.

You can't leave me too. I'll be completely alone. He could speak, tell her that. Except he couldn't.

"...with me...can you? ...think...can," He couldn't understand, except she was leaving him. Just like everyone else. Sam huddled into himself, fell over. His shoulder slid across the frosty ground.

"...get answers. ...where the Drain went...sky...others."

"Don't," he croaked out, but he couldn't tell if he had said the word or not. His eyes closed. He tried to open them. He got one open, enough to see Enos' boots walking away from him.

Time passed.

Sam felt a shiver course through his body. *Cold. The Drain.* He was on his side, in the alley. *How long was I here?* Moving his head was a challenge.

She's gone. She's had enough and finally left me. He was curled up on an alien planet, somehow populated with humans—*Don't think about that for now*—having survived a disaster defying the laws of the universe. And aliens and magic were real. And he could use magic.

Why the hell can't I be normal?

Sam felt strong enough to look around the alley. His view was sideways, as his face was in the dirt. It was cold, and Enos was still gone.

Unclench your muscles. His watch had made an impression in his hand. He lifted it to his ear. He was breathing several times for every beat. *I'm hyperventilating. One beat, one breath.* A little slower. *One beat, one breath.* Better.

Sam put one shaky hand to the wall behind him, pushed away. *Sitting. I can do that.*

More time passed.

Sam checked his pulse, his breathing. It wasn't normal, but he was out of the worst of the attack. He checked the alley. *I've been here for a while. It's not so strange to me. We all walked here together.* He'd have to walk to the end of side street to find the main road.

Standing is a good start. He got to his knees, his feet. The watch timed his movements, letting him know time was still passing.

He took one step, and a gust of wind blew against him. Then he was back against the wall, curled fetal. *Try again. You cannot stay here forever. You must move forward.* Even his thoughts felt strange to him.

Sam closed his eyes, blocking out the unfamiliar city. In the darkness, the Symphony came to him, no longer fractured, but beautiful and whole again, if wounded. It was slower, in a minor key.

The music relaxed him, playing against the notes that made his song. He let the Symphony of Communication unfold in his mind, tracing the trills and cadenzas of weather patterns in the sky. He caught the trail of bird flight above his head, a series of tremolos. However, the ground beneath him was dead and drained of energy. There were no grace notes of insect signals. It would take a long time for this city to recover.

Gradually, he realized his own notes fitted into the Symphony, outlining his impact in this environment. It was hard to hear, like looking at the back of his head between two mirrors. He felt far back into his mind, where panic always reigned. It affected him and this place too. He was communicating with his surroundings.

Does my song show what I do? My experiences? Is that in the House of Communication? He traced themes and solos, connecting his actions to the alley, to the fading piano of Enos' words to him. There was a broken strain, a dissonant percussive piece far louder than it should be in relation to the others around it. His panic, as others saw it. It was in syncopation with his heartbeat, in sixteenth notes.

He grasped the notes of his song, lowering the pitch and the strength of the music, until it was not a mad race, but a soft beat. *I just used my song to adjust—my song?* Fatigue bit at him, not quite like when the Drain had taken his notes. *Was that a permanent change?* He wasn't sure.

Sam opened his eyes, and the alley seemed less strange. He unclenched his muscles, took a deep breath of fresh air. He stood up. *I can do this. One foot in front of another.*

He met Enos at the arch with the dead flowers above it. It was a walk of maybe a city block, at a halting pace, but he had done it by himself—no one else helping. The edges of his mouth pulled up.

Enos looked startled as they rounded opposite corners and came face to face. "You are up," she said.

It was the defining struggle of his life summed in three words. So simple. His smile faded.

"What did you find?" He tried to keep frustration from his voice. Enos couldn't know what he went through. She hadn't asked, either.

"Come see," she said, and he followed.

On the main street, Sam walked close to Enos. Yes, he had moved through the strange city on his own, but that didn't mean all of his anxiety was gone. He took her hand, and Enos knitted her fingers through his.

"Are you well?" She was watching him.

"Better." Sam tried out a shaky smile again. "I had a little break-through, while you were away."

Enos raised her eyebrows in invitation, but she didn't press, and Sam had no idea how to express his contemplation of the Symphony, especially to one of another house.

"If you can, take a look." She lifted her free hand.

Sam hadn't raised his eyes past Enos' face, and she was shorter than him. *Try looking up. She's there to help. You can do this.*

The Drain was gone from the sky, and streets previously in shade were now in full sun. It had vanished like the one in ChinRan, but the devastation here was far worse, as if a giant had taken a melon baller to the city, scalloping out buildings. At its fullest, the Drain had touched down only a few blocks farther on, making a spherical depression in the foundation of the city. It must have disappeared minutes after they passed out.

"I wonder if the others are alright," he said.

"We cannot know," Enos answered. "We could try looking. I wanted to, but I told you I would come back."

"Thanks," Sam mumbled. His legs were jelly. *She came back—she can't think I'm worthless, can she?*

"I wonder where it went." Enos was looking up, but Sam kept his head down. He had seen enough.

"Did the Drain in ChinRan do the same thing?" he asked.

Enos shook her head. "My brother made his portal before—" She blinked rapidly. "Before it was finished." Then she turned to him, brows drawn in tightly. "Could you make a portal?"

Can I? I have before. He had no idea how. It had been an instinct, a flight mechanism. "Majus Cyrysi never got that far. I can barely make simple changes with my notes. Portals seem even more complicated." *So why can all maji make them?* He would have to ask when they got back. "What about you?"

She wilted slightly, before recovering. "No. The councilor has not taught me either." Now Enos' back was straight, chin up, as if she was receiving important guests, and hadn't been knocked unconscious in an alley.

"What were they waiting for?" Sam said, frustrated. "Portals should be the first thing we're taught." He shook his head. *Getting angry won't help.* "I don't think anyone else is in the city. Where do we go?"

Enos looked down the street. The buildings had been eaten away to below street level. Sam looked where she did. They walked nearer the worst of the devastation, by unspoken agreement. "Down here?" she suggested. She squeezed his hand.

"Maybe there's some clue where it started," Sam said. "We were taking samples, after all. Maybe there's something left. We never got all the way to the center. We've got to get back to Inas and the others."

Enos squeezed his hand again, then Sam realized she was pulling him to her, crossing the small space between him. Her face was close, dark eyes looking into his. Then her lips were on his.

Sam's eyes went wide, his heartbeat spiked, and the Symphony bloomed in his mind. *Oh!* He relaxed into the feeling, closing his eyes.

After a moment, Enos pulled away and Sam stared, at her eyes, her lips. "What—"

"Thank you," she said, "for being so good to me and Inas. For helping us. For saving me."

Helping you? Sam almost laughed, but that would have spoiled everything. "I...I'm really glad I found you two." Now he did laugh, a snort of disbelief. "I wonder what Rey's doing?"

They started walking again, Enos swinging his hand. "Probably sleeping in, or getting into trouble. The usual. When we get back, we'll finally have our own stories to tell instead of those far-fetched things he's always spouting."

Sam bumped her shoulder, just for the contact. *She kissed me.* He waited for the fear to rise up again, but it didn't, even as he watched the buildings on either side of the street, carved down to sloping ruins. "I thought some of them sounded too incredible, even for the Nether."

Soon they passed where he and Majus Cyrysi had collected samples from the Drain. They were only a block away from the epicenter. If they hadn't left, it would have consumed them. Sam shivered, not because of the lingering chill.

Something caught his eye in the middle of the dead street, and he released Enos' hand. Near a drift of fallen, blackened leaves was a small pile of metal containers and plates—Professor Riteno's equipment. He gathered it up reflexively, then stood there, looking around for a place to put it. He could try to stuff it in the many pockets in his now dirty vest, but they weren't big enough, and he would end up looking ridiculous.

Enos shook her head. "Leave it. We can tell them where it is if the professor needs them back."

She was right. *I can't hold her hand, either, if I'm holding this stuff.* He set the pile down carefully, plates stacked in order of size, jars and beakers on top. A little cairn, for Dalhni.

The last block of buildings was trimmed from head height, sloping down to ground level, then below. The Drain had started above a building, but now there was only a shallow crater in the packed dirt of the street. Enos dragged him over to a piece of iron buried in the dirt at the edge of the crater.

"What is it?" he asked. Enos didn't answer, and he leaned over her shoulder to get a better look, taking in her warmth, her smell, as he did. The silken shirt she wore had been a rich burgundy when they started, but between the ride back to ChinRan, the trip to Dalhni, and running from the Drain, it was stained with dirt and creased from being frozen and thawed.

She pulled the iron free and laid it on the ground. It was a piece of metal carved to resemble a dog's leg. Sam tilted his head at it. "What is that?" *I'm repeating myself.*

"I do not know." Enos stood and he followed. She looked up at him. "Though it tells us one thing."

He made a face. "Which is?" *Doesn't tell me anything.* He took in her face. A smudge of dirt spread from her temple to her cheek, and he gently brushed the dirt away. He couldn't get it all off, and Enos shook him away, then brushed her hair back over her ears.

"The Drains are not natural."

Sam stared, then realized his hand still hovered in the air. *I look like an idiot.* He let it drop. "How can you possibly know?"

Enos lifted her chin even higher. Any higher and she'd be looking up into the sky. "My family members were traders."

"I remember," Sam said. "What does that have to do with anything?"

Enos turned away slightly, pointing to the leg. "This is not something made by Methiemum hands. My guess is Lobath or maybe Festuour. Methiemum do not use such fine detailing." She pointed out deep crevices in the dog's foot, indentations between the toes. "See those? They are too impatient for such meticulous craft."

Sam raised his eyebrows. *They?* Well, if Enos' family had been merchants, she was probably used to clumping species together.

He thought about all the clothes and decorations he had seen here, whether in the Nether or on Methiem. They were incredibly detailed, more than anything he could buy on Earth.

"Someone could have bought it," he countered.

Enos shook her head. "This town is poor. People here buy little from outside Dalhni, much less from off Methiem. Our caravan never came here. It wasn't worth the travel fees. See how new it is?" she ran hands down the leg. "In the normal humidity of Dalhni, this would have rusted in a ten-day or so. It must be part of something larger, so why is this at the center of the Drain, when nothing else survived?"

Sam let out a breath and looked at the raw dirt around the depression. There was nothing else but dirt. The leg seemed like something left at the last minute. "I see. You think this might have had to do with the Drain? Could we prove it?" *If we can even figure out how to get back to the Nether.*

"This, it is not enough to prove anything," said a sibilant voice behind them. Sam spun, feeling Enos do the same. He grasped at her arm, panic rising. The voice belonged to a figure almost as short as Enos. They were dressed all in black—pants, loose shirt, a cowl covering their face, even down to a pair of black gloves covering their hands.

"You're a majus," Enos said. Sam stared at her. "She understood us," she told him in a low voice, and Sam grunted in realization. This person certainly couldn't understand English away from the Nether, unless she was a majus.

"Who are you?" Sam said. She was standing not ten feet behind where they had been examining the metal leg. Sam had seen the black-clothed species before, but didn't remember the name offhand to match to it.

"Me, I am a majus, as you say," the figure confirmed. "We are looking for survivors of this catastrophe." She spread her arms wide, taking in the ruined city.

Enos' grip on his hand tightened, and he frowned at her. *Scared?*

Why? We're saved.

"You will take us back to the Nether, then?" Enos asked.

Why would they not?

"I, and my search party, we will take you to safety," the figure said. "I am Dunarn." The Nether wasn't here to help with the subtle body language, and the black clothes hid everything. Sam realized how much he had depended on the intrusion of the Nether in his head.

Dunarn turned and gestured sharply. Two more black-robed figures stepped out from behind a sloping building down the street and approached. The majus gestured to one of them.

"Gaotha, take these two with you. We will all leave here together."

Sam moved forward, to the Nether, to safety, but Enos' held him back. "I do not like this."

"They've come to help, haven't they?" *Is it normal for maji to pop up right where they're needed? They can use portals, after all.*

Enos only shook her head. Her eyes were wide, and Sam felt puffs of her breath on his arm. She was exhaling heavily, and he wanted to comfort her, but what was there to fear?

"Come on," he said, and pulled her with him. She came, but grudgingly. She was going to leave marks in his arm. *Now I'm the one going toward new things.* His heart raced, but it was as much pride as terror.

"You two, you will come with Gaotha," one of the two figures repeated, in a much lower and gruffer voice. Sam was fairly sure Gaotha was male, where Dunarn was female.

Gaotha reached out a hand, but jerked it back as they got closer, as if unwilling to touch them. He and the unnamed other turned back down the ruined street. Sam started to follow, but Enos poked him.

"What—" He started then followed her gaze. Dunarn was watching them go from under her cowl, standing near the destroyed building. The metal leg was gone. He looked back to Enos, slowly figuring out what she meant. *Someone looking for survivors wouldn't pick up random trash. Even if they did, they wouldn't hide it.*

Sam dug for his watch. Enos' fingernails were biting into his skin, and he let them. Dunarn knew what the metal leg was.

"Sam," Enos whispered.

"I know. I figured this one out." He tried to watch Dunarn out of the corner of his eye. She hadn't moved. Sam looked ahead to Gaotha, a few steps ahead.

"Gaotha, wait for one moment please," he said. *We can sort this out now.* He was panting. *If I don't faint.*

Both figures in front turned. "You two, you will come with us," Gaotha repeated.

"He cannot understand us," Enos said. "He is not a majus."

"Do you know their language?" he whispered. She shook her head violently.

The guards had stopped. Gaotha took a step forward. "You come with us," he said. He took another step.

"I don't think so," Sam said, and took a step back, Enos with him. *Hide. Get away. Open a portal!* The panic filled him and he reached for the Symphony, but it pulled away, chords fading into the silent air.

"We will take you to safety," Dunarn said behind them. Sam jumped and turned. The majus had come up quickly. Enos hissed out a breath, and stepped away from Sam, her body suddenly lighting with a white aura.

"No, thank you," she said.

Dunarn ignored the aura Sam knew she could see, stepped closer. "This, I think is the best course for you. You should come with us."

Breathe. Relax. He heard a few measures of the Symphony before it faded again.

"Do not come closer," Enos warned. The aura concentrated on her right hand, and she raised it toward the majus. *What has Councilor Ayama taught her?*

Dunarn reached out with a gloved hand, glowing with emerald green and specks of burgundy.

"Don't—" Enos broke off as Dunarn grabbed her arm. The white warred against the green, until a spike from the House of Strength drove Enos' color back, and he heard her gasp.

"Now, now, apprentice," Dunarn warned. "Using your song against a full majus, it is not a wise thing to do."

A hand fell on his shoulder and he tried to twist away, but it held like a vise. *Should have been doing something.* He snatched at the Symphony but the notes slipped out of his grasp. He turned to confront Gaotha, but there was a sharp pain in the back of his head, and his eyes rolled back.

CHAPTER SEVENTEEN

An Unexpected Prisoner

-So little is known of the Aridori's abilities that a thousand cycles after the last one was seen, people still ascribe new stories and powers to them. Examples include telepathy, moving through shadows, impersonating leaders, and disrupting transportation between the homeworlds. There is, of course, no evidence for any of this.

Excerpt from "A Dissertation on the Ten Species, Book XII"

Origon checked on Rilan several times the next morning, but she hadn't gotten out of bed. Each time, she told him to go away, in a small, sad voice, like nothing he had heard from her before. He strained for some way to help.

It was nearly lunchtime when he knocked once more on the door to her room—Sam's room.

"Go away." The growl was still quiet, but this time it had a little of Rilan's usual force behind it.

Coaxing was not working, and he tried a different tack. "We must be going back to find the apprentices." Rilan's sense of duty had dragged her through much over the cycles. It might get her through this.

"They're lost. Dead," Rilan said through the door. She sounded dead too, and Origon's crest spiked in shock. This was not like her. He had never seen her so helpless.

"We will not be knowing until we look." There was still a chance.

There was a heavy thump, and slow footsteps. The door creaked open enough for Origon to see one bloodshot eye.

"I'm through, Ori," she said. "I have no power to make these choices any longer. The Council and the Effature made sure of that."

Origon snorted. "When has their opinion ever meant anything to you?" Rilan was strong enough to have been Speaker for the Council, instead of Jhina, if its members hadn't been arrayed against her.

Rilan's eye considered him a moment. "The other councilors, yes. I can do without those blowhards." The one eye squeezed shut. "But the

Effature, Ori. He was there. He has *never* shown such disapproval. He thinks my tenure on the Council was a mistake."

Origon almost spit out the first thing on his tongue, stopped. Then he cocked his head. Why not say it? It was true, or at least he had always believed it, and an angry Rilan was a Rilan in motion.

"Maybe it was."

The eye indeed grew angry. Ah. She was still in there. He could get her moving again, get her out of the self-loathing she was trapped in.

"You are knowing my original opinion on your nomination."

"You said I wasn't ready."

"I am proved correct."

"For *eleven cycles* I have been on the Council, Ori." The door opened more and Origon kept his crest neutral. "Some maji say I'm the best councilor for the House of Healing in two hundred cycles. I've proven again and again I know what I'm doing." The door opened farther and Rilan took a step toward him. Origon suppressed a toothy smile and took a small step back.

"Were you simply proving yourself, the entire time?" he asked.

Rilan growled, stalking toward him, and Origon wondered if he might have gone a little too far. He backed up. He was trying to get Rilan moving, not make her eat him.

"You have done good work, I agree," he said, serious now. "It is time to continue it. We are maji, Rilan. Yes, *maji*." He brushed away her grimace's meaning with one hand. "The councilors have no more power in the Grand Symphony than we do, and we are having so much more than those who cannot hear it. We are *bound* to use it. This is why I am spending so little time in the Nether." He flicked an angry finger at the walls of his apartment, letting his crest bristle. He had spent too much time here already. More than about three ten-days and he got itchy. "The maji here huddle in their own little worlds, thinking they can make a difference by telling others what to do."

"The Council isn't the only reason—"

"Your father." He didn't try to soften the words, and Rilan's face crumpled as he said it.

"He's gone."

Origon had lost his own parents before he met Rilan. She had helped him through the loss of his brother, and he remembered the numbness when they viewed the body. Had it really been so long? Almost twenty cycles. They had both been so much younger.

"You will never forget him," Origon told her. "There will always be sadness, but you know what he would be doing now." Origon had a few meetings with the man over the last twenty-odd cycles. He had been nearly as terrifying as his daughter when he saw an injustice, or a danger, or when something had to be done.

"He'd be cleaning up, and rebuilding. Making things better." Rilan pursed her lips, then reached back and pulled her braid into order. The little white bell on the end jingled.

"Yes. Come and hear what Caroom has thought of," Origon said.

* * *

"Targeted?" *What would father do about it?* Rilan was seated next to Ori on his mint-green couch. Caroom stood opposite them.

"The idea is bizarre and terrifying," she said. The others nodded. "If it's natural, then the coincidence is too much. If by plan, that's even scarier." *Someone planned to destroy Dalhni? Why, when the other voids were isolated? Did they think about what it would do to the people who lived there?* She kept upright with effort. She wanted to curl into a ball, go to sleep. That wouldn't get anything done.

Father would be rebuilding.

Rather, he would start by scolding her about wasting her blessing from the gods. He had been so proud that she was a majus. She swallowed heavily and blinked her eyes. *Focus.* "As the news from Dalhni gets out, if anyone else has seen a void they may come forward."

Ori's crest rose. "The hypothetical perpetrators of the *Drains*, if this is not to be natural, cannot have many members."

"Then if there are maji involved," Rilan said, "they will be much easier to find."

Caroom's eyes were flickering agreement. Ori's crest fanned out in disbelief. "Yet the Grand Symphony cannot touch it," he protested.

"Who else could create such a thing?" she asked him. *Only maji. Which means maji killed him.* Maji—the only people her father had deferred to.

"The Grand Symphony cannot touch this aberration, but in order to know how to, hmmm, create such a thing, there must be input from one who knows as much," Caroom answered.

"Then we must be going to the Council," Ori said. "They can be directing a research project into the history of the maji to see if anyone has studied such a thing. I have certainly never heard of it before Ksupara."

"I'm not going to them," Rilan said flatly. *Useless, all of them.* "Not for anything ever again, if I have my way." She crossed her arms. "They're too caught up in the Aridori. They're going to try to make the Servants rejoin the Assembly tomorrow, and if they can't see the problems the voids are causing, I have no use for them."

"Bofan A'Tof?" Caroom asked.

Rilan paused, her mouth open. That was no longer her problem. "Feldo said he was attacked by Aridori, but his conclusions are circumstantial at best. Back in his prime, Bofan was a master of strategy. He could have handled twenty non-maji opponents at once, though no one would have dared. More likely it was the anti-majus sentiment, the protests. People are scared." She tapped her thumbs together, thinking of her father's pride when she and Ori visited him after she was raised to majus. That led to thinking of her time with Ori, traveling across the ten homeworlds. Were they all so old now?

"Still, the Council should know what we know. It is our duty to inform the maji of new information," Ori insisted, though he looked as if he had swallowed a particularly bitter grub.

"Is the loss of your apprentice giving you a sense of responsibility? I'm not interested any longer. Not my problem. They've made that clear." *Here, have an apprentice and get out of our hair. Except now I've lost her too.* If the Great Assembly fell apart because she wasn't on the Council, they had bigger problems.

She and Ori stared at each other, and Rilan felt as terrible as he looked. *Father never quit. Just because he's gone, that doesn't mean I can.* Even her defiance was pitiful.

"Fine, tell them, but go without me," she said.

* * *

It was the next morning before Origon was allowed to see the Council—only for a short time, and only because he told Jhina he had been at Dalhni. News of the Drain had spread and the Assembly meeting had been pushed to later that day, to allow time to collect all the information available.

The location of the new portal ground outside Dalhni was just being disseminated. As such, Origon could not look for Sam and Enos. He could have made a portal to a nearby city, but the travel time would have been as long as waiting. In addition, Mhalaro had reported no new findings on the samples he took, saying they were as inert as sterilized earth. Origon was not in a good mood.

"What this time?" Freshta barked at him when he was finally let in to see the four-person Council. Origon's crest expanded in amazement. Not four people, but five. Yet the seat for the House of Power was still empty. It was good Rilan had not come.

"If you have come to contest the removal of *Majus* Rilan Ayama, I'm afraid that matter has been settled and closed," said Majus—no, unfortunately—*Councilor* Vethis. "There is no need to sneer," he continued, drawing fingers across his ridiculous moustache. It extended past the sides of his thin face, waxed to within a feather of its life. Origon itched to stroke his own chinfeathers in sympathy to make sure they were lying flat, but he held his hand back. How had the slippery man worked his way on to the Council? Most likely with large sums of Nether glass and blackmail.

He pointedly ignored Vethis, directing his comment at Jhina and Feldo, the only two of any use.

"We have more news of the Drains," he said.

Vethis rolled his eyes in the corner of Origon's vision. "Not this again. What are we supposed to do about it?"

"It destroyed a Methiemum town. You should be caring a little more," Origon said, then instantly regretted taking Vethis' bait.

"Cleaned it up, you mean," the oily man answered. "It's gone, now."

"Enough," Jhina said, a little sharply. "What is your news, majus? We are busy today."

"The Drains are not natural," Origon said.

"You have told us this before," said Feldo, his dark eyes boring into Origon from behind his round glasses. "Well?"

Origon wet his lips. "I have said they were *unnatural*. Now I am saying they may not be *naturally occurring*."

"You play word games," Vethis said.

Jhina held up a hand, silencing him. "Do you claim—and think very carefully before you answer this, Kirian—that some person or persons may be responsible for *making* the voids? Because that would be an act of war against the Great Assembly." The speaker bent her long neck, fingers twitching.

Origon didn't pause. "I do."

"Don't believe you," Freshta said in response. Scintien Nectiset had been silent, but shook her head as well, her crest flaring in surprise and disbelief.

"I do not either," Feldo drawled. "Yet." The others turned to him, and he shook his head. "Strange things are happening lately, and I would like to give full consideration to all tales brought to us by reputable people." He glared at a snort from the other end of the table. "Majus Cyrysi is reputable, Councilor Vethis, no matter what we may think of his ways. In fact, I would like his viewpoint on my own recent issue."

"That is business of the Council only!" Vethis was actually pouting, and Origon ignored him, turning back to the head of the House of Potential. If anyone from this inept bunch was fit to lead the Council, it was Feldo.

"I am making it the majus' business," Feldo said. "He is friends with one who I still hold in greater respect than you, Fernand." Vethis shrank down in his chair, glaring death, which affected the other councilor not a bit. Origon kept his crest flat with an effort. At least he could pass on Feldo's opinion of Rilan. It might cheer her.

"Do you still say the Aridori are an illusion?" Feldo asked Origon.

"I have not seen true evidence of their presence," Origon answered carefully. He knew the Methiemum councilor aimed at something, and Feldo was rarely without a reason. "Thus I am concerned the Drains are not getting the attention they are deserving."

The councilor nodded along, and took up when he finished. "Then if you bring me evidence—real evidence—they are not natural I will give you more attention on that matter." He fell silent for several moments, fingers idly playing with his bushy white moustache. Jhina began to twitch, and he spoke again. "What would you say if I told you I had been attacked, as were the Councilors Bofan A'Tof and Rilan Ayama?"

Origon's topfeathers went rigid. Three councilors? Half the Council. "I would be saying we have a serious problem."

"I agree," Feldo said. "Further, what would you say if I told you I captured one of my assailants, and conclusively proved it is one of the Aridori?"

"You have it captured still?" Origon asked.

"I do."

"It changed shape before you?" This had to be another trick—another false alarm.

"It attempted to mimic my face as I overwhelmed it," Feldo said. The lines in his forehead were deep with worry.

Origon's mouth worked. *By the ancestor's egg teeth.* The Aridori were gone; a children's story. A live Aridori would be definite proof. He looked at the other councilors, found they were all—even Vethis— deadly serious. They waited, while responses flew through his head, most inane. Feldo wanted another viewpoint.

"There are too many coincidences lately." Origon crossed his arms and rubbed them under his brightly-colored sleeves. Cold shivered down his spine. "The Aridori, the Drains, the Sathssn secession, the attacks on the maji— There is to be something connecting them. There has been relative quiet among the ten homeworlds, save petty rivalry, since the Lobhl joined fifty cycles ago."

Feldo gave him an approving nod. "Some citizens of the Nether have begun to speak of the coming Dissolution, since other old myths are returning." The councilor tilted his head one way, then the other. "I find I am less disinclined to believe them than I was before."

Were any old stories false? Would the monsters outside his window take him away if he did not finish his grubs? "Would I be able to see this Aridori for myself?"

Feldo wobbled a hand through the air. "That would be something the full Council would need to agree upon." Origon resisted looking at Vethis. "For now, I wish whoever is responsible brought to light, and soon." He stroked his beard. "You seem to have already begun on this path."

"Feldo," Speaker Oscana said warningly. "The Council has its arms full with the Assembly."

"The more reason we should allow a small group to investigate," he replied.

"Not them," Freshta complained.

"At least Rilan will be occupied," Vethis said, looking thoughtful. Councilor Nectiset glared at Origon, her crest flat and antagonistic.

Feldo studied his fellow councilors, and Origon had enough sense to stay silent. He had a feeling the councilor had tolerated him over the cycles mainly because of his competence, though he would take one ally instead of none.

"What better group to keep this quiet than one with a former councilor?" Feldo stared down the others from under bushy black eyebrows. One by one they looked down, not disagreeing, in any case. Origon would take what he could. Feldo turned back to him.

"Sort this out," the older man said tersely. "With as little mess and exposure as possible."

Origon heard the dismissal but ignored it for one more moment. "Then we will be having your support in the investigation?"

"At the moment, the void is believed to be a natural, if unfortunate, event," Jhina said, her words sharp and distinct. "The Council is heavily involved in the cleanup, but if we wanted this *conspiracy* public, we would do it ourselves. Figure out who is behind the voids. Then ask us for favors."

Origon pursed his lips, but carefully kept his crest neutral. He gave a minute nod to Feldo and Jhina, and left.

* * *

"A real Aridori? Feldo has it captive?" Rilan asked. *Undeniable proof, though of course they're unwilling to share.* If this got out, there was no way the Most Traditional Servants were coming back to the Assembly, and she was sure the Council wouldn't tell them, with their fears of being persecuted for hunting the species. There was little chance of the factional group even showing up to the debate today.

She paced Ori's apartment. Every thought not on the voids or the secession twisted inward, to her father. Proof of the Aridori gave her something else to think about.

"We have to find where he's holding the Aridori," she told Ori. They would need to tell Caroom. They were involved now, and she missed their clear head in these matters.

Ori was shaking his head, large purple eyes tracking her movements. "Feldo made it very clear this investigation was to be below the water line. I am not thinking the Council will want us close to their prisoner."

"Since when have I cared about what they said?" she asked him, taking another turn around the small room.

He held his hands up to make peace. "I agree, yet you are no longer on the Council. You have power, yet you do not have the same political heft."

Rilan tossed her head, letting her braid swing with a satisfying smack against her back. As much as she was enjoying being rid of the blowhards, she didn't have the power to go against them. The prisoner—*an Aridori*—would be held in the tightest security. No telling what it was capable of.

"Ah, this may not be the best time—" Ori continued, de-railing her thoughts. She glared at him, but it slid off. He could be stone-like when he wanted.

"What?" *Maybe the rest of the species have left the Assembly. Or Ori has decided to climb to the top of the Nether.*

"They have elected a new councilor for the House of Healing."

Rilan's brow pulled down, though she didn't stop her restless walk. "Though not one from the House of Power to replace Bofan? How did that happen?"

"It may have something to do with their selection of councilor," Ori said. He was tapping his fingers together, his crest spiky. He was nervous now, but not when he told her bedtime horror stories were real?

She sighed. "Who is it? I assume Vethis has propositioned one of his important friends to take the post."

"Ah. Not exactly," Ori said. "It was to be more," he paused, "direct than that."

"More direct?" Rilan stopped her pacing. "You can't tell me he—?" The look on Ori's face confirmed it. "Shiv's ears! How did he wriggle his way into that? Will I never be done with that no-talent, boot-licking, manipulative, immature—"

Ori patiently waited for her to run down. "He would technically be in the candidate list, since he has been a majus nearly as long as you."

"Maji aren't picked on their age, they're picked on talent and merit," Rilan shot back. "He has precious little of either. At least that's how councilors *used* to be picked. They probably picked him because he knew too much. Ever since the Council chose Freshta, it's all gone downhill."

"You had a hand in that," Ori reminded her.

Rilan waved a hand at him. "I disagreed. The others wanted one of the newer races to be represented, and the Pixies were ready to start a war if one of their own wasn't chosen. Freshta was the least unqualified at the time." She gave him a long stare. "You know you could have had the position if you had bothered to show up."

Now Ori looked hesitant, his crest drooping. *Fear, from him?* "So much responsibility and red tape would have been killing me," he said in a pained voice.

"Is that why you never took an apprentice until now? You didn't want the responsibility?" It was one reason she took the position on the Council when Karendi offered it, back when the old Kirian had been Speaker. She mentally weighed the good she had done, in such a visible position, against traveling with Ori. She still wondered, every once in a while, what the other choice would have meant.

"Speaking of our apprentices," Ori said. He was changing the subject, but he was right. They had to find out what happened to Sam and Enos. It was another failure—how could she have *lost* her apprentice? She would either have to wait for the Council to share news about the secessionists, or attend the Assembly as a majus. She wasn't doing that.

"Did you get the location of the new portal to Dalhni?" she asked.

Ori nodded. "From Aditit Baska on the way in. Most of those in the House of Communication have it now, and it is being passed to the other houses."

"We should go look for them before too many others return," she said. *Enough of this. The secession is not my problem any longer. Neither is the Council.*

"Now?" Ori looked surprised.

"You have more pressing business than finding Enos and Sam?"

"No—I was only assuming—" He cut off. "You are willing to go back?"

"I have a few things to tie up in my old home town."

CHAPTER EIGHTEEN

Bars of Music

-For cycles, the Great Assembly has pampered its maji, teaching them only of the scientific and diplomatic uses of their song. What of war? It is often in war that the greatest breakthroughs are found.
Toblerimat Unnistratude, often called The Heretic, 483 A.A.W.

Sam woke on the ground, cold, with something wet seeping into his pant leg. It was pitch dark, but he heard dripping water. *Where am I?* He sat up, pulled into a ball, hands around knees. A shiver ranged up his back, and he nestled fingers into his vest for warmth. *Where did they take me?* One hand gingerly felt the lump on the back of his head. A headache threatened to form, or maybe to reappear.

"Enos?" he called. *Did they take her too? I can't see anything. Did they do something worse?* Dunarn was a majus. *Why would—*

"I am here," Enos answered, and Sam's head collapsed to his knees in relief.

"Are you hurt?" he asked, groping out with one hand, trying to get a sense of her location in the dark. She was to his right somewhere.

"No," she answered. Silence.

He couldn't hear her moving. *Is she frightened? Angry? At me?*

"Have you been awake long?" he asked.

"A while," she answered, and he heard her inhale, a long hiss of air. "The Sathssn blindfolded me when they brought us here, but we passed through a portal. You were unconscious."

"Sathssn?" *Is that what Dunarn's species is called?*

He heard Enos' clothes rustle as she shuddered. "I must admit, they are not my favorite species."

"Why?" *Specism, from Enos?*

There was a silence. Finally, "We must try to escape."

"I agree," Sam said. "Any ideas?"

"We need light," Enos said. "I cannot see the extents of our cell."

Cell? That would explain the dark. Then we are prisoners. Oddly, the anxiety he felt was a small thing, beneath his concern for Enos' well-being. Sam brushed hard-packed earth beneath him. "There's a wall behind me," he told her. "It's hard—possibly earth or rock—and there's a little trickle of water. And my pants are wet." *A cave? If so, it's sealed well to be this dark. I can't even see my hands.*

"It is the same for me, save for my pants," Enos said, and fell silent again. After a moment she spoke again. "Maybe if—" It sounded like she was speaking half to herself.

"If what?" Sam asked. He was waiting for the panic to rise up and take him away, but it didn't. Maybe because he could hear his voice defining a small space, and because there was not enough definition to his surroundings.

"I'm listening to the Symphony of Healing. There are small creatures living in the water," Enos told him. "I am not very good, but I may be able to change their song and make them luminesce."

"That would help." Sam heard her shift. A hand touched his arm, drew back, then ran up and around his back. He leaned into the comforting contact.

"I must get closer to change their music. Where is the water?" Enos asked. Sam guided her hand to where he felt the trickle. Her hand was smooth, cool to the touch, much smaller than his. He let his thumb slide between her fingers.

Once they found the water, Sam let go reluctantly. "Can you do it?" he asked.

"I believe so. One moment." There was a pause, and Sam tried to listen for the fractal music. It slipped away and he tried again.

There was a flash of white in the darkness. As in Dalhni, the color did not illuminate, though he could see it. Then it disappeared, and Enos yelped.

"What? What happened?" Sam groped for her, finding the bumps of her spine, rested one hand at the base of her neck.

"My notes—they're gone." She made a small sound. "That has not happened to me before."

"It happened when Majus Cyrysi and I tried to get too close to the Drain," Sam told her. "It's not a good feeling."

"It is not," Enos agreed. She sucked in air through her teeth. "Does it always sting so? It tingles all over."

"Sting?" Sam asked. "For me, it was like...like a piece of skin tearing away from a scab, but on the inside." *Do other houses feel it differently? Why would she lose notes in the first place?*

"I feel that too," Enos said. "This is something else, then." Sam heard a flapping sound. She was shaking a hand, as if trying to get feeling back.

"Let me try." Sam didn't want to lose any more of his notes—he could still feel an absence in his song from Dalhni—but he had to know what happened. This time when he listened, the Symphony of Communication unfolded in his mind.

It was a sparse thing in the cave. The microbes Enos found created their own small melody, which would have been drowned out normally. There were echoes of sound and speech between the two of them, in trills and cadenzas, but barely any air stirred in the chamber, and Sam followed its source to a tiny exit, only a few steps away.

He took the fewest notes he could, creating a measure to bring a draft of air toward him. The yellow of the House of Communication blossomed, around his unseen hands. As soon as he applied the change something snapped down between him and his notes, like the teeth of a trap.

"Ahh!"

"Then it is not just me," Enos said.

Sam gasped, his whole body stinging. *Like touching a live wire.* It almost masked the loss of his notes. "It's not just you," he said, panting.

"Are our captors keeping us from using our song?" Enos asked.

"Is that even possible? How could you know which house was changing the Grand Symphony?" *Trapped.* Terror welled up.

"It must be a System, but not one I have heard of."

"What do we do?" *Keep it together. Only rock and dirt around you, and Enos is close.*

"Where is the air coming from?"

Sam found her hands again, taking comfort in his friend's touch. It was off-balance, without Inas on his other side. They made a circuit, finding their prison was maybe six steps across, and as many deep—even smaller than he thought. The trickle of water vanished down a little hole to one side, but it wasn't even big enough for Sam to get his finger into.

The door was hard to identify, though Enos finally discovered the crack running around the edge. The surface was slightly smoother than the walls, and there was a small slot cut into it near the bottom, where Sam had felt the airflow. The door didn't so much as budge, even with both of them pushing on it.

He left Enos' touch for a moment to kneel and press his eye to the slot, but could see nothing. They regrouped near the trickle of water.

No one knows where we are, Sam thought. He groped for his watch. The pocket it was in had a button, fortunately closed. He found the smooth oval with a sigh. "I'm out of good ideas. Do you have any?"

They settled on the floor, shoulders together, one of Sam's hands in hers, the other on his watch. The ticking was loud, in the stillness, now it was out of his pocket.

"Not now," she said. She rested her head on his shoulder, and Sam gently rested his head on hers. His stomach gurgled. *No idea when I last ate—was it this morning in ChinRan? When Inas and Enos and I were talking in the tent?*

They sat in the dark for some interminable period of time, occasionally trading a few words. Neither wanted to speak, and Sam took comfort in Enos' nearness.

It could have been hours or half a day later, when he glimpsed light, outlining the rectangular opening in the door. It was enough to see faintly, and he could make out Enos leaning against him.

"Are you asleep?" he whispered.

"Hmmm? Not any longer."

"There's a light." *We're not completely forgotten.*

Enos kept close to him as they stood.

The room brightened, and Sam's eyes watered from the flickering light. *It must be a torch.*

It was bright enough to see the rough-hewn cave now. It was oval, the ceiling close above their head, and the walls only far enough away for them to sit a few feet apart at most. There was no exit but the stone door with the little hole.

"Little birds, are you awake?" came a voice. *Gaotha.*

Sam looked to Enos. *Should we answer? Maybe if we don't, he'll come in and—*

"We are awake," Enos called out.

There goes that idea. Sam frowned at her, but she wasn't looking.

"You are hungry?" Something clattered, and obscured the light for a moment.

"Eat, and I will come check on you later. Gaotha, he must know his little birds are kept safe. The form must be whole, in all who are here." There were footsteps, and the light dimmed.

"Wait!" Sam called, rushing to the door, but the footsteps didn't pause. *What did that mean?* His foot hit something with a *clack*, and he bent down while there was still enough light to see. It was an uneven wooden bowl filled with odor-less glop. He poked a finger in it and felt a cold wetness.

"Dinner is here," he told Enos. "Or possibly breakfast." *How long have we been here?* He still expected a spike of anxiety, but it didn't happen.

They sat down, and split the goop in the dark. It wasn't very good, but Sam was hungry enough not to complain. Enos ate as quickly as he did. When they finished, he put the bowl back near the door. Maybe when Gaotha came back next time, he could...grab it? *At least he seems to want us alive.*

"Who are they?" he asked.

"Sathssn." Enos' words were flat, harsh. Even though he couldn't see her, he could hear the shaking in her voice. *She really doesn't like them. Why?*

"Surely a few of them don't represent the entire species," Sam said. "I don't think *all* of them captured us. Why do these Sathssn want to capture apprentice maji? What do Sathssn need to hide from the maji? What about the 'form'?" A flash of insight singed through his brain. *Oh.*

By the sounds of Enos shifting, she had come to same conclusion.

"The secession," they both said at the same time.

"I've heard how strict the Most Traditional Servants are, but that doesn't tell *why* they captured us," Sam said. "Nor does it explain why they were near the Drain. The secession was about the Aridori rumors. This might still be something else, but if it is, I have no idea what."

He waited for Enos to speak, but she didn't. He squeezed her hand, and the minutes stretched out. She shivered, and made a strange sound, like a whimper. *Is she crying?*

"What's wrong?" he asked. He reached for her face, one hand moving up her shoulder, to her cheek. It was wet.

"I—I can't," she said, her voice hitching.

"Can't what? What's the problem?" *I'm missing something, between the Drains, the Sathssn, and the Aridori. I wish Inas was here.* He turned his head blindly in the dark. *I wish we were with him.*

"We must escape," Enos whispered. "We must change the Symphony to get out."

"I...I agree," Sam said. "But I don't want to lose any more of my song to whatever field they have around this place."

"Can we break through?" Enos suggested.

"Break through what? The System cut us off the moment we started to change the Symphony," Sam said.

Enos scooted around in the dark, and put one hand on each of his shoulders. He could feel her breath on his face. *Is she going to kiss me again?*

"I do not know if it will work, but we *must* get out of here." Her words were fast, nearly hissing out of her. Sam flinched back.

"I don't care about losing some notes." Her hands gripped tighter, almost painfully so, and Sam scrunched down. "We can't just sit blind in this little box until they kill us. Help me!"

"They didn't say anything about killing us," Sam said. "Gaotha said they want to keep us safe." Sudden heat boiled up in him. "Why are you so scared? What did he mean about 'the form'?"

Enos was silent, her fingers digging into his shoulders. "The Sathssn Cult of Form," she said, each word a puff of air.

"What does that mean?" Sam felt the beginning thrill of tension in his gut, heard his breath get faster. *I was doing so well.*

"It's the religion many Sathssn follow," Enos said. She pushed up from him, her voice fainter and then stronger as she paced back and forth. "They think the body is holy. Anything physically wrong must be culled. Few follow it like they used to, but the strictest adherents are the Most Traditional Servants."

"Culled, like *killed?*" Sam said. *Keep it together.* His heart was starting to race, and he palmed his watch. "But that's their own species, not the other species in the Assembly, right? So why us? We're not injured, and they don't have any reason to hurt us." *Is Enos hiding something?* He imagined her pulling up a sleeve to reveal a hideous scar, or a third arm.

She didn't answer for a moment, and Sam's thoughts spiraled. She broke in before he got too far. "They referred to our forms. I have never heard a Sathssn apply their religion to one outside it, so this is something new. We aren't injured, but there is no telling what they might do, if the Servants are making up new rules. We have to escape. I'm going to try again."

"Don't—" Sam got out before he saw the flash of white, followed by a moan of pain. He stretched out a hand, found her, shaking and spasming. He rubbed her arms until it went away.

"It was worse this time." She sounded terrible. "Will you try?" Her voice still quavered.

"After that?" Sam could still feel little judders, as the muscles in her arms contracted.

"Yes, after...after that."

She's desperate, terrified of something, but what? Sam kept rubbing, but didn't answer.

"Please. We have to get out."

Sam took in a long, deep breath, let it out. *For Enos, for getting back to Inas. I'm an idiot.* "One more time."

"One more time," Enos repeated. "If it does not work, I will try alone."

I can't listen to her go through that again. He would try as many times as it took for them to escape, if that was what Enos wanted.

He heard the strains of the Symphony almost immediately. He could listen, but the System reacted if he changed anything. Could he overwhelm it and change all the notes in the Symphony at once?

Sam held measures in his mind, listening to the Symphony play over itself. Air was the most basic thing the Symphony of Communication affected, but the air in the cell was sparse, simple compared to the riot of music he normally heard. *Find the core of the piece, change each and every note and maybe the System won't be able to stop me.*

It was like trying to cram all of calculus, or the French language, into his mind at once. Every other sense fell away, until the music ran through him, intertwining with his song. *Will it still be air if I change all of it? Overlap the notes of my song, all at once.*

His new creation was a screeching, jarring mess. It wasn't pleasant, but he could feel the notes buzzing, trying to become a different melody. *A Mozart sonata becomes a punk rock ballad.* The air thickened around him, and Sam struggled to inhale. *Can't breathe if it's not air!*

The System slammed into place, splitting the notes of his song. Some came back to him, others were ripped away. Sam fell to the floor, jerking uncontrollably. Enos was a presence over him, and he tasted fabric—an obstruction to keep him from biting his tongue.

Thoughts scrambled, and Sam shook. The feeling lasted an age. It lasted an instant. Wet warmth trickled down a leg.

Then his fingers and feet were his again, gently twitching in a discordant rhythm.

"Sam—I'm so sorry." Enos hovered over him, touching his face, his chest, his arms. "I did not know—mine was not—"

"I'm—" He swallowed. "I'm alright, I think. God. It feels like a chunk missing from my—" He searched for the right word. "Mind? Soul?" *Did I pee my pants?*

Enos' weight moved back, still over him, but not keeping him down. "I will not ask again."

The shaking was almost gone, and Sam struggled to sit. Enos heard him, and groped for a hand, helped him up. "Something happened," he said into the silence. Cloth scraped the earthen floor from Enos' direction. "I changed the whole melody of air at once, or started to. It was going to change, though into what, I don't know. Then the System they have here won out." There was no answer, and he almost asked if she had heard.

"You changed the *entire* melody of the air?" Enos asked.

"It wasn't easy," he said.

"No. It is impossible," Enos corrected. "Councilor Ayama told me: maji can change part of a Grand Symphony, but there must be something of the original. One cannot make a Symphony fundamentally different."

Then what did I do? The room grew brighter. "Gaotha," he said. They scooted to the other side of the cell, away from the door.

"Your food, is it all gone, little birds?" Gaotha's wheezy voice drifted through the slot at the bottom of the stone door. "If the plate, it is all clean, then push it back to Gaotha and he will bring you more later."

Sam reached for the bowl, but Enos' hand stilled his. In the low light, he could just see her head shake.

"Come now, little birds," Gaotha said. "Majus Dunarn, she says you can understand Gaotha. Push the bowl back." His voice was louder than before.

Enos got to her feet and quietly stepped to the door, white glowing about her fingertips. She reached for the surface, color dividing into smaller and smaller tendrils around her outstretched hand, encompassing the outline of a figure.

There was an audible snap, and Enos crumpled to the floor, twitching. Sam was on his feet in an instant, by her side. *Enos, why?*

Outside the door, there was a guttural laugh. "Little birds, you should not do that. Gaotha can see what you do with the toy the majus gave him. As long as it is on, you cannot do your magic tricks. It will hurt more each time, little birds, and we want to keep you safe and keep the form whole. Bad, if not." He paused. "Now, the bowl. Push it back to Gaotha."

Sam snatched up the empty wooden bowl, and Enos put out a shaking hand to stop him. He pushed her away and fit the bowl through the slot. *I won't let her kill herself. I can make Gaotha go away, make her stop trying to use her song.*

There was a scrape outside the door. "Good, you are eating well. Tomorrow, one of our doctors will tend you. He will make sure you are healthy before you meet the leaders." Gaotha's footsteps left them, the light receding.

"They'll let us out tomorrow," he said. "They'll just check to make sure we aren't missing limbs or something. It's fine." He forced his mouth shut. He was babbling. He tended to Enos, soothed her shaking.

* * *

Enos didn't try again, and at some point, Sam must have slept. When he woke, he was alone, in silence. In darkness. "Enos? Enos?"

"I am here," she said. She was right next to him, sitting quietly.

"How long was I asleep?" he asked.

"A while. I slept a little."

There was no way to tell time in the dark. *I should be nervous. I should be panicking.* A small dark place was perfect, especially with his friend beside him. It couldn't hit any of his buttons. *I'm a coward, comfortable in the dark.*

The brightening light heralded Gaotha, calling for his "little birds." Neither of them answered this time and the Sathssn went away, chuckling to himself.

They ate the sludge in the bowl rapidly.

"Why are they keeping us here?" Sam finally asked. "They're just going to check us out and what? Let us go? It makes no sense."

"This cannot be all they intend." She scooted closer, and Sam gravitated to her heat. "I'm scared. I should try—"

"No," Sam interrupted. "Don't hurt yourself again—it will only be easier for them to find something wrong. We'll wait until they let us out."

Enos leaned against him, and he realized she was shaking. *I should be more scared.*

Later, Gaotha came again.

"Little birds, there is more food." The bowl pinged in the slot.

Gaotha came back for the bowl when they finished. "The doctor majus, he will come soon to inspect Gaotha's little birds, to make sure they are fit for the True Form. You will be honored."

Enos pulled Sam close, her grip like a vice. "Did he say—"

Sam shushed her until Gaotha's footsteps died away. "What is it?"

"They have someone from the House of Healing. I thought it was a regular physician. He will examine us." Her hands were shaking on him, and her voice cracked as she spoke. "They cannot. They cannot do that." She was panting, an anxiety attack. Sam held her close, taking her shaking into him, absorbing it. He was used to the feeling. He could handle it. Sam remembered Enos' reluctance to let Councilor Ayama touch her with her song.

"It won't be fun," he said, "but I don't think they'll hurt us. They would have done that before."

"They are Sathssn." Enos shook in his arms, her breathing tickling his ear, too fast. He tried to count, to calm her, but she didn't seem to hear. "They are the Servants. The majus is House of Healing."

"They won't hurt us," Sam said again. *Don't know if that's true, but if it helps—*

"You do not understand," Enos said into his shoulder. "If we do not pass inspection, we will be unworthy of their idea of form."

"Which means?" Worry grew in Sam.

"The souls of the unworthy must be sent back to receive a new form."

"They kill people who don't live up to their standards?" Sam asked.

"It is their way. For any deformity, or large injury, or major disease, they kill instead of treating the problem." Enos sniffled, shifted in his arms. She was tightening into a little ball. "You will pass, Sam," she whispered. "I will not."

"Why not? Do you have a disease?"

Rather than answering, Enos struggled against him, and he let her go. She stood, and he stood with her. The air shifted around her, a change to her posture, her intention. *She's made a decision.*

"I am going to leave this room," she said. "I will try to move the door from the outside, or at least turn off the System keeping us here."

Sam tried to answer, but no words came out. *There's something wrong. Something I haven't realized.*

"How?" he managed to ask.

"I will change my shape to squeeze through the slot," Enos answered.

Sam laughed, and heard the high-pitched panic in his voice. "Enos, I can't fit my hand through that slot. How could you get through?" He heard her kneel, presumably feeling the slot's dimension. "There's no way anyone could fit through there."

"There is one way I could."

Sam frowned. "That's impossible. They're all dead." He listened in the darkness, heard no response. "Right?"

"Sam, I am Aridori."

CHAPTER NINETEEN

A Cold Trail, a Geometry of Actions

-Besides translating, the Nether also aides in understanding across cultural barriers. Among the ten homeworlds, it is rare to find different species living together in large communities, but in the Nether, species freely mix with far less tension.
A study on relations between the ten species, 856 A.A.W.

Rilan stepped out of Ori's portal into the remains of Dalhni. The profile of the city was a silhouette against the light of the early dawn, carved and restructured. *How could such a deadly object simply disappear? Like a tornado, or a flood.* Her hands clenched in folds of her heavy pants—ones her father had made by hand. They weren't the first pair he made, but they were still old. *I wore the first pair when Ori's brother was killed. Now Ori's beside me again, when we're going to—*

"Come on," she said, making sure her voice was steady. She led him into the city.

Dalhni was sprawling, though it took much less time to get to the city center this time. They saw only five others as they walked, dark figures slinking through the broken city. There were surely others here, but the Council must still be restricting access.

The city looked like it had been ground down with a giant ball. Buildings creaked and swayed. The center area wouldn't be livable for cycles. *What will happen to the families who lived here?* Some had escaped, but they passed many bodies.

Ori's crest was spiking and waving as they walked. "This place will be stinking, before long. The cleanup alone will be massive. Such a catastrophe has not happened for as long as I am remembering."

Even to Ori, it was a catastrophe, something terrible to be fixed. Rilan realized tears were running down her face, and there was no way to stop them now. She knew many of those who lived here, knew their children, had shared feast and holy days with them. She stared at what used to be Mr. Andryanti's grocery store, now the merest stub of a building, shorter than her. *Did he get out in time, or was he stubborn too?*

She could see a man lying on his side in the alley next to the ruined store. She knew him—Kevayn Wilder—a local artist who had made daguerreotypes of families in Dalhni. Her father had one of them taken on her twentieth birthday hanging beside his front door. She could remember the jolly man setting up his equipment, positioning them just so, her father's hands on her shoulder, her holding on to a smile for what seemed like forever, waiting for the plate to take down their image for eternity.

"Ah—Mhalaro's things," Ori said, breaking into her reverie. Rilan gasped in a ragged breath, and he turned to her, his crest wild. "I—oh, I did not realize." He had been watching the city, not her. "To see it, like this—" There were two more small still bodies, not far away.

We can't give all of them the respect they deserve. She shook her head, dashing at her eyes, then shivered. It was still cold. "No—that's alright. Maybe we can give the equipment to Mhalaro. He may be able to get more information from them, though I doubt it."

"They are stacked." Ori pointed to a small pile of glass plates and beakers. "I did not think Mhalaro left them in any order."

Rilan shrugged. She couldn't raise an interest in the question.

"Could it be meaning Sam came back here, afterward?" Ori asked. "It is a small thing, but we have little to start with." He looked around the decimated city, as if their apprentices would spring out of the ground.

We're here for more than one thing. Rilan forced away memories of running through these streets as a child, visiting friends. *One I can do something about. The other is a finality.*

She pulled in her awareness, listening for the scant melodies of life. Down to the very crawling things beneath the earth, their songs were silent measures. Plants were dead and wilted, with only a few tremolos left in the hardiest tree roots, far underground. Strains of a rolling jig told her there were a few birds coming back, though there was almost nothing to eat. They wouldn't stop long.

She reached toward the lumps of cloth and flesh across the street from them, but there was no music. The bodies were nearly devoid of nutrients. It would take a long time for the ecology to rebuild.

Death wasn't the only reason she was here. She searched for vibrant life in the Symphony of Healing. It stood out, an old rhythm, but still there. Rilan turned in a circle, listening to the Symphony flow and ebb around her.

"Anything?" Ori asked. She shushed him.

There. "They came this way." She pointed across the street, and moved to it, stepping over debris, and things that were not debris.

At the edge of the void's crater, the echoes of their apprentices' paths were etched into the melody, a faint backbeat. Normally she would need an object to match the musical sequence of the past. Here, there was so little, the residue stood out as a duet, softly playing.

"They stood here for a while," she told Ori. "After the void left. They survived it somehow." They were alive, and she had two less deaths to occupy her.

She oriented on the music, hope fluttering in her chest. Ori kicked a rock, the toe of his boot disturbing his hideous robe. The one today was green and lavender striped.

"It will take a minute," she said. "This sort of thing isn't easy to hear, so go stand somewhere else. Your melody is interfering." He stilled his boot, and though there was a frown on his face, his crest lifted in amusement at her bossing. She felt a strange smile, like a sunrise at midnight. She would have thought her humor was gone. *How did he survive without me?* She was surprised something hadn't eaten him because he wouldn't take the time to get out of its way.

She followed the faint duet Sam and Enos left, moving as they had. A few steps away from the center of the void, it got muddy. She went back to the path of song, tried again. The trail stopped again, abruptly.

Rilan looked to Ori. "They disappeared," she said.

"Disappeared where?"

"I don't know. It cuts off like they—" She smacked her head. "Like they went through a portal, of course. Where? They can't have created it themselves, because they're not in the Imperium. We would have heard something."

Ori's generous eyebrows creased together. "They could be in another city, or in the grainlands somewhere. Are you sensing anything else?"

Rilan listened to the duet. "No, nothing else—wait."

"Yes?" Ori's crest puffed.

It was not just a duet. There was a small chorus behind it. "They weren't alone. There were two, no three, other beings here, but arriving later." She paced along the ground, following their paths, walking in circles. Two were over here, one there. She held her hands out, holding their positions in her mind. "They...talked to the apprentices?" Finding that meaning in the music was more art than certainty. "I can't tell anything else, but Sam and Enos must have gone with the strangers. Maybe they rescued other survivors when they left through a portal."

"It is still leaving the question of where they went," Ori said.

Rilan nodded. "The song ends here, but perhaps the other direction may give us information."

The other end of trail led them to the street outside her family home.

"I, I can't hold it any longer." As her chest tightened, the music escaped her, as it hadn't since before she got her seat on the Council. There were too many thoughts pulling at her. *Why did they come here?*

She didn't look across her yard, but instead swiped a finger across an eye. They had to find the apprentices. There were important matters she had to take care of. There wasn't time—

Then Ori was close, holding her, and she realized she was leaning against the alley wall. Her hand hurt, and she looked at it to find scrapes all down one side. *Did I punch the wall?* It was a blur.

"Why?" Slowly she sank down against the wall. Ori was there in an instant.

"You must acknowledge it," he said.

"Acknowledge what?" she said.

"Your father is dead."

"I know."

"You have lost your position on the Council. They took your power, your accomplishment away."

"I know that!" Rilan screamed back. Part of her was astonished at the lack of control. "Who's the psychologist? Don't you think I know?"

Ori reached out a hand, then hesitated. When she didn't flinch, he gently stroked her hair. He hadn't even started when she shouted into his face. "You do not *feel* it. Being on the Council has sucked the emotion from you." She wanted to push away from him, wanted to hug him close. "Your father was a strong man. This *should* be painful for you. You were the best one on the Council. It was taken away. How have you been so calm, so long?"

Every word was a stab in her chest. She bent around the wounds, curling in, letting Ori support her. It was easy to do, though they had been separated for cycles.

"We will not be finding the apprentices here," he said. "Let them go, for now. Find yourself before you find them."

Then Rilan was crying, wailing, into Ori's horrible robe. Maybe she would ruin it with her tears. It would be the only good to come out of this. She had to be strong.

"You are not needing to be so hard," Ori said, as if reading her thoughts. "Be soft today. Let it go. Later, we will find them."

Rilan stayed next to him for a long time, crying into his robe. He smelled like old leather—not a bad smell, but comfortable. He was a spur of rock, in the chaotic river that flowed around her.

She had been happy when they traveled together, then given it all up for the power of the Council—the chance to make real changes. Then, while incompetent maji pulled the Council apart, she had lost her father. She could have visited him more. Could have done so many other things. She was crying again, hot tears cutting down her face.

* * *

They buried him afterward, arranging him in the grave behind the house. It was warming in the city, though gradually, as if the void left a part of its coldness behind. It was a relief, because it meant nothing had disturbed her father's body.

They buried the chickens too, little balls of limp fuzz. They had been part of her father's livelihood, and Ori, shyly, suggested they might at least make use of them. Rilan checked the Symphony, and found the carcasses starved of nutrients, like the void had eaten them already and spit out the leftovers.

They both said a few words over the new grave in the backyard of the house. Rilan's mother had died long ago in the consuming plague, and Rilan had no other siblings. They were the only ones left to say anything. Those in the town who knew him would be too busy with their own problems.

There was little danger of anyone claiming the house and property, at least anytime soon. Rilan would stake her claim to the land later, once people came back to Dalhni. Maybe she could rent the small yard out when the city was rebuilt. If the city was rebuilt.

For now, she took only the silvered image of her and her father from its place by the door, both its creator and one of the subjects given back to the great wheel of life and death in the same disaster.

As they trudged back to the edge of the city, Rilan squeezed Ori's arm. "Thank you," she said.

"I have not been here for you," he answered. "I have been out of reach and—selfish. I am here now."

It was a hard thing for him to admit. "I know," she said. "I was far away from you, too." She let the silence build, considering her next words. She thought they were right, but her decisions lately were all suspect.

"I've been thinking about how things were, before I joined the Council."

"Really? What—things?" Ori's eyebrows lifted, intrigued, and his feathery hair made that certain pattern it did when he was anticipating something. She hadn't seen that expression from him in a while. It pulled her face into a smile despite her mood.

"Us, for one," she said, turning her face to his. Maybe seeing those three apprentices together had biased her. She hadn't been with anyone in a long time.

Rilan brought her braid around and thoughtfully thumped the bell into her hand, chiming with every beat. "It's just a thought." But Ori knew her too well. He'd been thinking about it too. She could tell. His smile picked up even more, his pointy teeth showing. She remembered those teeth nibbling on her ear. They walked in time with each other for a few beats, her lengthening her stride, him taking short steps. "For now, let's get back to the Nether. We need to find our apprentices."

* * *

Origon puttered aimlessly through his apartment. Sam had cleaned at some point—it no longer looked like he had spent the last several cycles traveling. If the young man hadn't done it, Origon might have even considered dusting. Anything to keep him from interrupting Rilan's rest.

He might test, over the next several days, how much she meant what she said in Dalhni, and how much was her grief talking. If she was serious. He forced his crest back to neutral. A man of his cycles should be able to control his emotions better. Yet Rilan's smooth brown neck, her wiry, strong arms, kept forcing their way into his head, and he firmly put them out. She had required a little convincing to rest, but she needed the sleep, if only for her mind. They had both slept for a little—in separate rooms.

With the time difference between Methiem and the Nether, they had been up most of the night, and the walls of the Nether were brightening into morning. Rilan might not want to be alone during the next few days. She was still so brittle, even after their trip to Dalhni. It would be the work of many months to help her through her grief. She didn't show it well. Like others of the caring profession, physical or mental, she was always her own worst patient.

Just then a knock sounded at his door. He frowned, and went to answer it. Caroom's wide, placid face stared back.

Origon shook his head. "We were not finding anything useful in Dalhni," he said.

"This one is sorry to hear, but that is, hmm, not the reason for coming."

Origon raised his eyebrows and took a step back, waving a hand for Caroom to enter. As they did, the Benish's passage revealed not only Inas behind them, but also a Lobhl.

"Oh," Origon said, surprised. "Be coming in, please, all of you." The Lobhl were still a rarity in the Nether, and Origon was ashamed to admit he sometimes had trouble telling aliens of that species apart. All their faces were remarkably without distinction, and many wore covering shawls around the lower half of their heads. This one waved a tattooed hand in thanks.

"Nothing about my sister or Sam?" Inas looked unwell. There were deep discolorations under the young man's eyes and his hair was uncombed.

"No, not yet, but we believe they are alive and well. We will find them soon, I promise," Origon told him. He had no idea if he could keep that promise.

He got the three seated, or standing in Caroom's case, and even remembered to ask if they wanted refreshment. The movement and talking woke Rilan, and she appeared from the spare bedroom, looking as if she had been crying. He hoped she had been. That often flushed stress away, in Methiemum. He sat her next to him, refrained from patting her shoulder. It would only make her edgy.

"Hand Dancer," Rilan said. "I didn't expect to see you here." She addressed the Lobhl, and Origon squinted at the alien's hands. That was where the distinction for this species rested, but he would be a rotted egg if he could remember one from another. Even the Nether wasn't a lot of help.

<Forgive our intrusion, Councilor,> Hand Dancer signed. Origon watched the large and expressive hands twirl through the sentence. The five fingers and two thumbs on each hand curved and twisted in a different direction, and both hands were heavily tattooed. It was disconcerting talking to a Lobhl. Most of the time, Origon could ignore how the Nether changed speech so other's words were in his native language in his head, but the Lobhl communicated almost entirely with their hands. There were no facial expressions, and the bald creatures didn't even have a crest to communicate. The meaning appeared directly in Origon's head, as if Hand Dancer had said the words a moment before and Origon was remembering them. It made him want to itch something, though he didn't know what.

"It's no bother," Rilan replied. "How should we address you today?"

<I am male this morning,> Hand Dancer signed.

"Very well, let us know if anything changes," Rilan said. Origon had never gotten used to that bit of etiquette when speaking with the Lobhl, but the species usually preferred others ask rather than misgender them. Rilan took in a breath, then added, "It's just majus now, Hand Dancer. I see the word hasn't gotten out yet."

Origon watched the Lobhl's eyes hover around Rilan's middle, rather than her face. He always wondered how the translation looked to them.

<Yes. Majus Caroom told me, but I had no wish to presume.> The Lobhl had strange ideas about propriety and honor.

"The Council hasn't communicated with you, has it?" Rilan asked.

<They have not.> The large hands paused in the air for a moment, then fingers described a question. <Should they have?>

Rilan waved it aside. "No matter." Origon gave her a look, which she ignored. She rarely dismissed things so easily. Left-over business? She had been definite about separating herself from old Council matters. She pulled her braid over one shoulder. Her dark hair draped like coils of oil, down her chest.

"Hand Dancer came to this one yesterday evening," Caroom put in. "He heard this one had been in this company lately, but could not, hmm, locate either of these ones, for reasons we know." Their flickering eyes danced between Origon and Rilan. "This may greatly interest both of you." They moved a thick mahogany hand for Hand Dancer to continue.

The Lobhl turned his bald, bland head toward Origon, whose eyes slipped away from Hand Dancer's head naturally, down to his hands, already in motion. <You spoke of the voids you are investigating, in the Great Assembly.>

Suddenly, Origon's attention was in the conversation, his crest rising. "Yes. What is this to be about?"

<My homeworld has recently seen one of your voids. It is possible there were more, but this one was observed outside the major city of Shifting Winds. No one was injured, as the void was away from habitation. Word was transmitted to the Assembly this morning.>

Origon looked to Caroom, who nodded back. "It seems, hmm, this one's proposition was incomplete," they said.

"Then the Drains could be naturally occurring after all, but happened to hit Methiem in force." Origon ran a hand down his moustache. "Other homeworlds could have also seen them. We should ask." The data were frustratingly sparse. If he could only learn something, *anything* about how the Drains formed. He put hands on the arms of his chair, made to rise, but Rilan waved a hand.

"One moment." Her head was tilted, her eyes narrowed. She had hold of some feather, feeling to which bird it led. "Maybe I'm paranoid, but lately I feel I have reason to be." She turned back to Hand Dancer. "Is your birth city, by any chance, Shifting Winds?"

The Lobhl indicated surprise—a gesture with hands stretching out to the sides, thumbs curled. <It is, majus. How did you know?>

Rilan stared at Origon a moment, trying to force some concept through the air between them, but it had been too long since they worked and traveled together; he couldn't catch her meaning. Though the situation felt familiar—had she told him something about it?

"I asked whether the Council had contacted you for a reason," Rilan said. "I recently put forward your name for consideration."

Origon's crest flattened, contracted. The news about Bofan was still not common.

"That recognition may have brought you too much attention, if councilmembers, and potential councilmembers, have been targeted," she said. "If correct, the issue is larger than we suspect."

Caroom swung their head from Rilan to Origon with a creak, putting pieces together. They also knew of Bofan's murder. "Does this mean the, hmm, *coincidences* these ones spoke of before may rise higher in the maji's organization than anticipated?"

There was silence for a moment. "That seems to be one interpretation," Origon said, carefully. If this was true, all the homeworlds could be affected. His crest fluffed in fear of what this would do to the Assembly.

"We should move fast," Rilan said. "I trust Hand Dancer. Considering he may have been targeted as we were, I think it's time to make our three into four."

"You mean four into five."

Origon blinked, and looked at Inas. The young man had been quiet the whole time, knees pulled up in front of him on the couch. "I want to help find my sister, and Sam." He looked at the maji and licked his lips. Nervous, Origon thought. The young man was hard to read, even in the Nether.

"This is to be something for full maji," Origon said. Apprentices were a risk, as they all well knew.

"If Majus Caroom is going somewhere, I will have to accompany them," Inas said. "I haven't gotten any work done since they were lost. I can't think."

"Inas is a part of this, as much as those ones', hmm, missing apprentices are," Caroom added. Origon saw Rilan wince, and he carefully kept his crest neutral. *He* hadn't gotten the two lost, after all—they did that themselves. "That one has already led this group to the site of one of the, hmm, voids, and may be of more use."

<As I seem to be included, may I ask what is going on?>

Origon started, and saw the others do the same. How they could hear the signing when they weren't looking at the Lobhl, like a cough in an echoing building, was beyond him. He would never fully understand the Nether.

"Any disagreement?" Rilan asked. No one signaled a negative. "Then we will become five, as Inas says, and after we find our apprentices, seven. This investigation is getting larger. Something is happening, and we must all be careful our information doesn't spread."

She explained the events of the last several ten-days to both Hand Dancer and Caroom, starting with the assassin on Methiem who sabotaged the space capsule. Origon broke in a few times to add corrections, especially how he had found Sam. Inas, in a shaky voice, told of the Drain that took his parents.

Last, Origon revealed Councilor Feldo's news of a captured Aridori. Hand Dancer's fingers fluttered in mute astonishment at the pronouncement and even placid Caroom jerked upright from their perch on the wall, their solid green eyes flashing. Inas' fingers gripped the arm of the couch until they turned white, his back rigid. His face was pale, and clammy.

<There is *something* missing here,> Hand Dancer signed. <May I extrapolate from what you have told me?>

"I'd be interested in your input," Rilan said. They were all fishing for data. Origon studied the Lobhl, wondering what he would do. Laying out everything at once had jogged something in his mind, and he sat back, letting the Symphony of Power in, listening to echoes of the connections between their stated facts, a five-part harmony in sultry horns. It was good for that sort of thing. The music was complex, a spiral of phrases bridging and building on each other.

Hand Dancer listened for a moment as well, in him, a stretching of thumbs. Then his hands moved again. <I must be female during this task, for concentration.>

"We understand." Rilan passed a look around at them. Inas shrugged.

Hand Dancer was listening to the same music Origon heard, as he—she—was also of the House of Power. The Lobhl's sense of hearing was not as strong as the other species, and Origon wondered in what way the Grand Symphony appeared to Hand Dancer. A faint orange haze surrounded her intricate hands as they wove a complex tapestry in the air. It was laced with her personal bland gray. She traced lines in the air, each a different chord, a roadmap of the events. Origon had never had much patience with the technique, preferring his own mind to leaning on an artificial construct of the Symphony.

Hand Dancer snapped another orange line into existence with three of her thumbs, then lightly adjusted its place, as if painting a landscape. She shook a hand loose to communicate. <I agree, there must be some purpose behind these voids. They cannot be completely natural.>

"We know this," Origon said. He didn't bother to correct the Drains' name this time. "What we are not knowing is who."

Hand Dancer pushed her construct, the lines connecting like a spider web on the edge of chaos and order. She plucked a strand with a finger and one thumb, and Origon heard a new chord in the melody. The construct was a masterpiece of the technique, and Origon thrust down a stab of jealousy. He could see why Rilan had wanted the Lobhl on the Council. Her analytic thinking would greatly offset Freshta and Scintien's weak strategy.

<The assassin on Methiem,> Hand Dancer explained, one hand blurring in clipped speech as the other held on to a glowing line. Another finger and thumb of the same hand plucked a different strand, intersecting the first, <the attack on Councilor Bofan A'Tof. Both included murders of maji—something unheard of for many cycles.>

Origon hadn't thought of Teju—the assassinated majus who was originally supposed to pilot the Methiemum's space capsule—for several ten-days. He had sent a gift of Nether glass to the young majus' family, unable to think of anything else to do.

"Must the attacks be connected?" Caroom asked.

<I think they must,> Hand Dancer signed, releasing the strand to gesture with both hands. <The music bears a similarity in style, and composition. In any other situation, there would be no cohesiveness to the recent events. The similarities would be random coincidences otherwise, and I do not believe in coincidences.>

"It isn't likely," Rilan agreed, and Inas nodded. He was sitting forward now, and drew his hair back behind his ears. Origon thought Rilan looked a little better already. Something to focus her. That was what she needed right now.

<There is a significant chance the unusual occurrences are connected.> Hand Dancer reached out again, pulling at strands of the orange web as if playing a harp, making chords chime in Origon's mind. <The assassin. The mobs. The voids. The Aridori. The—forgive me—incompetence of the Council. Each by itself or connected to another forms a part of a pattern, as we see here.>

"If they were are all to be connected?" Origon asked. He was beginning to hear the convergence of the chords into a new, deadly chorus, but he couldn't quite make it out. He squinted at the glowing lines.

Hand Dancer gestured a smile, her hands opening out, one above the other. <If *all* the pieces are connected...> She pulled at one strand and then another, pushing them into a different place. <Then this happens.> She spun the construct in the air, and Origon heard Rilan take in a breath.

The lines became a complex geometric shape, trilling a series of harmonics in Origon's mind. It was beautiful, a riot of stars and triangles folded into a sphere.

"What is it?" Inas asked.

<I believe it is the sixteenth stellation of an icosidodecohedron,> Hand Dancer answered. At Inas' confused look, she continued. <The shape is not important, save that it is useful to model a complex situation where all aspects must be connected to the origin.>

Rilan poked a finger into the center of Hand Dancer's creation. "If all the events are connected to the origin, then why is this model hollow?" The latticework of lines formed intricate shapes on the surface of the model, but the middle was bare.

Caroom suddenly leaned forward from their perch with a creak. "Because that is where the originators of this, hmm, this *conspiracy* are located."

<Correct. That is where we must look; at the center of the events.> Hand Dancer's digits signaled mystery.

Rilan leaned back in her chair. "A conspiracy. Within the Assembly and the Council. A ten-day ago I would have called you crazy, but now,

I wonder if whoever is behind this could really be controlling all these pieces?"

Origon nodded. This was what he had been worrying at the past ten-days. There was some intelligence at work behind all of this. Maybe he would look into Hand Dancer's technique. "We must be finding the spider at the center of this web."

CHAPTER TWENTY

Aridori

-The Most Traditional Servants of the Holy Form are a small splinter of the Sathssn Cult of Form. In past cycles, they have caused little problem with their eccentric and unwholesome practices, but they are lately gaining power in the governance of Sath Home. I am worried.

Thesna, Sathssn representative for the Southern Coastal Coalition

Sam's back hit the wall of the cell. *Aridori.* Things—little gestures, looks, reactions—all began to fall into new places in his head. Councilor Ayama's warnings played on a loop. *Never trust what an Aridori says or does. Slip through a crack like an Aridori.*

"Sam?" Enos' voice was soft. *Is she getting nearer? Should I wave my fingers in front of my face? Will it help?* His breathing was fast, too fast, and his hand curled around his watch. *I trusted her—kissed her.*

"Sam, it is still me."

He shook his head, knowing she couldn't see. Now Rey's words came back: *planning, for cycles on end, your best friend becoming a different person, revealed as a spy.*

"Does Inas know?" She'd been leading him on the whole time. What else could the Aridori do besides shapeshifting?

There was a sharp exhale. Not a laugh. "He's like me. He is Aridori too. We are—it is complex." He heard a step, and pressed himself into the wall. She was close. "We wanted to tell you so many times," she said, "especially when you helped us, at the place our family...was killed." He could hear the hitch in her voice, knew how her chin raised when she was uncertain. *Real, or an act?* She was very near now, and he shifted sideways, trying not to make noise.

She gave a hitching laugh, or rather, somewhere between that and a sob. Sam cringed. "I was scared senseless to tell you, but now I'm light as a feather."

He took another step to the side, and yelped when his arm touched her hand. She had been coming from the other direction. *The echoes threw me off. Sneaky.* He pulled his arm away from her.

"Sam, you must say something." He could almost see her small hands, clasped together. "Please."

The silence lengthened. *What* can *I say to her?* "What are you? What is Inas? I...I trusted you."

More silence. "I am Aridori." Her voice sounded surprised at the word. "Inas and I are—a pair. A set. Two instances."

Sam worried at the strange descriptor. "Why did you lie to me?"

"That, I think, is obvious." This was the old Enos' voice, sardonic.

He imagined her half-smile, mirrored by Inas. *Two instances? What does that mean?* "I suppose it is." He shifted again, away. It wouldn't help in this tight place. *Observe my own reactions, then make a choice.* Odd that advice about anxiety came in so handy when one of your closest friends betrayed you. "Why tell me? Why not slip through the slot, disable the System, and slip back in?"

Now Enos was silent. He felt her come closer, heard the strains defining air change in the Symphony that now buzzed in the back of his head. He curled in, but didn't move. There was a scrape as she slid down the wall, sitting. Slowly, he followed.

"The process takes time, and it is likely you would have noticed anyway." He heard her pause, felt "but" hanging in the air. "I wanted to tell you, rather than have you discover it." She sighed, but sounded relieved rather than sad. "It is so good to let go of this secret for once."

"We could have found another way out, eventually." He offered. *Never trust what an Aridori says or does.* She wasn't doing anything to him. In Rey's stories, the Aridori attacked as soon as they were found out. *What's different?* "You could have stayed hidden."

"No. The majus from the House of Healing will be coming," she said, her tone flat again. "They *will* kill me, once they find out what I am."

"Then Councilor Ayama—" He thought about how Enos shied away from the mental probing the councilor favored.

"Yes. The House of Healing can determine species, if a majus looks close enough. The Sathssn Cult of Form abhors any physical injury or change. How do you think they look upon a species who can change their shape at will? The Most Traditional Servants executed many of the Aridori, after the war." There was heat in Enos' voice.

"That's why you told me." He gripped the watch, swallowed hard.

Can't trust an Aridori. His breathing was leveling out, but now he felt heat rising up. "Only at the risk of death. You and Inas were fine with playing my friends," *or more than that,* "but wouldn't commit to the whole truth." It wasn't a fair accusation, but Sam didn't want fair.

"We could not, Sam," Enos pleaded. "I told you, we wanted to. You of all people could understand us." Fingers touched his shoulder and Sam shuddered away from them, like insect legs climbing up his back.

"This imprisonment was forced on us," Enos said. "It's not fair, to me or you. I would not even think of changing, normally. We do not shift our shape except in emergencies. It has its price."

Sam tried to keep the rage going. If he could see her face, it would be easier to hate her. Instead, the darkness made his imagination blossom, and he shuddered at the thought of her head, like putty, squeezing through the slot in the door.

"Will you let me change my shape to free us?"

I can't stop you. "What kind of question is that? Otherwise they'll kill you. Maybe both of us." He couldn't get the images out of his head. "Fine, do it." *Might as well ask me to kill her myself.*

He heard her get up, and walk to the door.

"It will take a few minutes. We do not have much time before their majus comes. Be ready when I call for you to push on the door."

Sam grunted, and sat in silence, listening and trying not to. *What should I do?* When—if—they escaped, what then?

There were sounds at first, murmurs and sounds of effort, and then all vocalization from Enos ceased. There were other small things, twitches and whispery sounds, and Sam put his fingers in his ears. Skin like putty, arms and chest and legs all mashing together in a shapeless horrible blob. He took his fingers away. They weren't helping.

There was total silence.

"Sam," came the whisper, minutes or hours later. *I can either sit here, captive of people I don't know, or get up and help an Aridori who's been lying to me.* There wasn't that much to decide.

"I'm ready," he said.

"There is a bolt here, but the door is extremely heavy. You must help me move it."

"What if we get caught?"

"We *are* caught. Do you want to get out?" She sounded so normal.

It took both of them at the door, Sam pushing and Enos pulling, before it ground outward with a heavy growl. Sam expected someone to come running at any second, but no one did.

Then he was outside the cell, with Enos. It was still dark, but a faint slip of air moved against his face. He hesitantly listened to the Symphony, gauging where the wind was coming from. He reached for notes of his song, and placed them in a single phrase to show him the direction the air movement. There was no shock, no response from the System.

"We can use our songs," he said.

"Which way out?" Enos asked. She touched his arm again, and he flinched away. "We do not want to get separated," she said.

Sam forced himself to relax and accept her hand. He was going to hyperventilate. *Any second, her hand will grip, puncture the skin—* No.

"There's only one way forward." He started walking.

A little way down the tunnel, light bloomed in front of them, concealed from the cell by a sharp curve in the tunnel. Sam winced at the brightness, and looked to Enos. She was the same as always, dark hair, round face, short. *Did she pick how she wanted to look?*

The walls arched overhead, to make a tunnel carved from dirt. The top was just past his head, comforting as it enclosed him.

"We must hide," Enos whispered.

"Why?" Then Sam realized the light was coming toward them. Gaotha was coming back to get them. "Where? Back in the cell?" There was nowhere else to go. His heart raced, and he turned to Enos. "Can you, you know, *do* anything?"

She frowned. "I told you it takes time. You also seem to have forgotten I am an apprentice majus of the House of Healing."

Sam blinked. With her revelation, he had forgotten. *Not only an Aridori, but a majus. Are there others?* Later. He would deal with it later.

"Back a little," he said quietly. "We can get a moment of surprise where the passage curves."

Enos nodded and hurried back, close to the open stone door of the cell. There was a device attached to the wall, softly glowing brown and white and blue. Enos closed her eyes, head tilted. "I can hear him, in the Symphony. There is only one."

"Get ready," Sam whispered. He crouched, hands out. *I have no idea what I'm doing.*

"I believe you are also an apprentice of some sort," Enos hissed.

Sam felt the blush heat his face, and listened. The music of the air diverged into two strains as it went around a form, the air describing a jig in the eddies from a torch. Staccato beats came from booted footsteps, and steady breathing. Quiet echoes of their speech made little cadenzas.

As Gaotha's black cloak rounded the corner, Enos' hand shot out to touch him, white blossoming from her fingers. Instead, a black glove caught her hand, white with turquoise accents beating down her color.

"Do you not think, young one, that a majus of the House of Healing could tell when two apprentices are hiding around a corner?" It was not Gaotha. The words were quiet, sibilant. The glow enveloped Enos' arm, spread. "Back to your cell. Your escape, I do not know how you managed it, but it will not happen again."

White flared from Enos, fighting the other, but it died quickly and she gasped as if hit.

"You have not been taught well if you try the same change to the Symphony twice," the Sathssn said.

"Sam, do something!" Enos shouted, and he jerked. The smooth voice had lulled him into a stupor.

Air can be compressed. The medium to allow communication can also stop speech. The thought was odd, separated, but Sam adjusted his notes, condensing the melody of the air around the Sathssn into an abridged version, tighter, quicker. He cupped his hands, and a wash of yellow left him and condensed around the black robes. The Sathssn tried to step back, but moved slowly, in molasses instead of air. Sam plucked out more notes, tightening the melody further, making the air denser. The tunnel was heating up, almost sweltering. He heard a rasp of breath, as the majus' cowl jerked. The white and turquoise faded and Enos wrenched her hand back.

"Run," she said, and tried to dart around the majus.

Faster than thought, one black-clad arm shot out to grab her again. It glowed white and turquoise, sped up somehow, with the House of Healing, but the rest of the Sathssn was stuck in the sphere of condensed air. Sam grabbed Enos around the middle, pulling her away.

"You will be good candidates for the Life Coalition's new army," the Sathssn said. His voice sounded like it came from underwater. "You are strong, and resourceful. If you are free from defect—"

The cowl bent forward, and white and turquoise reached up Enos' arm and shoulder, reaching up to her head. She strained away.

"No! Don't let him, Sam!" Her own white flared against the majus', but died quickly. Sam pulled, but she was stuck fast to the Sathssn, who gasped.

"Another. How curious. I knew we did not capture them all." The colors intensified around Enos.

"No!" Instinctively, Sam pushed his notes into the Symphony, bubbling and writhing around him, music discordant and complex. The Sathssn was talking, but cut off as a blast of air, tinged with Sam's yellow, shot toward him. The torch flickered low, casting weird shadows down the corridor. The majus fell back, oddly slow. Sam found the link of communication between the Sathssn and Enos, separated one melody from another.

The black-gloved hand spasmed and let go, and Enos staggered toward Sam. The sphere of compressed air he created fractured and flowed away, and the Sathssn fell hard to the floor, his cowl falling back.

Surprised red eyes, catlike, stared at Sam out of a face halfway between reptile and mammal. Delicate scales, light green and gray, covered the Sathssn's face in place of skin, and his elongated snout, a wispy white beard beneath, opened to show remarkably human teeth.

Enos tugged him forward. "We have to go."

Sam left the majus sprawled behind them, snatching his notes back as he did. A hole in his being refilled. The Sathssn wouldn't be far behind.

"He knows I am Aridori," Enos panted as they sprinted down a long corridor.

Is that good, or bad? What happens when we get back? Another curve was ahead, illuminated by the torch sputtering by the Sathssn majus. They turned the curve, and almost bumped into a thick door of raw wooden planks.

"Push!" Enos said.

Sam took a quick look at the hinges—rough iron—as Enos leaned forward. "No, pull," he said, and grabbed the wooden block that served as a handle. *Rough rock walls, an unfinished door, a block of wood for a handle?* He had seen so much beautiful handiwork in the Nether that the contradiction registered in his mind.

Gaotha stood behind the door. "The little birds, they fly from their cage," he said, deliberately blocking the tunnel. "Zsaana, he will not like that. He is only trying to help—to make sure you are fit to serve the Holy Form."

Sam's hand came up, yellow flaring, the melody of the alien's words singing through the Symphony. *Stop the words, push him away.* They had to get away from the majus—Zsaana.

Enos' arm came up at the same time, dripping white, contacting Gaotha's cloak with one finger. She changed some phrase at the same time Sam did, and Gaotha gurgled, catching at his throat. He collapsed.

"What did you do?" Sam said, alarmed. *An Aridori trick?*

"I slowed his muscle reactions. What did you do?"

She's a majus too. "I stopped his speech. It's too much." He took his notes back, as Enos' white glow returned to her. Gaotha still gurgled and gasped. Sam stooped to help, but there were footsteps behind.

"No time. Run!" Enos suited words to actions. Sam spared only one glance for their jailor. He wasn't breathing. *Did we kill him, by changing too many notes?*

"Sorry," he whispered, and sped after Enos. Hopefully the majus, Zsaana, would tend to him. *Death follows the Aridori. No. Not fair to think that.*

Past Gaotha, the excavated tunnel was lighter, an occasional torch splitting the darkness. Sam caught up to Enos at a branch in the tunnel.

"Which way?" Enos panted. Sam closed his eyes and listened to the Symphony. Air flowed equally from both, but there was a trill of voices to the left.

"Right," he said.

Three more times the tunnel branched, and each time Sam picked their way. He thought briefly about separating from Enos, running the other direction. *No. Have to take her back to Majus Cyrysi and Councilor Ayama.* It was the right thing to do.

A last tunnel ran into another crude wooden door. Even without the Symphony, Sam could hear voices.

"Back the other way?" he whispered. Enos waved him to silence, took in a shaky breath.

"We may be able to find out where we are." She pressed her ear to the door. Sam kept a wary eye back the way they came, and let the Symphony flood his mind, picking his notes to amplify the chords he heard. *A change to this phrase, to make it a little stronger.* Each change to the Symphony came easier. Voices filled his ears.

"Zsaana, he should have been back with the apprentices." The speaker had the same sibilant quality, though in a higher register. Another Sathssn, then, probably female. Was that the only species here?

"Maybe he found them wanting to the Holy Form." This voice was lower.

"If so, this, it is a waste. We will need all the aid we can find. Must we test these blasphemers? Them, we know they are wanting. It is a farce to test." Another low voice.

"I will not abandon the precepts of the Most Traditional Servants, even if you do so, Iano," said the first voice again, cold and haughty.

"Not all here fit in that category, Janas," said a fourth voice, equally as cold. Sam thought he recognized Dunarn, the one who captured them, but couldn't be sure. "Eventually, the Life Coalition, it must spread past your limited branch of the religion. What then?"

Enos tugged on his arm, and Sam flinched, then realized she was trying to tell him something. The voices faded away as he pulled his notes back.

"Footsteps. Zsaana." She pointed the way they came. There was nowhere to go. Sounds echoed far in these tunnels, and he couldn't be sure of the distance. He found the Symphony again and tried to bridge a phrase to bring the sound closer, as he had done to the voices in the room. The notes slipped his grasp and he gasped at a shock like a glass of water thrown in his face. *Can't make the same change twice.*

"A portal. We need a portal back to the houses." Enos said.

"I don't remember how," Sam argued. He had done more with the Symphony today than since he had arrived. His song was stretched, and he had trouble grasping his notes.

"Try. You've done it before." Enos held his eyes. They were the same as they had always been, dark and serious.

How can she be an Aridori? It's not fair.

"It's still me, Sam," she said. "Inas will be his same handsome self. We both like you. We'd never hurt you, or anyone else, I promise."

Sam thought of Gaotha, choking on the ground. They had both done that. He closed his eyes, distancing her from him the only way he could. They had to get away.

He rifled through fragmented memories of his escape from Earth, but they slipped through his fingers, their terror making his heart race. He felt for his watch. There was no context. Sam had known nothing of the Symphony or his song. *What happened when Majus Cyrysi opened a portal?* He opened his eyes.

"I don't know how," he told Enos. *If she's caught, won't it be better?*

"Then we shall both be killed." She wasn't accusing. Her voice was empty.

"I'm sorry," Sam told her.

A voice rang out from behind the door. "Yet we *are* still pure. Now go, check outside again and see if Zsaana is coming with them." There was the sound of boots.

What do I do? He curled in, ready to squat to the ground. The panic was welling up in him. He couldn't think.

This way. Tie the two Symphonies together. You know of the Nether. It was a far-off thought, disconnected, like someone pushed a memory up into his consciousness. Then, abruptly he knew how to create a portal. Had the Nether communicated with him somehow and thrust this into his head? Were they even in the Nether? Yet it was simple. Make the Symphony of this place and another place he knew so similar that they occupied the same location.

He placed his notes in the Symphony, building a phrase he knew well. *Damp air between wooden alley walls. Birds overhead. A crowd outside the exit, feeding panic with their voices.* He stared at the tunnel in front of them and a speck of black appeared, whirling and twisting. A yellow ring grew, and the whole thing turned in a way that made his eyes water. A portal stood before them, and it connected to the Nether, in the alley where he had first arrived.

"You remembered." Enos' eyebrows rose. "Know where we are?"

Sam shook his head. He couldn't tell that. "You first." He gestured and she vanished through the portal, either trusting his novice ability, or terrified of staying here.

He faced the blackness, tried to calm his ragged breathing.

The door behind him creaked, and Sam threw himself through the portal.

CHAPTER TWENTY-ONE

Gathering Information

-The Effature, Bolas Palmoran, acts as caretaker of the Nether—the glue between the different areas of government. While he nominally presides over the Great Assembly and the Council of the Maji, his office is largely legislative, handling the minutia of trade, taxes, immigration, and fees. The Effature is famed for his knowledge of history and incidentals, for the fairness of his decisions, and he is consulted by diplomats from all ten homeworlds to find particularly reclusive pieces of information.
From "The Great Assembly through the Ages"

It took Origon a tram ride, a short trip in a cart, and a full lightening of walking to become wholly entrenched in the worst part of Low Imperium. He let the Nether guide him with the intention of heading to the Water Gate docks, which connected the shipments coming in by way of Lake Thaal. The great walls of the Nether gleamed behind him with afternoon light, and a column ahead reflected it, a shining pillar rising from the mess of ramshackle buildings.

He wore a simple robe today, half yellow, half orange—his colors. A pouch of Nether glass hung from his belt. His outfit practically shouted that he was a majus who had wandered far out of his usual habitat. He also wore his heaviest boots, just in case.

Hand Dancer could impress all the others with the fancy web of interactions the Lobhl put together. So what if it was something Origon couldn't replicate. He pushed his crest flat. There were other ways to get information.

While he walked, he placed his notes into the themes from the House of Power he heard, amplifying the connections between the poor shacks piled on each other, built on top of sturdier stone foundations. The ones who lived in this section of the Imperium changed addresses as often as he changed his robe. Slowly, a web of glowing orange lines grew in front of him, not a neat geometrical shape as Hand Dancer had made, but a mess of angles and intersections.

The thing collapsed into a flash of orange sparks and Origon hastily snatched his notes back, panting. "May the ancestor's beards fall out," he cursed, then glared at the surprised looking Pixie wheeling a cart loaded with shipping crates. She looked back to her work and attempted to push the cart faster.

Origon walked on. Hand Dancer had made the web of connections look easy. Ever since the space shuttle, his song was too frail, his notes too thin. He listened, trying to thread the various songs together again.

A tap on his shoulder broke his concentration, and he looked up quickly, trying to gauge his surroundings. He was in a particularly dingy alley, dwellings made of cargo pallets leaning together over his head. Hanging lanterns gave weak light, as the walls did not illuminate here. He wrinkled his nose as a breeze assailed him, driving a decomposing stench off the shallow lake against which the Imperium nestled.

"I said, got a coin handy, sir?" a voice said to his left. A rather ugly Methiemum in a wrap that might have once been blue held out a hand. There was nothing visibly wrong with him, aside from his smell. Origon listened to chords of meaning in the Symphony of Communication, between this man and several others behind him. He didn't turn.

Finally.

"I do not," Origon told him sternly, refusing to acknowledge the pouch hanging at his side. "I am not appreciating being disturbed. Did you know I am a majus?"

"We do, that," the man replied, with a haze of halitosis. "Me and me friends were thinkin' what with all the trouble you maji are diggin' up with the Aridori, you could spare some coin for the lesser privileged."

Origon pretended surprise, his crest spiking up. He turned, taking the chance to swing his robe out of the way, and took in the three others he had heard in the Symphony. There was another scraggly Methiemum woman, a stocky Lobath, hir head-tentacles an unhealthy gray, and an Etanela barely taller than him. She must have been severely malnourished growing up. Only four? How disappointing.

"The maji have not caused any recent problems." Origon feigned haughtiness. "You should not be believing such stories about the Aridori. Likely they are lies. The maji help with large matters, not handouts." A few days ago, he had believed the Aridori were rumors. Now, he was reserving judgment until he saw the one Feldo captured.

"We're happy to *earn* our wages from you," the Lobath said, and something shiny in hir hand caught the light from the lanterns strung above.

Origon tried to disrupt the jigs and dances of power between this gang, but it was too similar to what he had done before and the Symphony resisted. Stupid of him. He waved away the tingling, taking his notes back.

"He's doing magic," the woman said. "Stop him!" The Lobath thrust the knife toward Origon's shoulder.

He smiled, showing pointy teeth. This, he knew. A few notes added to the Symphony of Communication created a blast of air to push the thin knife off course. He recaptured the notes and the wind died.

He closed the distance and stuck a fist into the Lobath's stomach—a short punch to the ribs, the thumping beat of the strike amplified in power by his song. The Lobath turned even grayer and buckled, gasping for breath. Origon scarcely stopped his own gasp. This should be a simple matter, but each breath felt labored.

He sucked in breath, and spun to the Etanela and Methiemum woman, who were both circling in. He brought measures closer together, arpeggio, in the melody of the air. At the same time, more of his notes went to the long, smooth tones defining temperature. With the House of Power, he shortened them, making them faster, creating heat.

He pushed one hand toward the woman, the other toward the short Etanela. Spirals of yellow and orange spun toward them, a sudden change in air pressure and temperature. There were two short *thuds* and both fell, clutching at bleeding noses and ears.

The man barreled into him. Origon hit the flimsy alley wall with a grunt, the breath driven from him. Something cracked as the man punched him in the stomach. It was the thin boards of the wall, not his ribs, thankfully. Origon shoved the man back, tying the music of power and communication into one measure, endlessly repeating.

"Stop."

The man swayed, then stood, blinking at Origon. It was a trick he picked up many cycles ago, rarely used, and only by a majus who could hear both the Symphonies of Power and Communication. If the Council knew about it, they would have forbidden its use. The endlessly repeating measure short circuited the man's connection to his body. He would break through it eventually, but not before Origon had answers.

"Tell me who sent you." Origon put out a hand to prop himself up against the alley wall, slumping. The changes had taken more out of him than they should.

Instead, the man gathered air to yell, and Origon immediately tapped into the Symphony of Communication. He used more of his notes, muting the noise until it was a squeak. A sharp pain ran through his head and he fell against the brittle wall.

That had been a permanent change. He was using too many notes. He glanced at the other three long enough to tell they wouldn't be getting up for a little while.

"No help will come. You are at my mercy. Tell me who sent you." The threat was laughable, as Origon fought to stand upright. Veins stood out in the man's neck as he struggled to make his body obey. Hopefully the command would not wear away too much before he could reverse it. Every bit the man struggled would lose Origon more notes.

"I will free you if you tell me," he bargained.

The man still didn't answer, but he watched Origon warily.

"Did someone pay you?"

After a long moment, the man answered him. "Yes."

Origon smiled in response. "See, that was not hard. Has this same person paid other groups in the Nether?"

There was a shorter pause this time. "Yes."

"How much did they pay you?"

"A large triangle," the man answered immediately. He was probably lying—that was a cycle's wages for a menial worker, and Origon doubted this man had a steady income. Still, he needed information. He fished in his coin purse. Luckily he had a triangle on him. He found that and five small circles of the denomination below. It was most of his stipend as a majus for the last month, but he could get more. This was in the service of the Council, after all, if not official. He showed the translucent coins to the man.

"One and a half times your payment. Yours if you tell me the truth. I will know if you lie." Though it was possible with the House of Communication, Origon had no energy to spare.

The man's eyes—the only part of him that could move—followed the coins greedily. His mouth trembled.

"Nakan," he finally spat, then the words tumbled out. "One of the Sathssn. He were another majus, like you. He's been funding all the groups in Mid and High Imperium. We tell him what we see about you maji." He panted, as if the words had tired him physically.

"He gave you his name?" Nakan was a Sathssn name, but probably assumed.

"Some other snakey with him used it once. When he saw we heard, said he was not going to sneak about like you 'Nether maji'."

Origon gave him another toothy smile—the man's eyes grew large—and then pressed the coins into one of his limp hands. Let the four of them scrabble over how to divide it.

"You have been most helpful. I trust you will not be attacking any more maji in the future?"

Origon held the man's eyes. He still couldn't shake his head, though he trembled with effort, and finally said, "No, we won't," with obvious sullen resentment.

"Make sure to be passing that recommendation to the other groups." Origon kept his steps slow, as he strolled past the man and the fallen, still gasping Lobath. The woman and short Etanela were unconscious from his attack, the trickles of blood from their noses and ears slowing.

"Go help your comrades," he said over his shoulder, and snapped his fingers, releasing the command and reabsorbing his notes. He didn't need to snap, but seeing the look on the man's face as he slumped was worth the dramatics.

Origon strolled away, whistling tunelessly through his teeth. He had a name and information. This walk had been most informative.

* * *

"Nakan," Ori said as he walked through the door to Rilan's apartment and around a stack of crates. The large set of rooms near the entrance to the House of Healing was inhabited by the councilor and house head, but she was neither, now. Usually the process was controlled—councilors were very rarely removed from the Council—but

Vethis had been by twice to gloat and hurry her along. She hadn't hit him. Yet.

"What's a Nakan?" Rilan said, looking up from the box she was filling with Council documents. They were her private notes, and Vethis wouldn't be getting his hands on them. The whole Sureriaj-Methiemum poison incident was recorded in these papers, though no one else had ever seen them.

"The name of the majus who has been riling up the street gangs," Ori told her. Rilan stopped packing. "He is also not wanting to associate with the 'Nether maji'."

"A rogue majus?" Some maji grew tired of being ruled over by the Council. There were no hard rules to stop them, though the Council also controlled their stipend, and to an extent how easy it was to find work. Some still took that option. "How did you find out?"

"The direct method. By being attacked."

Rilan raised her eyebrows. "On purpose?" She saw Ori frown, then smooth the expression away hastily, innocent. His crest looked like a feather duster, however.

Rilan dropped the stack of papers in the box and crossed the room to him, smoothing out the wrinkles near his eyes with one hand. "You're pale. Sit down. How much of your song did you use?"

"These groups are not only attacking councilors, but tracking any maji they see," Ori told her, ignoring the question, but sitting in a chair with a small sigh.

"Then we have to warn Caroom and Hand Dancer," she said.

"I sent a message to them before I was coming here. They will soon arrive."

Rilan frowned. "I'm packing, Ori. I'm no longer head of the House of Healing, if you didn't catch that part. If I don't move out soon, Vethis will come sit on my doorstep, and that will not end well."

"Then we will be helping you while discussing what happens next," Ori said.

Considering how Ori looked now, she didn't want him fainting if he did pick up a crate, so when the others arrived, Rilan set them to work before Ori could capture their attention.

"Pack while you talk, or talk later," she said, directing Inas to a stack of small boxes.

"Third floor, room eight," she told him. "It was the closest to the ground floor I could get at short notice, and only by pulling some strings. Caren E'Bon is having her second child, and has to move her family out. They're going to a separate apartment in High Imperium."

She kept them moving for the next few darkenings until true evening, prodding even Ori to help when she didn't think he would fall over. It was time for her to become invisible. Her new status and the disgrace that followed it would help. Her list of friends had dried up significantly in the past three days.

"Nakan. That is a, hmm, Sathssn name, is it not?" Caroom asked that night, when they were resting in Rilan's new, smaller, apartment. The furniture was cramped, but she wasn't going to move it again today. Between the return from Dalhni, the few of hours sleep, and the morning meeting with Hand Dancer, it had been one of the longest days in her memory. She'd find the best place for each piece over time.

"It is," Ori confirmed. "This Sathssn is seeming to be behind many of the recent attacks, and is spying on the movements of the maji society."

"What of the attack on Councilor Feldo, by a, hmm, confirmed Aridori?" Caroom raised one massive burnished hand. "Is this Nakan connected with them as well?"

Rilan eyed Inas' wince. He and his sister flinched at any mention of the Aridori. What had their parents taught them? "If they are connected, then this is an even larger piece of puzzle."

<Big enough to be the center?> Hand Dancer signed. The Lobhl had informed them zie was a third gender this evening.

"Possible," Rilan said. There was still something they were missing. She could feel it. "Shiv's tongue and teeth, why would a majus prey on his own? Anyone know of this Nakan?"

"This one has not heard of that one," Caroom rumbled. Their flickering eyes passed over Rilan from their perch against a wall.

Rilan tucked a few errant strands into her braid, loosened during the move. "So he is rogue, or keeps to himself. We don't even know which house he belongs to. If he isn't rogue, he must have a very weak song for none of us to have heard of him."

Ori shook his head, crest rippling in thought. "How is this to be affecting the web of power?" he asked Hand Dancer. An orange and gray glow surrounded the Lobhl's hands, strings coming into existence. Ori watched the color intently, listening, and Rilan hid a smile. Sometimes he was as petty as a child.

<What variables shall we assume this Nakan affects?> zie signed. Rilan watched the complex shape twirl in the air.

"The attacks on the maji, hmm, obviously," Caroom said. Hand Dancer nodded and plucked a string. One side of the shape began to look more solid.

"Potentially the rising rumors of the Aridori," Ori mused.

The structure changed again as Hand Dancer's large and tattooed hands touched more strings, compressing. Suddenly, another strand popped into being and zie made a surprised gesture.

"What happened?" Inas asked.

Hand Dancer took a long moment before answering, carefully looking over the glowing structure hanging in the air in front of hir. Zie looked to Ori, and their eyes met. Ori gave a slow nod. <It seems this also affects the disappearance of the apprentices.> Hand Dancer signed. Rilan sat up in surprise. So did Inas.

"It does? What about it? Can we find them?" Inas' voice rose with each word. Rilan raised a hand to quiet him, but Hand Dancer was already answering.

<I am unsure> The Lobhl's fingers twiddled in concentration as zie peered from all sides. <There is still data missing. Can you tell, Majus Cyrysi?>

Ori looked at the web before also shaking his head. "We know they are connected, but I am not certain—" He rose to stare at the representation of glowing strings from another angle, running clawed fingers down his moustache. He closed his eyes for a moment, surely listening to the music.

"We must find my sister and Sam," Inas said, half out of his seat.

"Shush, boy," Rilan said sharply. She glanced to Caroom afterward, realizing she had corrected another's apprentice, but they nodded slightly and closed their eyes in acceptance. "We will find Enos and Sam. One is my responsibility and I've already lost a Council position over it. They are part of our group. Do you not think I want to find them?"

Inas looked embarrassed at that, and fell silent.

Ori stared at the construct, his head tilted, crest expanding and contracting. He reached out one finger. "May I?"

Hand Dancer gestured acceptance. Ori gently hooked one claw around a string, tugging. Both he and Hand Dancer winced at the same time and the string fizzed with a silent chord.

"Excuse me. Wrong note."

Rilan was glad she couldn't hear the Symphony of Power.

Ori tried again, repositioning the string. His face was strained, Hand Dancer's fingers crooking, as if they listened to a sustained dissonance. He let go, leaving the construct in a slightly different shape, but the connections at the center were closer together.

<It is a possibility, though less likely than some other iterations,> Hand Dancer signed.

"What is?" Rilan asked, and Ori started. Hand Dancer's fingers spread wide for a moment.

<Majus Cyrysi has made an interesting connection,> Hand Dancer's fingers gave the emotion hir shrouded face could not.

"The Aridori prisoner," Caroom said. Inas jerked. Everyone looked at Caroom and the Benish spread their hands, eyes bright. "There are other ways to logically deduce than, hmm, this." They pointed a thick finger at the construct and Ori frowned at them.

"I sent a communication to Feldo yesterday," Rilan said. "I haven't heard anything back, and there's been no announcement." It was a safe bet the Council wouldn't let them talk to the only representative of a species thought extinct.

"As Caroom says, there are other ways." Ori looked innocent.

"Sneak in to see the Aridori?" Rilan hesitated. She would be going against the Council, and the Effature. Inas was sitting bolt upright, nearly vibrating. His eyes were wide. Whatever he had been told about the old monsters must have scared him silly.

"Think of it as a way to be undermining Vethis," Ori said.

Rilan threw a black look at him. "Don't assume that will assuage my moral sense."

"Hmmmmm," Caroom hummed, the emanation from deep within their chest. "The Council is not aware of the connections these ones are." They gestured toward Hand Dancer. "If that group was, surely those would jump to the same conclusions. So should this group assume this act is in the interests of the Council, even if these ones do not inform them?"

Rilan threw back her head and laughed. It was the first time in...gods, how long? "Caroom, I didn't think you had such subversiveness in you."

"Maybe Caroom would be interested in traveling together for a while," Ori mused. "They remind me of someone else, many cycles ago."

Rilan punched him in the arm—not too lightly—and he tried to hide a smile, but his crest gave him away.

<We could simply take our information to the Council,> Hand Dancer signed. Zie looked around the silent room, until Caroom lifted one large finger and tapped their stubby nose conspiratorially.

<But such an action may easily be forgotten in the heat of the moment,> Hand Dancer concluded, hir deft fingers implying they would all be blameless.

"Any other objections?" Rilan looked around the room. Only Inas looked worried, but as she watched him, his face went carefully blank.

"Then the Aridori is our next source of information," Rilan said.

CHAPTER TWENTY-TWO

The Weight of Repeating History

-There are prisons in the Nether, built to hold common criminals. What of when our illustrious maji do wrong? Who then shall guard our most powerful wrongdoers and keep them from repeating their offences?

Plea from Roftun Befurtyon, Sureriaj Speaker to the Great Assembly, 382 A.A.W.

Sam came out of the portal on Enos' heels, and kept his head down as he blocked the alley's exit. *Don't look up. I've been here before.* It seemed ages ago that Majus Cyrysi had pulled him through from Earth to this exact location. The rotting musk of the dead-end alley was almost comforting. Now, the sounds of the Imperium were quiet, the walls dark. It was late at night, or very early morning. If he didn't look around, he could pretend this was like the tunnels they just came from.

"Sam?" Enos sounded scared.

He didn't want to meet her eyes, look at her dark hair curling over her ears. "I can't let you free," he said. "Not knowing what you are." *Have to take her to Councilor Ayama, and Majus Cyrysi. Can I face Inas?*

He looked up slowly, though he didn't want to. Enos was frowning. "I thought you, of all people, would understand," she said, and the words were a punch in his stomach. He curled around them. "You have not heard a lifetime of made-up stories about my people. You only have Inas and me to judge by. What of the connection between the three of us?"

Sam wanted to reach out to her. *Take her into my arms; tell her everything is alright and I understand her. Tell her we and Inas can still be together.*

"Do we seem like monsters to you?"

He curled in tighter, arms crossed, head down. *Were we ever together? Were they both pretending at this relationship?*

"Well, we are not. You have no right to keep me here." Enos brushed past him.

Sam almost let her through. Then at the last moment the Symphony of Communication flooded his mind. It came easily now, air currents whispering the weather, lullabies of sleepy nighttime speech. The exit to the alley was a doorway, and another place of communication. He stuffed his notes into the holes in legato passages, making them overcrowded with music, and the air thickened to a block of jelly, glowing yellow. Sounds from the marketplace outside cut off. Enos halted and placed a hand against the wall of air. It resisted her movement. She turned and glared up at him.

"You aren't monsters," Sam told her. *I have to know.* "But those stories came from somewhere. There's a reason mobs are searching for Aridori. Can you promise your family didn't do anything I've heard about? Were the Aridori not the cause for the Aridori war?"

Enos hesitated, her chin up, hands clasped by her sides. The panic started to well up in Sam at last. It was comfortable. Familiar. He dug a hand in his pocket for his watch.

"A faction of the Aridori were responsible for the war," Enos said. "My family knows—knew—that much. *We* were not responsible. Those of the Aridori who did not agree with the violence fled. All the others were wiped out."

She didn't do it. Inas didn't do it. Can I trust what she says? "That was a long time ago," Sam said. "What about all the rumors? Did the Aridori suddenly become peaceful after the war?"

"You assume I was warlike at some point."

"But everyone says—" Sam looked up again, despite himself. Enos' face was tight, closed off. He understood why, understood that he was attacking her, but he had to know.

"Are all Methiemum greedy traders? Are all Etanela artists or all Lobath dull and lazy?"

Sam swallowed. Everything he knew about Enos told him she was a good person. The stories he heard of the Aridori told him they betrayed those closest to them. Both couldn't exist together. *Which do I believe—my eyes, or knowledge a thousand cycles old?*

"Why do I have to prove myself to you?" Enos said, her volume rising. "Can you not trust me by what you know of me?"

Tension swelled in Sam's chest like a rising tide. His breathing was faster than his watch. Too fast, and his knees buckled.

"Sam—you do not get to hide from this." Enos' voice was closer. "You cannot blame your prejudice on your anxiety. Talk to me. Say something."

What can I say? "I...need more information." It was all he could come up with. *What would prove Enos and Inas are good people?* He croaked out a laugh. He knew how bad that sounded.

"Why do you look like me?" He wasn't aware of the question before it escaped his mouth. It was, if not neutral, then at least not as inflammatory.

He heard Enos sit, close, but out of arm's reach. She made a noise at the condition of the alley. "My family has always looked like Methiemum. Inas and I were born as Methiemum. My father, mother, aunts and uncles, and all their ancestors have looked like Methiemum for so long they did not remember how they used to appear."

Two instances. The thought intruded into Sam's mind. He kept his head down, speaking into his arms. It helped if he didn't have to think about where he looked. "You and Inas are linked?" The same half smile, his attraction to both of them—sometimes it felt like they were two halves of the same person.

"Aridori are born as twins," Enos said. "Two chances to choose what to be. Two paths in life."

"Are you telepathic?" *Can she call to Inas for help?* The prospect of Enos doing anything to hurt him was farfetched. *Isn't it?*

Enos snorted a laugh. "I wish we were. I could have told him where we were and avoided all this." Sam finally looked up, his breathing slowing. "When we are very close, there is a...feeling from our other half. Otherwise, no." She shook her head.

"All of you are like that?" When had anyone last interviewed an Aridori to prove the validity of the old stories?

Enos nodded. "My father's other chose to be male as well, but never settled with anyone. My mother's other chose to be female when young, but male when he decided to bring a Methiemum man along with our merchant group."

"Did he know? The other man?"

Enos shook her head. "You are the first, as far as I know."

"Are there others?" Sam envisioned Aridori spread through the ten homeworlds. *Just like when the war started.*

"We reproduce slowly," Enos said. "Inas and I are the last ones born. All our family lived and traveled in the convoy that was destroyed." She blinked rapidly, several times. "My parents never spoke of others. As far as I know, we are the last of our species."

Sam watched her for a long moment. "I don't want to go back to the others yet." *She's lied to me since we met.* "I need to rest for a while. Then I'll decide what to do."

"You assume you have a right to judge me." The heat was back in her voice.

"I don't, but I'm too tired and scared to just let you go. I know you're a good person, Enos. Give me time." Sam deliberately closed his eyes. *Show me, one more time.*

"At least let us get out of this stinking alley," Enos said. Sam opened his eyes. "Let me go—we'll find a place to sleep out in the market, if you don't want to go back."

"I...yes. That'll be better," Sam said. *I've been in the market. I can handle sleeping out there.* "I'm sorry. I know you and Inas." He took back his notes blocking off the alley and the wall of air thinned as the yellow dissipated.

They found a sheltered area under an awning where a merchant would sell goods during the day, and settled down for the night.

As he heard Enos' breathing slow, Sam looked up at the starless sky above, feeling his heart race. *I know this place.* The Symphony of Communication played, in the back of his head. The shape of a massive column rose into the darkness, and far above, a night animal flitted away from the surface.

I've made a portal for the second time. I could find home. The knowledge was slipping away, like someone else had poured the information into him, then sifted it out. *Change this Symphony to match that one. How do I tie them together?*

He imagined a blank crater where his house had been, like a giant melon ball had scooped through the yard. He tried to push his notes into the space between those measures and the ones for the alley. The music resisted, he pushed more notes into the space, and chords made a discord in his mind. His notes rushed back as he gasped with the shock. *No good.*

* * *

Sam woke to find Enos watching him. He shifted, turned his neck, and winced at a sharp pain. *Sitting against a hard wooden stall and falling asleep was not my best idea.* It was morning, to judge by the light from the walls, and the marketplace was filling. A Lobath trailing a cart with fruit behind him waved them away from their spot.

They walked through the market together, Sam noting the stalls he had seen before.

"Well?" Enos said after a while. "Have you had enough time?"

Sam made a show of checking all his fingers and wiggling his toes in his shoes. "I seem to still be alive," he said. They stared at each other. "That was a joke."

"We could have alerted the others of the Sathssn's connection to the Drains last night," Enos said. "Instead, we slept like homeless people because you were unsure."

Sam cleared his throat. "You lied to me, from the moment we met. Lied while I depended on you and Inas to help me cope with *this* place." He threw a hand out, then sighed. He wasn't angry or frightened of Enos. She was his friend, and she deserved that respect. "I'm sorry. I've just heard so much about the Aridori. So many people are frightened of them. But you're not like that." He took in a long breath. "Let's tell the others about the Sathssn."

Enos paused at the archway that marked the end of the market. "Will you keep my secret?"

Sam nodded. "The information we have on the Drains and the Sathssn is more important than a war a thousand cycles past." He reached for her hand, and she didn't pull away, though she watched him. "You and Inas mean a lot to me. I, I had to let what you told me sink in and fight off what everyone else has told me. I'm sorry I take so long to process things."

Enos looked at him for a long time, head tilted just a little, eyes moving over his face. Then she stepped in and kissed him lightly on the lips. Sam responded late, unprepared, but she was already stepping away, her gaze avoiding him. "You mean a lot to me and Inas too. I can feel that much from him, when we are all close together."

Sam pulled his courage from where it sat, deep down. "Then this between us isn't weird? That I can't pick between the two of you?"

Enos shrugged. "Two iterations, each free to choose. We both chose you."

The walk through the Imperium to the Spire was much different from the first time he had done it, drugged with Councilor Ayama's magic. This time he had Enos to hold on to, and the Symphony of Communication singing in the back of his mind. The chords cut off sooner in the Nether, rather than trailing wild and free like above Dalhni, but they also meshed with the ever-present music that floated to them from street musicians they passed. The melody and Enos both kept his panic away, though it bubbled below the surface of his mind.

They had slept for several hours, and Sam was starving. The Sathssn hadn't bothered to take away Sam's coin purse with Majus Cyrysi's money. His once-green shirt was very worse for wear, and he didn't want to know what he looked like. There were mud stains on both his pant legs. He spared a glance at Enos, whose silk shirt was even dirtier than his. *Her clothes have been through a mailbox-size slot.* He shook the thought away and steered them toward a food vendor, happy to use the Nether's directional prodding again. *I need to stop anyway.* The expanse of the Imperium was getting to him.

They stopped for bowls of Etanela barnacle stew, perching on the high stools outside the café. Sam looked around, making sure no one else was in earshot.

"Can you change into anything you want?"

Enos gave him a sharp look.

"Come on—you can tell me that much. I'm curious. There's no one near." Sam tried out a smile, letting his mind wander, just a little.

Enos looked around too, then combed her hair back with one hand. Sam watched it curl around her ear. "Neither of us have changed often. Our parents taught us only to do so in emergencies. We can mimic biological things. It is not as easy to copy inorganic items."

"All at once, or can you do different parts?"

"What are you getting at?"

"Just asking." He shrugged. Images of Inas and Enos floated through his mind, both changing size and shape, both very close, at the same time, their clothes too loose, too tight, falling off— He looked down, his face hot.

"Uh huh."

He could hear that half smile.

They turned in their bowls and covered the rest of the distance to the Spire. It was easy not to get lost. It towered over everything else, snugged against a column.

When they finally got to the House of Communication, Majus Cyrysi was not home. It was early evening, as they had wandered slowly all day, Enos letting Sam set the pace. He wondered where his mentor could be. Had he returned to Methiem to look for them? They tried the councilor's apartment. Sam tried not to complain about going back down all the flights of stairs.

The Councilor Ayama's apartment was empty and dark. Soft, high chimes floated through chords and arpeggios, a background lullaby. There was a little window by the front door, and Sam looked through it, peering between cupped hands.

"All the furniture is gone. It's like she's moved."

Enos frowned, gestured to a plate set into the stone of the wall, stating in small letters, 'Head of House of Healing.'

"If this is the apartment belonging to the councilor, and the councilor has moved out, then where is she?" Sam asked.

"And where did she take my things?" Enos said.

"Surely you children are not speaking of *Majus* Rilan Ayama?" came a smooth voice from behind them. It had a slight lisp.

They turned to see a Methiemum of medium build, with greasy black hair and a ridiculous looking moustache. Sam tried to keep his expression straight as the man reached up with a hand and twisted one end to make it stand straight out. *Don't laugh.*

"Majus?" Enos asked. Sam hadn't registered the word the first time, but now he started.

"You mean the councilor?" He didn't know who this man was, but he took an instant dislike to him.

The man twirled a hand in the air to force back a length of dark blue lace overhanging his wrist. He pointed back toward the main building.

"You'll find the *majus* back there. Floor three, or something. I can't keep up with where all the lower maji live, of course. I'm only just getting into my role as councilor, after all."

"Excuse us," Enos told him, and pulled Sam along behind her.

* * *

Rilan looked up at the knock at the door, raising a hand for silence. They were discussing undermining the Council's power, and not all that quietly. Were her new neighbors nosing in on her lowered position already?

"Shiv's knobbly kneecaps, but that had better not be Vethis coming around to gloat. I might just forget he's a councilor for a moment or two." She pushed herself up, and Ori laid a brief hand on her arm.

"Careful." *Now* he got cautious. Not when facing down one of his voids.

Rilan glanced around as she went to the door. There was nothing to say they had been actively hatching a plan in opposition to the will of the Council. She rubbed at her forehead like there was a target painted there. The others adopted poses of innocence, but no one said anything. They were all watching her.

She looked through the peephole just as a hand reached out, obscuring who was on the other side. She jumped back as the knock rang out, cursed, and then jerked open the door in irritation.

"I'm coming. Brahm's balls, you can't wait a moment to let me—"

Her words cut off as her mouth hung open, probably making her look like a gasping fish. Then she was thrust aside by a bolt of red and silver silk from behind her. Inas dashed through the door and embraced his sister and Sam.

"You are alive," he murmured into Enos' hair as he crushed both the apprentices close. Enos hugged him back equally as fiercely, though Sam tensed, only for a moment. Then Inas drew back, looking between them. "What?"

"Later," Enos said. The two shared something in their look, though Rilan couldn't make it out.

Rilan pulled Inas away from her apprentice, looking into her face. "How are you?"

"We are well," Enos said.

Sam nodded. "Just a little dirty."

"I have been missing you, boy," Ori said, behind her. She could hear the smile in his voice.

Rilan shook her head. Was everyone going to go all gooey today? "Come in—no sense standing about in the hallway. Quick." She ushered them back inside and risked one peek back down the corridor after them. No suspicious heads poked out of doorways. She shut the door firmly and locked it.

Sam and Enos found seats in the chaos of chairs that filled Rilan's new, smaller, front room. Inas sat next to them, beside his sister. For once, Sam wasn't in the middle. The two looked like they had crawled through mud.

There was a silence, and Rilan searched for words.

"So. These apprentices are back," Caroom said.

"Um. Yes," Sam said.

Rilan rolled her eyes. "Let's start at the beginning. How did you survive the void?"

Enos seemed about to answer, but a movement from Sam stopped her. He was staring at Hand Dancer, frowning.

"Zie is with us, as you will soon be learning," Ori told him. "Zie knows of the Drains and is helping us with our investigation."

<My name is Hand Dancer, currently third gender,> the Lobhl gestured. Hir name was a complicated movement echoing its meaning. Both Sam and Enos jumped as they responded to the Nether's disembodied translation.

<I am a Lobhl, and I am very happy you are both well. Not only for the obvious reasons, but I believe you may be crucial to the puzzle we are currently investigating.>

Sam exchanged a long glance with Enos. Now that was interesting.

"Um, Majus Ayama?" Sam spoke the words hesitantly, and Rilan pursed her lips, but nodded once. They were well informed for going missing for three days. "It might be better to skip over how we survived and how we got back for now," the young man continued. "We have something more important to tell you."

Rilan saw the others were just as confused as her. Only Hand Dancer made a gesture of half understanding.

"Four things," Sam said, ticking points off on his fingers. "First, we were captured by a group of Sathssn, with maji leading non-maji. Second, we heard them call themselves the 'Life Coalition.' Third, they have cells that suppress the use of our song. Fourth, they know something about the Drains."

Rilan whistled a long low note. The others were putting the pieces in the same places she was. So Nakan was not the only rogue.

"Were you in one of these cells?" she asked. "How did you get out?" She was watching carefully, or she would have missed the wince Sam tried to hide. He cast a worried look at Enos, but her face was blank, like when she was being particularly obstinate with a lesson.

"We'll tell you the whole story," Sam said, "but can we get cleaned up first?" He gestured to his ruined pants.

"Of course," Rilan said. "You can use the facilities here. It's on the left, across from Enos' new room."

"I will be fetching you some new clothes," Ori chimed in. "The walk will be giving me time to think."

"Be quick," Rilan said. "It's late, but I want to hear this tonight. Caroom, Hand Dancer—maybe you can find a food kiosk still open. I don't remember when I last ate, what with moving." She hid a yawn behind her hand.

Rilan showed Sam and Enos around her new apartment. Ori, Caroom, and Hand Dancer all left, promising to be back soon. Inas volunteered to stay, hovering protectively around his sister and Sam.

"We are not responsible for your situation, are we?" Enos asked her softly, when the others were gone.

Rilan hesitated only a moment. "No. Of course not."

"Will you be able to rejoin the Council?"

She looked down, thinking. She hadn't even thought about getting back on the Council. Not in the near future.

"You know," she said, "I don't think I'll even try. The past few days have been freeing, in a way. It's nice not to listen to those blowhards anymore."

Enos gave her a tight smile, and went to get cleaned up.

CHAPTER TWENTY-THREE

The Prison

-Although Gloomlight was chosen as a place of punishment for inhabitants of the Nether, it was first settled by the Lobath as their town of choice. This mix of punishment and segregation has done little to improve the other species' view of my people.
Kruten A'Gof, Lobath representative, 203 A.A.W.

Sam faced Enos and Inas in the small bedroom. Boxes were piled around them, the low frame of a bed hastily pushed in one corner. One lamp sputtered around its wick, making shadows dance. There wasn't a lot of room.

"I will clean up first, if you do not mind," Enos said.

Sam shook his head. "Go ahead." He was staring at Inas, who was staring back, his dark hair unbound, wringing his hands. Sam wanted to comfort him, but Inas' true identity held him back.

"I'll be quick," Enos said. She rooted through a wardrobe, slightly off-center in one corner, and re-emerged, clutching new clothes. She looked between them. "Don't do—I will be quick," she repeated, and bolted from the room.

Inas turned to him, one foot forward. One hand rose, then fell. "What happened to you?"

We were captured. You are an Aridori. The Sathssn were going to kill Enos, because they think you're a danger to the ten species. You've lied to me.

"We got taken by some rogue maji, but we escaped them," Sam said. He couldn't bring up the words he wanted to. He couldn't just accuse Inas. Inas had confirmed nothing, as Enos had. *Enos might have been lying. Again.*

Inas stepped closer, took Sam's hand, and Sam's heart began racing. He forced himself not to pull back. Instead, he grabbed Inas' hand back, squeezing hard. *Don't be one. Don't be.*

"Something happened between you and my sister. Something's changed." Inas stepped closer, pulling Sam in. His eyes flicked down and up, marking Sam's mouth, throat, eyes. His other hand brushed down Sam's cheek. Inas' lips were slightly open. "I missed you, Sam."

"I...missed you too." *Please don't be true.* He wanted the universe to give him this one little thing. He leaned closer to Inas, searching, their noses almost touching. His eyes closed as Inas' lips pressed to his, and Sam tried to let the kiss burn away all his suspicions, but he couldn't. He pulled back, turned his head.

They stood like that, close together. Minutes passed. Sam's head bent to breathe into Inas' shoulder, feeling his warmth, smelling his heady, spicy scent where his neck emerged from his shirt. It was just like before he knew about Enos. *Stay like this. I won't cry.*

"She told you, didn't she," Inas whispered into his ear. Sam almost knew the words were coming before Inas spoke them, betrayed by puffs of breath against the side of his face.

"Yes." The word was too quiet to hear, but he could tell Inas understood him by the little tremor that went through him.

"What do you think?" The words quavered and Inas stretched back, signaling an end to their closeness, without an answer to the question.

Sam drew back to face him. He still held on to the other man's hand, like a tether connecting him to a fantasy he wanted to believe. "I...I don't—"

The door opened, and Sam heard a sigh from Enos, whether in relief they hadn't torn each other apart, or from something else, he didn't know. *Either she was very quick, or we've stood here longer than I thought.* He turned away, swiping the wetness away from one cheek with a hand.

"I'm going to bathe and change," he said. Majus Cyrysi wasn't back with his clothes yet, but he couldn't be in this room any longer. He didn't look at either of the twins as he slipped past them and out of the room. Away from Inas' question.

He was quick, filling the tub with water from a spigot that glowed blue as the water poured out—a System of the House of Grace. He tried not to think as he washed away dirt from ChinRan, Dalhni, the cell, and the alley.

He got back to the bedroom a few minutes later, with his dirty pants on again, and his green shirt loosely draped around his shoulders. It stank. Enos' new shirt was blue silk with a silver edge. A towel was wrapped around her hair and twisted up on top of her head.

Inas was sitting on the bed, playing with one of his sleeves. His gaze moved up Sam's chest, but Sam curled away from the scrutiny.

"Shut the door," Enos said. "We need to talk." Sam did so. "Can you do something to keep us from being heard?"

This was it. *They'll tell me to get out, to never talk to them again.* Sam barely kept his hand from going to his watch, tucked in his pants pocket, though his breathing was speeding up.

He reached for the Symphony, and the calm that came with the fractal music. There was so much life and communication here, in the middle of the Imperium. The door was like the entrance to the alley, but sound would travel through the walls too. This was not simply changing phrases in the melody of the air, but also in the paths of communication between this room and the rest of the world. He set his notes into the music, closing phrases away from each other, tying cadenzas in the paths of the air into perpetual repetitions. Some other score rumbled beneath what he did, too low to hear. Majus Cyrysi never said anything about doors as communication, but it was easy for him to think that way.

The room was ringed with a curtain of shimmering yellow, and Sam felt the loss of his notes, tied up in the Symphony. He couldn't avoid looking at the twins any longer.

"We're safe," he said.

Inas erupted from the bed. "I wanted to tell you, but we could not. We have never told anyone." He took a step forward, and Sam took a step back, hitting against the door. The sound was muffled. He saw the hope fade from Inas' eyes. *Well, I guess that's the answer to his question.*

"Then she was right. You are like everyone else. Are you going to turn us in? Was that kiss a goodbye?" His eyes were bright, shining in the lamplight.

"I won't," Sam said. He wanted to deny his retreat from the kiss, wanted more than anything to go to Inas. He couldn't move.

"Now you are afraid to come closer? Are you afraid I may kill you and take over your body?" Inas was pleading. "Is that what you think will happen?"

I've been through this already today. He should be over it. It should be easy to go to Inas. He lifted one hand, let it drop. "You lied to me."

It was the wrong thing to say, and only after he said it did he realize he was angry. "You lied!" This time it was a shout, and Inas stepped away, blinking.

"It was not solely her secret to tell," Inas said, flinging a hand to his sister.

"Would you prefer we were still trapped in that cell, or Enos was taken by the Sathssn?" He looked over to Enos, who had dropped to sit on her bed, silent. "She seemed to think the Sathssn knowing was worse than telling me."

Inas jerked, his hair falling around his shoulders as he swung around to stare at his sister. "The Sathssn know?"

"You didn't tell him that part?" Sam asked. *Why keep anything back now?*

Enos stared back. "I did not want to worry you any further. They are an offshoot of the Servants, we think—the Life Coalition. They likely have few resources."

"That won't stop them," Inas said.

"Stop them from what?" Sam asked. In an instant, Inas had grasped his wrist. Sam stared down, every muscle tense. *Oh God, he's going to do it.* That was silly—wasn't it?

Inas' fingers were vibrating, but he kept his eyes locked with Sam's. "Despite everything between us, you still have this reaction. Imagine the fears of the Cult of Form, whose tenets tell them one must be so pure of body that any major infection requires killing the host." Sam frowned, and Inas nodded, but his face was still hard. "They search for birth defects and kill children who have them. Anyone who has lost so much as a finger must be euthanized. They worship an *ideal* form. What do you think they would do to one who could change his shape?"

"Will they come after you?" Sam looked to where Enos sat. She lifted one shoulder in an indeterminate gesture. He looked back to Inas, still gripping his wrist. "How do we stop them?" Then he had it. "We can tell the others. They'll understand. They can help us."

"No!" Enos sprang off the bed.

Inas jerked at his wrist, grip tightening. "You said you wouldn't tell. You promised!"

Sam tried to pull out of Inas' grasp, but it was like iron. He glanced back down and gasped. Inas' fingers were fused together in a collar around his wrist. He was shackled to an Aridori.

"Get off me!" Sam pulled, fighting the grip, but Inas was reaching for his free wrist with his other hand, fingers already trembling and elongating. *Changing.* Sam clawed at the Symphony, listening for anything he could use.

"Stop it, both of you." Enos was suddenly between them. She grasped Inas' wrist as he had Sam's and stared her brother in the eyes. "I've changed recently. You have to fight it like I have been. *Fight* it, Inas!" A haze of white surrounded her hand and Sam could feel a tingle in his own arm. Misty green rings, like little scales, emerged in response up Inas' arm.

What did that mean? *Can't think. Too close.* Sam's back was to the door, both Aridori closing him in. *Too close!* He scrambled through the Symphony, his heart racing. He was sliding down, Inas' grip the only thing keeping him upright.

"Do not fight me," Enos warned. "Stop your change."

Then Sam heard the phrase he needed, buried deep in the Symphony. It echoed far away from other music in the House of Communication, a deep resonant measure. The grasp of hand to wrist, though physical, was a way of communicating. Sam threw his notes into the music, blocking it, and something stopped. Yellow mist warred with both the white and green. Inas' fingers—and they were fingers again—slackened and Sam jerked away, rubbing his arm. He slid the rest of the way down the wall, the others looming over him. Belatedly, he took his notes back, and a breath of energy flowed back into him.

Both twins were staring at him.

"What did you do?" Enos asked.

"I...I think I stopped his communication with his shifting," Sam said. He only knew that the phrase felt right.

"I do not think it works that way." Enos held her brother's hands. Inas made a gasping noise, turned away, and she drew him back to give Sam room. "It's over. We won't do anything more."

Enos was giving him room to recover. *If they were enemies, they wouldn't do that, would they?* Inas wouldn't look at him.

"It's like how I stopped the Sathssn from attacking you in the tunnel," Sam said. "Why did he—"

Enos shook her head, stopping his question. She pushed Inas back, made him sit on the bed. "I changed recently, and my brother and I were too close. The reunion between the three of us was too emotional." She combed her fingers through her brother's hair. "I should have warned you. Clear your mind. Find the Symphony. Let your emotions go, like our parents taught us."

A muscle in Inas' cheek jumped, then he closed his dark eyes. He took a long ragged breath in, held it, and let it out. His eyes opened and when they found Sam, they were filled with shame. *He looks so lost.* Sam almost went to them. Almost.

"Want to tell me what that was?" he asked Enos. Words she said in the cell came back: *We do not shift our shape except in emergencies. It has its price.*

Now neither of them looked at him. Enos' mouth worked before she answered. "It is an Aridori ghost story, or at least it may have started one." She stopped.

"Keep going," Sam said.

"It separates us from the Aridori who fought the war. We keep the changes from affecting our emotions. The others did not. Changing shape raises emotions and magnifies them."

"I was afraid. For all of us," Inas said. His voice was harsh.

"This happens every time you change?" Sam pushed up from the wall. His heart was slowing, and he hadn't even needed his watch this time.

"It is worse when we are already stressed, or feeling strong emotions," Inas said, his head still down. His hair was loose and fell around his head, hiding his face. "I did not want you to leave me."

Sam went to them this time. Enos and Inas were sitting on the bed, and Sam stood in front of them. He made his hands find theirs, squeeze them. "I couldn't leave either of you, not any more. I care too much for you." Enos smiled her half-smile. Inas only looked up, his eyes soft.

Could the others understand them as I do? What if they have to change shape, like Enos did?

"The others must be getting back," Enos said. "We need to go talk with them—tell them the rest of what happened."

"Without saying anything about *us*," Inas added.

* * *

Origon ate his mushroom stew and fried swampflower as he listened to the apprentices' accounts. The meal was good, but it lacked the flavor and texture a few wriggling maggots would provide.

So, the Servants were building an army and capturing maji? There were ways to stop maji from changing the Grand Symphony, but he would wager few others had heard of them. His research sometimes led him into odd areas. Rilan looked disgusted, perhaps thinking of their first excursion, with the revelation that the Grand Symphony could be altered mechanically. To his knowledge, neither of them had ever spilled that secret.

While Sam and Enos glossed over parts of their escape, they shared enough to reveal who was involved with this Life Coalition.

"Old Zsaana?" Origon said. "I was thinking the decrepit bigot was dead the last twelve cycles."

"No one could find him when he disappeared. Opened up the House of Healing seat on the Council," Rilan said. "Took another cycle before they confirmed me as councilor." She fell silent.

The apprentices had more names of Life Coalition members, but unfortunately none of them were Nakan. Nor did Sam remember how to get back to wherever they had been imprisoned.

Caroom harrumphed from where they were balancing a bowl of something fibrous on one large hand. "Then shall this group go with the plan these ones, hmm, discussed previously?"

"What plan?" Sam asked.

<We talked while you were changing. Our new source of information may be able to tell us more,> signed Hand Dancer.

Origon looked at Sam and Enos with a grin. "We will be going to Gloomlight prison." Inas, next to them, sat straight, wide eyed.

"Where is that?" Sam asked.

"In the center of the Nether," Origon answered. The twilight city was placed just far enough from the Imperium to create a portal. "Councilor Feldo was attacked recently, but managed to capture his assailant."

"They're being held in this prison?" His apprentice was fingering his watch.

"That is what we are believing. We are going to interrogate an Aridori."

* * *

It took a day for Origon and the others to scope out the prison, a massive stone and resin construction, dome-shaped like other Lobath dwellings. It loomed over the rest of the structures in the town save the columns, their immense radii a constant reminder. Whenever they approached the prison, Origon saw the serious-looking Lobath at the entrance, all in matching purple jumpsuits with the emblem of Gloomlight prison on the upper arm. Their head-tentacles were uniformly braided, large unblinking silvery eyes flicking right and left in the drizzling rain.

Gloomlight had been settled by the Lobath back when the Nether was first colonized, before the Aridori war, as one of the best places to farm the fungi and spices the Lobath traders lauded. Now it was where many of the Lobath in the Nether lived, enough so their party stood out. When it was first built, the Lobath had protested the decision to house the largest prison complex in the Nether. Now, keeping it was a source of pride to them.

Origon's apprentice had gone off with the twins, taking walks in the continuous rain. Sam's excuse was he wanted to grow accustomed to Gloomlight so he would not have a panic attack when they broke into the prison. Origon wondered what really happened when he and Enos were captured. There was some secret there, that none of the maji were privy to. Sam nearly had to hold Enos back when Origon told them about the Aridori. That incident, combined with Inas' reactions, ruffled his feathers, and made Origon suspect unpleasant connections where there were none. He determined to get the answer to it soon, if only to ease his mind.

They were staying near the center of the city, where a column, even thicker than the ones in the Imperium, speared up to the Nether's ceiling. It gave off a faint light that made the city center slightly brighter than the surroundings. Gloomlight stayed dusky twilight throughout the day, and pitch black at night.

<The Lobath my cousin Finger Nib knows has promised to meet me tomorrow,> Hand Dancer signed. They were sitting in the common room of the hostel where they were staying. She had a cup of some thick liquid, and had pulled down the scarf that usually covered the

lower half of her face. She carefully sipped at it with the tiny opening serving as her mouth. <Only me. No one else must be there. He has said he will have proof whether the Aridori is in this prison, or held somewhere else.>

"I'm sure it's held here," Rilan said. "Still, good to be sure."

"Have these ones heard the news?" Caroom asked, reading a paper while propped against a wall. "Hathssas will be the new, hmm, councilor for the House of Power."

"A weak choice," Origon said. "She likely has ties to the Most Traditional Servants. In the worst case, now that Hathssas is in the Council, the Life Coalition may be hearing news before we do." It was an unsettling prospect, and he felt his crest flatten.

Origon idled badly. The next day he worked with Sam a little, on listening to the Symphony, and was surprised at the progress his apprentice had made. From being unable to hear the music to having themes of Communication rumbling in the back of one's head usually took months, not ten-days.

"What is this about cutting Zsaana off from the Grand Symphony?" he asked, halfway through their lesson.

The young man shook his head, his hair swinging from side to side. It had lengthened since he had been here, yet still could not signal any emotion. Methiemum were very odd. "I don't remember much, except it was buried deep under the rest of the music. It was hard to change the notes."

"I am not surprised. The deeper the music in the main fractal of the Grand Symphony, the harder the notes are to change. They are being more fundamental to the nature of the universe." He looked his apprentice over. Thank the ancestors he had learned to control the worst of his anxiety. Origon supposed the twins had helped with that, as strange as the pair was. He had been all over Methiem, and had never seen a culture with quite their combination of speech and clothing patterns. It was similar to those who lived in the Ofir archipelago, but subtly different. The inconsistency was like a feather going the wrong direction. It constantly irritated him, and he knew it was tied in with the rest of the strangeness surrounding the twins. A question for later. Not much later, but later.

"Have you done this any other time you can remember? Against anything inanimate?" If he could track down Sam's strange talent, they might be able to put it use when infiltrating the prison. He would admit one could loosely group information transfer of any type as Communication, but there were limits to the range of houses of the maji. It was why maji could only hear the music of one house, or two, in his rare case, but no more.

Sam chewed his lip, and the Nether translated it as thoughtful, but maybe also reticent. "I...don't think I've done it to anything inanimate, though I don't see why it wouldn't work, if I can find the notes, right?" Sam looked up to him.

"Keep it in mind," Origon told him. "It may be useful."

* * *

It was several darkenings later when Hand Dancer found them in the common room of the hostel. Origon saw his many-fingered hands twitching from across the room. "You have information?"

Rilan cut off her conversation with Caroom. Sam, who was sitting with the twins at an adjacent table, leaned over. Hand Dancer plopped into a chair. The recliners had a strange dip near the back, forcing Origon to sit lower than he would have liked. They were suited for Lobath forms.

<There was a box delivered to Gloomlight prison three days ago,> Hand Dancer signed. Origon's eye twitched as the Nether translated the hand motions to the memory of speech. The Lobhl was excited, his fingers twitchy, the intricate tattoos hard to see. The remembered sound was breathless. Sometimes he thought the Nether tried too hard. <It was disguised as a food delivery, but my contact, a very reputable Lobath who works in the kitchens, said the box was taken downstairs before they could open it. It was heavy iron, chained closed.>

"That would have been the same day Feldo was attacked," Rilan said. "It's got to be the Aridori."

"They aren't taking any chances," Sam said.

"Would you, with a live Aridori?" Rilan shot back, and the young man hunched back, exchanging looks with Enos and Inas. Both twins were expressionless. Origon peered at them. His subconscious was formulating a nasty theory and was nagging him to pay attention, but it was not something he would say without proof, or at least very strong suspicion. Right now it was only a tickling of his feathers.

"The box was headed to the, hmm, lower levels of the prison, as this group guessed," Caroom said, and Hand Dancer's fingers signaled agreement.

"Then all we need is confirmation of the prison layout," Origon said. This was coming together better, and faster, than he could have anticipated. He looked to Rilan. "Unless you remember the layout well enough?"

Rilan waggled a hand, and Origon caught Hand Dancer's amused gesture. How did the Nether translate their hand motions to the Lobhl? "Not well enough for my comfort," Rilan said. "It's been cycles since I've been there, and never to the lowest levels." She looked around. "If we have to, we'll make do—"

Caroom's eyes flickered, then shone bright green. "This one will handle this concern. One more day."

"One more day," Origon sighed.

* * *

It was only midday, though one couldn't tell that from the sky, when Caroom limped into the hostel, holding a massive brown hand over their left arm. A thick, greenish substance leaked through their fingers, but they waved away Hand Dancer and Inas and crossed to the tables the group had appropriated at the hostel.

"It is, hmm, worse than it looks," they rumbled.

Rilan sniffed the air. "It smells like something's burning." She batted away Caroom's hand, revealing a crater in the Benish's arm, still smoking, green fluid slowly bubbling out. "Are those burn marks? Did you get shot, Caroom?" White and olive surrounded her hands, and she made a smoothing motion around the hard, blackened flesh. Origon knew she was terrible at healing, but she had many ways of soothing pain away.

Caroom grunted, but their eyes glittered in thanks. "This one has a map of the prison," they said. Origon sat forward. Was this the last piece?

The Benish produced a rolled up sheet of parchment with their good hand, from inside the flimsy tan vest they wore. Benish skin was plenty thick enough to resist most temperatures, as evidenced by the crater in their arm.

"This group may, hmmm, want to enact any plan these ones have sooner, rather than later." Their eyes scanned the rest. "This one might have to leave Gloomlight, hmmm, quickly, if certain things are discovered." They raised their injured arm.

Rilan closed her eyes. "If we were not already so deep in illegal action, I would ask what happened to you."

Origon grinned at Rilan. Just like old times.

CHAPTER TWENTY-FOUR

The Break-in

-The Symphony of the House of Communication is built on the theme of a wind instrument, like the currents of air those maji can manipulate. The house is not restricted to manipulation of nature, but also with how one person connects to another. Often, the councilor for the House of Communication is also the Speaker for the Council of the Maji.
Treatise on the six houses, approx. 224 B.A.W.

That night, the seven of them gathered outside the stone hulk of Gloomlight prison. On the way, Origon and Hand Dancer muted the legato strains coming from the orange lights at each intersection, casting their party into a traveling patch of darkness. Several streets later, they took their notes back and let the light shine again. It made their progress slow, and Origon felt his notes stretched thin by holding a sustained change so long, but they were also much harder to identify.

"The fence first," Rilan directed, pointing to the massive vertical resin planks barring their way. "See the brown aura? From the House of Potential. There could be a System to shock you, or a complex piece composed to drain your stamina. We should have brought Inas' Sureriaj friend to help—what was his name? Rey? Who's his mentor, anyway?"

"Majus Kheena, I believe," Origon said, scanning the roof. No figures watching them yet, but it would only be a matter of time. Rilan stared at him as if it was a surprise for him to remember another majus' name. "Though Kheena is Sathssn," he continued. "Alerting him to our operation might not be advisable."

Rilan tsked. "Just because he's Sathssn, that doesn't mean he's Life Coalition. I think Kheena's from the Southern Coalition. Doesn't even follow the Cult of Form, if I remember. Really, Ori."

Origon let his crest flatten in chagrin. "Of course. Merely taking precautions." There was too much developing all at once, for his taste. He turned to his apprentice. They should focus on getting into the prison rather than idle speculation.

"Now, Sam, as we practiced," he said. Creating the type of camouflage they wanted was not a simple matter.

He moved through the Symphony, picking out phrases defining the air around them. It was for once not raining, though he heard the far off strains that told of another storm coming, in another darkening. They would need to work quickly.

He heard other changes as Sam began his section of the composition. Origon placed his notes in the refrain, adding solidity to the phrase, then switched to the Symphony of Power, doling out a few more precious notes to slow the andante temperature to a legato. Uncontrolled changes to the air tended to heat the surrounding, unless a majus used the House of Power to negate the effect. Above their group a dome shimmered into view, reflecting the dark of the cobblestones up and around them. Enos lit a small lantern, half covered to hide the light.

Hearing a set of intricate chords, Origon squinted at Sam. The young man was doing something different, deeper in the music, and he couldn't quite follow it, but the other half of the dome was tighter-woven than his, the notes all in time. Origon felt his crest flatten and scowled. He couldn't help it if his potential had been damaged by what the space capsule took from him. It would take many more cycles to get back to his old potential. For now he would have to content with a fledgling majus showing him up.

Rilan and Enos were moving among them as he and Sam worked, touching each one in a flare of white. Enos kept to the apprentices, her lantern illuminating their faces, Rilan to the maji. When she touched him, he felt his boots settle differently around his feet. He would make less sound as he moved.

Caroom and Inas were already working on the fence, half-spheres of green spitting sparks as they dug into the brown aura. It would indeed have been easier with one from the House of Potential. However, the light show was contained under the dome he and Sam had created.

"It is not yet shorted out," Caroom rumbled. They forced a hand forward again, and the brown flickered, then grew back.

<The System is feeding from the rest of the fence, regenerating itself.> Hand Dancer kept her finger movements small—the equivalent of whispering, the way the Nether picked up her intent. <I believe I

may interfere with the source of the power.> She waggled her fingers in a circle, describing a patch on the fence for all of them to pass through. What she did was intricate, technical, and very fast, as with the geometry she had created before. Origon would have liked a few moments to understand. <Try it now,> she signed.

This time when Caroom and Inas pushed forward, the aura dimmed, then died within the outline Hand Dancer had described.

"That will do," Caroom said, and wove their fingers between the thick planks, made of some resin the Lobath produced. When they pulled, green and tan grew from their fingers, pushing the material back. Something creaked in Caroom's back, and they emitted a deep grunt. The resin flowed, for just a moment, resetting in a passage through the fence.

"Inside, but be careful of the plants," Rilan said, and ducked through the hole in the fence. When Origon came through after her, he saw the field of low growth, shadows in the dark. Sam pressed in behind him, then the others. He could feel his apprentice shivering. Now was not the time for a panic attack. He hoped the young man could hold it off.

Inas took a step forward, but Rilan threw a hand out to stop him. "The bulbs on top are filled with spores. They will explode if you touch them. The spores fluoresce and will give us away, even with Ori's bubble." Origon looked up to make sure the opaque reflecting bubble was still refracting the ground rather than their figures. It had traveled with them, his notes dragging the melody along, but the diversion would not stand up to heavy scrutiny.

<I may be able to dull the connections between the plants and their spores,> Hand Dancer signed, but Rilan shook her head and the Lobhl's fingers stilled.

"Enos and I will have to do this. The spores are also toxic. Even if they didn't give us away, they could put us to sleep if enough of them touched our skin." She suited actions to words, hands out in front, white and olive green spreading in a wave before her, the plants bending out of the way. She whispered to Enos, gesturing, but her apprentice shook her head, as if unclear. Then, with a start, she leaned in to what Rilan was doing, and in a moment, a wave of white flowed from her, too.

Origon followed them, stepping carefully through the plants, now hanging limp and deflated in the light from Enos' lantern. He heard rustling behind him, as the others came after.

The wall of the prison loomed in front of them, stones fitted together with almost no space between. Origon felt the camouflaging bubble around them press into the surface. He adjusted the placement of his notes, melding the low rhythm of the air to the flat slope of the wall. He heard an echo of what he did. Sam was next to him, watch in hand, his eyes closed. "Steady, boy," he said.

Sam nodded. "I'm okay for now. The Symphony helps." He was breathing too fast, and Origon had to hope he could stave off the panic. They did not have time for error.

Caroom and Inas were at the wall, the Benish already pulling a block out, the green of the House of Strength imbuing their arms with great vigor. The small amount of mortar between blocks, permeated with green and tan, crumbled, and Inas, spirals of green running from his fingers, funneled the extra material away.

The block came away, and Caroom started on the next one, but a surge of orange and brown flashed from deep in the wall and Caroom shook, falling backward. Origon and Rilan tried to slow the wide Benish's descent. He had forgotten how solid the species was.

"It drained his strength," Inas said, his voice higher than normal. "I can try again, but I do not know if—" He trailed off as Hand Dancer pushed forward.

<It is another System, deep in the wall.> Her dexterous fingers, sheathed in orange and gray, crawled into the hole in the wall, like two spiders seeking shelter. Her body shuddered as she encountered something, shuddered again, then Hand Dancer slumped back, still.

Origon looked to Rilan, to Sam, to Enos. "Is she—?"

Hand Dancer spasmed again, then straightened. In any other species, Origon would have expected a scream or even a grunt of pain, of acknowledgement. Eerily silent, Hand Dancer raised her hands. They shook, and the Nether gave him no translation. White and olive emerged from the backs of Rilan's hands like drops of sweat.

Hand Dancer shook again, and her fingers moved, this time with purpose. <I am recovered.> The ghostly echoes chimed in Origon's head and he released a breath he had not been aware of holding.

<The System is complicated and intricate. It protects itself. I do not think I will be able to dismantle it in time.>

"Let me see." Origon pressed in, between Caroom, pushing themself up from the ground, and Hand Dancer, dazed. He peered into the pitch black hole, a rectangle wider than his shoulders. If they could get past this barrier, they could break through to the prison. There couldn't be any more traps. It had taken a concerted effort by seven maji to get this far. He listened, his crest brushing the stones as it flexed up and down. The music was faint, sotto voce. It was another disguising mechanism, to make the System harder to defeat. He reached for the music, trying to decode it. Parts were likely of the House of Potential, cementing the music into the System by making the measures permanent and unfading.

The rest of it—Origon felt his crest rise, up and out. This was *intricate*. There were glissandos, trills, and other extraneous notes that added inflection and personality to the music. It was almost too fast to hear. He could barely catch one phrase before another overrode it, the music flashing by. Hand Dancer must have tried to place one of her notes somewhere and slow down the tempo. Only because he was expecting a trap, did he hear the repeating atonal motif, interweaving through the larger melody, the one that would snatch such placed notes away and make them part of the barrier. He could not bear to lose any more of his notes. Hand Dancer was right. This would take *days* to unravel. Maybe working together, they could—

"Majus Cyrysi." Sam's whisper was intense. "There are guards talking above us. I think they may have seen the bubble of air, or maybe—" A pause. "Majus Hand Dancer's attempt alerted them? It's hard to make out words in the Symphony."

Dear ancestors, he could hear *words* in the music?

"They sent someone down!" Sam's voice was too loud.

"We have to go," Rilan hissed.

<This will be our only chance,> Hand Dancer signed. <If they see our actions here, they will certainly heighten their security.>

"Can we stop them? Set up a barrier?" This was from Inas.

"To do what? Attack the, hmm, Lobath guard?" Caroom had finally gotten upright again. "This one will not condone such violence."

"There has to be another way in," Enos said. Sam, next to her craned his neck, watching the shaking outline of the bubble. Origon could see him trembling, and his knuckles were white around the watch. His apprentice looked to Enos, then to Inas. His eyes were wide, mouth opened as if he wanted to speak. What was between them? It must be something that could help, but what could apprentices do that maji could not? The same feeling that had been pulling his feathers for days crept back.

Origon's mind whirled. Was his guess about the twins correct? It was impossible.

"No other doors but the front entrance." Rilan said, interrupting Origon's thoughts. "We checked the entire complex."

"The roof?" Origon offered, halfway in an attempt to stifle his traitorous thoughts.

Rilan shook her head.

"We have to get in!" Sam's voice rose, ringing in the night's stillness. "Are we just going to wait until the Drains destroy everything?"

"Calm down." Rilan crossed to him, putting her hands on the young man's shoulder. "You'll give us away. Unless you know of a way to impersonate a councilmember, there's no way in. We have to take our losses. We'll find something else."

If Origon hadn't been watching, he wouldn't have caught the twins stiffening in unison. Impersonate a councilmember. Aridori could do that.

He caught Sam's eyes and held them. "Can they get us in, Sam?"

Sam's face was white in the low light from Enos' lantern. Then, very slowly, his chin dropped in a nod. It was as much an answer as a shout.

Inas' mouth was open, his eyes wide. "No, Sam," he said. "Not this way."

"How could they get us in?" Rilan asked. Origon recognized the focus on her face, the little pucker of skin between her eyebrows. Then her face went blank, and she waved two fingers in front of her eyes once, twice. "Oh. Oh Brahm preserve us."

CHAPTER TWENTY-FIVE

Trust is a Fleeting Thing

-The House of Strength is both defensive and nourishing. While many study the foundational aspects such as masonry, personal defense, and transfer of constitution, no few turn their paths toward the herbaceous aspects.

Part of "A Description of the House of Strength," 421 A.A.W., author unknown

"These ones are Aridori?" The question, which must have come from Caroom, gouged at Sam. He was curled inward, sucking his notes back. His half of the dome collapsed, leaving them partially visible if anyone was watching. *I hope my friends aren't looking, aren't seeing how I failed to keep their secret.*

Majus Cyrysi was altering his dome. Sam could hear where the majus forced his notes to bend the melody farther, thickening and lowering the tempo until the air was barely moving. He could tell the music was bending toward the twins, and he could help, or hinder. It was in his power. *Has Enos or Inas fought back?* His heart beat against his chest, and the darkened sky threatened to cave in on him. *Why can't I do anything? Why am I useless?* If he moved, he would drown. He forced his eyes up. At the very least he could watch what he had unleashed. He had almost told their secret with no prompting, but then his mentor had guessed. Would he have known if Sam hadn't frozen?

Enos slowed as Majus Cyrysi's yellow dome solidified around her, leaving them all visible, and she strained against air like thick mud. Inas was close by, green of the House of Strength running down his arms and legs. None of the maji approached. *It's my fault. It's all my fault.*

Majus Ayama cornered Inas, holding her arms out to either side, not touching him, but threatening. There was a white and olive haze around her, and an emerald green wall rose from Inas, resisting her, matching each pulse from the Symphony of Healing.

"Maji, assistance please," Majus Cyrysi said. "We must prepare a containment, and we have only seconds." His words were rough, his crest flared up and out. Enos had spheres of white around her joints, somehow counteracting the compressed air holding her. The notes Majus Cyrysi had placed in the Symphony of the air crumbled where they touched her.

Get free, Sam thought at her. He cleared his throat, found his voice. "Run! Don't let them catch you!" It came out as a whisper.

<We must have all the houses present for a full containment,> Majus Hand Dancer signed. They were ignoring him.

"Then it will be a partial containment," Majus Cyrysi snapped.

Majus Hand Dancer stepped toward Majus Caroom, her hands flickering fast and vague, the words oddly muffled. One of her eyes had a film of orange and gray over it and she pointed to a spot near the wall.

In response, Majus Caroom took one step forward, their massive gnarled foot striking the ground, and a wash of emerald and tan flowed out. Their change bolstered his mentor, and the Symphony of Communication surged. Enos slumped in response, while Majus Ayama herded Inas toward his sister. Sam could hear boots, far above them, pounding along the roof.

Sam struggled to get to his feet, pushing against the sky pressing down, the terror welling up from within. He had no idea how fast his heart was pounding. He couldn't feel his fingers any more. *I have to get them to see reason. It will be better for everyone, now they know.* If they don't kill each other first. He couldn't move.

Majus Cyrysi joined hands with Majus Ayama and their colors intertwined. The other two maji stepped forward and added their own. Enos and Inas struggled against them, but they were forced back against the prison wall. *They're going to push them into the field that shocked Majus Hand Dancer.*

"Stop." His voice was weak, and he struggled up. *Stand, damn you!* "Don't hurt them!"

Majus Ayama spun to him, her eyes blazing in the reflected light from Enos' lantern, lying sideways on the ground. "How could you hide that *my apprentice* is an Aridori?"

If he couldn't pin his anxiety down in this moment, then he never would. He had to keep them from hurting Enos and Inas. He clutched his watch. *I'm better than this.*

"We don't have time to fight," he said. "Majus Cyrysi is right—they can get us in to see the prisoner." If Enos and Inas were useful, the maji wouldn't hurt them.

"Out of the question," Majus Ayama hissed. "You expect me to trust an Aridori? A live Aridori—my own apprentice! Vish's knees, I'm dense. I should have seen this." Her words were fast.

"Please," Sam said. His knees were weak. Seconds were ticking off in his head. *How long until the guards get here?* "They won't do anything. They can help us. They're not like the other Aridori, in the stories."

"How would this one, hmm, know?" Majus Caroom's eyes were flickering fast, more emotional than Sam had seen them before.

"They told me," Sam said. "Enos rescued me when we were captured. She could have left me there." Enos and Inas were standing, defeated, not attempting to escape. *Stay there, stay helpful.*

Majus Ayama snorted, loudly. "It is the most foolish thing to trust an Aridori. It is their nature to betray. Everyone knows that."

"How do you know?" Sam asked her. He was almost shouting. If the guards hadn't been alerted before, they would be now. A warmth rose in him, washing the panic away with its strength. Enos' words in the alley came back to him. "Have you met any before? Is it like how people say Lobath are stupid, or Kirians are arrogant, or Sathssn are fundamentalists?"

Majus Ayama narrowed her eyes, turned to the twins. "Give me one reason not to leave you to the guards," she told them.

Sam ached to go to them, force his way through that ring of color, but the majus had already ignored his words. The twins had to speak for themselves. Enos had Inas by the hand, both of them small against the four full maji. She stared at him, and closed his eyes against the pain, the betrayal he saw in her eyes.

"We can help you, as *he* says," she spat. "None of you know anything about the Aridori. We are not like the stories. We may be the last, in any case."

"Save for the prisoner we're trying to see," Majus Ayama said.

Inas raised his head. His didn't even look at Sam. "We want to know where this Aridori comes from too. The rest of our family was destroyed in the Drain."

"They were targeted as much as Dalhni, and Earth," Sam said.

<And my homeworld,> added Hand Dancer.

"As was the, hmm, Methiemum space program," Caroom said.

Hand Dancer suddenly let her change fade, the orange disintegrating. She stepped backwards. <These two can help us, and we have leverage against them. We must decide now.> Her hands commanded attention. <Remember, the Lobhl have had to argue for every benefit and accommodation to be heard by the Great Assembly. We are familiar with prejudice.>

Majus Ayama actually growled, and Sam took a step back involuntarily. Then her white and olive faded, followed by Majus Cyrysi's yellow and Majus Caroom's green. "We will figure this out when guards are not coming for us, or we'll all be in the same prison cell. The Aridori in front, where we can keep an eye on them. Sam, you're behind them." She waved them forward. "Quick! Now!"

Sam pulled his feet forward, stumbling behind Enos and Inas, along the path of wilted plants and through the fence. He could feel the disapproval of the maji, as bright as the searchlights rounding the side of the prison.

* * *

They kept to the darkened streets, Rilan herding the Aridori in front, Caroom next to her. Ori kept up a whispered stream of strategy for their next attempt, and Rilan nodded along. If they were to follow this crazy plan they would need to act quickly, before the next day, capitalizing on the chaos they had created, and giving the Aridori as little chance as possible to escape.

Ori's apprentice was huddled as near the twins as Rilan would let him. It must be his naiveté that had let the two get so close to him. How long had he known?

Hand Dancer followed, keeping an eye on the Aridori—no, Enos and Inas, they had names—from the rear. Rilan made her jaw unclench, forced herself to stop grinding her teeth. "Let's get this over with."

The rain had started again, a steady drizzle. They stopped under an overhang built out from a building constructed from a section of giant mushroom. The shelters were dispersed around the town, giving relief from the constant rain.

Sam was the first to speak. He hunched inward and the little majus-light overhead cast shadows lengthening his bent shoulders. "They can get us in. They just have to look like councilors, coming to check on the break-in. We can walk in the front entrance."

<It is a workable plan,> Hand Dancer said.

Caroom crossed their arms, leaning against the wall. Their fluores-cent eyes flickered at their apprentice, who stood quietly next to his sister, both staring back with little expression. It was the same stone wall Rilan ran into when she pressed too hard into Enos' past. That made a lot more sense now.

"What do, hmmm, these two have to say of it? Will they go along with this plan?"

Inas clasped his hands together, knuckles whitening. "It seems we have little choice."

"We will not force you," Ori said. He was pacing the edge of the overhang, only three strides across, his crest flaring and collapsing. Then he stopped to peer at the twins, like they were a particularly interesting species of grub. "Amazing, really. I would be quite interested to be seeing the transformation process."

"We are not your toys," Enos told him, her voice acid. "If we wished to be imprisoned and analyzed, we would have told you our species *voluntarily*." She directed the last word like a spear at Ori, but Sam was the one to duck his head, face crumpling.

<Yet you are able to do it,> Hand Dancer signed. <This would be a good step to proving you mean to help us.>

"Which we would not normally need to," Inas replied.

<Oh, I am not condoning this,> Hand Dancer signed. <My species has had to fight for every right the others come by naturally. It is why you see so few of us. Just to have others ask our gender rather than assuming is a major battle for us.>

Rilan stared at the Lobhl. She didn't know it was such a challenge for them. She looked back to Enos—her apprentice, after all. The young woman had given no indication but that she wanted to excel at being a majus. It was just what Rilan had done as an apprentice.

Enos drew in a deep breath and sighed it out. Her breath misted into the rain. "If we were to do this for you, we would need to be familiar with who we were to impersonate."

"Councilor Feldo, for that one was the one to, hmm, capture the prisoner," Caroom said.

"I am familiar enough with him to impersonate him, I think," Inas said, and his sister stared at him.

"So quickly?" she asked.

He shrugged. "I would rather do that than stand in the wet being stared at."

Enos raised her hands, palms wide. "Fine. We might as well. This is surreal as it is." She shook her head. "I would rather be back with my family—" She cut off, abruptly, blinking.

Never trust what an Aridori says or does. The phrase ran through Rilan's head before she could stop it. Did she really believe Enos' grief was a farce? No. She knew her apprentice that well, didn't she?

"Hathssas," Rilan said. Sam and Ori looked confused for a moment. "The new councilor for the House of Power. She's not well known. Easier to impersonate."

Enos surprised her by nodding along. "I am familiar with Sathssn, if the face and mannerisms do not need to be exact."

"I do not think the guards would be able to tell," Ori said. "She is very new."

The twins turned to the wall of the shelter, but Rilan could see their skin begin to crawl and change. Rilan thought about insisting they face them, but once the fleshy sounds of skin rubbing on skin and joints popping started, Rilan faced away, to leave them with some dignity. Ori was fixated, of course, but the others gave them privacy. Fortunately their change was a slow process. If the Aridori took time to become another person, then they could be caught in the process and found out. It was little comfort.

* * *

Soon after, they found the entrance to Gloomlight prison a kicked ant's nest. Lobath guards and police officers from the city were describing complicated arcs of their investigation with lanterns. It was too early for the city to be up, but past midnight.

Rilan trailed behind Councilors Feldo and Hathssas—she automatically thought of the twins that way, so perfect was the approximation. Feldo especially, had every hair and wrinkle in the correct place. *Eerie.* Hathssas, as Enos had imagined her, was a dark green Sathssn woman, from what Rilan could see under the cowl covering her head. The two even copied the clothes of the councilors from black cloak, gloves, and boots, to Feldo's brown suit and collection of artifacts. The range of the Aridori ability was impressive and troubling, offset only by its speed. *How many more are hiding among us?* The twins said they were the last, yet that was already a lie, because of the one imprisoned.

Rilan pinched the bridge of her nose, trying to relieve the pressure in her head. *Shiv's teeth and tongue!* Her hands clenched into white-knuckled balls, fingers tingling as her nails bit into her palms. The collected guards let them through automatically, until they came to a lone officer, a badge of rank on the shoulder of her jumpsuit. The Lobath frowned at them.

"We are here to investigate the disturbance of a few lightenings past," Enos hissed in a fair approximation of a Sathssn accent. Hopefully the Nether's translation would blur any incongruities.

"We wish to make certain the *special* prisoner is unharmed," Inas said, and the familiar deep timbre of Councilor Feldo's voice made Rilan shiver. It wasn't the words the councilor would have said, but the inflection was correct, and evidently enough for the officer.

"Yes, Councilor," she said.

"Councilors," Enos corrected.

Rilan barely kept in a manic giggle. *Brahm, they're going to bury us so deep no one will ever know what happened to us.*

The officer stood straighter, the tips of her head-tentacles twitching. "My apologies. Councilors." Her large silver eyes flicked over the group. "How many are there?"

"Just us two." Feldo—Inas—Rilan had to keep that forefront in her mind—gestured to him and Hathssas. "We cannot send the entire Council for every emergency, especially at such short notice. The others are helping in this investigation."

"I—yes. One moment, please." The officer frantically gestured with long fingers to another guard. "We were not aware you would visit so soon."

Rilan traded glances with Ori. So the councilors might be on their way. If she knew the real Feldo, they would be. Their group would need to be in and out quickly, then disappear.

The other guard brought a sign-in sheet, making quick notes as he scanned their party. Rilan looked back to others. If they had full descriptions of their group, they could be tracked. She glanced around, looking for a solution, and saw Hand Dancer had both hands up, fingers flying through a complicated knot of orange. Zie took a moment, one hand away from the construction, to make a placating gesture toward her. Was zie camouflaging them somehow? Could the House of Power do that? It must be something with the connections in their group and the way people recognized them. She would have to ask Ori later.

"—only four at maximum," the officer was saying. She had missed a few words, but the twins were looking between each other, and Enos turned back, her cat's eyes passing over Rilan with a question.

If they would only let four of them in, Rilan would be torn apart by elephants before missing out. She swiveled two fingers between her and Ori. Enos faced forward.

"Councilor Feldo and I, we will take two of our assistants." She marked Rilan and Ori with a black-gloved hand.

Rilan spun to the others, whispering. "Get away from here before they make too many guesses. We'll meet back at the same overhang." Caroom's eyes flickered in agreement. She looked to Sam, huddled in the back. He was shaking, breathing hard, and he was holding his watch against an ear. He looked pale. "Take care of him." No matter how much he had been drawn in by the twins, revealing their secret, even accidentally, must be very hard for him.

Hand Dancer made a motion of agreement, and zie guided Sam away. Caroom stumped after them.

The guard who had taken their descriptions, hopefully muddled by Hand Dancer, gestured them forward. His head-tentacles were tied in a neat knot. They followed him into the depths of the prison, down stone corridors with flickering torches. They did not use Systems where they did not have to in the prison.

"The System Sam encountered would have been useful here," Ori whispered on the way.

Rilan nodded. "I believe Zsaana had something to do with those plans being 'lost.' When I was first accepted to the Council, they spoke vaguely of the possibility, but I got the impression the development was tied up in technical difficulties."

Ori snorted. "I am wondering how long this Life Coalition has been working behind the scenes."

Soon they hit the bottom of the Nether, the floor the same rough crystal clarity of the walls. Looking through the vast distances of the crystal always made her uneasy, and she focused ahead.

Two more guards were stationed at a solid door in a solid wall. Their guide held a low conversation, gesturing back toward them. One attendant opened the door with a hiss, and Rilan saw Ori's eyebrows go up, his crest perk. There was a faint yellow haze visible, which must indicate a seal on the door.

Inside the cell, Rilan nearly bumped into Ori. She peered around his shoulder as the door closed behind them.

In the exact center of the room was a small box, no longer on a side than her forearm. It was solid steel with no symbols or decorations save one small hole in the center of the top. There was a film of glowing yellow and white surrounding it.

"A filter," Ori whispered to her and she nodded.

"It won't let anything organic through."

Enos reached a shaking gloved hand toward the box. She hesitated a mere breath above the metal surface, then pushed a finger down to touch it. Immediately, she snatched it back with a moan, and swayed. Inas moved close to her.

"There is someone in there," she said, her cat's eyes locked on her brother's.

CHAPTER TWENTY-SIX

The Prisoner

-Those from the House of Healing are thought of as healers, but in truth, they are better described as biologists. Only rarely is one of the maji able to speed the healing process, and only at a great cost. More often those of the House of Healing occupy the forefront in positions of learning and science, though I have seen as many become great fighters or politicians.

From "A Discussion on the House of Healing" by Ribothari Tan, Knower

Enos pulled her finger back as if it had been burned. One of her species was in that box, though not a close relation. The subtle link pulsed in her head—the same one that bound twin instances at close range, and evident when many of her family came together. It was normally only felt when both halves of an instance were together. This one Aridori exuded more of that link than the rest of her family combined. Who was it?

Inas caught her arm, offering assistance in response to her thoughts. She shook him off, gently. She could feel Majus Ayama's eyes on her without turning her head. For cycles, her family remained hidden in plain sight, only to be exposed by Sam's innocence and his mentor's observation. She clenched pointed teeth. Even the thought of him sent spikes of rage through her, though that was the effects of her changing, ramping up emotion and every feeling. She hated that too.

If she was rational, if she had not had to change twice in five days, she knew she would have expected their secret to come out, after his first reaction, and inability to keep his mouth shut. She knew he cared, and she still cared for him, as did Inas, no matter what came between them. Right now she wanted to tear him apart. Only the threat of the maji revealing them had kept her from running.

Their parents warned them, as all children of the Aridori were warned. Once free, knowledge of their species could never be contained. They each had to be vigilant for themselves and each other.

Their family had kept their nature secret for hundreds of cycles, until she went and told Sam. Stupid. She was mad at herself too, if she was being honest.

Enos looked to her brother. The Drain, their capture, both of them revealed as maji—everything at once was too much. Sometimes it threatened to break all the bounds inside her, gush out over all the homeworlds. She tightened one hand into a fist.

"There is someone in there," she told Inas, willing her eyes to give him the rest of the information. He felt enough, through their connection. He was never as composed as he appeared. It was one reason Sam was so good for him, for them.

Though he appeared as Councilor Feldo, he was still the same underneath. Curse this Sathssn skin she wore—it was like a thick wool cloak, blotting out everything she was used to, living as a Methiemum. The Sathssn panted more than sweated, and her breath felt short. Yet to change again would give them away, raise her emotions more, and take too long, all at once.

"Is it anoth—is it an Aridori?" Majus Cyrysi asked her. Majus Ayama threw the Kirian a dirty look. Enos wanted to do the same for his sloppiness. Was everyone so careless? Did everyone not have some secret they wished guarded? Who knew who was listening to them?

Carefully, she nodded once, making sure both maji saw.

"Can you talk to it?" Majus Ayama asked. Emotions ran across her face, too fast to catch them all. There was distance between them, a barrier made of centuries of hatred and bigotry, yet Enos still wanted to be apprentice to the woman. Could time heal this rift? Or were Inas and she headed to another cell in this prison?

"I believe I can," Enos said.

The majus gestured awkwardly to the small box. "How is it surviving in there? Is it curled up? Is it in its natural shape?"

Enos was uncertain. She and Inas never changed unless absolutely necessary. She also did not want to give any sign she or Inas were unfamiliar with this Aridori. She was useful for now, as an expert.

"I will attempt to find out," she said, and steeled herself to touch the box. She subtly changed the surface of her hand—it would not affect her emotions much more—by removing the fingertips of the black glove and transitioning back to flesh, even if green and scaled. It should make no difference, but psychologically, the contact would be fuller, and she needed the reassurance. She was used to wearing clothes, not making them of her own substance, but there had been no time to search for a suitable black cloak and accompanying accessories. She reached out and down.

Free us—

The words caught her by surprise and she jerked back, air escaping her alien throat in a hiss. It—they—must be pressed against the inside surface of the box to transmit so clearly. Even with Inas there were never transmitted words, just images and feelings. With all the family gathered, there were only vague sensations of intention. She eyed the maji, and gave a quick shake of her head to Inas so he wouldn't come nearer. She pressed her entire Sathssn palm to the metal.

Free us to slash, to tear, to bite and squeeze and pull and rip and taste and—

Enos gasped before she could help herself. A smell of dark, rich blood welled up in her mind. Inas was at her side, offering comfort.

"What is it?" he whispered.

She eyed the maji. Too close for truth, for what they might overhear. "There is more than one in there," she said.

Inas' eyebrows lifted, coarse black and white hairs in his disguise. He understood. Both instances were in there, together, *mixed.* A muscle in his jaw jumped. "Shall I try?" Even his voice was different.

Enos shook her head and shoved him away. Keep him in shadow, out of the maji's notice.

One more time, she pressed a hand to the cold metal, feeling the rush of insane words and images rush over her. Curtains of blood. Striking for hot flesh, tearing, using knowledge of weak spots. The non-Aridori, they were frail, unmalleable. There was a need to make them malleable, maul-able.

Enos cleared her throat.

"Can you hear me?" she said out loud, aiming at the little hole, covered by an aura of yellow and white. She could hear some of the phrases in the House of Healing. The regimented rhythms were like bars, keeping the unwanted songs from coming through.

—to drink sweet and thrive in the sun and the rain and the blood with the change and...

The rambling broke off.

Another part of me? Come back at last? Where are more?

"I said, can you hear me?" Enos repeated out loud. *Please speak,* she begged mentally. *Don't just be a voice in my head.*

The box vibrated, grew warmer, and Enos drew back. Something was forming, from a constant state of flux. Bile rose from her Sathssn gullet. The prisoner was completely without a shape.

Thoughts swirled together without separation—more than one consciousness, thinking at once. She concentrated. There was no telling how many instances were fused together. She coughed, hiding a gag. This was all her family rejected.

Air whistled through the little hole, and Majus Cyrysi leaned forward, his crest rising, maybe listening to something in the System. Enos took her hand back hastily.

The prisoner spoke, an oddly melodious voice. "It has been long cycles since we voiced our thoughts. Could voice our thoughts. Was free to have voice." The speech grew hoarse. "Voices. Longer cycles since speaking to one of our kind, separate from us." The timber was rusty chains now, dragged along rock, blood dripping from walls.

Four sets of boots, shuffled back.

"Why did you attack Councilor Feldo?" Majus Ayama asked. Her voice wavered, just slightly.

There was a pause, long enough that Enos almost spoke again. Then the dead voice issued from the little hole.

"We would see who questions us." It grated against her ears.

"No," said the majus. "Answer." Her voice was steady now.

There was another silence.

"Let us see you, smell the air, taste for us the fear you drip and sweat."

Enos put her hand against the box again. That was too close to the insane thoughts she had heard before.

Drip and sweat and bleed the blood that fills the rips and tears and scars and—

"Talk to us," Enos commanded, breaking into the thing's mindless gibbering—she couldn't think of it as an Aridori, or even multiple Aridori, not like her family.

"We must see to whom we talk," the grating voice insisted, and an echo drifted through the strange link to Enos. *To whom we talk to shred and gaze upon the death and loss and—*

"We're getting nowhere," Majus Ayama said, sharp and low. Enos looked up, at the mental prodding from Inas. It was weak, compared to intense insanity from the box. Her mentor was close to losing her temper. Majus Ayama couldn't hear what it thought, how dangerous it was.

Her mentor flicked a finger at Majus Cyrysi. "The risk is worth it."

Enos realized too late what she was doing. "Don't—" she began, but it was too late. Majus Cyrysi leaned forward and waggled long fingers at the yellow glow over the hole in the top of the box. Majus Ayama closed a fist. The melody of Healing describing the bars shredded into dissonance, and both colors vanished. The thing's litany soared as the filter keeping it from the rest of the Nether was erased.

The smell of fear and sweat is close! It comes we come to see to treat and rend extend and form oh form of constant sight and smell—

Enos pulled away from the box, shaking her head, driving the voice away. Inas was tense beside her, taller than usual, covered in false hair, wearing glasses he didn't need. He reached for the Symphony of Strength. She could almost hear the music when he did, as he could almost hear her changes to the Symphony of Healing. Could he feel the words the thing in the box thought?

Out of the opening a pseudopod extended, probing like a blind worm. The hole was only the width of two of her fingers, but once through, the questing stalk thickened, as if something inflated it from the other side. It was purple and yellow and blue like a deep bruise, the surface mottled and pitted.

Majus Ayama drew in a breath as the end of the mass changed shape and color, forming a single eyeball, the size of Enos' head. It looked them over one by one, unblinking. Even Inas took a step back. It changed fast, from a constant state of flux. The emotional turmoil that would rise from that was more than she wanted to think about. Cold rose, deep in her belly, and she reached back for Inas' hand, right where she knew it would be. Enos was suddenly positive this creature had been around since the war, maybe had been one of those—several of those—who had killed innocents.

A gash opened across the center of the eye, splitting the pupil in two. Each half contracted, still seeing. Strands of flesh linked the sides, stretching as it moved.

"We speak," it said, and Enos could almost hear the continuation of the sentence contained in the thing's thoughts. *We speak to treat to ply and learn and slide—*

"Why did you attack? Do you—do you work for someone?" Majus Ayama asked, and this time the waver in her voice was very clear.

"We do the work of ones of black and cloaks that set the path to ripe blood's drip and color mighty color pooling above to sing the song of stars and planes and—"

"Shut up!" Majus Ayama shouted, and the thing ceased its babble. The large bisected eye, like an overripe melon, hung suspended toward her, the mouth in the middle gaping open in silent laughter. Her face was gray, as pale as Enos knew she must be. Majus Cyrysi looked surprised and disgusted, one hand stroking his thin feathery moustache repeatedly. His feathery crest was disarrayed. Enos clutched at Inas, his steady warmth a bastion. They couldn't think this insanity was anything like her.

"Majus," she began.

"You shut up too," the majus snapped. "I only want to hear answers from the Aridori here, or by Brahm's sacred hands, I'll—" She trailed off, shaking her head.

"We are not anything like that, that abomination," Inas growled. His voice was taut as a wound string. Deeper than normal. His lip curled, covered in a bristly moustache.

"I'll be the judge of that," the majus said, though Enos saw Majus Cyrysi cock his head in thought.

"Why have you attacked the maji?" Majus Ayama tried again. The thing in the box eagerly strained forward as she spoke, talking over her last word.

"The souls of songs that sing of life and death and color and fear to take and wind and coil inside to hear the pain and blood the pounding voids that still and kill and die and—"

"Enough!" The majus shook, then clasped her hands, fingers knotted, as disarrayed as Enos had ever seen her.

Majus Cyrysi put a gentle hand on Majus Ayama's shoulder. "It spoke of black cloaks. It must have been in contact with Nakan and the Life Coalition."

Enos waited for their condemnation. Surely they couldn't think she was anything like this? She looked to her brother, who sneered at the eyeball with its gash of a mouth. His expression, on a different face. She should be angry, but she only felt cold, and afraid. The dank space stank of fear and, somehow, blood and rot. The thing in the box had no blood—no rot. Where was the smell coming from? Was it projecting the smell into her mind?

Majus Cyrysi was obviously contemplating something. "Is it to be talking of the Drains?" Majus Ayama's brow lifted slightly, her eyes focusing.

"Voids, yes. Could this thing be connected to them too?"

"Connect the pain and drain and stars and song and all the dark extends unseen to pass the rift and block and patch of pain on wounds of time and place—"

Majus Ayama shot the thing a look. "Shut it." It subsided into a barely audible chant of gibberish. "It's clearly insane, just like the stories of the old Aridori." She glanced at Enos, who swallowed a lump in her throat. That was the look she expected. She couldn't even defend herself looking as she did. She flexed her Sathssn hand, watching the little scales move against each other. She was stupid to have agreed to do this.

"Surely we can be getting more information?"

Majus Ayama shook her head. "The only thing it's told us is that there are Aridori still in the world, and they are just as deadly as we thought."

"I will admit I was not thinking that was the case a ten-day ago," Majus Cyrysi said, his crest fluttering as he watched the pseudopod.

Enos clutched her brother's arm. They would leave here, and the maji would lock them up. There was no defense that could save them. *I cannot think of anything. Inas, help us.* He was her rock, her protector, her other half.

She wanted to save the mess of Aridori captured in that box as much as she wanted to run from them. They might represent the rest of her species, but they were also insane—hardly even sentient. They must have lost their minds while forced to stay in a permanent state of change, in a space too small for them.

No. That wasn't right. Enos frowned, and the little scales at the corners of her mouth flexed. It had been captured only days ago. There was no way that short amount of time would have driven them mad. The Life Coalition must have held them, in some other small container. Where had they been when the rest of their species were traveling as merchants to the ten homeworlds? Were others still out there? What was in the box was in no way a viable being, or beings.

Inas patted her arm and she looked up at him. He was staring directly at her, through Councilor Feldo's glasses, trying to tell her something, in the way they had. Maybe it was this Sathssn skin. She didn't understand.

"Watch over me," he said. What was he doing? He brushed her arm off his, cutting the contact between them.

Majus Ayama was turning to leave, but Inas took one step forward to the pendulous eye and maw.

"I can help," he said. Majus Ayama turned back around. Majus Cyrysi had been watching the whole time, but made no move forward. He still had his head cocked, like some giant bird.

"What are you—?" Her mentor's words cut off as Inas reached a calloused hand forward, the fingers slowly blending together into a mass of flesh. Out of the bloodshot white of the thing's eyeball another pseudopod extended, reaching hungrily toward her brother.

"No!" she said, but he ignored her. She reached out one hand, drew it back. The maji were making similar protests. What would happen if all three of them made contact? Did she dare contaminate both her and her brother?

Too late. Tentacle and hand touched, blurred, came together. Something like a sigh escaped the thing's mouth and the eye melted back into flesh. Once there was no distinction between the two, the animation went out of the extension of flesh emerging from the box.

"Ask again," Inas said, staring at nothing, and the echo came from the gaping slit of flesh:

"...again and hear the words of death and birth and rain of blood..." They cut off sharply.

Majus Ayama was looking at her now. "What did he do?"

Enos shook her head. "I am not certain. He was always better, the few times we were allowed to change. It is something our parents may have taught him."

"Ask again," Inas repeated. "...again and hear of slashing claws and shadows..."

Majus Ayama seemed frozen, and Majus Cyrysi spoke for her.

"Are the attacks on the maji having anything to do with the Drains?"

Inas and the thing in the box responded at almost the same time, his voice coming just a fraction of an instant later, enough to set a discord to the speech.

"The attacks are distraction (of sweet flesh and tearing ripping...). The Life Coalition (life and death and dripping pus of infection...)—the Life Coalition has another goal (of sucking space like marrow from bones so sweet like honey...)."

Inas' voice was strained, and Enos could tell he forced himself to stop after each phrase. The thing would rattle on a few words before falling silent. Sweat was dripping through the thinning hair that was not his, his eyes rolled back. Enos hovered. She wanted to make contact, to touch her other half, to comfort him. The touch of this thing was poison.

"What is the other goal?" Majus Ayama asked. Her voice was soft, as if the question would be easier for Inas to answer. Her eyes flicked back and forth between the thing in the box and Enos' brother, brows creased.

"The goal of life from death (and death of life of pushing through the rot and springing forth in fount of blood...). They are making (making hurting seeding sucking...)—making the voids themselves. The Aridori are to distract (and rend the flesh so sweet in blood like rain to suck the flesh...). They distract from the voids (of death and life of all that is so empty place of nothing send us nothing there to die in pain for all...)."

Inas was trembling, near to a seizure. His knees wobbled, beneath the hanging coat of the councilor. Enos stood as close as she dared, regretting not finding real gloves. Could she shield herself from contamination? Maybe with the House of Healing? She listened for the Symphony, but it was spotty, coming in and out of clarity. She was too anxious.

"What is it to be a distraction from?"

"They take the Assembly's focus from the voids (oh nothing cease to be to die and color blossom in the nothing take us kill us send us...)."

The thing was losing cohesion. Bits of it rotted as she watched, and plopped to the surface of the box. It spread like a pox along the pseudopod extending from the small air hole.

"What is—" Majus Ayama began.

"Leave him alone!" Enos shouted. She moved around him, shielding him, but Majus Ayama raised her voice.

"What is the Life Coalition going to do?"

"They will open (and send us promised oh they promised sing of death and nothing free from pain and life of prison save us free us kill us send us...). They will open a huge void (we helped them help us send us free inside to die the nothing silence of the pain so long to stand to wait on them we wait and act...)."

Inas panted, sagging. While he fought to get his breath, she forced her hands forward. The Symphony surged in her mind and she put her notes into the rondo of music along the skin of her hands and arms, making it thicker, stronger, keeping her own brother out. When her hands, shining white, touched his other arm, she felt nothing from the thing in the box. It was dying quickly from injuries sustained while fighting the councilor, and with her brother's help, she suspected. It was dissolving in body and mind. Silently, she supported Inas, leaning her weight into him. The tentacle was almost gone, rotting fast, dripping like a putrescent fruit left in the gutter. Only a string connected Inas' hand to the air hole.

"*Where?*" Majus Ayama hissed. "Where will they make it?"

"—opened in (so big so large it kills and kisses sweet like honey of oblivion takes all away the pain away...). Opened in the Nether (it kills the others dissolve dissolute it brings and hates the others so perfect form unchanging why the void of ending death it goes we go...)"

Inas' head snapped forward as the last string of flesh melted away. "In the Nether," he gasped. "They will open it in the Nether." He fell back into Enos' arms, an unfamiliar weight and smell, but she hugged her brother to her, relishing his touch.

A stench rose in the little cell, like carrion and feces and all things foul. The maji gasped and stepped away from the box. Enos almost gagged, but held on to her brother.

"Get out!" Majus Ayama commanded, and pounded on the door. "Open up!" she said.

A bolt screeched as it moved, agonizingly long in the overpowering stench. Enos raised an arm to cover her face, even as she supported Inas. He was unconscious. Finally the door creaked open, and Majus Ayama pushed through. Enos heard surprised murmurs from the guards. She didn't care if her cowl was back, revealing her supposed secret Sathssn form. She had to get Inas away.

Enos followed the maji quickly down the hall, ignoring all the questions from the surprised guards, dragging her brother's body. Partway down the hall, her load lightened, and she glanced up. Majus Cyrysi was helping, and gave her a tentative, but tight, smile.

CHAPTER TWENTY-SEVEN

New Information

-Is the music of alien worlds more familiar to us in the confines of the Nether? Certainly some say it is better to appreciate the great Etanela operas in their natural semi-submerged element on Etan. Others insist the Nether's translation allows one to appreciate it as a native would.

From "A Dissertation on the Music of the Ten Homeworlds," by Festuour philosopher Hegramtifar Yhon, Thinker

Sam heard the others coming, their themes twining through the Symphony of Communication. He shook the rain off his overcoat, a hot thing with some sort of oiled-suede outer lining. The steady dripping wetness hadn't stopped with the night. He was sheltered with Maji Caroom and Hand Dancer under the same communal corner overhang as before. Waiting had been an agony, with both Enos and Inas away from him. *I need to make it right between us.*

The rain made a steady drumline through the Symphony of the air, and the four coming out of the prison cut through both in a shrill accelerando.

"Get ready," he told the maji. "They're coming fast." Caroom shifted with a creak of splitting wood, and Hand Dancer made a nervous gesture with hir hands, one twisting over the other. *Something's wrong.*

They intersected Majus Ayama, then Majus Cyrysi and Enos disguised as Hathssas. She was half-carrying Inas, still wearing Councilor Feldo's face. All four were huffing, almost jogging.

"No time for explanation," Majus Ayama said, preempting any questions. "We got away from the guards for now, but we need to get back." She pushed past, and Sam joined them.

"Back to the, hmm, rooms?" Majus Caroom asked, catching up with their constant stumping rhythm.

Majus Ayama shook her head. "To the Imperium. Something will happen soon, and I'll be Shiv's breakfast if I'm going to let it threaten the Nether. We need to get back to the portal ground."

"Will the Council be watching the portals?" Majus Cyrysi asked.

Majus Ayama shrugged. "I don't know if it's worth worrying over yet." They fell to discussing logistics of travel, Majus Hand Dancer gesturing broadly to speak over the others, and Sam fell back to the twins in their disguises. Majus Cyrysi had abandoned his post and Inas/Councilor Feldo was stumbling, his head lolling. *He looks drunk. How did they get away?*

"Is he alright?" Sam asked, ducking to Inas' other side.

"I have nothing to say to you," Enos hissed back, and turned her head away, but she let him help.

"Nothing ever again, or nothing right now?" he asked. *I can't let them leave me, no matter who they are.* They didn't look like his friends right now, but he could see Enos, through her mannerisms and the way she walked.

She didn't answer, and Inas' head, with its full beard and wild hair, wobbled side to side as he lurched along. He was mumbling something too low to hear.

"Look, I don't know what went on in there, but Inas obviously needs help," Sam said into Enos' silence. The maji were still arguing, heading toward the edge of town and the portal ground. There was no one out yet, and this path was familiar from walking it for the past few days. His breath came fast, and his heartrate was elevated, but that could have been from supporting Inas. His mind went to his watch, then found an outlet in the continuous fractal Symphonies always in the back of his head. *Have to try again. She has to say something.*

"I'm sorry for what happened. I wish to God it hadn't. I wish Majus Cyrysi hadn't figured it out so soon. But now that he did, can you forgive me? Can we still be together?"

Enos kept her head forward, the black cowl blocking her face from view. "You nodded. You confirmed what the majus only suspected."

Inas briefly raised his head, seeming to continue some sentence he had started beneath his breath. "...to free them to find their way. I had to do, we had to do what we did. What we have done. It was the only way. Tell him sister tell..." His voice faded away.

What happened to him? Aridori or not, Sam pulled Inas closer to him, his chest tightening with concern. Inas even smelled different, old, disguised like this.

The black cowl turned to him, and Sam caught a worried cat's eye.

"Yes, I nodded. Would you rather I didn't say anything and the maji suspect all of us? This way I can stand up for you. You need me," he told her. "*He* needs me. I can at least start to make up for what I did. You don't have to tell me. Just let me help."

Enos sighed, but didn't object as they followed the maji through the dark of Gloomlight. Finally she spoke.

"We still want to be with you. I—we—will forgive you, in time. It's only, this is something new for us." She paused under an overhang to readjust her grip on Inas. "Our family was careful with secrets. This is why we do not give them out, and what we were warned against."

Sam ducked and swung Inas' limp arm around his shoulder. *His fingers aren't right.* They were always so warm, but now they were ice cold, strangely stiff. Enos looked over at his indrawn breath.

It looks melted. The fingers were stuck together in a claw, what remained of the thumb tucked into the palm. He looked to Enos for an explanation, but she was staring at the hand too, Sathssn eyes wide. *She didn't know about it either.* There was no time to ask the maji, and Sam wasn't going to without the twins' permission.

Majus Cyrysi didn't let the tired-looking Lobath majus at the portal ground ask questions, talking over her objections. After the one hissing chemical light illuminated Majus Ayama's face, tightened into a rictus of anger, the Lobath backed off to a corner of the fenced-off ground, her head-tentacles trembling. Majus Hand Dancer opened the portal to the Spire, the dark hole ringed in orange and a bland gray.

Enos went through first, dragging Inas. Sam swallowed against the lump of fear in his throat and closed his eyes. He let the others pull him through the blackness.

At the Spire, the maji discussed where to go, finally settling on Majus Hand Dancer's apartment in the House of Power, mainly because zie was less implicated than the other three.

Sam helped Enos lay her brother down on the springy, cork-like floor of a side room. Enos lay down next to him, and was asleep almost immediately. Sam watched them for a moment. Both their faces were softening, Enos' scales already losing their green tint, Councilor Feldo's beard growing shorter. Sam waited for the surge of disgust at seeing them change, but it didn't come.

He set a low, flat chair just outside the room and fell into it, drifting off in moments.

* * *

A faint but insistent buzzing woke Sam, and he blinked blearily at light from an open window, through which he could see part a wall of the Nether. *Where am I?* Colors swirled through the air, combining and dancing like fireflies painted in many hues. The vision changed, becoming a vast swirl, which gave way to a vista of a moon over a dry planet, or was it a sun reflecting in water? The sun, or moon, took flight, changing to a fantastical bird—white and silver with scales for feathers—which dove into the waves and became a fish. The colors changed and flowed. Sam's lungs complained and he realized he was holding his breath. He sucked in air.

The vision faded, and Sam saw Majus Hand Dancer sitting cross-legged on the floor, large dexterous hands splayed into crevices in a fluted box of shining wood and glass. The buzzing faded as the Lobhl lifted hands away, tattoos catching the light from the window.

"What was that?" Sam asked. He—she?—zie?—had been making the visions. "Um. How do I address you today?" The Nether wasn't giving any clues.

The majus started, and fingers twisted around words. <Forgive me. I did not mean to wake you. I was practicing, and am but the method of expression. While practicing I am devoid of identity, an "it.">

"Were you changing the Symphony?" Sam asked.

Hand Dancer made a negating gesture, tempered with a motion expressing a shy smile. <Hardly. I am a musician by profession. I was simply warming my hands up with practice exercises.>

Sam looked at the strange box it was holding. "Music? I only heard buzzing."

Majus Hand Dancer gave him another finger-smile. <Music is what one perceives.> It made an unusual gesture indicating its face, tapping a small hole on the side of its bald head, above the covering on the lower half of its face. Even with drawing attention to its head, Sam couldn't make an impression of facial features, as if his memory slid off the contact. <My kind does not put so much emphasis on sound as on sight.> Sam frowned and stood up, stretching. He came closer to where Hand Dancer was sitting.

"It was very beautiful. Is that the, um, instrument?"

<It is.> It clicked a switch and warm light suffused the box. <A gesture conveys the emotion of the artist.> It swirled fingers, and lights popped into existence in the room, blue and gray and purple. They changed into triangles and then pentagons, before disappearing. <It is called the Hand Dancer.>

"The Hand Dancer?" Sam was sure he looked confused.

<I was called after it, on my second naming. I picked one up when young and composed my first symphony. I was considered quite a prodigy in my early cycles.>

A rumble of conversation started in the next room and Majus Hand Dancer looked around vaguely, as if unsure where the sound was coming from. Sam peered around the corner to see Enos stirring.

Majus Hand Dancer carefully tucked the instrument—the Hand Dancer—into a little ornate box and put it on a stand. <I believe the Aridori are awake. I shall be male for this meeting,> he signed.

In the other room, Majus Ayama stood over Enos, Inas lying beside his sister. His eyes were open now, and he looked like himself. Enos' skin was still freckled with little scales, as if someone had drawn lines on her, but they were fading.

Maji Cyrysi and Caroom appeared, carrying boxes which smelled of fresh hot bread. Sam's mouth watered. *When did I last eat?* From the light of the walls, it was still fairly early in the morning. Even Inas perked up a little, though he swayed when he sat up.

"Time to tell us the rest of what you found out," Majus Ayama told them. "We can do it over breakfast, but I want to know every scrap of information you got from the thing in that box."

Soon, they sat around a low round table, except for Majus Caroom, who leaned against a wall as usual, nibbling at their bread. Majus Cyrysi had a little box of his own, with things that wiggled inside. He slurped them up with a pointed utensil, and Sam tried not to watch.

They split the warm fresh bread, with generous slabs of butter and jam from some fruit Sam couldn't quite place. It tasted a little like strawberries, but also like oranges. Enos spread butter and jam for her brother, and Inas kept his left hand beneath the table.

After they were settled, Inas spoke, slowly, his voice raw. "I saw into its—their mind."

Their? Sam looked between the twins. *Like two instances?* Enos saw him looking, and as if reading his thoughts, gave him a very tiny nod.

There was fear in Inas' eyes. "This is not something I knew Aridori could do. You must believe me." He shook his head back and forth. "We know little except what our family told us, and that many of the rumors about us are false."

"This creature was a thing of nightmares," Majus Ayama said. "We saw what it could do. Can you do the same? Can you prove you can't?"

"Not reasonable to ask this one to prove a negative," Majus Caroom rumbled, and Majus Ayama accepted the correction with a wave of one hand.

"We cannot do what they did," Inas replied. His voice was getting smoother, closer to what Sam remembered. "You have seen us change. It is normally a slow process. Maybe multiple minds, melded together, have other powers." He shivered, and sniffed. Was he crying? Sam longed to go to him, but it was too soon. Enos put a hand on Inas' shoulder, her eyes hard. "They were old, so old," he continued. "They did not have names, not that they remembered. They were completely insane."

<Yet I gather you connected to them in some way,> Majus Hand Dancer signed. <Should we be concerned?>

"He will not hurt you," Enos retorted, clutching at Inas. "You think the worst of us, but it is lies!" She stared around the room and Sam rushed at a chance to defend the twins.

"Surely it's been long enough since the war. Can't we convince people that there are good Aridori too?" He looked between the two. "You told me you were descended from the peaceful ones." Majus Ayama regarded him for a long moment. *Wondering how long I've kept this from her. Let her wonder.*

Enos took in air through her teeth. "There is not some artificial line demarking the 'bad' from the 'good.' Part of it came from changing too much, raising the emotions."

"These ones are not, hmm, accusing," Majus Caroom said. "Still, those two understand this group must be cautious. These ones are still unsure of the hidden species that appears to be living in hiding, while in plain sight."

"We were minding our business, living our lives," Enos shouted. "He and his mentor forced us out!" She flung a finger at Sam and Majus Cyrysi.

"Calm. This is not to be getting us the location of the Life Coalition, nor where they will make the next Drain." Majus Cyrysi stared Enos down. Sam didn't think she would have reacted so strongly, save that she had recently changed form. *I hope not. She said she would forgive me. I can't protect them if she won't let me.*

"They were insane," Inas continued, speaking to the table as if he hadn't been interrupted. "I could still tell the difference between my mind and theirs. I believe I am safe from contamination."

Sam stared at where Inas hid his hand under the table, wondering if he was really was. *Should I ask about his hand?* It was further betrayal of his friends. No, he couldn't do it.

"They shared things with me," Inas continued in a monotone. "Mostly they begged me to kill them. Those that captured them have held them a long time. I do not know how long—they had no sense of time—but I got the feeling of centuries upon centuries. Their mind no longer operated as usual, but there was an original design, some reason of working with the Sathssn. They had been captured longer than the Life Coalition existed, kept somewhere secret from all but one family of Sathssn. They must have known of our merchant group, for the Drain to have caught us." He stared down, right hand drawing an invisible doodle on the tabletop. "In the end, I helped them find their way."

Sam gripped his hands on the edge of the table, fingertips scraping across the wood. *I have to help them. I can't help them until the maji get their information.* He didn't know if Enos would let him get close.

<Did they say how Councilor Feldo captured them?> Hand Dancer asked. <It must have been difficult, to contain such an old and experienced creature.>

"A good question, especially since it could change so quickly," Majus Ayama added.

Inas shook his head. "They did not say."

"It was likely to be a shield of energy, or something similar," Majus Cyrysi said. "The House of Potential can come closest to approximating a full containment without the other houses present. The resulting prison could also be moved, so Feldo would have been able to put it in the box we saw."

"How old was it, to know of your family of hidden Aridori? Do you know if any of your people ever went missing?" Majus Ayama asked Enos.

Enos shook her head angrily. "You accuse us of knowingly letting one of our people suffer this? No one could be that cruel!" She was shouting again and Sam stood up. At Majus Cyrysi's glare and flared crest, he sat back down. *Have to do something.* He checked his pulse. Too fast.

"Peace, child," Majus Caroom ordered, and their voice held a deep resonance, like a thrumming cello.

Enos' eyes widened. *Maybe she'll realize what's happening.* Sam sat forward.

"The majus asks only if this one's family may have known of these beings from before their capture."

Enos was silent, as was Inas. When she spoke again, her voice was restrained, but Sam could hear the stress underneath. He wanted to go to her, comfort her. "Our family was very close. There were so few of us. I do not recall any member of our caravans going missing in our lifetimes."

"What of the information it gave you?" Majus Cyrysi said. "Anything of the Drains?"

"There were images of black cloaks—of their captors," Inas intoned. He at least raised his head, but his eyes were sunken, staring into nothing.

"Sathssn," Majus Ayama said. "Like Sam and Enos reported. The Most Traditional Servants must be funding this Life Coalition."

<Why would they do this?> Hand Dancer asked. <What is it they wish to gain?>

"During our 'interview'," Majus Ayama filled the word with distaste, "the creature said the Aridori scare was a distraction for the voids. What would the Sathssn—even the most fundamental of them— want with the voids? They will be destroyed just like everyone else."

"Do they want to get rid of those different from them?" Sam hazarded. He hunched his shoulders as the others looked to him.

Then Majus Cyrysi answered, and Sam let out a breath. "What is to be gained now? The fundamental Sathssn have always had a dislike for those they saw as blasphemers." He paused, looking unnaturally worried for the generally confident majus. "The prisoner mentioned both 'dissolve' and 'dissolute' in close proximity. Normally I would not even consider such an idea, but recent occurrences have, well, adjusted my perspective. Could they have meant 'Dissolution'?"

No one answered, though the maji's eyes darted to each other. Sam didn't have the confidence to ask what the Dissolution was.

Then Inas cleared his throat. His eyes were focused far off, but his posture was erect. He looked more like himself. "I've remembered. They knew something else. The next void would take place in the Nether."

"We already know that. Where?" Majus Ayama said, but Majus Hand Dancer raised long fingers at her and she fell silent.

"They did not know where in the Nether," Inas answered. Something like a sigh went through the group. The Nether was vast.

We won't find it in time. They could pick any place.

"But," Inas continued and they all stared at him, "it will be in the Nether, because...because something special is to happen." He screwed up his face. "Many voids—at least one on each homeworld—they will converge on the Nether. I cannot recall. A meeting? Between—"

"The Life Coalition is meeting?" Majus Ayama said. "Where? When?"

"There will be...a meeting." Inas said the words slowly, as if tasting them. "Yes. There will be a meeting in the Nether. In the Imperium." He paused. "Tonight." He seemed surprised by his own words.

The maji sat forward. "Better," Majus Ayama said. "Where is it?"

Inas closed his eyes, then opened them. He met Sam's eyes, frowned slightly. "I think I can take you to it."

CHAPTER TWENTY-EIGHT

The Bazaar

-The Imperium is divided into three sections, High, Mid, and Low. There are no borders to mark them, but from a high vantage point, the divisions are easy to see. High Imperium holds the Assembly, the Palace, the Spire, and the wealthy and elite. Mid Imperium consists of many of the shops and entertainments, and Low Imperium contains much of the industry, machinery, crime, and finally, the Bazaar.
Morvu Francita Januti, Etanela explorer and big game hunter

It had been late morning when Sam and the others left Majus Hand Dancer's apartment, and it took most of the day for them to reach the other end of the Imperium. First they traveled by hired cab pulled by a pair of ostrich-like System Beasts made of creaking bronze, then by the tram, rumbling along a raised line that sped through and above the buildings of the Imperium.

Around them, the warren of interconnected structures making up Mid Imperium fell away to something fundamentally different. There, the dominant feature was commerce; signs waving in a breeze, or vendors out boasting about their wares, or smells of cooking meat or vegetables. Here, it was industry. Even in the tram, the sound level rose, dopplered rhythms of great presses striking metal, or sizzling fires, or carts filled with sheets of strange bark-like material rattling along underneath nearly as fast as the tram.

The others took it in stride, and Sam's eyes darted between the maji, and his friends. Inas and Enos had their own bench, across the aisle from Sam, near, but not by his sides as when they had traversed the Imperium together. *Was that only a few days ago?* At least they looked at him now, though as often Inas' gaze was lost in the distance, as he tried to recall details of what he had learned from whatever had been in the box. Sam tried to pry more information out of them, but they wouldn't tell him. *It was an Aridori, but not like them. It was like the ones in the war—different enough to make them afraid.* It was easy for him to see, but the maji didn't understand. He wished he could press his knowledge into the others, but the prejudice against the Aridori went deeper than simple words could fix. It would take time for the maji to trust them again, as it had with him.

The walls were shading toward twilight as their tram slowed, pulling into the terminal station of the Low Imperium line. "I didn't know the Imperium was this big," Sam told Majus Cyrysi. *Too big, too crowded,* his mind screamed at him, and Sam tried to regulate his breathing. His watch and the Symphony had been constant companions through many of the stations, as he'd seen various beings join or leave the carriage. *It's all so new.*

"It is to be quite large," Majus Cyrysi answered. "Larger than Kashidur City on Methiem, even." A pair of Pixies buzzed past them, speaking rapidly as they flew to the next carriage.

"Low Imperium is practically a city in itself," Majus Ayama said. Her eyes roved the crowds outside the tram, their clothes plainer than what Sam was used to seeing near the Spire, and often smudged with dirt or soot. "If High Imperium is a bright jewel, reflecting the light from the walls, then Low Imperium is cut glass trying to pass itself off as a diamond."

He saw nothing resembling a diamond—it was more like coal. This was a place work got done. He peered out of the tram's windows at the maze of low brick warehouses, then pulled back, breathing out in measured time. Hand Dancer leaned forward. <It may not look so here, but Majus Ayama is correct. Wait until you see the Bazaar,> she signed.

Sam felt his stomach clench. He knew the Lobhl was trying to help, but the anticipation only made things worse. They got up, Sam keeping hold of the cloth seat backs as he walked, forcing his legs forward. The smell of old wood varnish and unclean bodies made him mildly nauseated. *We'll be out in the crowds soon.*

Inas and Enos were behind him as they exited the tram terminal, and Sam focused on their presence, hearing echoes in the Symphony of their subtle body language, communication the three of them shared. *When did I learn to hear that?* He glanced down to Inas' left hand. *Have the others noticed yet?* Enos followed his eyes, then looked back to him and shook her head, just a little. Inas had his eyes forward, his steps taking him to the head of their group. Sam was forced to follow, his steps and heart too fast. *Too much new.* He kept his head down, reached for Enos' hand. She didn't pull away, for which he was thankful. At least the fading light reduced how much he could see.

They turned a corner, and the sound level increased again. The metallic buzz of industry gave way to the organic soup of many voices, all together. There was a group of three Etanela banging out a frantic jig on a set of dented pipes and found percussion. Sam winced, and squeezed Enos' hand. *More crowds.*

"Will the meeting be in the Bazaar?" Majus Ayama called.

"Nearby," Inas answered, his voice distant. Both twins had calmed during the day, regaining composure after returning to their everyday forms. *Are they natural forms? What do they really look like?* Sam stared at the back of Inas' head, his hair bound up again. *Does it matter? No. It* didn't. Their personalities were what he liked. His gaze trailed down Inas' lower back, moving over the curves below. *Well, mostly.*

"They knew the chaos would be a cover," Inas continued. "Those who gave them orders met with them there."

Sam guessed he meant the thing they had found in the prison, which the twins said was multiple things. He rubbed fingers over Enos' knuckles, and she squeezed back. *Like two instances? Mashed together with no escape?* He couldn't imagine Enos and Inas like that. No wonder it had been insane.

"The Life Coalition?" Majus Caroom asked.

"Most likely," Inas answered.

They came to a balcony, overlooking a field—even larger than the grounds of the Spire, and Sam let go of Enos, grasping the rail to combat the vertigo that pulled at him. There was a column to one side, reflecting soft dimming light from the walls. *There are so many people.*

It was absolute chaos, beings of all shapes and sizes moving back and forth in the twilight, between tents and tables, like a massive flea market. It was on open ground, divided into sections by temporary barriers and structures. Trees from many worlds ringed the area.

Spicy aromas drifted up to them—meats cooking, and sweet fruits, and the unmistakable sour scent of fermented drink. Inas said the meeting would be at ninth darkening, near midnight. It wasn't that late yet, but close. Even at this time, the Bazaar was filled to bursting.

"The meeting is on the far side," Inas said.

"Through that?" Sam felt his knees go weak, and the railing he clutched was the only thing holding him up.

Inas turned to look at him, as if seeing him for the first time that day. "Yes. I'm sorry." He reached out his good hand, hesitated, then grasped Sam's shoulder.

Sam closed his eyes. "Will you stay with me?"

"We will," Enos said.

Sam kept to the middle of their group, between Inas and Enos, hemmed in by Maji Ayama and Cyrysi in the front and Caroom and Hand Dancer in the back. He had a wall to look through and observe life outside of his anxiety.

Others brushed by the group and Sam flinched inward, even sheltered as he was. He held his watch, thumb rubbing the engraving around the rim. *Listen for the Symphony. Feed the worry into it.* It helped a little.

All ten species were in evidence here, some manning the myriad stalls, some buying from or trading with them. Sparking gas lights with halos of orange threw long shadows. People called prices, questions, and insults, the Nether translating everything with the trademark accent of each species—the fast and weird tenses of the Kirians, the gruff words of the furry Festuour, the smooth fluid slurring of the Etanela. Anything and everything was on sale, from raw materials, to food and drink, to clothes, jewelry, weapons, tools, vehicles, technology, and, of course, sex. Sam tried not to stare at a bare-armed and legged Kirian, her brightly colored open shirt revealing the curve of breasts touched with downy feathers. Next to her a lengthy Etanela, which the Nether identified as the subordinate male gender, sat with no shirt, his tall blueish torso smooth and hydrodynamic. Both Majus Ayama and Enos gave him an appraising look as they passed.

Many of the stall owners were the enterprising Festuour, and Methiemum, but tentacled Lobath and even the tiny winged Pixies ran many of the stands.

They passed around a cluster of whispering Sathssn, arguing with an Etanela over a painting of sunrise over a watery landscape. One had her cowl back, and watched their group with red cat's eyes. Orange light glinted off the tiny bright green scales on her face.

There were even a few Benish stumping along, each as wildly organic and different as two gnarled trees shaped by the wind, and Sam picked out a bald Lobhl gesturing in barter to a Pixie over a set of elongated pipes which could have been musical instruments, tubing, or some sort of food processor. Behind them, a group of three Sureriaj stalked, glaring suspiciously at others, and whispering back and forth in their brogue.

Boots and cart wheels had churned the ground, and Sam picked his way around mud puddles and the papers and rags of garbage, strewn on the ground. As they moved through the crowd, Sam's breathing gradually slowed. *Enjoy the sights while you're here.* Their group opened enough to let him feel the surface of a smooth twisting sculpture which reminded him of torrents of water, frozen in the midst of falling.

"That way," Inas called, pointing to a corridor between two stalls, veering away from the crush of the Bazaar. Their group had been pulled apart by the allure of the displayed wares. Caroom stopped for a moment to admire a selection of standing poles. They knocked a complicated rhythm against one and Sam was surprised by the smooth ringing. Another musical instrument? At their apprentice's call, Caroom stumped back.

Majus Ayama seemed less drawn in than the other maji. "Is the meeting place in one of those?" she asked, pointing to a line of wood warehouses, presumably where items for sale were stored.

Inas nodded. "It will be the one with no guards."

"Ah. Naturally." Majus Cyrysi was in a good mood, humming as they walked. Sam wondered if his mentor had a death wish, or just liked walking into dangerous situations. He was short of breath, both from walking, and from the lingering panic clawing its way up his throat. Even with the others protecting him, every step was a struggle. His blood rushed in his ears, and he thought he might be sick.

The third warehouse from the left lacked the Lobath and Methiemum toughs that stood around the others, and who paid them little attention anyway. Only a lone light pole stood nearby, throwing illumination. It was late—the passage through the Bazaar had taken a surprisingly long time. Behind the warehouses stood a stand of trees with no leaves, and little tendrils covering the trunk. The branches pointed nearly straight up, and some animal flitted between branches as Sam watched.

"Assume we will meet resistance here," Majus Cyrysi told them. "Rilan and I have experience with these situations. We will be directing our approach."

Sam felt a tide of uncertainty rise up. *What's that supposed to mean? Does he think we're going to fight someone?*

* * *

Origon noted points around the perimeter of the warehouse, entries, exits, and weak sections of wood. They would need to get in quickly and quietly. In the past, this had been Rilan's forte, but she was likely out of practice, with her cycles on the Council. He had honed his skill during the time he traveled alone.

Several points of entry, and they would have to block any participants from leaving. The others were looking around as if they had no idea what to do. Rilan at least, had a finger to her lips, studying the warehouse.

The Aridori, however, were hard to read, though they had done nothing that could be construed as offensive, and he wasn't as taken with the terror stories as Rilan was. He was more concerned with the news of this Life Coalition. Had no one else really understood that they might be *creating* Drains? How could it be possible to artificially make something no natural object could touch? The imprisoned Aridori had been taking orders from the Life Coalition, and had seemed to know a lot. It was almost a shame they were dead. No way now to determine who was giving whom information. He would wager a who-knows-how-many-centuries-old Aridori would be very good at making secret plans.

"Apprentices with your mentors," Origon called quietly. The young ones could at least aid their maji, even if they did not have much experience. "We must be dividing into two groups to make sure those inside do not escape. Caroom with me, Hand Dancer is to go with Rilan." The House of Strength could physically shore up weaknesses in his two houses while engaging offensive opponents, especially as Origon's song was still weak. If he had been at full strength, he would have entered the warehouse by himself, and left the others to stand staring.

He ignored a babble of concerns, flattening his crest and turning to Sam. "What of you? Will you and the twins be able to aid us? Any problems with your panic?"

Sam gaped at him, like a fish out of water. "I, um, what are we—" He looked to Inas, moving closer to the other young man. Enos glared back at Origon.

So none of them would be much help. "Stay behind us, and follow the changes we make to the Symphony. You will be doing quite well, I am certain." Positive encouragement always improved things.

By the weak light of the lamp pole, he quickly outlined how the building was constructed, and where Life Coalition members would likely be placed. Any place an opponent was constricted, there was opportunity.

He was relying on Rilan to remember their old tactics, back when they traveled together, though it had been many cycles and she was still distracted by the death of her father. Understandable. "You are remembering the dual-flanking action we used in the hive on the Pixie homeworld?" he asked.

Rilan stared at him a moment, blank-faced, then understanding came over her. "With the rebel group challenging the queen. Yes." She looked to the warehouse, to Hand Dancer, then back to him. "Yes." This time more certain.

Good. "Are we all ready?" he asked, looking at the others. There was a round of agreement. "Apprentices, be following your master's instructions to the syllable, yes?"

Sam stared back, wide-eyed. "What are we going to do in there?"

Origon sighed. "You are going to be following my instructions."

"But, I mean, are we going to *fight* them?" Origon drew in a breath again, but then saw the others watching, save Rilan, who was staring at the warehouse, calculating something.

Origon stroked his moustache down flat, and attempted to keep his crest from flaring in alarm. "We are going to be invading a meeting of hostile individuals, who have been working with an insane Aridori." He glanced to the twins. "No offense. Potentially some or all will be maji. We must do so with surprise, silence, and efficiency. They will not be expecting us, and the more we can incapacitate and capture, the more information we will be having about the Drains."

"As well as about the murder and attempted murder of half the Council of the Maji," Rilan put in, and Origon waved a hand to acknowledge the point.

"Then are we ready?" he asked again. There were slow nods all around. It would have to do. He pointed Rilan's group to the other side of warehouse, and stalked around the nearer side with Sam, Caroom, and Inas in tow.

There was a large door on this side, in shadow, and they had seen two more, on other sides. He would let Rilan pick her entry. As they pressed against the splintery wood of the door, Origon cocked his head to listen for voices. He let the Symphony run through his head, cataloging applications of Communication and Power. In this tight a space, he would only be able to use each one once, or maybe not at all if another used something similar.

Suddenly, yellow light bloomed around his apprentice as notes bridged two melodies in the air, one farther off and fast, the other near and slow. Conversation surrounded them.

"What are you doing?" he hissed, and Sam jumped.

"I figured out how to do this this in the cave the Sathssn trapped us in," he explained. "I thought you wanted to hear them better."

Origon tsked at his apprentice, letting his crest expand in annoyance. "Do not be using your song before I say so, boy. We must be sparing with application." He attempted to mute the sound of their footsteps, but his attempts encountered resistance. "May your ancestor's beards fall out!" he cursed, quietly. "The effects are too similar. Do *not* do anything without my telling you to!"

He pointed a finger at Sam, intending to continue, when a low rumble came from behind him. "Hmmmmm. Perhaps these gathered should listen to the advantage this one has given?" asked Caroom innocently. Origon scowled at them, but cocked his head to hear the now clear voices.

"—time yet, Nakan," one was saying. "If we move too soon, the Council, it will not be properly prepared. Past the date and we will miss the Assembly sessions." So, two Sathssn, at least, one speaking and one the mysterious Nakan. They were speaking of the timing of the Drain, maybe?

"A squad, can we not send it into the city at the same time?" Another voice spoke, even more sibilant than the first speaker. "We attacked for a reason. Not only for distraction."

Other voices chimed in at that, and Origon picked out three, four, five, six. Put a rough estimate at ten of them, then.

"Where are they?" he asked Sam.

"Um?" The young man looked baffled.

"You were redirecting their sounds toward us. Where did they come from?" he asked.

"I...I don't know," Sam stuttered, folding in. "I just made it happen. I'm not sure how."

"Perhaps this group should, hmm, enter," Caroom interrupted. They stepped forward, their whole body sheathed in a thin sheen of green, freckled with their bland personal color. Inas was behind his mentor, looking into his right hand. A sheath of green climbed down his arm, mimicking Caroom.

The Benish reached for the slat door, one large hand pushing to one side. There was a moment of hesitation, then a slight pop, and the door slowly slid on tracks.

Origon hastily grabbed for the shrill notes that would become a shriek of metal on metal tracks, muting them with a couple of his notes.

Caroom turned their wide body sideways, slipping through, and Origon took his notes back, breathing in at the return of energy.

Origon shooed Sam and Inas ahead of him. It was dark in the warehouse, save for one light in the distance. A chemical tang filled the air. Crates, barrels, pallets, and a few metal containers were stacked to their sides, lining the entrance. Origon peered around them, through the gloom. At least they would have plenty of cover.

* * *

Rilan waited in the darkness, a familiar tightness in her shoulders. Enos and Hand Dancer stood to one side. She motioned the Lobhl closer—she could hardly see in this gloom. "As our illustrious leader gave us a locked door to enter, can you find a weak point, quietly?"

Hand Dancer assented with one hand and stepped to the rough planked building. She splayed both large and crooked hands against the door, and rivulets of orange and dull gray splashed out, running along cracks in boards and circling nail holes. They centered around the lock, and began to glow. The boards grew warmer, smoking, as condensate appeared on the metal of the lock.

Hand Dancer got a firm grip on it with both hands and tugged. The lock popped in half with a small squeak and Rilan winced. The heat in the door faded as the orange aura did—Hand Dancer reabsorbing her notes. The Lobhl went through first, followed by Enos, and then Rilan.

Inside were stacks of shipping containers of all sizes—items to be sold in the Bazaar. Enos sniffed audibly. The scents of spices, tar, and drying teak filled the air. Though the large marketplace was technically illegal, the Effature turned a blind eye. It earned a tidy profit for the Imperium in trade, and introduced rare items to the Nether. Warehouses like this contained objects that couldn't be found without a trip to some remote place on one of the ten homeworlds.

<What is next?> The faint words echoed in her head. Rilan could just make out the Lobhl's fingers moving in the darkness.

"There's a light over there," she said, pointing. All three peered around a wall of stacked barrels.

At a quick count, there were twelve figures at least, all in black cloaks, standing around several lanterns resting on top of crates, and directly in front of the main door. *Vish's knees. Good thing we didn't come in that way.* Rilan ducked back behind the barrels and the others mimicked her. They hadn't been seen—likely the group of Sathssn was night-blind from staring at the lanterns.

"What do we do?" Enos asked in a whisper. There was so much unknown about her apprentice and her brother. Unfortunately, nothing Rilan could do about it now. She'd rather have the young woman in her sight than out of it. Just thinking about the Aridori brought to mind the fleshy, pulsing, thing in the cell. It was enough to make her feel sick.

Trusting them is the greatest stupidity. It is the same in all the stories. It is how they infiltrated, by gaining trust. I cannot let my guard down for a moment.

Would the new councilor, Hathssas, be here? The one Enos had impersonated? Rilan flexed her fingers, and checked her belt knife.

CHAPTER TWENTY-NINE

A Surprise Meeting

-The House of Grace is little understood to those who have not some personal experience. Its Symphony envelops all aspects of everyday life, making them easier. The most advanced maji of the House of Grace can walk through a packed crowd of people carrying a saucer brimming with water, yet touch no one and spill not a drop.
Jhina Moerna Oscana, on the House of Grace

Origon contemplated the group of Life Coalitioners, gathered around three lanterns placed on a large crate. All were facing inward. Were they so confident they set no guards?

As they carefully crept closer, he reassessed his original count to more than ten. He glanced around at the squeak of wood against wood. "Sorry," his apprentice whispered. "Boot got caught." Origon sighed and slid one eye around a storage chest with a rounded lid. There was something fragrant, like rich incense, inside. One of the cloaked heads rose slightly, then lowered. The sheer number of untrained members in his band would give them away.

A scrape and a shuffle made his head whip around, crest ruffling. Inas was off balance, leaning into a large banded box. Origon sent an incredulous glance his way, and reached to help the Aridori back up, but his boot twisted under him on nothing more than a division in the floorboards. Origon pitched forward into the massive Benish's arms, scraping fingertips on rough bark-like skin. Contrary to their bulk, Caroom began to tip backward.

Origon barely caught his balance. Otherwise, the four of them would have ended up on the floor. Only then did he see the faint blue haze hanging just at the floorboards.

No one was this clumsy. "House of Grace," he whispered. The practitioner was skilled to steal the grace of others. It would require a permanent investment of the majus' notes.

The robed figures were repositioning. "Be very careful when you move," Origon said, keeping his voice low. "You are more clumsy than normal." Hopefully they would exhaust the trap's stored notes soon.

The gathering of black cloaks was silent, arranged and alert. Eight were on the outside, four inside that circle. The nearest one scanned left to right, dark hood twitching with the movement. Gloved hands threw the hood back and a chill ran up Origon's spine. The person was Methiemum, not Sathssn. Why were other species wearing the clothes of the Cult of Form?

"We have lost our surprise." He would have liked more time to prepare offensive phrases and melodies. "Caroom, to my left. You are on defense, with Inas. Sam, follow my lead."

The Symphony of Power was thrumming a base beat of connections—three separate measures, one for them, one for Rilan's group, and one for the Coalitioners. The Symphony of Communication trilled above, air currents chiming with quick motions. Origon began composing with his reduced song, keeping his hands low so the color would be hidden from any Life Coalition maji.

* * *

"What by Shiv's great hangnail is that oaf doing?" Rilan muttered at the scuffles and creaks from the others side of the warehouse. The figures around the lanterns had turned outward save for four, who faded into the center. A defensive posture, and she would wager the four inside were maji.

"They're going to get slaughtered," she said. "Let's see if we can't provide a distraction to let Ori get his act together. Hand Dancer, is there anything that could smoke or catch fire nearby?"

Hand Dancer made an agreeable gesture, then grasped the air with one hand, leaving a trail of orange leading back to a package wrapped in layers of cloth above their heads. <I think I know what you want, majus,> she signed.

She made a quick jump and caught the edge of the package, bringing it down. There were dark fibers inside. She busied herself with them as Rilan gauged the situation.

"Enos, can you do your—" She trailed off, waving a hand vaguely and looking a question at her apprentice. She couldn't believe she was asking an Aridori to perform what generations of people had used to scare their children.

Enos shook her head, hair swinging. "It will take far too much time. Besides, I would rather help as majus, than as something you look at in fear."

Rilan lofted an eyebrow. A fair argument. "Then try to be helpful," she said. "I assume you no longer have an objection to using both physical and mental techniques?" She saw confusion on the young woman's face for a moment.

Then Enos nodded. "I will attempt to follow your mental changes too."

Rilan snorted. So her apprentice's resistance had only been to keep her from discovering Enos' species.

Hand Dancer had the fibers ablaze in one arm, and her orange and gray herded the smoke and flame in front of them as a screen. Under cover, they made their way forward, Hand Dancer's free hand conducting her melody. A snake of pure flame, wreathed in dark smoke, rose above them.

Three figures headed toward Ori's group, but with a noise like a tram rushing by, a fierce gust of wind staggered the Life Coalitioners. It also made Hand Dancer's flame dip to the floor of the warehouse. Rilan swore by all the gods under her breath. She should have remembered Ori's predictable opening move.

"Keep it steady," she told Hand Dancer, who flipped an agreement with two fingers. "He rarely does two of those." She could see him now, stooped. Before the space capsule, he had performed far more complex actions without pausing.

Something whizzed past her face and she shifted to one side. Crossbow bolt. "Smoke them," she told the Lobhl, and the flame flowed to the group, trailing thick smoke. The dark cloaks fell back and several took down cowls to wrap them over their mouths.

They aren't all Sathssn.

She counted two Methiemum, a Lobath, and a Sureri. The Lobath went for the door, but Hand Dancer sent the serpent of flame dipping and coiling to block the path. The Life Coalitioners were trapped with them in the warehouse.

Then, in the center, one of the Methiemum stood, his cowl down, clearly showing his smug face. Rilan hissed in a breath, rage blooming in her belly like bloody roses. Of course *he* was the traitor, not Hathssas. That skinny, mustachioed, be-laced, traitorous...

"You bastard," she growled. Then, "With me," to Enos. Rilan strode forward through the chaos, lost in the Symphony of so many bodies.

* * *

Origon winced as his gust billowed the column of smoke and fire Hand Dancer was controlling. He hadn't anticipated that part, but he could hear the faint echoes of the capering melody, new notes adjusting the tempo and key. Working with all these half-trained maji was disrupting his attack.

He took notes from his song, intending to hem in the slow phrasing in the air, compressing it to enclose the Life Coalitioners with the smoke. His notes slipped away, back to his song, and he staggered and bent over. Had he copied another change? No, he could no longer do what he was once able to. He cursed the ancestors of the lazy engineers who had sent him to Ksupara in nothing more than a steel box on a jet of flame.

Origon saw a flow of fire block the exit, casting long shadows toward them. One shadow contained a figure with a crossbow. Origon fumbled through the music of both his houses—a shield of air, a burst to overpower the mechanism, a twist of air current—but he was exhausted; weak as an apprentice after his first use of the song.

He heard the click and the bolt flew toward his face.

A hand like a plank of thick mahogany passed in front of him, jerking with impact. Caroom grunted. "Hmmmm. Careful. That one's body has not the density this one has." The green glow shielding the Benish was like liquid emeralds. Beside them, Inas' own shield was dull and spotty.

Caroom snatched an iron strong box from a second shelf as if it were a pillow, and tossed it toward Origon's attacker. The box arced, but another dark form stepped forward and caught the iron box with an upraised glove. Origon's crest rose in surprise. The box weighed more than any two of them. The majus of the House of Potential shone with a rich brown aura, and twirled in place like a top, sending the projectile back toward them. Origon bent forward, arms up, though he knew it would make no difference.

* * *

Sam flattened into the shelving as the box descended on his mentor. *I can't help. I can't do anything.* Even the Symphony faded from his hearing.

Then Majus Caroom was there again, moving with Inas, who kept a hand on his mentor's back. Their combined green glow pulsed as the iron chest impacted the Benish majus' raised arm—and bent around it.

There was a deep rumbling creak from Caroom, and Inas stooped as if he carried a bag of cement. Then both straightened, and the wooden floor around them shook and creaked in an expanding circle, warping, but never quite breaking, until the impact finally dispersed. The crate fell to the ground with a ringing *clang*, bent beyond repair.

The House of Strength. Sam turned to where the Life Coalition were recovering, waving smoke and fire aside. One re-cocked a crossbow, five others drew heavy swords. *They have a majus from the House of Potential.* The transfer with the box was like what Rey had done, back in the alley, but on a much larger scale.

Inas is helping Majus Caroom. I've only hindered my majus. Majus Cyrysi was still shielding his head, straightening. Across from them, four of the figures in black whispered together, pointed to targets, and raised their blades. *Do something! Stop being useless!* What could he do? What did the House of Communication do?

Communication. Separate species talking. The Nether was the only thing keeping them together. He closed his eyes, and the fractal Symphony blazed in his head. He stepped under a rack of hanging fabric as the black cloaks advanced.

Where is it? He let the music in his head fill him, like listening to all the songs he owned at once. Themes built under and over each other, even dissonant sections supporting the main harmony.

Communication should be—there? One Symphony-in-Symphony gained more meaning, the notes becoming clearer. It was deeper in the pool of music than he had ever been. The phrase was rolling and complex, with a rondo of iterations, each set of measures subtly different.

This is the link between species, interpreting and aiding each individual song. The voice was in his head, but Sam wasn't aware of thinking the words. *Here is the intersection of song.* It was like someone taped pages of music from different pieces together. *This is the translation we hear.*

Sam listened to the Symphony around the cut—the taped page—and found something deeper yet. It had a strange harmonic, both higher and lower than the key of the House of Communication. He shoved notes between the taped pages of music, twisting the connection for their opponents.

He peeked out from the hanging fabric. Two of the robed figures were rearing away from each other, slowing. Another attacker faltered as he saw his fellows, and asked them something Sam couldn't hear. The first attacker, a Lobath who had pushed back his hood, said something else angrily, and the other shouted back, just as loud. Sam grinned as Majus Caroom lowered their head and bowled the fighting attackers over, sending them sprawling. A ripple was running through the line of dark cloaks as they found they suddenly couldn't understand their compatriots. Behind them, he caught a flash of Majus Ayama running, Enos by her side.

He *could* help. Majus Cyrysi was back on his feet now, chest inflating, as orange and yellow spiraled up about his neck and face. Sam clenched his hands. His heart was trying to beat its way through his chest, and not just because of panic.

Inas, coated with a sheen of emerald green, glanced at his good hand, then up to Sam. He winked, then touched one of the long brown and gray floor planks. A crackle of green ran down its length, the wood creaking in protest. The other end pulled up in a curve, tripping an attacker sighting down a crossbow.

Majus Cyrysi's boot heels thumped on the planks as he ran toward the circle of light from the lanterns. One hand rose, and Sam's ears popped in protest. The Symphony of Communication was in chaos, measures playing over each other, tied together with the majus' notes. The Lobath across from him shook his head violently, splattering drops of dark blood from his pug nose.

Majus Cyrysi spoke a single word and all was silence; white noise buzzing like flies in Sam's head. His vision wavered, and Majus Caroom and Inas staggered. Two of the cloaked figures fell with muted thuds to the ground, and the others shook their heads.

Sam pinched his nose, fighting off a sudden headache at the dip in pressure. Clanks and yells drifted back into audible range, and his mentor swam into focus, too close to the cloaked figures, bent on one knee. His head was bowed, thin hands clasped across the feathers on his head. Sam ran to help him.

* * *

Rilan batted away smoke to reach the traitorous piece of slime at the middle, her rage trying to strangle her brain. She didn't even look toward the metal crate Caroom had thrown. Another maji intercepted it and threw it back.

"You took my seat, you Brahm-cursed monkey dung!" she yelled at Vethis. She threw a punch from her hip, and the oily man fell back, robes billowing. She followed with a front kick that would have doubled him over, had he not scampered out of the way.

He was off balance, and she grabbed a wrist, twisting Vethis' arm back and up. His head followed his body as it tipped forward. The Symphony of Healing blazed through her and she added notes to the drumbeat that was the density of her bone. She took notes away from his. Her fist would go through him like a mallet through a cantaloupe.

"No! I can explain!" All trace of Vethis' affected lisp disappeared, his face just above the floor. Rilan raised his wrist, forcing him closer.

"Should have thought of that before you decided to betray the Council of the Maji," she spat at him, and plunged her fist down.

It hit nothing. She blinked, realizing she was tumbling to the ground. Her notes came back with a snap that almost made her eyes cross. The edge of a dark cloak brushed past her vision.

She rolled, coming up on her heels, hands out. Vethis was on the ground, cradling an elbow out of joint, pale white and deep blue misting around the fingers of his other hand, his face pasty. He must have hated to wear that black cloak instead of his usual lace.

In front of him was a smaller figure, clothed all in black, with its cowl pulled down. The figure raised its head enough for Rilan to catch a flash of light on predatory teeth.

"I look forward to dancing against you," the figure said, sibilant. "This, I have long been waiting for, to show the Nether maji their weakness."

Rilan flicked her eyes once more to Vethis, and then all her attention was on the newcomer. "So be it, Snake," she said, trying to goad the Sathssn.

It didn't work. She feinted forward with a wrist strike to the cloaked head, intending to follow up with a reverse punch augmented by her song. Neither strike landed. Arcs of sapphire blue and a dark, bruised purple swirled around the Sathssn's feet and he was out of her range. She moved again and he was behind her, slipping past in a waltz-step. A strike to her kidney staggered her and she grunted.

"Nakan, he shall show the Nether majus who is more capable. We have all heard of the prowess of Councilor—ah, *Majus* Rilan. Will she stand up to me?"

Rilan whirled, barely catching Nakan's arm with her fingers before he could slip away. *Shiv's dagger, he's fast.* She added notes to the melody of her fingers, turning major chords to minor, fixing her fingers in claws, dragging herself along with the Sathssn.

He moved a step, then spun, tilting her off balance. She felt a knee buckle when he kicked, and turned piano to forte, strengthening the tendons.

Must get on the offensive.

No time for her mental tricks. This would all be physical, and she had to make changes to Nakan, not herself. She recognized some of his steps, had fought against them before.

"Zsaana can't have taught you all his tricks," she said. Her fingers were still on his arm, giving her a connection, and she burrowed into his music, turning solid measures into trills, loosening his tendons in a flush of white and olive. Nakan stumbled, but his aura pulsed against hers, blue and purple against white and olive.

"Old Zsaana, he was my teacher as he was yours," Nakan said. His movement was drunken with his loose tendons, but he used one arm as a whip, flicking the fingers of his glove out to her temple. She stepped back, looping an arm around his attack, but he stepped in with a strike from the other side. "He recounted your matches many times. This, I have been excited to see for myself."

Rilan countered with a double-arm block, and muted notes, intending both his arms to go numb. *Not enough time to grab my knife.* Something went wrong when she did and Nakan snapped upright, stable again. She shook tingling fingers, eyes wide. There were extra notes in her song. He had made her reverse her change to his tendons. She didn't know the House of Grace could do that.

Her foot came up to knee Nakan in the gut, but the Sathssn moved fluidly around it in a flash of blue and purple, flipping over her head. His hands caught her shoulders, pulling her backwards. She made quarter notes into eighth notes, then sixteenth notes, adjusting the curvature of her spine. She accelerated his motion and slammed him into the floor with a crash. Rilan rolled over, pinning his arms across his neck, choking. The majus growled as blue and purple fought against her white and olive, but she locked the joints in her elbows, shoulders, and fingers, pressing down. Above her head, an impact shook the air, and her ears popped. Must be Ori. That would take down two or three of the thugs, if they were lucky.

"How's Zsaana's training going for you? The old bigot must have forgotten a few things." She breathed into Nakan's face. "Is the Life Coalition so arrogant it separates itself from the Council of the Maji? This traitor—"

"Has something you should see," interrupted a smooth voice. The lisp was back. Rilan looked up to see Vethis clutching Enos to him, one hand pulling up under her chin, keeping her head back. The skin of her neck had gone an unhealthy color of purple, as if it were being crushed. Vethis winced with the effort to control her, and his ridiculous moustache was all awry. Little sparks of white passed between them, with splashes of dark blue on his side, and Rilan could hear warring strains of music, each trying to go dissonant against each other. Enos looked like she had swallowed a bee. Her face contorted as she warred against Vethis, but there was no contest.

"I propose a trade, Rilan," Vethis said, and she bit her tongue to keep from spitting at him. As he spoke, a spiraling portal opened behind him, ringed in green and burgundy. So the last majus was House of Strength. Rilan glared at Enos, willing her to understand.

You have another power, girl, she thought at her apprentice, *use it and you make this much easier for me.* Enos was staring back at her, and pursed her lips, though whether in concentration or reluctant agreement, she couldn't say.

"Why, Vethis?" she asked. "Why betray the Council?"

"Your precious Council," Vethis sneered, giving Enos a jerk, "is falling apart. You've seen the same thing. I'm only aligning myself with the winning side."

"The Life Coalition will attack the Nether!" she said. Impossibly, she could feel her grip on Nakan slipping. He was using the House of Grace against her, sliding away. She couldn't keep this up for long.

Enos, do something, she thought.

"I know that," Vethis replied. "I gave them the best time and place to attack."

Rilan gaped. She couldn't imagine even this social climbing rat doing anything so blatant. She struggled to keep Nakan immobile until he passed out.

"The Dissolution will be upon us soon," Vethis told her, and Rilan screwed up her face against the incongruity of the old fairy tale. Yet it kept coming up. "Always, I've been second place to the noble, the brilliant, the *special* Rilan Ayama," Vethis spat. "Let the universe burn, if one time I can come out first—Ow!" Vethis jerked, and Enos slipped away from him like a viper. Vethis was staring in shock at a trickle of blood running down his arm—the one that had been holding her wrists. "She bit me!" he cried. "How did she bite me?"

Nakan writhed and Rilan saw him grin under his cowl as he wriggled free. "Take the rat with you," he ground out as he slipped away. "He is lazy and dishonorable. You, you are a good fighter. I wish to test you again before the end." Then he was gone, a shadow, heading for the portal. Rilan reversed the changes to her body, her notes a welcome warmth. She sprang up, ignoring Enos' hand, and stalked toward Vethis, who shrank back in fear.

* * *

Origon could do little more than stand and observe, with Sam holding his elbow. A voice called from the center of the confused Life Coalitioners, and Sam looked up in interest. His apprentice had done some other impossible thing, twisting the communication between the non-maji. Later he would get an explanation. For now, they would mop up this bunch. Hand Dancer was bringing her column of smoke and fire to circle around the defeated group.

Rilan and her apprentice were fighting with two of the maji, and Caroom had a hold on the much smaller maji from the House of Potential, pulses slamming back and forth between them, green and brown and tan. Energy ripped and transferred and equalized.

The brown flared and Caroom went down to one knee with a creak like an oak swaying in a high wind. Inas was at their side in an instant, but the Life Coalition majus tipped a stack of barrels over. The barrels swayed, then righted themselves, swathed in a swirl of brown. Origon recognized the transfer of energy, and called out, but too late. The majus backhanded Inas with a lazy glove and the young man flew backwards, the weight of five tottering barrels propelling him.

Origon moved, painfully, to help them both, but the voice called again from across the warehouse and a portal formed, ringed in green and burgundy. The majus from the House of Potential looked back, swung one more massive punch at Caroom, who fell to the ground, and ran toward the portal. The non-maji still standing were already going through.

Origon crossed the distance to Caroom, Sam beside him. Was the Benish still alive?

"Hand Dancer," he called, waving a tired hand. His robe—singed during the fight—slipped down his arm, baring far too much skin. "You are needed here."

Hand Dancer glanced toward him, gestured an agreement, and made a rounding-up movement. The rest of the ash and smoke, still warm, lost its heat and drifted to the floor, behind the exiting dark cloaked figures. Hand Dancer helped him lift the heavy Benish up.

* * *

Sam saw the shadow flick by as his mentor helped Majus Caroom to their feet. The Benish was bleeding from a deep puncture on their chest—the same thick, greenish fluid Sam had seen in Gloomlight. They had scrapes and cuts all over. Sam aimed toward Inas, collapsed in a pile by a large barrel. His heart pounded, but he couldn't give in to the panic. His friend's life might depend on him. *Is he alright? He can't be dead.* Another shadow crossed his vision and Sam stumbled.

His foot slipped out from under him. *The House of Grace?* He fell, cracking his head on a board, and saw stars. When his vision cleared, another short figure in black was holding Inas in a painful grip, his arm twisted behind his back, walking him toward the portal.

"Our assistant, your cousin of sorts, told us you can help us in our holy cause," the Sathssn said to his prisoner. "You should be overjoyed to contribute so much as a blasphemer."

Sam tried to get to his feet, but sat down again heavily, dizzy. "Inas! Fight him! Change!" Inas only gave him a terrified look over one shoulder. Sam scrabbled forward, but his balance was off, and he collapsed on one arm. *Get up. Do something useful!* "Help him!" he shouted to the maji, but they looked around in confusion. When Sam looked back, the figure and Inas were gone.

* * *

Compared to Nakan, Vethis was easy. A fake to the left, a step to the right, and Rilan grabbed the arm she dislocated earlier. The scum must have been able to put it back in place. He'd always been good at healing. She twisted as she turned, sliding her grip up, and was rewarded with another pop and a gasp from Vethis. Dislocated joints took time to regain their strength.

"No Snake to help you out this time," she taunted, then heard his notes inserting between measures as he tried to break the tendons in her hand. It was clumsy, and she countered easily, olive flaring against dark blue in a wash of white.

The bell in her braid tinkled as she shook her head. "Hardly worth the effort. You're weak and lazy, Fernand Vethis, and as soon as we get back, I'll—"

"No!" The interruption jolted Rilan, and she looked to where Enos was blocking Nakan's path to the portal. Nakan held Inas immobilized.

"You cannot take him," Enos insisted, and a white aura gathered about her.

Rilan threw Vethis to the ground, then muted the music of the nerves in his legs just in case. Unfortunately, she had to keep a hand on him to keep from disrupting the change.

Nakan slipped around Enos so fast Rilan had trouble following his movement. "I will not bring you, girl," he said. "The Life Coalition, it has enough trouble handling one Aridori in our ranks. As this one has helped the other one to die, so he will fill its place." Nakan backpedaled toward the portal as Enos advanced.

Change, boy, Rilan thought at Inas, seeing his chance slipping. *They know about the prisoner already.* Was it through Vethis? The Council might know of the break-in to the prison this morning, but how could they know of the twins? Maybe the Aridori had another way to communicate to the Life Coalition before it died, though that was even more disturbing to contemplate. Something for later.

Regardless, she couldn't let the slime go, even to help. The moment he got up, they would have an enemy at their back and her chance to rescue Inas—the Aridori—would be lost. She dragged Vethis after her, but she was too slow. The twins had to save themselves. *They are so paranoid of being discovered, they will not act even when they are.*

Enos ran after the two, but they were at the portal. The Life Coalitioners all were through except Vethis, the majus from the House of Strength, and three non-maji, dead or unconscious. The majus at the portal gestured impatiently.

"Come, Nakan. We must be away." Enos froze at the voice, then ran for them. The majus from the House of Strength gestured, and planks curled up to block her path, dripping green. "Only one of you," the majus said, and disappeared into the portal behind Nakan and Inas. The planks collapsed as she did and Enos leapt to where the black hole in the air had been moments before.

"No!" Enos beat hands against her thighs and slumped forward.

Rilan dragged her prize, Vethis swearing and cursing and yelling in pain. "Hand Dancer!" she called into the sudden silence. "Get over here now! We lost one."

CHAPTER THIRTY

The Last Session

-The Great Assembly takes two long breaks each Nether cycle, which is modeled on the trader's calendar. This in turn was originally based on the seasons of Methiem, which indicates how much that species plays a part in the politics of the Nether.
From "The Great Assembly through the Ages"

Sam ran to Majus Ayama, Hand Dancer next to him. The former councilor was yelling at the majus she had captured, who was on his back. *They took Inas. He's gone, and they'll put him in a box like the other one.* Enos sat crumpled beside her mentor, head in her hands, and Sam threw an arm around her, his watch in his other hand. "It'll be alright," he told her uselessly, squeezing her close. She grabbed at him, pulling him in. She buried her face in his shoulder and wetness seeped into his shirt. The ticking of his watch didn't help.

"Where is it? Where will they make the void?" Majus Ayama shouted at her prisoner. Sam lifted his head. Two of the lanterns still rested on the crate, throwing weird shadows through the dark warehouse. The third was smashed, its flame extinguished. In their light, he saw the Life Coalitioner was the same greasy man they had encountered in the House of Healing, his moustache all askew.

"I could—I could not stop them," Enos said into his shoulder, barely audible. "Dunarn took him."

"And Nakan," Sam said, and Enos nodded, the motion working tears farther into his shirt. He blinked rapidly, heart racing. "Dunarn opened the portal. We'll find him." Enos pulled back and looked him in the face. *Can we find him? We still don't know where they held us.* Behind them, the maji grouped around the prisoner, but Sam didn't pay attention to their words.

"I'm sorry," he said, and Enos frowned. "I'm sorry I ever doubted you," he clarified. "I'm sorry I was afraid. I'm sorry I gave you away." He was breathing too fast, and had to pause to swallow. "If I hadn't let your secret get out, we wouldn't be here."

Enos stared at him a moment, then slowly shook her head. "I was so angry at you." Sam prepared himself for the outburst, drawing in. It didn't come. He realized she had spoken in past tense.

"And now?" he asked. He ran arms down her shoulders, waiting for her to push him away.

"We would not have gotten in to see our cousins, and I would not have learned about them." She twisted in his arms, looking over her shoulder. "I think it was not only Majus Cyrysi who guessed. Majus Ayama was also close to discovering us, and then we would not have found out what the Life Coalition was doing. We are not used to living outside our family, and certainly not with maji."

"Inas' hand," Sam said. It came out before he realized he would say it. "Will it get better? After we find him, that is?"

"I do not know," Enos said. "I've never seen that before."

"Then we'll have to find him and fix him up." He stood, then reached down to pull Enos to her feet. She squeezed his hand, holding on as they turned to the maji.

* * *

Origon watched, tapping his thumbs together, as Rilan kept up a steady stream of curses and invective at the prone Vethis. They had both expected the new Sathssn councilor, Hathssas, to be here. Instead there was this egg-sucking son of a turtle. Was Hathssas not a member of the Life Coalition after all? Or was she merely not at this meeting?

"Hand Dancer," he said to the approaching Lobhl, "check the portal. See if you can trace where it was going." It was something the House of Power could do, but not easy in the chaotic residue from so many changes to the Grand Symphony. Hand Dancer would have a better chance of finding something. Meanwhile, he had to make sure Rilan didn't do anything too permanent to one who was still technically part of the Council.

The Lobhl stepped closer to him, her hands making small gestures only Origon could see—the equivalent of a whisper. <I must apologize,> she signed. <I am not a fighter. I fear I was not much help. Perhaps if I had done more, or affected more changes, fewer of them would have escaped.>

Origon waved away the apology with one hand. "Do not be second guessing what is done. The flame was well made, and kept the Life Coalitioners from escaping through the other door. Check the portal before it is fading too much." He hoped Rilan would get something out of the slimy man soon. Hand Dancer gave a short twirl of her fingers in acceptance and stepped away to where the portal had closed.

Origon glanced to Caroom, but the big Benish's eyes were dimmed in concentration. An aura of green and tan surrounded their many cuts and scrapes, and they were not paying attention. He stepped close to Rilan and gripped her arm.

"Stop it," he hissed, letting his crest rise. Her stream of abuse cut off, and both she and Vethis looked up in surprise. "You two have been sparring with each other since you were in university."

"He is *Life Coalition*, Ori!" Rilan sputtered. "The little slug is sabotaging the harmony of the ten species, may Brahm give him boils and waste his bowels."

"And he can be giving us information," Origon added. His nails were digging into his palm.

"I won't give you anything," Vethis snarled up. Origon casually leaned over and cuffed him on the side of the head. Rilan gaped and Vethis shrank down, eyes wide.

"You are the son of a turtle and a jackal," Origon told him, keeping his voice calm. "Your ancestors must tear their eyes out rather than look down on you. You are a traitor and you will pay." He paused, took in a deep breath, and smoothed his crest. They were both still staring at him and he realized his teeth were grinding together, one cutting into his cheek. He did not like how the little wretch brought out the worst in Rilan. He forced his jaw to relax.

"We can be doing this the easy way, where you tell us where the Drain is to be, or we can do it the hard way, where I compel your body and Rilan your mind. I am tired, and may upset my composition so your mental acumen is affected. Rilan may accidentally cause you to forever be her admiring servant. We may make mistakes in our haste to save the Nether. What shall it be?"

There was silence. The apprentices were watching, silent and pale.

"The Assembly," Vethis whispered, and Origon's head whipped back down to the vile man, his crest stirring in agitation.

"What?"

"It will be in the rotunda of the Assembly while it is in session. The void will take the representatives, the maji, and the Effature."

"Why now? Why not sooner?" Rilan had finally found her voice.

"I'm not sure," Vethis muttered, his lisp gone. "I haven't been privy to all their secrets." He actually seemed disappointed he hadn't wormed his way farther in. "Something about a buildup of voids and energy to access the Nether. That's all I know!" He shrank in on himself as Rilan raised a menacing fist. Before she could do anything, Origon smacked Vethis hard, across the face. More physical violence from her would lead to further ties between the two. Origon simply wanted information from the traitor.

Vethis gasped, and blood ran from his nose.

"Think fast. What else?"

Vethis gasped like a fish and brought up a finger to dab at the blood. "I, I don't—" Origon raised his hand again. His nails had left red lines down the man's cheek.

"There's one on each homeworld!" Vethis blurted. Origon cocked his head and Vethis stuttered, trying to get the words out faster than he could speak.

"A void—a Drain. They've made one on all the homewords. I don't know why. No, wait!" Vethis raised both hands, warding off an attack that didn't come. "Something I heard—the ten homeworlds all connect to the Nether. The Drains reduce the amount of energy required to—to—"

"To create a Drain in the Nether," Origon whispered. He felt his crest rise in understanding. "That's why they were not attacking the Assembly directly. The Nether exists outside the universe, and it must take too much power to create a Drain here—there must be some protection." He could almost hear the chords of Power that separated the Nether from the homeworlds. It was a focal point, an anomaly. The differences had always confounded him. Maji could make portals to the Nether without having been here before. Why? "They were making the other Drains—Drains that destroy energy—to reduce a barrier required to create one here. They were making it into a distraction, with the secession, the attacks, and the Aridori."

Origon raised his hand again.

"By all that's holy, that's everything I know!" Vethis wailed, hands covering his face. Origon relaxed his hand.

<I cannot find the exit point.> The mental echo of words distracted Origon and he looked to where Hand Dancer had sketched a series of interconnected lines, blazing in the air in front of her. A new section appeared, wavered, and buckled under the combined harmonics.

"Someone from the House of Potential could trace it, even that young Sureri—Brahm's balls!" White and olive green flared about Rilan's hands.

A small portal opened underneath Vethis' head and shoulder as Origon looked back down, and his upper body slid through. Origon made a catch at the man's legs, but his long fingers closed on air and the portal disappeared with a swirl of white and deep blue.

"Shiv take his eyes!" Rilan punched one hand into another. Hand Dancer's construct collapsed in a series of harmonic resonances and Origon winced at the dissonance. With two portals occupying nearly the same space, and with a similar endpoint, any hope of tracing the connection was doomed. The Symphony would be resistant to any further such changes.

"That one will, hmmmm, not be treated well by that one's fellows," Caroom intoned. Their eyes widened and focused on Origon. "However, the Coalitioners may find out what this group knows and get to the Assembly first. These ones should hurry. Hmmmm." They gripped their chest with one large hand, rumbling in pain.

"Can you come with us?" Rilan asked them, stepping close. Hands spread on bark-like skin, Rilan probed Caroom's wounds, white and olive flashing between her fingers.

"This one's apprentice has been taken. Is there any, hmmmmm, question?" Caroom's pauses were longer than usual, and they took in a breath after each one. They must be in great pain, but they would also slow the group.

"Your, ah, tissue is broken along here." Rilan traced a line where a Kirian or Methiemum would have a rib.

"Hmmmm. This one is aware," Caroom said. "If there is a chance this group might save this one's apprentice, it must be taken."

"Even an Aridori?" Rilan asked, and Origon glanced sidelong at her. Had the twins not proven themselves in this fight?

"His name is Inas!" Sam called from the side.

Caroom's eyes flashed as they looked at Rilan. Some inner part of them creaked as they raised a massive finger. "This one shall not, hmmm, abandon a charge," they told her sternly. "The Benish have long memories, though this species is not considered a, hmmm, founding species of the Nether. Not all remember the Aridori with such fear and anger. Some remember when those ones were like the rest of the species. Hmmm." Caroom paused and rested three fingers along a wound, which was oozing thick fluid again. "Perhaps those two are merely what they, hmmm, say. Was that considered?"

Rilan blinked and looked away, though Origon had seen her stand up to screaming senators and charging beasts with equal poise. "Can you function without medical attention for now? I'm, ah, not much good at it myself," she said.

"A small investment of, hmmm, permanent nature will be enough," Caroom said, and set his words to action, a line of emerald green and tan tracing along several of his cuts. They stood a little straighter afterwards, but their skin was dull, lacking its usual burnish.

Rilan rounded on Origon, and he felt his crest flatten before he could control it.

"You. How long have you been hiding your weakness?" she asked. "You said your notes were almost restored."

Origon stammered at the sudden change in topic. He hoped she hadn't seen his actions during the fight. "It is not so bad," he said, but she obviously didn't believe him.

"The capsule took more out of you than you admit," she said, poking a thin finger into his chest. Origon stepped back a pace, though his balance was still off. "How much of your space flight was permanent?" she asked. "You controlled that shuttle for hours."

"Most of it was to be permanent," he admitted quietly. "I was speaking to the engineers for quite some time about it."

"What about now?" Rilan pressed. "Can you help me stop this? You nearly fell over when you had to fight another majus. It was four on four, and still they got away."

Origon's crest fell. Maybe he should be less concerned with Caroom and more for himself.

"I can help," Sam put in unexpectedly. He withered under Rilan's glare and even Origon cast an annoyed glance at him. The young man was talented, but he didn't have a full majus' training.

"No offense, boy," Rilan echoed, "but you're barely able to touch the Symphony. I was planning to leave you behind." Origon nodded along. Sam's anxiety would keep him from being much help.

Then Enos placed an arm around him, and Sam straightened. "We *can* help. We escaped the Life Coalition, Enos and I. We gave you the information you needed to get here. I broke the communication between the people who fought us today. We're going to find Inas."

Rilan turned a questioning glance to Origon. He nodded reluctantly. "I am not to be sure how he did it, but Sam garbled the Nether's translation, for the non-maji." He would be asking the young man about that. There were limits to what the House of Communication could do. One couldn't simply rationalize something as a subset of the music of Communication. Some parts of reality were under the control of another house, or of none. The Nether's music, especially, was impenetrable.

<I would like to come along as well,> Hand Dancer signed. <I hope to add more there than I did here.>

"I'm going with Sam," Enos said. She wiped at both eyes, and smoothed wisps of black hair back and out of her face.

Rilan's face closed in, calculating, Origon knew. "Let's stop standing around then," she said testily. "The Assembly's last session of the season is tomorrow. The Life Coalition can use a portal to arrive from the homeworld where they meet—Sath Home, I would guess—whereas we are much too close to open one."

When she slid the door back, the dim rays of first lightening illuminated her. They had taken more time than he thought for the walk through the Bazaar, the fight, and interrogating Vethis.

"We have only a few lightenings before it starts," Origon said.

* * *

They left the bodies of the Life Coalitioners behind them, and Sam gripped Enos' arm as they exited the warehouse. *Three people are dead, gone, because they were defending their beliefs.* The Life Coalition had killed many people, and there was no defense of that. Yet they had to have some reason, didn't they? *Why are they doing this?*

In their haste to stop the Life Coalition, Sam wasn't entirely sure the others had followed that train of thought. This was their home. They were protecting it. Sam, as an outsider, had a clearer perspective.

Why do they have 'Life' in their name if all they do is destroy? What possible reason did these people have to make Drains? How did they do it?

They had been up all night and Sam's arms dragged by his sides. Even his anxiety was a small thing, hammering at his mind as they walked. The Bazaar was nearly quiet at this time of early morning, with many stalls closed, and the smaller carts and blankets gone. Sam dozed on the tram, and then on a carriage, curled up with Enos. It would take several lightenings to get back to High Imperium and the absence of Inas' familiar warmth picked at his sanity.

He woke to Enos shaking his shoulder. "We're here," she said. Her face was tight, eyes pinching at the corners.

"We'll find him," Sam told her. *I hope we find him. Please don't hurt him. I don't know what I would do.*

They were at the terminus of the carriage system, right under the growing brilliance of the walls, stretching overhead. Sam fought down a stab of panic, and brought his watch to his ear. *Calm. You're used to this place.* He just hadn't been so close to the walls. They were rippled and smoothed, like glowing waves crashing vertically.

Even in early morning, it was bright, and rich, dense foliage sprung up in every crack and plot of dirt. A group of little birds—or bird-like things—shot overhead as their group descended from the station back to street level, and Sam heard the bird's chatter echoing as trills and glissandos in the Symphony. There were little creatures in the brush, too, finding and becoming breakfast, communicating in waltzes and gallops. He ducked his head, keeping out most of the vastness of the Imperium. There was no time for his anxiety here and he had to keep his triggers to a minimum.

Majus Ayama took the lead, as usual, heading to a huge cylindrical building with a dome of what looked like crystal. The former councilor's long black braid practically vibrated with energy, and her jerkin and pants creaked as she walked, stretching their range of motion, as if she was trying to pull herself along by sheer will.

Figures were already entering the Dome of the Assembly in the early morning light, and Majus Ayama hurried to intercept a lone figure in a black cloak and a hood. Sam traded a look with Enos. Was she going to accost every Sathssn?

"...heard about the program for today, Hathssas?" Her words drifted into Sam's hearing. Majus Ayama was gripping the Sathssn's shoulder, and the figure turned so Sam could see an insignia on its chest, half orange and half bright pink. He suddenly realized the Life Coalition members had not worn those insignia.

The others grouped around and the new Sathssn councilor for the House of Power looked between them, her cowl twitching from side to side. Sam saw a flash of dark green flesh in the bright morning light. Their group was bruised and dirty, clothes dusted with ash, Majus Caroom's shirt torn around the places they were injured. Majus Ayama had a splash of crimson on her jerkin. *Blood? From her or someone else?*

"What is it you mean, Council—Majus?" Hathssas quickly corrected her slip, ducking her head as she did so. She was short, like most Sathssn, not even reaching his chest. "Has there been a change? This, I would hope to hear of first since my rise to the position of councilor." She sounded unsure.

"What's on the schedule?" Majus Ayama demanded. "What are you discussing? What's the agenda?" Majus Cyrysi slipped fingers across her back, maybe attempting to quiet her.

"I—nothing special, I do not think," Hathssas stammered. "Today, it is the last of the Assembly for three ten-days. It should be only the ends of business." Then her cowl cocked to one side. "Although—"

"Yes?" Majus Ayama pushed forward. "What?"

"Let her be thinking, Rilan," Majus Cyrysi murmured, but the majus flicked a hand at him.

Hathssas raised a gloved hand to tap at the air, and Sam glimpsed fine dark green and yellow scales between the end of the glove and the robe's sleeve. She was showing more skin than most Sathssn. *Not as conservative as others.* It was a mark in the new councilor's favor.

"Now, I remember. Yesterday, late in the day, there was an addendum to the schedule for today." She paused to think again, and Sam thought Majus Ayama might throttle the little alien to make her speak faster. "The one who raised it, I am not sure who it is, but the motion was to pass a resolution on the attacks by Aridori in the Imperium today." Her cowl twitched again as she twisted to look at the streams of people going into the Assembly. "Maybe this, it is why so many attend today."

"You did not remember this until you were being prompted?" Majus Cyrysi asked incredulously.

Hathssas shrugged, the folds of her robe popping up and down. "Me, I was never convinced the Aridori were behind the attacks."

"Hmmmm. This one thinks we may have misjudged Councilor Hathssas," Majus Caroom rumbled.

"Agreed," Majus Ayama snapped. "She isn't one of them." She turned back to the Sathssn, who was peering at them all in confusion. "If you see anything *strange* happen today, be ready to get the others out of the Dome as fast as you can."

"Which others?" Hathssas asked.

"All of them."

CHAPTER THIRTY-ONE

Aberration

-The Drains were to be formed by one of each house of the maji, in conjunction. All the greatest works were done so, but never were any so destructive. It is still beyond my understanding how a negation, or void, can be generated by melodies existing in the Grand Symphony. Were they able to counter every strain of music with an inverse vibration? It seems an impossible act.

Journal of Origon Cyrysi, Kirian majus of the Houses of Communication and Power

Rilan struggled through the halls of the Assembly that circled around the main chamber, swimming through throngs of delegates on their way to the floor. The Assembly was big enough to hold over one hundred thousand representatives of the ten species, and even the lower floor was packed today.

"Out of the way! Move please! Majus coming through, on service of the Effature." Well, she would be once they talked to him. She elbowed and pushed. They were surely behind the Life Coalition, with so much time wasted traveling between the Bazaar and High Imperium. The others strung out behind her. She hoped Enos was helping Sam deal with the crowds, and then shook her head at the thought. *How easy to fall into trusting the Aridori.* One hand rose, almost by itself, to make that stupid warding gesture. Rilan forced it back down.

At last, the crowd thinned near the Speaker's Entrance, and soon she was in the Assembly proper, Ori beside her, ignoring confused and hostile looks from the guards. The loss of her seat, to Vethis no less, fed a pit of ice in her belly. Her one shred of hope came from the certainty that Vethis wouldn't be a councilor much longer.

Among the chairs of the speakers, most still empty, she searched for the one face that could help her. Ori was past the guards, and so was Sam, hanging from Enos. They were near one wall—Sam would likely stay there a few moments, acclimatizing to the new surroundings. She scanned the Assembly, ignoring rising calls and shouts that she was not in the correct place. Jhina glared over from the sparse seats for the Council. Hathssas was beside her, and Freshta, but the others had not yet taken their places.

Before any of them could accost her, or thankfully, question her part in the recent events in Gloomlight, a quiet voice addressed her, near her left shoulder. "Majus Ayama."

She turned, feeling like an apprentice called to the house head, and found the Effature standing behind her. He looked ancient and time-less as always, his little wisp of a beard trailing in the breeze from her movement. The coronet of Nether crystal on his head glowed faintly.

"Sir," she began, but the Nether's caretaker held up a hand and she stopped.

"I have no doubt you have something of great importance to tell me, but I believe we should leave the floor first." He raised one pale white eyebrow and glanced over the gathering speakers, many of whom were turning their direction.

"Yes sir."

She followed him to a nook in the wall rising from the Nether floor, which supported the rings of seats above. The little setback was behind his chair. Along the way, Ori collected Sam and Enos from where the young man was pressed against the wall, urging him forward with one hand. Sam clung to him as much as to Enos.

Hand Dancer and Caroom were just entering the rotunda, the Lobhl supporting the Benish. They were arguing with the guards, Caroom holding one hand to their chest, and Rilan made sure they saw where she was going. They would have to talk their own way in.

The little indentation in the wall of the rotunda was cramped with the five of them. It was inside the thick rock wall that supported the first row of seats, dark and quiet, distorting the sounds of the Assembly. She had seen the Effature vanish in here before, to rest in the middle of a long session, but she had never been here before.

The little man was facing a wall of the nook, and turned back with a miniature crystal goblet of clear liquid in each hand. His long green sleeves nearly covered his hands, and hung most of the way down to the floor. He offered a goblet to her and Ori, then went back to the wall the moment they took them. She stared at his back, tracing the intricate purple and green pattern of scales that reflected the little light in here, willing him to turn back. There was no time for cocktails. She sniffed the goblet. Not a cocktail—it was just water.

The Effature swiveled, again with two tiny goblets, offering one to Sam, and one to Enos. Sam, trembling, accepted, though his eyebrows almost disappeared into his shaggy hair. Rilan made a mental note to get him a haircut, if they survived the day.

"Majus Ayama." The deep words pulled her attention back to the Effature. He had his own glass of water, and reached for another object of Nether glass, this one hemispherical, carved like a curled animal—a cat, perhaps. He tapped it twice, and it rang. Then Rilan realized it was ringing not only in her physical ears, but inside the Symphony of Healing, tuning notes to true. She traded a glance with Ori, whose eyes were as wide as hers.

"I hear it too," he said. So that was why they were speaking in here.

The Effature crossed his arms, hiding them in the opposite sleeve. "Please, drink. You look quite tired."

"Effature," she said, trying not to let the words rush out. "We must hurry. You are in terrible danger. If you would just let me show—"

"It is pure water," the Effature said. Rilan fell silent, then raised the crystal goblet to her lips. "From my estates outside the Imperium. There are some mineral deposits filtered in the stream, and I find they improve my constitution." The water was light and clear, with a faint taste of iron.

"What about the System?" Ori asked, pointing a finger at the carved hemisphere—how had the Effature *carved* Nether crystal? It was glowing with a rainbow of colors, all houses of the maji involved.

"Something left from a long time ago," the Effature said. "It helps to clear the mind. Now, what is so urgent?"

Indeed, Rilan found her thoughts more ordered than they had been in days. "There is a splinter of the Fundamentalist Sathssn called the Life Coalition, though they employ other species. We believe they will create a void during the Assembly session today." Her mouth closed almost by itself. Yes. That was what she had to say, short and succinct.

The Effature only nodded, then looked between them in expectation. His eyes lingered on Enos for a split second longer, and the young woman looked down into her drink. "I have suspected a rift forming among the ten species," he stated. "How will you handle this?"

"We were nearly apprehending the Life Coalition a few lightenings ago," Ori added, "but they escaped here. According to Vethis, who was among them, they will be creating a Drain. We must apprehend them before they start."

The Effature didn't bat an eye at Vethis going turncoat. "I have the utmost confidence in you and your friends," he said, then motioned for them to finish their drinks. They did, Rilan licking her lips at the metallic taste, and he returned the crystal glasses to an alcove. "I will organize the retreat of those in danger, and handle the organization in the Imperium," he said. "For now—" he paused, and Rilan heard a scream echo from inside the rotunda. "You should hurry."

* * *

Sam heard a clink as the man, the Effature—from what he could tell, like a president or prime minister for the Nether—returned the glasses to a concealed bar. The water wasn't the reason the man brought them in here. *That crystal he tapped is doing something to our notes. It's adjusting us. Cleaning us?* Time felt stretched. The Effature's glittering, scale-like suit whispered as he moved. Enos was near and Sam could even smell her more clearly; a fresh, mint scent, mixed with sweat and smoke. She was shivering. *She's thinking of Inas. I can't believe he's gone.*

Majus Ayama and Majus Cyrysi traded looks only they could interpret. When someone screamed outside the Effature's nook, Sam didn't even flinch, but squeezed Enos' hand, pulling her forward as Majus Ayama brushed the fabric hanging aside. As Sam entered the massive stadium of the Assembly, the anxiety that slowed him was buried under the little crystal carving's effects. He let the Symphony fill him, tracing shrill paired fourths in the screams, how they rippled out to others in the music.

A portal was open in the exact middle of the rotunda, green and burgundy rotating around it. *Dunarn made this.* Enos gasped, and Majus Cyrysi murmured something Sam couldn't hear. The portal was wide enough for three, and rank after rank of black-cloaked figures spilled out, forming an ever-increasing circle around the entrance.

There are so many. None of them wear the badges the maji do. His breathing spiked, and his hand was suddenly slick with sweat, sliding in Enos' grip. He was certain there were maji mixed in the crowd. No way to tell who could encase you in air or break your arm with a touch, or whether they would just shoot you with a crossbow bolt.

Maji Hand Dancer and Caroom were outside the Effature's cubby. The orange and gray film was over both of Hand Dancer's eyes and he scanned the gathering. Sam thought he used the change as a strategy overlay, letting the Lobhl see the connections between things. Majus Caroom wore a skein of green, though it was patchy in places and they moved slowly, keeping a thick hand near the wound in their chest.

"Is Inas with them?" Enos leaned forward, peering into the emerging Life Coalition troops.

Majus Hand Dancer made a negative with his hands, and Sam shook his head. "They probably have him wherever they came from." No sense in bringing Inas here. *That means we have to stop them, and find out where the Life Coalition is hiding.*

Diplomats and speakers stood, some yelling at the invaders, or scrambling to get away. A few auras of color showed where individual maji were trying to help. The Effature directed his guards with hand signals, and they rushed to evacuate the Assembly. Sam recognized a few members of the Council trying to help, though Councilor Feldo was absent.

"Hand Dancer and Enos, come with me," Majus Ayama said. Majus Cyrysi had Majus Caroom behind him.

Enos turned to him, worry in her eyes. Sam's heart rate spiked as she drew her hand away. *I'll be alone. It's too much.* He was curling in again. He was so weak.

"I have to help, Sam," Enos said.

"Go," Sam whispered back. *First stop the Life Coalition.* "I'll be fine." It was a lie, and both of them knew it. He fished his watch out, thumb running down the raised design on the edge, and held it to his ear. *Breathe evenly. React to what you have to.*

"Sam—can you be helping me and Caroom?"

Sam's knees buckled and he fell against the wall beside the Effature's niche. "A minute," he managed.

"We do not have a minute," Majus Cyrysi said. "We must act now, or not at all."

"Go," Sam whispered again. "I'll, I'll help when I can." *Just have to survive this attack. Too many people here. Too many things happening.* Even with the soothing of the Effature's crystal, he was too weak.

Majus Cyrysi shook his head, crest high and tight. Distress, the Nether told Sam. Torn between his apprentice and the approaching threat, no doubt.

"Go!" Sam shouted, and the maji turned away. Sam slid down the wall, watching; the most he could do. After a last figure appeared, who must be Dunarn, the portal closed with a pop. Several other figures stood near her, and auras popped into existence, tinted by secondary colors—blue, then yellow, orange, and white. Dunarn glowed green. They were creating some melody, and Sam could almost hear snatches of it, a strange thing with more pauses than notes, like the melody was halting more than moving. Inverting. A last figure set down something heavy and metal on the Nether floor with a boom that echoed, quieting the chaos for a moment. A rich brown enveloped the figure. There were maji from all six houses.

Sam reached for the Symphony, letting the intricate music calm his heart, his breathing. Almost without thought, he placed notes around the melody of the air in front of him, making parts of it harder, stronger, more *forte*. The air coalesced, becoming a magnifier, and Sam got a good look at the instrument on the floor of the Assembly. It had three finely wrought legs, holding up the barrel of something that looked like a cannon. Each leg ended in a foot carved to look like a dog's.

Thoughts of Dalhni flashed through his mind; Enos picking up a similar leg, Dunarn hiding it in her robe.

You know how to stop this.

The thought resonated through his mind, like the other thoughts that weren't his own. He hadn't realized then. The Effature's System was running his brain in a higher gear. The voice had been speaking to him for days. He blinked, his brain finding the other moments, like when he had made a portal from the Life Coalition's prison, or when he created breezes under the Drains in Dalhni, and outside ChinRan. It went all the way back to...back to when he opened the portal from his house on Earth. The voice had told him to take the fire's heat, showed him how to build a portal. Whatever it was, the voice was helping him. Was it the Nether?

How do I stop them? he asked, but the voice was silent.

Through his magnifier, he could see Majus Ayama and his mentor reach the edges of the rotunda and signal the maji in the stands above, coordinating the houses. First a swath of green, then another of yellow beside it, then orange, blue, white and brown, making a circle. A vast network of maji, all connected. *Why wasn't the Council already doing this?* The Etanela councilor was gesturing to those of the House of Grace, but the councilors for Strength and Communication were just standing there, watching frantically between the approaching army and the rest of the maji.

The six Life Coalition maji paid them no attention. Their troops held position, a shifting mass of black, with multiple species represented. Many had crossbows cocked and aimed, but they weren't attacking. *What are they waiting for?* Through his magnifying glass, Sam saw the six Coalitioners gather around the metal contraption and put their hands on the body of it.

It begins. The voice echoed in his head, like his thoughts, but not.

"No!" he called, but there was a puff of smoke, and a fraction of a second later, a *boom* shook the entire Assembly. Sam pushed back into the wall as his head was drawn up, following the path of something glimmering like glass. It tore through the air, up to the clear ceiling of the Assembly, then slipped *inside* the air, winking out of existence.

There is a way to end it, the voice in his head told him.

Who are you? he shouted back. No answer.

The air far above rippled and bubbled, like plastic burning in focused sunlight. It darkened, until it was an ugly sallow off-white sphere, like a blister. Panic spread through the gathered diplomats and maji as a hail of crossbow bolts arced up and out.

Sam rubbed at his arms as the first chill raked his skin.

* * *

Origon gaped at the Drain forming high above. Even through the sleeves of his robe, he could feel the temperature dropping. He stared at the cannon the Life Coalition used. How had they done it? They created something, using all of the houses, but the Drain was the negation of matter. It was a work of un-creation. It defied everything about the universe. It destroyed energy itself.

"Majus, we are lost," Caroom rumbled. "We must go." Origon noted individual faces in the crowd, positions of the Life Coalition's troops, lines of attack and defense running through his head. He was unaccountably clear-headed from the Effature's System-imbued Nether crystal, but still, all scenarios ended with the Drain as victor. Yet it had been created. It could be destroyed.

Something pulled at his sleeve, and he realized the Life Coalition troops were shooting at anyone who approached. There was a hole the size of his fist in the sleeve of his robe, and a trickle of blood ran down his arm. Sounds he had been ignoring reached him; people screaming, and dying. He smelt the sharp smell of his own blood. Some of the maji were down. Others were fighting. The diplomats and representatives of the Great Assembly were being herded away by the Effature's guards. Several speakers were motionless, dead or knocked out. They had been closest to the incoming troops, but the Effature's guards were fighting back, working with the Council and the maji. How long had he stood devising strategy? Where had that Nether crystal come from?

Origon poured notes into the Symphony, but it resisted. Too many were changing it at once. He backed between two speaker's chairs, finding the smooth rolling rhythm of heat and the tumble of notes in the circulating air. He bridged the two, heating the air even as he compressed it, forming a shield of air far harder than just the House of Communication could make. It was unique enough that the shield popped into existence between the two chairs barely in time to reflect a bolt back toward the black-cloaked figures.

Origon inhaled, and hung on to the shield. In his weakened state, it was the most he could do. Then Caroom's hand laid heavily on his shoulder, and a wave of well-being washed over him as the Benish passed a portion of their breathing and body regulation on. Origon nodded and stood straighter. If only Sam was here.

Origon spotted the young man, back by the Effature's hidey hole, scrambling to avoid the flying bolts. Ancestors take that anxiety of his. Together they might be able to reverse the Drain's effect. He couldn't do it on his own.

* * *

Rilan bolstered the resonance of her voice with her notes, increasing the volume of the melody, and bellowed above the sounds of the battle. Vethis wasn't here, of course, and Scintien was less than useless, though she was the councilor for Strength. Rilan would have to step in, where the members of the Council should take control. She shouted up to the first row of maji from the House of Strength above her, fixing on a senior majus she knew in the front row. "Give support to the others, Majus Rubin. Link up!" Beth Rubin was a few cycles older than her, a solid majus excelling in defense. The majus gave a quick nod and an aura of emerald and orange rose around her, spreading to the maji on either side. She stood quickly, leaning to one side to pluck a crossbow bolt from the air with a fist as dense as stone. With augmented muscles, she threw the bolt back into the mass of black-robed attackers at lightning speed, where it pierced a soldier, sending them tumbling backward.

"We have this fight," Majus Rubin called down to Rilan.

Rilan nodded back, then turned away, to where Hand Dancer was frantically weaving a map of the power play in front of him, gesturing to the captain of the guard—an immense Etanela, who bellowed orders to her sub-commanders. Hand Dancer jerked the tall captain to one side, and a bolt passed through the spot where her head had been. Explosions echoed through the chaos. The Effature's guards had blunderbusses against the Life Coalition's crossbows. Both took time to reload, and close fighting would become an important factor as the two forces engaged. The rotunda was huge, but the guards would only have a few shots before they crossed the distance.

Other maji were beginning to come down from their seats. A tall Kirian, his crest feathers unusually dark, vaulted down, then carefully adjusted his silver and blue robe to cover ankles and wrists. The majus—she thought his name was Magoula—stalked toward the Life Coalitioners, an aura of sapphire and pale green surrounding him, and he moved through a hail of bolts, using the House of Grace to pivot around shafts meant to take him down as easily as if they had been stationary. Nearer the attackers, he gestured, and ice began to creep across the floor, cracking and shifting, making black-robed forms slip and tumble. He pounced on one, punching down at a surprised face.

But despite the maji's help, they weren't going to win. Even if they defeated the black-robed troops, even if the Nether maji overwhelmed the handful of Life Coalition maji, none of it would make a difference. She eyed the void increasing above her head, shivering in the chill air.

Rilan ducked a figure running at her, swinging a scimitar. They had gotten through the ring of guards, and must have thought her an easy target. With the Effature's System cleaning her notes, her opponent was moving in slow motion. She caught the elbow of the arm still holding the sword high, and pulled upward, using the sword-person's momentum against them, turning and slamming the figure into the rock wall behind her. They didn't get up.

Rilan looked back to the void, now the diameter of a man's height. Was there any way to stop it?

* * *

Sam scooted forward, keeping close to the ground. *If crawling is the best I can do, I'll do that.* Every time he tried to stand, vertigo at the size of the arena, the noise of the two armies, sent him spiraling back down. It was safer down here anyway, away from projectiles. He ducked behind a speaker's chair.

Who are you? he sent inward. *Those are not my thoughts. What are you doing in my head?*

Nothing. He rubbed the goosebumps on his arms, and wished he had earplugs to guard against the clangs and shouts. It would have been easier to push the panic away. The old-fashioned guns the guards used boomed again, making him wince. The shooters fell silent, frantically reloading, while a cloud of smoke rose around them. Others with spears and swords battled the Life Coalition troops. They were less ordered than the guards, but a steady stream of crossbow bolts flew in every direction.

Flashes of green and blue showed organized efforts from the maji. The Houses of Strength and Grace were enhancing the guards. It wouldn't do any good, in the long run, and Sam wondered why the Life Coalition was still here. They had gathered the speakers, diplomats, and representatives of the ten homeworlds in one place, with an army. It was like they were trying to assassinate both the Assembly and the Imperium.

The Drain overhead was gaining speed, growing faster. The crystal dome of the Great Assembly arced above, lines of frost reflecting the morning light from the walls. *There has to be a way for the Symphony to stop it.* Majus Cyrysi huddled behind a shield of air, his head also turned upward, and Sam scuttled to the next speaker's chair, trying to close the gap.

I am the Symphony. The voice resonated in his head, jerking Sam to a halt. It was the first direct answer from the voice.

He frowned. *You aren't the Symphony. If you are, tell me how to get rid of the Drain.*

There was a different tone to the other thoughts. *I can show you knowledge. There is so much you don't know.*

Right now, I only need to stop this thing, Sam furiously sent back. What was he doing? This was insane.

You are not crazy—no more than I. Let what you call the Drain persist. I can show you how to protect yourself from it. It is a natural thing, a harbinger of what must come. It is merely a seed of the coming Dissolution.

Sam frowned. *It's not natural—show me how to stop it! Or are you not what you claim? Maybe you're a majus from the Life Coalition, messing with my head.* He glared through the chaos at the six maji surrounded by their troops. All of them were ringed with color. Which house could do that? Communication? Healing?

I am no house member, came the voice, and a strange feeling came along with the sending, like...laughter?

The Assembly maji were fighting back, and the Symphony was fitful in his head, resisting changes from the large group of maji. They were not working together. Several of the House of Healing were climbing down the steps, ready to fight the Life Coalition hand-to-hand. Many others in the Dome were fleeing toward the doors.

You aren't the Symphony either, Sam thought. *Help, or get out of my head so I can fight against the Life Coalition.*

Now the feeling of laughter stopped, became a colder emotion.

You are no fool. I am bigger than the Grand Symphony. I control it.

The coldness gripped the inside of Sam's mind as the Drain's cold gripped him outside, like an icicle plunged down his spine. *Leave me alone.*

If I was not what I say, could I do this?

The panic climbed up into his mind.

Sam gasped and scrabbled at the ground. The crowds, the newness and size of the Assembly, all crushed him down, a frog beneath a tire. He curled around his knees, covered his head. He hadn't had such full paralysis since the first day here. The floor was freezing, but he couldn't push up from it. If he did, he would float away, into the crowded rotunda.

He gripped the leg of the chair he lay behind with one hand, the other holding his watch to his ear. He was so close he could smell the wood and varnish. *Recognize small details. Accept them. Make landmarks.* His eyes flicked to the Drain, sitting like a blind and jaundiced eye. He began to hyperventilate, breath far faster than the ticking of the watch. He looked down again, saw little cracks in the material of the Nether, then looked away before it could affect him. *If I stay here, I'll be killed.*

He expected a retort from the intruder in his head, but none came. *What did you do?* he called, but there was no answer. Eyes closed, Sam reached for the Symphony. Like his heartbeat pounding in his head, the melody fretted and started, describing his own body.

What can the House of Communication do? If he could get rid of this fear, even for a few moments, he could go to the others. They would think of some way to the stop the Drain.

The melody was a mess of intersecting rhythms around his brain, connections firing in a way that created his own private brand of suffering. He sorted through it, trying to recognize a tune he could adjust.

Underneath was an ouroboros of music, ever repeating, different from the rest. He slipped through and around the tune. Was this the key? He blocked the repeating section with his notes, and the music slid apart into separate themes.

Pathways appeared, spearing from one thought to another. He opened his eyes and saw paths in the air, following actions, showing him cause and effect. A crossbow bolt flying to a target, hitting it, and being cocked in the crossbow, all at once. That guard would be cut down. This majus would change the Symphony. The battle was won, and lost, and not even begun, all at the same time. He looked at the Drain, where all pathways died, save one. It was hidden in shadow, difficult to bring to fruition in reality. He could *almost* see how to make it happen.

Sam blinked, and the pathways were gone, the ouroboros whole again. *What was the answer?* The clarity was fading, as the fear crashed back, bending him to the floor. His eyes swam in and out of focus.

All that mattered was that there was a way to stop the Drain, even if he couldn't remember. Part of it was so easy any majus could do it. *Think. What was the solution?* He rolled, pushed his feet to the floor, and levered up on the chair. With his eyes trained on the base of the Assembly wall, he backed to its safety. Slowly, one hand on the stone at all time, he made his way to Majus Cyrysi.

CHAPTER THIRTY-TWO

Fate of the Assembly

*-The maji of the House of Potential are the least like other houses.
Their abilities lie in the transfer of energy, and conversion from kinetic to
potential and back. Their house fuels the Systems underlying our society.
Without them, no change to the Grand Symphony could be sustained
barring direct involvement from a majus.*

From a lecture on the House of Potential, by Mandamon Feldo

Origon saw Sam coming closer, one agonizing step at a time. The
young man must be fighting another of his attacks. Understandable.
Origon was sweating even in the chill air, his crest flaring as he
searched for anything he could do to stop the Drain. If Sam could
change the Symphony in his state, there was a chance they might be
able to do something to the Drain together.

Origon turned to Caroom. "Can you be helping with more than one
change to the melody?" The Benish was still feeding him strength, but
didn't look very sturdy. They oozed thick fluid from their chest
wound, and from a large cut along their left arm where a bolt had
passed Origon's shield. But Caroom's eyes were bright on him, and the
chill at least might numb their pain. It would soon be cold enough to
freeze water.

"Hmmmm," Caroom rumbled. "This one will try, but the effects to
the body are draining." They gestured down their body with a thick
hand.

They still needed to keep the shield going while Origon tried his
idea. Hard to handle both changes at once, in his diminished state. He
eyed his apprentice, halfway to him. The likely key was to use all six
houses. He could only test his theory with Caroom. Once Sam got
there, they could make their way around to Rilan and Hand Dancer.
Then they would only need the Houses of Grace and Potential.

"We may be able to use a containment, as we began with the
Aridori in Gloomlight," Origon explained.

"For, hmmm, a full containment, there are only—"

"Yes, I am aware," Origon cut in testily. "We need all six houses, but we can test the validity. Join with me, but keep the notes in your other change. If I am losing your strength, this shield will fall, and we will be cut down in moments."

The Benish nodded—more of a small bow from their torso—and their flickering eyes dimmed for a moment as they looked inward. Origon did the same.

The Symphony was in chaos with this many maji affecting it, and it pushed back against changes. He didn't hear the chords of a containment circle though. He placed his notes in a perpetual repetition, not borrowing from the existing Symphony, but crafting an arpeggio. He felt it harmonize with something he couldn't quite hear—Caroom was doing the same. Origon panted at the effort, but kept his head up and his shield stable. What irony, if he were finally to affect the Drain, only to be cut down by a stray piece of iron.

"Give me control of it," he told Caroom, his eyes shut, the better to listen. He heard a hitch in the rhythm as something was thrust on top of his notes, making the music more complex.

Origon pushed the partial containment up, making his arpeggio rise several octaves to circle around the growing Drain. There was a horizon to it, where the Symphony crumbled to meaningless notes. If he could get it close enough to encircle without touching, this one small melody by itself, maybe he could contain—

Something drew at the warding, dissolving part of the rhythm. Origon desperately pulled back on what notes he could, but most were gone, sucked into the Drain. His eyes snapped open as he bent forward, and Caroom grunted like they had been hit with a club. Origon's shield wavered, and he clung to it like a raft in a torrent of water. He could not lose that too.

"That won't work," a voice said. Sam was pale, pressed against the wall, and shivering. He shook his head as if clearing it, and his eyes slowly focused on Origon. "It's a good idea, but I don't think it will work," he repeated.

Origon felt his crest surge in annoyance. What did this refugee know? He had been using the song for all of a couple ten-days, against Origon's more than fifty cycles.

"I am supposing you have a better idea?"

"Yes," his apprentice said, surprising him. "Though I can't quite remember. I think it's about openings." What was he talking about? He must have seen Origon's scowl.

"We need a door. Or not exactly a door, but something between that and a portal." Sam's voice was getting more confident. "You saw the sliver the Life Coalition shot into the air?" Origon nodded, starting to see what Sam meant. "The Drains don't follow regular rules of the universe, but if we cut off Communication between what's on the inside of the Drain," he put a hand out to one side, "and on the outside—" He put out his other hand. It held the watch the Methiemum used to focus.

Origon drew his brows down as far as he could. "You are not understanding what the House of Communication is about," he said. "This is not something it can do."

"I've done things like it before," Sam said. His voice was shaky, but confident. "See if you can hear what I do. I'll need all the help I can get. Majus Caroom, can you try as well? I don't know how to explain it any better." He swallowed, his eyes flicking down, then back up.

Sam's face contorted, and Origon, despite the young man's impertinence, dove back into the Symphony to follow him. This was not the time to be a stickler. He waded through music. Communication wasn't about doors. It was the medium of transference.

A note sounded, close to him, and he followed the Symphony through fractally separating strands, deeper than he usually went. The rhythms here were simpler, but more powerful, harder to change. They reflected parts of the universe more fundamental, containing rhythms other music was built on.

"Slow down," he panted, marveling at how *strong* Sam was. He could hardly keep up as the young man's song nudged notes aside. If he had been at his full potential, maybe he could have followed. Suddenly the Symphony wavered, and Sam's touch disappeared. "Where—"

"Right there, can you hear that?" Sam said, his face alight. He straightened, coming off the wall. "That's the place where the Drain joins the Grand Symphony." His smile turned down in what the Nether informed Origon was distaste. "It's eating the music, taking it somewhere I can't hear."

"I cannot—" Origon trailed off, and looked at Caroom, who shook their head.

"This one was, hmmm, able to hear an occasional note, but all is opaque now."

"It's right there," Sam insisted. "I've almost got it." He gritted his teeth and screwed up his face, and just for a moment, Origon thought the Drain paused and shrank, but then it resumed its growth.

Sam gasped, and bent forward, hands to his knees. Origon backed up, in case he might vomit. "I lost it, and my notes."

"Sam, I am not knowing what you do." Origon paused, loathe to speak the next words. "This is past my ability. You must do this yourself."

"It's okay." Sam raised his watch and closed his eyes. His shoulders relaxed, just a little. "I think I can try again, in a minute."

Origon glanced across the circle of black cloaks. No bolt had impacted his shield recently. The guards, backed by the maji, were pushing the Life Coalition inward. His ears twitched as the guards' guns sounded. Dark cloaks littered the floor, and the six Life Coalition maji were pressed together, still guarded by several ranks of their army. The stink of gunpowder was in his nostrils, and he swiped at his nose with one hand. The Life Coalition weren't trying to win. They had already done that, unless Sam could do something. The army had been only to give them time.

He looked back, saw Sam watching him. "I'll be alright, now the fighting is dying down," the young man said. "I think I can do it. Go get Maji Ayama and Hand Dancer, and Enos. See how they're doing."

Origon turned without question, then realized he was taking an order from his apprentice. He turned back, oddly confused. "You stay safe as well. I am wanting to have a long talk with you, on the other side of this."

"If you have to leave me here to rescue Inas, do so," his apprentice said, almost offhand. "Tell Enos that."

Origon let his confusion show in his crest and his face. "Why would I do such a thing?"

"Just a hunch. He's in more danger than me. I'll be fine. I've survived one Drain, you know." Origon checked over Sam, to make sure he was not delirious in his panic. He seemed serious.

"As you wish." With everything he had seen in the last few days, Origon had no idea whether Sam would be safer with him or on his own. The young man could always leave the Dome, after all.

He gestured for Caroom to follow, and reabsorbed the notes in his shield with a sigh of relief. They crept around the side of the Assembly to Rilan. Whatever Sam was attempting, there was a good chance it wouldn't work. Best to also attempt his containment plan, just in case. Tendrils of frost were creeping down the walls. The dome, high above, glittered with ice.

* * *

Rilan looked over the guard commander's strategy with Hand Dancer, though by this point it was academic. Most of the delegates and speakers were gone, herded out in a more or less orderly fashion. The bulk of the maji were left.

She shivered, and her breath fogged. The void was big enough now to feel it draining her energy. The maji on the top tier of seats were crowding down, near the railing.

She had assumed control, in Vethis' absence, of the segment of maji from the House of Healing. Jhina led the House of Grace, and Strength and Communication were largely self-sufficient, or at least Scintien and Freshta weren't screwing things up. Rilan was strangely happy to see Hathssas' black cloak leading the House of Power. Hathssas had the darker green scales of one born in the equatorial regions, near the more liberal Southern Coalition of states. It was a stereotypical assumption, but Rilan hoped it was accurate. The only other councilor missing was Feldo, though Rilan thought he'd be the first one to lead the advance. Where could the old man possibly—

"A full containment."

Ori's voice startled her and she whipped around. He'd come half-way around the rotunda without her seeing. She'd been caught up in leading the fight.

"What about it?"

"It is what I am wanting to try against the Drain. Did you see what the Life Coalition maji did?"

"The cannon? Yes." Rilan stared at Ori. His liver-spotted skin was not just pale, but gray, his crest drooping. Caroom looked little better, like a piece of ambulatory driftwood. She studied the Symphony around them for a moment, adding a few notes to smooth transitions from key to key. It would help their mental state, though she could do little for their bodies. She could spare a few notes in the permanent investment. The Effature's strange crystal still buoyed her. Both maji breathed deep and stood straighter.

"This one gives thanks, Majus," Caroom said.

Rilan nodded back, accepting the thanks. They had little time here before they would need to evacuate. "The Life Coalition didn't use a containment. It was something else."

Ori brushed this away. "It required all six of them. Reversing it will also require all six houses."

Rilan eyed the void. She was actively shivering, though Ori looked too tired to even notice the cold, and Caroom wasn't as affected.

Hand Dancer blew on his hands, flexing his long fingers. <There will not be time for a trial run.>

"The Grand Symphony would resist another full-scale change, in any case," Rilan added. She glanced around at the masses of maji in the Assembly. "Shall we rouse the maji?"

<You are thinking to use all of them? We must gather them, quickly. The void is continuing to increase.> Hand Dancer looked upwards. Some maji were discreetly leaving.

Rilan saw other sparks of color, followed by the respective majus looking gut-punched. They were going through the same experiments Ori and she had already tried.

"We will be needing to add notes simultaneously to lessen resistance to the change," Ori said. He had his hands on hips, breath frosting. His crest ruffled.

"Fine." Rilan looked back and forth between the other maji. "Any other arguments before we get eaten by the void? Good. Go to your respective councilmember. I'll take the house of Healing. Those who finish first can talk to Jhina, for Grace, and whoever's leading Potential. They'll likely have caught on by—"

"Majus Ayama." Enos had been watching the fight.

"What? We're a little busy here."

"The Life Coalition maji are departing."

Rilan swung around as the others moved to their sections. It was true. The Life Coalition majus from the House of Strength had another portal open, ringed in green and burgundy. The remaining troops were filing through, pressed from the rear by the guards. The majus holding the portal open would have to be last.

She looked down at Enos. *I can't believe I'm trusting an Aridori with this.* No, that wasn't correct. She was trusting Enos. Rilan could see this young woman one day taking a place on the Council.

"Convince the maji of the House of Healing, Enos," she said. "Make them work with the others to create a *full containment*, like we—like we used against you. You have it?" She waited for a hesitant nod. "Good. Don't let them argue with you. They will. Make them wait until everyone else starts. The more chuckleheaded buffoons who think they can take this by themselves, the harder it gets. Be firm." She made eye contact, let the young woman—*oh Brahm, the Aridori*—know she trusted her to do this task. Then she ran for the center of the rotunda.

While running, Rilan worked through the Symphony, picking out the phrases, chords, and strains of melody she would string together.

Then she was pushing, shoving, elbowing—everything she could do to get through the mass of armored guards.

"Move!" she shouted. "Majus coming through. Get out of the way!" Some moved aside. Some didn't move fast enough. She tried to throw apologies over her shoulders to the ones she had knocked out of the way. She had to get to the center before the majus went through her own portal.

Rilan forced her notes into the music she held in her mind, and then she was hitting black cloaks mixed in with the guards. These she didn't apologize to. Her bones were dense now, their baseline augmented by her song. Each punch was along lines of force of the Methiemum body, hitting with the impact of a hammer. Soldiers flew out of her way. She must be glowing like a full moon to other maji.

As she passed, she counted. Not even half the Life Coalition were Sathssn. Many were Methiemum. There were also Lobath and Kirians, but there were representatives from nearly every species. How long had this faction been operating without the Council or Assembly's knowledge? There were only a couple rows of Life Coalition left, and she knocked down a particularly robust Lobath, sending hir to the ground tumbling over hir head-tentacles.

Rilan pulled up, face to face with the Life Coalition majus. There was a glint of eyes widening under the black cowl, and Rilan threw out a fist. A gloved hand, shining with emerald and burgundy, stopped it cold. Rilan gritted her teeth and shook her hand. *Hope I didn't break any knuckles.* Never fight the House of Strength straight on—wasn't that the rule she learned long ago? No house had more sheer defensive might.

Something whirred behind her and she threw notes into the melody of her skin, turning quarter notes to sixteenths, hardening it. She felt the impact, before whatever it was bounced off her back. There would be a bruise later. A soldier rushed past her through the portal, and another behind him, each taking potshots as they went through. Rilan swung around and the majus' cowl swiveled, trying to follow. Rilan came up on the other side, forcing the majus to turn away from her troops. "How long can you hold this portal open, after you're unconscious?" she whispered.

"This, it does not matter," the majus answered, the voice feminine. She was between Rilan and the mass of troops now, and they were too busy fleeing to attack. "The great seed is growing. Our task, it is done."

"Seed?" Rilan glanced up, wary of tricks, but the majus seemed content only to defend. "The void? Why? Is this just for some insane plot of secession? You could have left the Assembly in peace. Why do this?"

The Sathssn chuckled, a dry hissing sound. "The secession, it was merely a stepping stone. The seeds will usher in the Dissolution, clear our species' name, and heal our wounds. It will make our forms perfect for the Holy one who brings the change."

"You're crazy," Rilan said, and leapt forward, but the shorter majus was ready, and ducked back, a green aura lending her strength.

"You will not stop us—not now. These changes, they are necessary. You will see, like us, the change will be for the better. We lead the ten species into a golden age."

She ducked back again, passing into the portal, and Rilan threw out a hand, clutching the tip of her cloak as it flared out. Her other hand slipped her belt knife free, and she sliced a section of fabric away. The portal dissolved as a cry went up from the remaining Life Coalition forces.

Rilan swiveled a full circle. *I'm in the middle of a hundred angry and lost soldiers.* "Guards—defend me!" she called, then blocked a scimitar with her knife, twisted it away, and thrust. There was a grunt of pain from her opponent. These troops were woefully untrained, as if the Life Coalition had hired them on, but didn't tell them they would have to fight.

She only had to bring down two more before a wall of guards in the Effature's green and purple pushed them aside, surrounding her. Rilan glanced between their helmets. The sections of seated maji were each glowing with their own color.

The void above her was close—too close, and it was hard to move or even to breathe. As in Dalhni, she had no idea how close the void had to get to be fatal.

She stretched the section of dark cloth. The House of Healing had some tracking ability. It would have been best if they had someone from the House of Potential down here as well; Feldo if she had her choice. She closed her eyes and dove into the Symphony, safe in the ring of guards.

The organic traces were complex strains of music, twisting around each other. Those of the cloth were organic, but simpler, as the death of the original plant removed chords. She used the fabric as a compass, training her mind to find those same complex rhythms, wherever they were. For a few moments after it closed, the connection the majus used to create a portal would linger. Where the majus stepped through, the Symphony was slightly different, sharing another location, on the edge of her hearing. These complex organic strains now existed there, if she could only make the connection.

The two places were more similar than she thought. The Life Coalition maji had not departed to another homeworld. They were still here in the Nether! She had been there before. It wasn't Gloomlight. Some other city, farther away. *Aha. Poler.* She had only been to the city a handful of times. It was on the opposite corner of the Nether from the Imperium, set up as a mirror of the capital city, though it had never achieved quite the same greatness. For the first time, they knew where the Life Coalition was.

Her eyes popped open and flicked up. A great ring of all six colors rotated and mixed above her head, one sixth of it weaving through music she could hear. It was surrounding the void, compressing. *Is the void slowing?* Rilan held her breath. If this worked, they could go after the Life Coalition. If not, they'd have to leave in a hurry.

One side of the containment wavered, then the other. She crushed the fabric between her hands, her nails digging through it into skin.

The circle held, and she forced breath back out. The ward slowly drew closer to the pus-like surface of the void.

Then a tendril swirled too close, and touched the surface of the void. The color bleached and disappeared, the change moving up the section, unraveling the music. Rilan heard shouts and a group of maji from the House of Potential went to their knees as one.

No. Keep it steady. They only had one chance.

The containment stabilized, but another tendril touched, and another section unraveled, like knitting pulled apart. Rilan caught snatches of the melody, discord weaving through it like one out-of-tune instrument in an orchestra of thousands. Other instruments around it faltered.

Hold it together. She was gritting her teeth.

As it compressed, the containment faltered, and places touched the void. In all those places, the void won, tearing through the Grand Symphony like a harpoon though a piece of paper. A great groan arose from the ranks of the maji as their construct began to fail. It wobbled, colors dropping in and out of existence.

Then some part must have become overbalanced, and the whole containment skewed wildly, impacting the surface of the void and dissipating in a puff of sparks, some even visible to non-maji. Cries of pain echoed around the rotunda, and several maji collapsed.

Rilan shook with cold and with rage, staring up into the bulk of the malevolent thing, untouched by the combined might of the maji of all ten species. *The Life Coalition will pay.*

CHAPTER THIRTY-THREE

Restitution

-The House of Power brings to mind the majus of stories, setting his enemies alight with well-placed fireballs. In reality it would be far too much trouble to create anything greater than a spark of light. The notes used could never be reclaimed, except maybe in fading body heat from one's fallen opponent.

Part of a lecture on the use of the aspect of Power, by Bofan A'Tof

Sam shuddered as the great circle of color collapsed. *So many notes.* He pulled most of his back from the collapse in time. It almost worked when he acted in conjunction with the rest of the maji. He had tried again to separate the deep rhythm Majus Cyrysi couldn't follow, to cut the Drain off from what it touched, but he wasn't strong enough by himself.

His heart hammered, and the watch nearly slipped from his sweaty grasp. The Drain was increasing again. The cold air rasped at his lungs as he drew in a long breath. He could not hyperventilate and pass out. The presence in his head had stripped away most of the progress he had made with his anxiety while living in the Nether. *Too many new things.* He held on to his vision of cause and effect. There was a way to stop the Drain for certain, if he could remember exactly how.

The guards were dispersing, some leading black-robed prisoners to the exits. *Maybe they'll get answers about the Life Coalition.* From their midst, a figure shot out, running to Majus Origon's group. Majus Ayama halted, then conferred with the others, throwing one arm back the way she came. Above them, crowded in the lower seats, the maji were scattering. The Drain was too strong, and their concentrated effort had failed. *Good. They need to leave. I remember that much.*

First the maji would leave. The premonition was hazy in his memory. Next, Majus Ayama jerked a hand in the air and Majus Cyrysi answered calmly, gesturing to where Sam was kneeling behind one of the great chairs. *We have to take Sam with us. But he was telling me to rescue Inas and leave him. He had some strange plan, and I think the boy might actually be on to something.* Sam waggled his head back and forth as he silently narrated the conversation.

He was up next. Shakily, he clutched the back of the chair as if it held him to the ground, used its weight to lever himself up. Without that and the remains of the effects from the Effature's device, he'd be curled on the floor. *So cold.* His breath was like ice crystals. The fireplace in his house rose in his mind, and Aunt Martha dying in the cold. *No. Can't stop. Have to keep going.* He had learned how to deal with new places and unexpected events in the Nether. He shivered, fingers and watch rattling on the back of the chair, then raised the other arm and waved.

The others were facing him, deciding, he knew. The maji in a little clump, Enos off to one side. He wanted to run to her, to go find Inas instead of this path, but that was death. There was only one way out.

They were too far away to hear, and Sam pointed one finger at an exit and jabbed at the air. "Go!" he shouted, and his breath misted out white in the cold. *Get out of here. Leave.* They would get his intent. His voice sounded dead, flat. *Is that the Drain's doing?*

Majus Ayama turned to Majus Cyrysi, gesturing angrily, and he once again made calming gestures, then pointed to Sam. Sam pointed back, and outside the Dome. The former councilor threw up her hands, and gestured for the others to stand back. A white aura surrounded her, the majus bowed her head, and jerkily, a portal formed, ringed in her colors. It was not the most probable option from the mass of cause and effect he had experienced, though he couldn't remember what other way she would have chosen. One by one, the others went through. Enos was second to last, and threw him a long look before she disappeared into the ring of blackness.

No, I don't know exactly what I'm doing, Sam answered her unspoken question. *I'm supposed to be here, though. You find the Life Coalition. Rescue Inas.*

He gave Majus Ayama one last wave, and she shook her head, then entered her portal. It closed, like a ripple on a lake.

Sam looked up and swallowed. His watch was digging into his hand, clenched between his fingers and the chair. The last of the guards and maji were almost out, and he was the only one foolish enough to stand in the path of the Drain.

He stopped trying to control his anxiety, let it flood him. *Start from the beginning.* Slowly, he sank to the floor, breathing escalating, heart racing. His eyes raced around the Assembly, and the walls seemed to waver, though he knew that was his own fear, distorting things. *Recognize what you see. Accept it. Move forward.* He closed his eyes. *Time breaths to seconds.* He held the watch to his ear. *Three breaths per beat. Two breaths. One.* He forced a deep breath in, opened his eyes, pried his hand from the chair, and took a step forward, toward the Drain.

You think you can stop this? The voice was mocking.

Back again? Sam thought to it. *Where did you go?*

I *went nowhere,* the voice taunted. *You will fall into oblivion if you stay.*

I *don't think so.* Sam listened for the Symphony of Communication, waded through the loftier phrases defining air, speech. Many were half-eaten by the Drain, limping discord instead of smooth harmony. Far underneath was that repeating, looping music, octaves lower than anything else in the Symphony. It would show him the truth. He pried it apart with his notes and pathways of cause and effect erupted again, far fewer choices now everyone was gone. Older lines displayed the chaos of the battle.

You have found that out by yourself. Clever. The voice was obviously a different personality. It had been speaking to him since he first arrived here. Sam didn't know how he hadn't realized the deception before now. *Shame you are too late. Now this seed has been planted in what you call the Nether, it is unstoppable. I have carefully prepared its field, over thousands of cycles, culminating in my little group of acolytes.*

Then you do *work with the Life Coalition,* Sam thought at the presence. He studied the possibilities, standing under the Drain, shivering. They were hard to see, ever shifting. The pathways also showed how long the Drain would take to kill him. *Comforting.* He could almost see the one way that didn't end in failure...

Ha! The laugh made Sam's mind throb. *Work with them? I am their god! As will you be.*

"What?" The lines dissolved. He shook his head, nearly fell. Watching those lines took away his notes, as if they poured into a chasm between raised cliff faces.

Yes! The voice was exuberant. *You can be the god of these little people. You are not like those so-called maji, those degenerate copies.*

I'm of the House of Communication, Sam thought.

You act as these maji taught you. Were there not times when you out-stripped your mentor, left him wondering at the chords of the Grand Symphony you could change? See your true color!

You're lying, Sam thought back.

Something happened, deep within the notes that made up his being, like two musical scores, base and treble clef, combined into one piece of music. They had been two things before. Sam gasped at the sting, though it wasn't like losing notes.

It didn't matter anyway. This time, he had remembered. In all the possibilities, there had been one opportunity left. He addressed the voice, wanting it to hear. *Nothing can touch this Drain, but the maji's ward fit around it. Could the Drain fit through a portal, if it was big enough?*

The voice in his head was silent.

Got you.

He only had to make a portal big enough to fit half the Great Assembly through. Where would the other end be? He searched his memory. Dalhni? Too changed from his memory for a portal to work. Gloomlight? He couldn't put a Drain there. Where else did he know so well he could place a portal? Where else was devoid of people?

Nowhere.

Searching fingers scooped and scoured his mind. Locations became confused, blurry.

What are you doing?

Ensuring my goals are not compromised.

Dalhni and Gloomlight grew fuzzy, indistinct, and the music that defined them faded. Other places disappeared from his memory, and Sam grasped at his notes, trying to get them back. The phantom fingers were far too strong.

Get out of my head!

No answer. Panic rose again, grasping at his chest, running up his spine. Sam shrunk to the floor—the crystal floor of the Nether below him. The whole Assembly was like one giant pane of never-ending glass. *The voice was silent when my panic was in control.* The voice was connected to the Drain, somehow. To stop one was to stop the other.

He looked down, into the repeating, reflecting, bottomless depths of the Nether and the tightness in his chest rose like a tide. The grasping fingers wavered and disappeared.

Sam curled on his side, on the freezing floor. The Drain was still growing, a malignant cancer hovering above his head. He dove into his anxiety, letting his fingers knot and his teeth clench, going the one place he never did. He was hyperventilating, colors flashing in his vision like a kaleidoscope. He relived the day his parents died.

* * *

Origon stepped into a cavern, dimly lit by a guttering torch, and instant warmth flooded through him. A shiver ran down his spine and his crest flared, then settled. He hoped Sam was getting clear of the Dome. It was lost, with the Drain so large. The young man had been quite certain about leaving him, that he had another trick to try. Maybe he also knew he would be a hindrance in this new environ. Yes, he could go with the other escaping maji. Even as strong as Sam was, surely he couldn't take on the Drain by himself.

A dark-cloaked figure was just visible, down a corridor to his right. Origon let the Symphony of Communication permeate him, listening to the way the air moved. He added a few notes here and there and started after the figure.

"Ori, wait," called Rilan as the portal closed behind her. "It might be a trap."

He skidded to a halt. By his grandfather's chinfeathers, of course it was a trap, how careless did she think he was? Too late now. The figure was gone. He turned to the others, Caroom wobbling on their feet, Hand Dancer bent-shouldered, and even Rilan, her jerkin all a mess and her hair coming out of her braid.

Enos stomped forward. "We have to go after them. They have Inas. I'm not losing both he and Sam today." She looked a challenge into Rilan's face. "We can't let them get too far away."

"I agree, there is to be no telling what the Life Coalition would do with another Aridori," Origon said. The musty air of the cavern tickled his nose. "Yet as Rilan says, we will need to walk carefully." He motioned them forward, into the dark tunnel connecting their dead-end room with the rest of the Life Coalition's hiding place.

"These caverns are underneath Poler somewhere," Rilan said. "Is anyone familiar with them?"

No one spoke. Origon hadn't known there were caverns in the Nether at all, but didn't say so. He had been to Poler once. The city was an oddity, like the Imperium in concept, but different. It was still almost a frontier town, though larger than Gloomlight. It was on the other side of the Nether from the Imperium. In retrospect, a perfect place for the Life Coalition.

The first tunnel they went through was deserted. It led into a "T," and one direction ended in another small cavern. The other direction split, and they went up the right path. Origon scanned the tunnel, both with his eyes and listening to the Symphony, hoping to catch changes left by maji.

There were no physical traps, no lethal Systems to catch the unwary. The caverns were empty. Gradually their group loosened, and Hand Dancer, Rilan, and Enos scouted side rooms while he and Caroom kept to the main corridor.

It was maybe half a lightening before they found the chamber with Vethis, still in the tatters of his black cloak. He was tied to a rough chair, inside a chamber with a rock door half open in front. The System clinging to a palm-sized artifact in the rock wall buzzed, surrounded with brown, white, and blue.

"It is the same device they used on us," Enos said. Her lip twisted as she looked at it.

"You're turning it off?" Rilan questioned as Origon reached for the button.

He paused, then shrugged. "Would you like to go in before I shut it off?"

"Very much so." He did not like the gleam in Rilan's eye.

<I would also be interested to go,> Hand Dancer signed. He cast a special flick of his fingers toward Origon, who understood it to mean the same as a significant look. They were definitely still in the Nether. Origon nodded back.

"Caroom, Enos, and I will guard the entrance. Be quick."

* * *

They pushed the rock aside, and Rilan and Hand Dancer went in. The others were watching the corridor, but Ori was keeping an eye on Rilan. She would not kill the traitor. Probably. She was already disconcerted by leaving Sam in the Assembly. Yet Ori had been insistent his apprentice had some other trick to try. It was madness.

Rilan slapped Vethis, not softly. His head lolled onto the back of the chair, and he jerked awake. His right eye was swollen shut and it looked like someone had been plucking out his silly-looking moustache.

"Oh, thank all the gods you're here," he told her. She snorted. His affected lisp was gone. "Untie me before they come back."

"Untie you?" Rilan asked. How stupid was he? "After you went traitor on the Council of the Maji?"

"I had no choice," Vethis pleaded. A trickle of blood ran from his nose as he spoke. "They knew about me, about—things I had done, people I owe. They wanted me to spy for them."

"Likely," Rilan grunted. She had suspicions, but no proof, of some less than legal actions the slippery weasel was involved in. "Yet they trusted you enough to bring you to their meetings."

"It was the first, I swear it," Vethis said. He jerked his bound hands against the ropes. "Get me out before they come back. They, they desecrated my form—so they would have to kill me, you understand. They're crazy Sathssn."

<We already know this,> Hand Dancer said, and the coldness of his translated words surprised her. <What useful information do you have to induce us to take you with us and not leave you to them?> Vethis' eyes widened in horror, and Rilan shifted her eyes to the Lobhl, but she stayed silent.

"Anything—what do you want to know?" How had a cowardly wretch like Vethis succeeded her in the Council of the Maji?

"What do you know of worth?" she asked, half hoping he couldn't think of an answer.

"Do you know where my brother is?" Enos called. Ori shushed her, but Rilan waved him off. The location of the Aridori was connected to the Life Coalition.

"It's a valid question," she told Vethis. "Answer that, and where they've gone, and I'll take you to the Council myself. Let them do what they want with you."

Vethis stared at Enos in confusion, the remains of his moustache sagging like a small, dead furry animal. "Her brother? How would I know—" Then he broke off and disgust washed over his face. "Oh. Oh, she's another one? I thought they made a poor joke when they said they captured an Aridori, but then they brought the boy back. There are some loose? I thought they kept the vile thing contained."

"Where is he?" Enos yelled. She was in the room now, and Vethis pressed back in the chair.

"They have him," he said, "and welcome to him. Bad enough you're still around." He looked up at Rilan. "You're so much better, aren't you? You judge the Life Coalition, but you're running around with the likes of *her*."

"I can still leave you here," Rilan warned, but Vethis only smiled back, a trace of blood oozing from a split lip. *He knows he has something we can use. I'll have to stop him talking about Enos. Somehow.*

"I'm beginning to wonder which is better." Vethis barked a laugh, and his stare took them all in. "You need me. I know other places the Life Coalition has been hiding, gathering adherents. They're all over the ten homeworlds. You'll never find a trace of them if you don't take me with you."

Rilan's lips pinched so tight her face hurt. "Help me get him out of here," she said, her voice flat.

* * *

Sam's parents died on a vacation in Alaska. The icy beach floated in his mind with perfect clarity.

I said I didn't want to go, playing in the sand and rocks. I pitched such a fuss, they kissed me, and sat me down to stack rocks into a castle. It was a deserted beach. What could be wrong with them walking just a little ways down the shore, to see if they could catch sight of whales on the ocean? It was what we had come to Alaska to do, but I only wanted to play with rocks, looking down at the ground as always. The cold of the rocks stung my hands, the salt stung my nose, but I was happy.

The angry storm front came down out of the sky like a tornado of ice. It was strangely small and concentrated, chewing through the beach like it was sugar.

I clung to the rocks, feeling a cold so much deeper than I had ever felt before. I thought the ocean was rising up to eat me, and called for Mom, for Dad, but they didn't come to save me. I'd never experienced anything like this before, flung side to side among the sharp outcrops. I could barely see for the sand and salt, like sandpaper against my skin.

It felt like one moment and a whole year, then the storm disappeared as suddenly as it appeared, leaving an eye of disturbed clouds in the sky, staring down at me in judgment.

Rocks were everywhere, and the sea was filling in a new hole in the beach. I ran across the sand, stumbling and tripping over loose rocks, and fish and shells thrown from the ocean. A sea lion called, a rasping, coughing bark, from where it lay on a huge boulder, a bloody gash in its side. I was screaming, crying for anyone to save me.

My parents were gone. At first I thought they were only hiding from the storm, but then I found the heel of my mother's shoe, sheared away as if cut with a knife. A little farther was half of the belt my father had put on that morning. I held it up, smelling the old leather, remembering it hanging in their closet. The spot where they disappeared seared itself into my mind, never to be forgotten, buried deep inside.

I called out to the empty beach for hours, shouting and yelling, but no one came. Only the gulls called back. The waves crashed on the rocks, and I clenched grit between my fingers and I searched. I found no other sign of my parents. It was hours before I wandered back to the fishing village, nearly dead from cold. They greeted me with suspicious stares when I told my story, crowds of people, twice my size, glaring down as if I had caused the storm that destroyed their beach. It was days until the police went away and I was sent to live with Aunt Martha.

On the floor of the Great Assembly, curled fetal, Sam created the dirge defining that place, a memory poised in time. He took every rock and pebble, the call of seagulls, the crash of waves, the salt and dirt and grit and skinned knees as he fell while running and shouting. Tears ran freely down his face as he melded the dirge to the Symphony of the rotunda, using his notes to patch minor chords and freeze sustained notes until the two were the same. It had already happened, but now he knew what made that terrible storm. In a way, he had known since he first arrived in the Nether.

Below the Drain, a black portal gaped, horizontal. Color surrounded it, but not the yellow of Communication. It was subtly different, shining, and gold.

Sam poured notes into the portal, expanding the measures. His song was base rhythm, unadorned, but he would get most of his notes back afterward, if he lived. *Have to make it bigger.* Sam uncurled, shoved up on his hands and knees, skin freezing against the Nether floor. *Don't look down again.* The edges of the giant portal slid past the extent of the Drain.

This was not enough. He had seen another shadow when he glimpsed the possibilities of cause and effect, a permanent change. He found another strain of music, this one high, almost sonic, and thrust more notes toward it, making a bridge to that other *time*—to the waves and the sand and the cold. Another color joined the gold, lighter metallic, like liquid silver. The music harmonized and the portal moved, spinning slowly upward, the black nothingness between *here* and *there* just touching the bottom of the Drain.

Sam gasped in air, though it froze his lungs. The Drain sucked at his song, eating notes, but he tugged them back, pouring them into the portal instead, feeling it slide up and around the malevolent sphere's diameter. The bottom quarter of the pus-like blister vanished into the blackness. *Just a little more. A little more.*

No! The voice was outside his consciousness. Some other force pushed back, as if from within the center of the Drain. *I will not let you do this.*

The grasping fingers returned, tearing out memories of his parents. Sam forced notes into the music, urging it faster, allegro. He tried to fend away the fingers at the same time, but there was not enough concentration in the universe. The portal wavered, and the Symphonies began to separate. Sam had no idea what would happen if the portal were unwound while open and while the Drain passed through. He reached for more notes, but there was not much left to his song, and the Symphony resisted, like someone had trapped the bow of the universe against the strings of creation.

Sam let his thoughts slide away from the mental fingers in his mind. This was why the Drain had disappeared, on the beach. It went somewhere else, but there was only one other place he could send it. He dared not even think it fully. To send the Drain there was unthinkable, yet if he let it destroy the Assembly, he knew something much worse would be freed, something connected to the voice that commanded in his head. He had to send it away from the focus point of the Nether.

He let the memory spring fully-formed into existence. He had spent the last ten years there. The Symphony of Aunt Martha's home appeared in his mind. He meshed it with the other two, and even as the opposing force swirled away the memory of the icy ocean in Alaska, Sam let the new memory take its place. This was no old recollection, buried at the back of his mind under layers of trauma. This was a memory he'd revisited every day since coming to the Nether.

Majus Cyrysi hadn't been able to open a portal because the Drain changed the house. Sam didn't connect this portal with the house in the present. He connected it to the past, like he had to his memory of his parent's death. *Mother, Father, Aunt Martha, forgive me.*

Liquid silver swirled around the edge of the portal, and Sam felt another portion of his song taken. A portal through time was a permanent change. But he would win this fight against the foreign presence, because it had already happened. He had already sacrificed so much, before he even knew he was doing it. *This Drain forced me from Earth. This Drain killed my parents. I will not let it win again.*

No! Stop— The voice faded from his mind as the top of the Drain vanished through the portal. It was above his house, weeks ago, no longer connected to the network the Life Coalition had created between the ten homeworlds. Sam let go, and notes snapped back to him, almost as painful as the cold. There was a large hole in his song, and another in his mind.

I am responsible for my parent's death. He couldn't remember their faces anymore. *For Aunt Martha's.* The thoughts drilled into him, and he curled again, fingers clutching to knees, shaking. *I did it because I remember it happening. I experienced it, so I knew it was the right thing to do. But did I cause it? Was there another way?*

The tears ran sideways down his face, rolling to the still frosty Nether floor. He listened, probed his mind, but the voice was gone, vanished with the Drain. Sam was certain the voice was connected, that the real aim of the Life Coalition had been to bring their god back to life. How could he tell that to anyone? To talk of some all-powerful mental presence would mark him as insane, even in this society.

His head knocked against the leg of a chair as he shook, and he welcomed the pain as a penance.

* * *

Rilan's stomach clenched as she helped untie Vethis. He stood on his left foot, shrieked, and collapsed into their arms. The Life Coalition had cut off his toes, and two of his fingers. A desecration of form. She almost felt sorry, for an instant. *Compare this to what is waiting in the Imperium.* She pushed away visions of the void eating through High Imperium, bodies of the dead in the streets, just like Dalhni.

The other chambers were empty, and they half-carried Vethis along. He was free with information about each room, from one used for studies of the Grand Symphony, to an armory with dozens of black cloaks hung up on one wall, to a cafeteria, remains of the latest meal still in massive iron pots. The space wasn't large enough to house the army that had attacked the Great Assembly. They must have funneled them through this cavern, with a second portal open to another hiding spot. Rilan clenched her fists.

"We have to go back," Ori finally said. They had searched through the tunnels for more than a lightening. There was nothing to tell them where the Life Coalition maji had gone, and Vethis hadn't been to another location. Caroom had stopped helping some time ago to tend their wounds. Green washed over their wide body, strengthening against their many cuts and injuries.

Reluctantly, Rilan agreed. "They've taken their records with them."

"They've taken Inas, too. We cannot go, not yet," Enos said. "We must find my brother." She looked a mess, her shirt stained with dirt, and tears in her eyes.

"Believe me," Rilan said, "I'm just as interested in removing him from the Life Coalition's hands as you are, but we won't find him here. Any portal is long closed. Our best bet is to reconvene with what's left of the Council of the Maji and the Effature, let them in on your secret, and organize a search."

Enos stared back, eyes wide. "You cannot," she breathed.

Rilan stared her apprentice down. "You've proved you're not a threat to us." *As far as I can tell,* she didn't say. "Prove your worth to them. At least three Aridori are alive, when we thought there were none. Who knows how many others exist? The leaders of the Great Assembly have to be told." If she thought about that revelation for too long, she might just collapse here.

"We will not be letting you come to harm, but those in power must know," Ori added.

"Those in power, like Councilor Vethis?" Enos asked, and Ori paused with his mouth open, crest fanning up. Rilan smoothed her braid back in place to give herself time to think of an answer.

<Enos is correct. We cannot let this get away from us,> Hand Dancer interrupted.

"What about him?" Rilan jerked her head at Vethis, propped against a wall. "The little sneak will let everyone know as soon as he can."

<He will soon be far out of favor, I think,> Hand Dancer signed. <We may reasonably be able to discredit anything he says.>

"It is worth a try," Ori said. "Though we still are needing the locations of the Life Coalition's other staging points."

"If only to find my brother," Enos said. She thrust her chin out. "He and I are the last of our family."

That remains to be seen. "We will find him, but we won't do it here." Rilan looked around the room. "Are we ready?"

"I believe so," Ori said. "I will be making a portal."

"To the Spire portal ground," Rilan told him. She hoped it would be far enough away from the Great Assembly to avoid the aftermath of the void.

The portal appeared, ringed in orange and yellow, seemingly without resistance. Was the void finished expanding then? If so, they still had to give Vethis over to the Council. She hoped leaving Sam with the void had been the correct choice. He must have escaped in time—no one could be that foolish. *I can't have another lost apprentice on my hands.*

CHAPTER THIRTY-FOUR

A Seed of Dissolution

-The Dissolution has come before, and it will—[text unreadable]—the beginning, and the end, and the end of the beginning. All things change before it, and—[burn mark]—still alive view creation in a new light. The Dissolution cannot be kept away, or hurried. This way lies only madness and—[parchment ripped]

Fragment of scraped parchment found preserved in the ruins of a structure underneath the Spire of the Maji. Dated at over twenty-three thousand cycles old (contested).

The hedges surrounding the Spire portal ground were untouched by the Drain. They rustled, healthy and green, in a breeze that brought scents of the Imperium. Origon hurried to the fence marking the boundary of the ground, the others following. There was no majus on duty, which in itself told of something amiss.

Origon peered between the Houses of Strength and Communication, toward where the massive walls of the Nether met. It was just after midday, when the walls were brightest. The dome was there, glinting in the light—no, there *was* something wrong with it.

"Are you seeing this?" he asked the air around him.

"I see it," Enos said, coming abreast of him. "The Dome of the Great Assembly looks squashed somehow. It must be the Drain." She held herself rigid, arms straight by her sides. "If Sam is gone then I will have lost my brother and...and a close friend in the same day."

Origon looked down at the short young woman. He let his crest spread out in sympathy. "Your species is much less an issue now, is it not?" Strange how Enos being an Aridori was such a concern only a few days ago.

"What's wrong with the Dome?" Rilan asked, on his other side.

Origon looked back to make sure the other two maji held on to Vethis. He need not have bothered. The Methiemum was as pale as a grub just dug from the earth. "We do not know. Shall we be going to investigate?"

<Someone must stay here with the *former* councilor.> Hand Dancer injected scorn into his signing, even using only one hand.

"Are you volunteering?" Rilan asked.

Caroom took an unsteady step sideways. Origon wasn't sure whether the Benish was holding Vethis up or using him for a crutch. "This one is, hmmm, very tired, and shall stay here with Hand Dancer to keep an eye on that one." They tilted their head at Vethis with a creak. Origon tried to ignore the ache in his own bones. They had all been up for more than a day.

<We shall attempt to contact the Council, or what is left of it. I hope they have found safety,> Hand Dancer signaled.

"Agreed," Rilan said. "Come on, Ori. We need to find where Sam has gone."

"These ones will take Councilor Vethis to, hmmm, the Spire, where maybe that one can help determine Inas' location," Caroom said. "In any case, that one will aid in ending the Life Coalition's influence." Their eyes flashed, and they stumped off with Hand Dancer, Vethis sagging between them.

The streets of High Imperium had fewer crowds than normal, but not abnormally so. Only when they got closer to the Dome did Origon see closed shops, and the Effature's guards in the streets.

"The void obviously didn't get this far," Rilan said. The Dome filled their view. "If it was as big as the one as Dalhni, it would have swallowed half the Imperium, and it showed no sign of stopping before we left." She shuddered. "It seems the Life Coalition failed to destroy the Assembly all the way."

"Drains are unpredictable," Enos said, then stopped. Origon gestured for her to continue, and she shrugged one shoulder. "The one my family, ah, encountered grew in starts, fast one moment and slow the next."

"Survivors reported the one at Dalhni flying up and out of sight," Rilan added.

"Then we do not know what this one would do," Origon said. "However, if they were being focuses for the Life Coalition, I would expect more signs of them in the Imperium. Did they merely hope to kill as many delegates and maji as they could? I feel there must be something more, an endpoint we have not yet seen." There was something unfinished, as if the Life Coalition was playing a game with different rules, decided they won halfway through, and abruptly left. It made his feathers itch, and he rubbed his hands together, unnerved and faintly annoyed.

"I agree," Rilan said. "We have to track them down, if only to find out what they thought they were doing—why they wanted to destroy the Assembly."

They reached the sloped road leading to the entrances of the Dome, bare of delegates and speakers. Two Lobath guards blocked their entrance, one wari, the other female, though both had their head-tentacles bound up under conical caps. They also held short blunderbusses.

"The Assembly is closed, by order of the Effature," one burbled in hir watery voice. Large, surprised-looking eyes stared up at Origon. "No one is to enter until the site is deemed safe."

His crest ruffled in anger. "Someone may still be in there."

"Do you know who I *am*?" Rilan asked, stepping in front of him.

The other Lobath guard poked the first with a long finger, and showed a card with faint sketches on one side. The first guard looked even more surprised than usual, and stepped back. "My apologies. You are allowed, also by order of the Effature."

Inside, fallen bodies of the Life Coalition troops, black cloaks splayed about them, littered the floor of the rotunda. There were fewer bodies of guards, mixed in. Insects and scavenger birds were already gathering. Though there was little structural damage, cleaning up the bodies would take time.

A few bodies of unlucky maji and representatives slumped in chairs above the retaining wall. Some were pierced by crossbow bolts, though bodies in the lower seats had crimson slashes—a sign of how far the small army had intruded.

"Look!" Enos pointed, and Origon followed her finger. Ah, that was why the Dome reflected light strangely, and how the animals got in. The great crystal Dome of the Assembly, made of the same stuff as the Nether walls, had a perfectly circular hole cut in it. A shiver ran up Origon's spine and his crest contracted. The material of the Nether was indestructible, the making of it lost. Yet the Drain had cut a hole through it as easily as it destroyed other matter.

They found Sam halfway around the rotunda from them, curled on the Nether floor by one of the speaker's chairs. Enos hurried to him, and Origon barely kept his crest straight. Was the boy alive? Why had he not run when the Drain came too close?

Enos touched his arm with two fingers, and he bolted upright, wiping his face with a hand. Origon breathed a sigh of relief. The young man would send him to the ancestors before his time.

"Oh! Oh, it's you," he said. He looked up at Enos, then took her hand. "Did you find him?" Enos shook her head. Their hands tightened together, and she rested her forehead against his. Their eyes closed for a moment.

Rilan cleared her throat. "You have a talent for surviving the voids." Her voice was sharp. "What happened?"

Sam hesitated just a moment while answering. "I...made it go away."

Origon thought Rilan's eyebrows might climb up into her hair. "You did *what*?"

"I'm...I don't remember everything, but I'm so tired. I fell asleep."

"You were making a permanent change with your notes," Origon guessed. He knew what that looked like, knew the bone-deep weariness. What had his apprentice done? "The Drain cannot be touched by the song."

Again, hesitation before Sam answered. "I, well, I made a portal that went *around* the Drain."

Rilan drew back, and looked up. "The void must have been half as wide as the Assembly when we left. No one can make a portal that big."

"I can." Sam pulled his lower lip up between his teeth. Enos sat beside him on the floor and he gripped her arm. His other hand snaked into a pocket for the watch.

"He is strong," Origon told Rilan. He had heard changes the young man made in the Symphony, controlling basic themes and multiple melodies at once. He pushed down the wave of jealousy. Origon could at least be the one to teach him.

"Any majus can make a portal, but not this big," Rilan insisted. She glared at Sam and he shrank down. Enos slipped an arm around him and squeezed. Sam looked back to her. "You're a Methiemum, but not from Methiem," Rilan continued. "You claim to be from a homeworld no one knows of. You say a void attacked your world—how I don't know, if the Life Coalition was creating them here—and now you make a portal large enough that the entire population of maji could run through at once. *Who are you?*"

Sam flinched at each accusation. Rilan was leaning over him, braid dangling over her shoulder. Origon almost defended him, but Rilan was correct. Sam was a mystery in a hidden egg.

"I...I don't know," he said. He was hiding something, but what?

Enos got up from the floor, making Rilan retreat. She still held Sam's hand. "Stop threatening him!" she said. "Can you not see how tired he is? Sam and I discovered the Life Coalition, not you. We survived the Drain. Inas is missing, and four full maji couldn't get him back. You mistrust me because of my species. So Sam is different too. Why can *you* not accept *us*?"

Rilan was silent, blinking at the young woman's onslaught, and Origon smoothed his moustache with one hand, recognizing the nervous gesture as he did it.

"It's alright, Enos," Sam said. With a grunt, he levered up from the floor, grasping at the speaker's chair, and she supported him. He was pale, and breathing hard. Origon thought he was hovering just above one of his attacks, but there was a core of steel there, under the young man's fatigue.

Sam pulled himself upright, pushed his shoulders back. "To answer your question, Majus Ayama, I don't know what I am, but I am fairly sure I'm not House of Communication." Now he looked to Origon, who frowned back. What nonsense was this? What else would he be?

"You won't agree until I show you," he said, neatly cutting off Origon's question. The yellow of the House of Communication glowed about him, but Origon couldn't hear anything. Also, the color was off— too bright, too metallic. Gold? A secondary color, at his age and experience? Where was the primary color?

Sam cast around, then jerked a wooden crossbow bolt from where it stuck in the chair back. He held it up, and the color drifted from his hand to the bolt. Sam cocked his head to one side and Origon listened along with him. There was nothing but the normal Symphony. What Communication would there be with a stick of wood and a bit of iron on the end?

The shaft of the bolt wavered, and grew darker. Sam's hand drifted down, then back up, as if the bolt had gained weight.

"Could I do this with the House of Communication?" he asked, and passed the bolt to Origon. It was now solid iron. No house could change matter at a basic level. Origon stared at him, then passed the bolt to Rilan.

"I need it back," Sam said. He was breathing heavily. "I don't have many notes to waste." Rilan handed the bolt to Enos, who passed it back. Sam closed his eyes for a moment, and a gold halo flashed around the bolt. When it passed, the shaft was once again wood, and Sam breathed out a relieved sigh.

"How?" Origon pressed close to his apprentice. He kept his crest down with an effort.

"I changed its melody," Sam answered, "just as with anything else. I think—I think I can hear more of the Grand Symphony than you. There are deeper layers. Each time I listen, I hear more."

Another house? Another way to change the Grand Symphony? This was treading on a path of feathers, which could collapse at any moment. Origon turned to Rilan. Her eyes were hooded, the mirror of his worry. They had both seen a way the Grand Symphony could be stretched, long before, and it had not ended well.

"Something for tomorrow," Rilan said slowly, and he knew she was thinking of the little piece of paper he had burned in his apartment, so long ago—the one with instructions on how to manipulate the Grand Symphony mechanically. "We won't figure it out here, and we all need sleep and food." Her tone promised they would come back to this topic. "We need to let the guards know the void is gone. We need to deal with Vethis." She tilted her head at Sam. "He won't mutate into something else overnight."

"Um." Origon's head snapped back around. He didn't like those little noises the young man made. Something bad usually followed them. "There is one more thing," Sam said. He looked between the three of them. "We've heard it mentioned before, but can you tell me exactly what the Dissolution is?"

Origon's crest puffed out like a feather duster before he could stop it, and his fingers tingled, as if the blood had left them. Why was Sam asking about this now, of all times, unless something else had happened to him? It was nonsense, of course, but when things like the Aridori and Drains appeared out of nowhere, even he would stop to listen to a rumor like this.

"Where did you hear it this time?" Rilan's dark skin had gone gray.

"It is the end of everything, and a time of great change." This was from Enos. "My father told us that once, when my brother and I were very young. I have never forgotten it."

"One of the Life Coalition soldiers said it, I think. Or maybe the maji." Sam's eyes would not hold his, and Origon let his crest show his disbelief. "They called the Drain a seed of the Dissolution."

The Dissolution was said to be an upheaval of space and time—some type of transformation. Enough change to bring a Methiemum from an unknown world? To bring back a lost species? He stroked his chinfeathers.

"I have a feeling we will learn more soon," Origon told them. "If it truly is coming, we will rebuild, and when the Great Assembly is repaired and cleaned, then the ten species—the eleven species," he nodded to Enos, "can face the Dissolution together."

END OF BOOK 1

If you enjoyed this book, please leave a brief review at your online bookseller of choice. Thanks!

Wondering about Rey's adventures? You can sign up for my mailing list and get a free short story – "The Symphony Eater."
http://williamctracy.com/mailinglistsignup/

Appendix: The Houses of the Maji

-For uncounted cycles, the six houses of the maji have worked together to uphold the Great Assembly of Species. They control the only means of transportation in and out of the Nether and between the homeworlds, and thus have a great responsibility to the non-maji members, who far outnumber them. As such, every majus has a say in the Assembly, a concept some non-maji are not comfortable with.

Houses of the Maji, often attributed to Ribothari Tan, Knower, later of the Council of the Maji

-Each house of the maji can hear and change one section of the Grand Symphony and thus affect reality, by the individual applying the notes that make up their own song. This application can be seen by other maji in a visual representation of color, often accompanied by a secondary color, personal to the individual majus. It is said each house's Symphony is based on a certain frequency or note.

From "Memoirs of Yaten E'Mez," Highest of the House of Communication and Speaker for the Council, 379 A.A.W.

House of Strength

The color of the House of Strength is bright emerald green, and the areas of the Symphony it affects often have to do with constitution, defense, strength, and growth, as well as soil and rock. A large portion of these maji have jobs as herbalists, veterinarians, or naturalists, though as with any house, the possibilities are nearly endless. Their Symphony diverges from the sound of a baritone resonant string.

House of Communication

Members of the House of Communication are the most common councilmembers chosen to become Speakers for the Council of the Maji. Their house color is pure yellow, and they affect quick thought, speech patterns, as well as air pressure, weather systems and avian creatures. Many of the House of Communication serve as diplomats of the maji, working less with the physical changes in their Symphony than those of interplay between the species. Their Symphony's fundamental tone is that of a low reed.

House of Power

The House of Power deals with the play of politics, movement of societies, personal relationships, as well as power generation, and simple heat. Their house color is fiery orange. They can as easily be found in the industrial districts of the Imperium and the homeworlds as in clandestine meetings and national assemblies. Their Symphony's base melody is of a sounding horn.

House of Grace

Those of the House of Grace are often subtle, with their control of liquids and ice, as well as efficient movement, cooperation, and coordination. Their house color is sapphire blue, and they work around transportation systems, food distribution, diplomatic intermediaries, and engineering positions. Many members are fond of kinesthetic movements such as dance, athletics, and martial arts. The founding tone of their Symphony is a passionate tenor.

House of Healing

The members of the House of Healing are best known as skilled physicians and surgeons, as the brilliant white of their house color seems to indicate. However, there is much more to the specializations of the house, including plant and animal breeding, psychology, profiling information on individuals, and even archeology through residue of living creatures on ancient artifacts. Their Symphony's fundamental tone is a high ringing of struck metal.

House of Potential

The House of Potential is the most directly tied to science and engineering. Its members are responsible for many of the technological improvements of the ten species made in recent cycles. Their house color is a rich rusty brown, and they are, at the very simplest, concerned with energy transfer. They are known to work with the House of Power on fuel and work generation and the House of Healing on ancient history, describing energy paths of artifacts. They deal with kinetic movement as the House of Grace does, transfer of force as the House of Strength, and energy of the weather with the House of Communication. Their members can also create Systems, or long-lasting changes in the Symphony, driven through a store of energy. Their Symphony starts with the shriek of whistling air.

Appendix: The Species of the Great Assembly

-The number of species in the Great Assembly varies over the cycles. Currently it resides at ten, including the recent addition of the Lobhl. The founding members are those who, according to tradition, started the first Assembly when the maji of their species discovered each other in the Nether.

From the notes of the Effature, Bolas Palmoran, 983 A.A.W.

-All members of the Great Assembly share basic similarity in form and function, though the species are physically spread far across the universe. The Nether helps to form connections despite differences, to the point where some scholars wonder whether the Nether has some impact on the species that find it.

From "Assumptions on the Nature of the Nether" by Festuour philosopher Hegramtifar Yhon, Thinker

Methiemum

The Methiemum homeworld is known as Methiem, and hosts a species well known as traders and decent scientists. They were one of the first to discover the Nether, as they are entrepreneurial and prone to adventure, though perhaps at the expense of long-term planning. However, this cannot have affected them greatly, as the common trading tongue of the ten species is derived from one of their dialects. In addition, they were the first to suggest an Assembly of all species who discover the Nether, probably to secure trading rights with the others. They are the most prevalent species of the ten, of medium height and coloring ranging from a dark mahogany to very pale peach, even with cases of albinism. They often have fine hair restricted to the tops of their heads and sporadically over the limbs and torso, more so on the males.

Kirian

The inhabitants of Kiria are known for their philosophy, debate, and ancestor worship. They were another species to discover the Nether early and became a founding member of the Great Assembly. They make fine statesmen, though they have a convoluted natural dialect in many of their nations, which does not translate as well inside the Nether as other species. Kirians do not let this stop them from expounding on any subject they know of, and some they do not. The males of the species favor long colorful robes in many cultures, while the females prefer to leave their arms and legs bare to show off their fine feathering and delicately curved nails. The species is generally tall, with wrinkled, liver-spotted skin, and feathers creating expressive crests on top of their heads. Males may also cultivate moustaches and thin beards, and both are sparingly feathered on the torso. Their pointed teeth can be unnerving when bared in smiles, though their dentation is mainly for gripping in their diet of grubs, beetles, and other slippery creatures.

Lobath

The Lobath are often looked down upon by the other species as dull and uninteresting, much like the prevalent mushroom farms on their rainy homeworld of Loba. However, Lobath are found at every level of society, from the menial to the most intellectual, and are one of the founding members of the Great Assembly. Consistently, they are defined as hardworking, compared to the other species, and tend to fill more physically demanding jobs. They are usually savvy with technology, especially new inventions. Other species may joke of the permanently surprised expression on the Lobath face, arising from their unblinking silvery eyes. They have a large range in coloring, from yellow, to orange, to red and brown, but are more easily identified by their squat neck-less bodies and three head-tentacles sprouting from the crown of their heads. The tentacles are often braided or tied together in certain styles. Males may have small rubbery growths above and below the mouth, while females have thinner head-tentacles and wari, the third gender, are generally of slighter, taller, build.

Sathssn

The Sathssn are unusual in that over eighty percent of the culture of Sath Home subscribe to various sects of the Cult of Form, based on perfection of the physical body. This invades every aspect of their society, from dark cloaks, robes, and gloves, to marriage rites, where the participants must be examined by other family for any illness or disfigurement, to livestock, bred to only descend from the most reputable lineages. The inhabitants of Sath Home are especially prone to cancers and tumors, and their winnowing practice began as a necessary response. Like many such things, it became religion. A notable exception is the Southern Coastal Coalition, a nationality where scales are allowed to be shown, and some may even go about without cowls and gloves and in short sleeves, to the dismay of the rest of their species. In the rare occasion flesh is shown, the Sathssn body is covered in tiny scales, ranging from yellow to green. Sparse hair may be present on the head and face, and eyes are red with yellow slitted pupils. Some Sathssn antisocial tendencies have caused interspecies conflicts in the past, yet they remain in good standing as a founding member of the Great Assembly. Despite their almost worldwide religion, many become scientists or statespeople.

Etanela

The long-lived Etanela are described as inherent pacifists, though the planet of Etan provides its fair share of malcontents, adventure seekers, and revolutionaries to the Great Assembly, of which they are a founding species. The Etanela typecast comes from their love of music, painting, sculpture, and literature. Many accepted great works were either created by an Etanela, or funded by one. Lots of educated Etanela are gifted speakers, and love to argue. Physically, they are the tallest of the ten species, with the largest individuals rising head and shoulders over even Kirians. Their skin tends to light blue, revealing aquatic origins, also noted in their large eyes and long fingers, and small, streamlined noses. The only hair the species exhibits is in a mane surrounding the head, often left to trail to the shoulders. The species is largely divided into four genders, with both dominate and subordinate versions of those who carry young and those who do not. Their mating rituals are often obtuse to those not of their species.

Festuour

Festuour can be hard to pin down to a stereotype. They thrive in the variability of professions and are well known for their philosophers, gourmands, mechanics, scholars, tailors, and explorers. On their homeworld of Festuour, once a member of the species finally discovers their chosen path in life, it is appended to their name permanently. Their inclusive friend-based society encourages members to do anything they set their minds to, with cheery acceptance. Children are reared communally to give the best options for advancement of themselves and society. Physically, Festuour are stout, covered in coarse greenish-brown hair. Their faces have long snouts with large noses, and nearly all members of the species possess piercing blue eyes, though a common failing is nearsightedness. The hairy Festuour do not often wear clothes, instead preferring accessories such hats, glasses, gloves, and belts and bandoliers with many pouches. They were the last of the founding members to convene the Great Assembly, though they have the distinction to be one of two species to share a galaxy, the other being the Methiemum. The two are often staunch allies politically and many of the Methiemum's customs and idioms have bled over to Festuour culture.

Benish

Even longer-lived than the Etanela, the Benish were the first newcomers welcomed by the newly created Assembly of Species. Most still live on their homeworld of Aben, and they are the least populous members both in the Nether and in the Assembly of Species. Cautious by nature, Benish are studious to a fault, often observing a situation from all sides before making even a preliminary decision. Little is known about their home cultures, save that the species is genderless, and propagates by a form of budding, where the parents, however many, share and mix memories, arranging parts of their history before dying to produce a new child or children, who inherit the progenitor's memories. Physically, the Benish are one of the most different species, with flesh made of a substance closer to plant than animal. They have no well-defined bone structure, and each member is varied in coloring, skin tone and roughness, and placement of internal organs.

Sureriaj

The Sureriaj are the most xenophobic of the ten species, surpassing even the antisocial tendencies of the Sathssn. Their culture is entirely founded on the concept of family, going so far as to have, instead of independent nations, major family lines that matriarchally govern their homeworld of Sureri. There is also a large group consisting of the disgraced—those who have lost their right to their family name— known as the Naiyul. Names are very important to the Sureriaj, and each individual has a hierarchy of names, the most secret known to progressively closer family members. Physically, the Sureriaj are tall and gaunt, with proportionally long legs. They have fine hair covering the entirety of their body, through which the skin can be seen. Their faces are not always appealing to other species, and that, with their aloofness, is the basis of the species slur "gargoyle." Their society is two thirds male, and two males and one female are required to create a viable offspring. The Sureriaj have the second lowest birth rate of the ten species, just higher than the Benish.

Pixie

This warlike and competitive species was the second to last to join the Assembly. To others, some of their members seem less intelligent to the point of an animal intellect, though this may be explained by their descent from a hive mentality, as well as their careful breeding of a fierce warrior caste, at the expense of progression in other areas. For each sufficiently courageous deed a pixie completes, a letter or syllable is added to her name, and many go by shortened nicknames. Pixies are short, blue to gray in coloring, with black compound eyes. They are capable of short flights with their gossamer wings, though often they will lift from the ground when speaking to another species, as if in recompense for being the shortest of the species. There are reports of members of another gender, hidden deep in their enormous city-hives, but all individuals who interface with other species are identified as female.

Lobhl

There is no proper spoken name for the Lobhl homeworld, so it is titled as the members name their species. The Lobhl have been members of the Great Assembly for only fifty cycles, and caused controversy when they joined for the amount of money spent on social restructuring, especially in the rotunda of the Assembly. Because the Lobhl have no vocal chords, they communicate entirely with complex hand gestures, and expensive visual displays were added in many areas to cater to them. Lobhl faces and heads are nearly featureless, leading to small problems in communication, even in the Nether. Lobhl hands are the points of reference for the species, widely different between individuals, and often tattooed. Each hand has seven digits, two of which are thumbs on opposing sides of the hand. Generally the Lobhl species is talented visually and mathematically. They also have a great love of what they define as music, though most is visually experienced. Their names are translations of actions they routinely perform, and their gender roles vary with the individual and the social situation. Their young are raised communally, and are neither carried in the body, nor in eggs. Many Lobhl worship the god of music, an incorporeal concept of light, like a personification of the Symphony, and most of their other religions focus on vision over sound or language.

Aridori

Little is known about this extinct species. They were rumored to be one of the founding members of the Great Assembly. However, many records were lost in the Great Aridori War, when the entire species suddenly turned on the others, often taking the forms of old friends, or even close family members. They were eventually eradicated, with many renegades hunted by teams of trained Sathssn commandos, but legends of their shapeshifting prowess and patient, long-term deception have provided generations of nighttime stories to scare children.

ACKNOWLEDGEMENTS

Way back when I first started writing, the original version of this was the "big story" I wanted to tell. It wasn't very good, and I knew it. That meant it had to wait until I felt my writing was ready to publish. Is it perfect now? No. Could it be better? Yes. However I feel confident this is the story I want to tell. It is an important part of the Dissolutionverse, but that world has grown a whole lot larger than my original vision, and I look forward to working on the next books in this series, as well as more novellas that let me delve into individual characters and smaller events.

This was also my first foray into Kickstarter, and I am very grateful to the friends, family, and strangers who were willing to help me fund this project. Because of you, there are five incredible illustrations by Micah Epstein, as well as his amazing front cover. Check out his paintings at micahepsteinart.tumblr.com. There is a very cool map by Damijan in the front. You can find him on Fiverr. In addition, thanks to Lindsay Flanagan and Chris Miller at Eschler Editing for the developmental edit.

Many others have also helped me out. The first thanks always goes to Heather, for "letting" me do this, putting up with paying more attention to my writing than to her, and still being willing to copy-edit for me. Second, a big thank you to my alpha and beta readers: Courtney Brooks, Reese Hogan, J.S. Fields, Robin Duncan, Katie Edwards, Daniel Eavenson, and all the folks at Reading Excuses for critiquing my submissions. Finally, thanks to the members of the Writing Excuses podcast for spending their valuable time teaching and encouraging new writers.

Of course, much of this wouldn't have been possible without my backers on Kickstarter. In no particular order, they are:

John and Nora Tracy, Mike, Rachel, and Luna Goffin, Miri G. Baker, Dyrk Ashton, Zach Chapman, Scott and Cindy Kuntzelman, Randall

Dameron, J. van de Erve, Mike McMullan, Daniel Eavenson, Reese Hogan, Tyler Bletsch, Emily Randolph-Epstein, Austin Alander, Susie and Ben Roberts, Elan, Matthew K. Burris, Courtney and Josiah Brooks, Kevin Wild, Rachel, Adam Nemo, Sarah F., Molly A. King, Ashley Capes, Becky Barnes, Caitlin Raine Fortin, Trever Peters, Jtifft, Adam Jackson, Katie Gomez, Joe Adams, Russ Wood, Ross Newberry, Ian Fincham, Greg E., Gustavo E. Alvarado, Kent Pittman, Knitdeer, Daniel Clouser, Chris Gerrib, Christina Gale, Noah Chan, Melissa Lee, Martin Severin, AnonyMouse, Dan Sloan, Alysse, Richard Pulfer, Michael and Brian Goubeaux, Margaret, Ryan Burke, Sarah Schweitzer, Robin Duncan, Penny, Mike Matthews, Eli McIlveen, Peter Schultz, Paul y cod asyn Jarman, Ethan Mosko, Christy Shorey, Anne and Patrick Emerson, Melissa Shumake, Amanda Grondalski, Joseph Rach, Jana Muduc and Traian Dorin, Tara Gazak, Mike A. Weber, Kriti Godey, Peter Asteriou Malousis, Stuart Turnbull, The Pillis Four, Steve, J.D. Allimonos, Benjamin Widmer, Elaine d'Ete, Y. H. Lee, Zachary Zientek, Henry and Julie Burroughs, SwordFire, J.S. Fields, Zaus, Kelly R., Matt Thompson and Family, Jennifer Nieuwstadt, Beth Rubin and Dane McGregor, Natty, Orusinfinite, Elí Freysson, Lisa Paciulli, Mike McCarthy and Miles, Katie Edwards, Leon Fairley, Bryan H., and Gabrielle Barnier.

Thanks to all of you, and I hope you enjoy reading!

ABOUT THE AUTHOR

William C. Tracy is a North Carolina native and a lifelong fan of science fiction and fantasy. He has a master's in mechanical engineering, and has both designed and operated heavy construction machinery. He has also trained in Wado-Ryu karate since 2003, and runs his own dojo. He is an avid video and board gamer, a reader, and of course, a writer.

In his spare time, he wrangles three cats and an ancient guinea pig. He and his wife enjoy putting their pets in cute little costumes and making them cosplay for the annual Christmas card.

You can visit him at williamctracy.com.

Please take a moment to review this book at your favorite retailer's website, Goodreads, or simply tell your friends!

82316405R00248

Made in the USA
Columbia, SC
16 December 2017